UNBURY
CAROL

UNBURY CAROL

A Novel

Josh Malerman

DEL REY • NEW YORK

Copyright © 2018 by Josh Malerman
Map copyright © 2018 by David Lindroth Maps Inc.

Published in the United States by Del Rey, an imprint of Random House, a division of Penguin Random House LLC, New York.

Del Rey and the House colophon are registered trademarks of Penguin Random House LLC.

Hardback ISBN 978-0-399-18016-3
Ebook ISBN 978-0-399-18017-0

Printed in the United States of America on acid-free paper

randomhousebooks.com

2 4 6 8 9 7 5 3 1

First Edition

Book design by Caroline Cunningham

For Derek, Ryan, Rachael, and Kevin

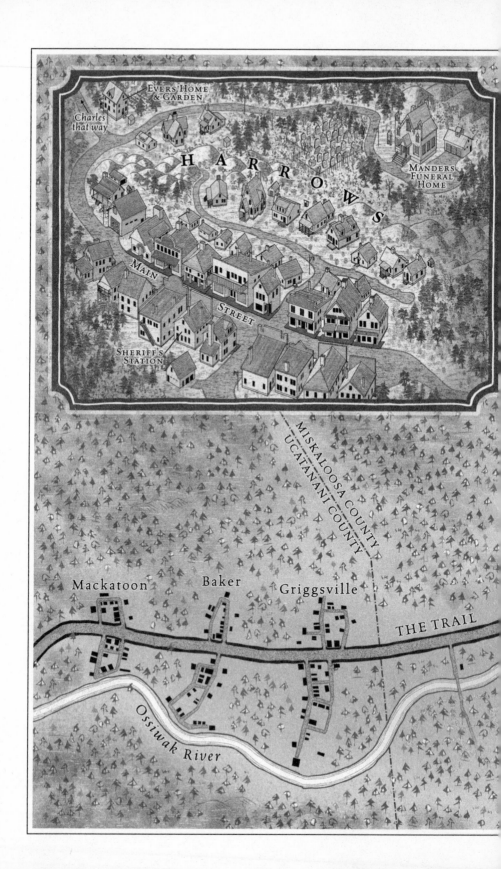

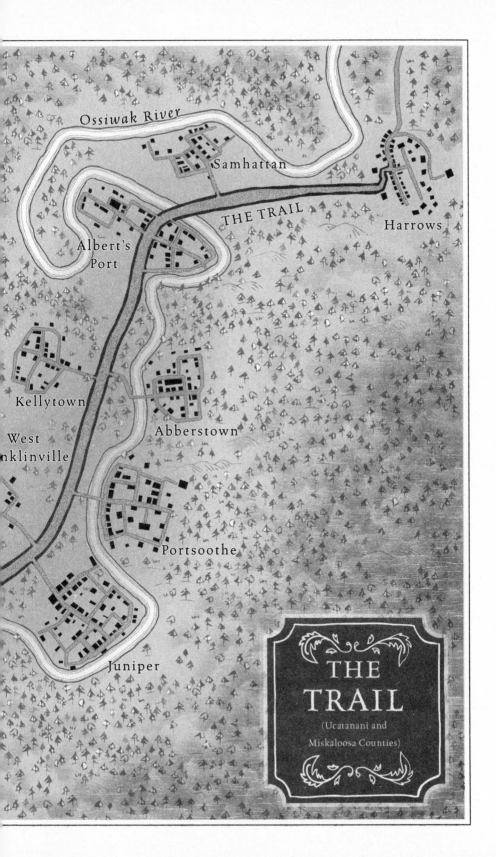

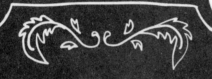

THE
TRAIL

Summer

(Ucatanani and
Miskaloosa Counties)

AT THE FUNERAL OF
JOHN BOWIE

Harrows, situated at the northernmost point of the Trail, savored its distance from the meat of the rabid road. It was easily the most affluent town in both counties; the homes of Harrows were larger, often constructed of stately stone, some with as many as ten bedrooms. The garden yards were as wide as the fabled Trail itself, some roofs as high as the willows. Even better: Harrows enjoyed more sunlight than the other towns, as the shadows cast by the arching of those willows concluded where the wheat fields began, just south of the border. Sunny and secluded, remote and rich, Harrows was a very desirable place to live.

But that didn't preclude its citizens dying.

John Bowie found this out the bad way.

"One of a kind," Carol Evers said, standing beside her husband, Dwight, looking into the open grave of her friend John Bowie. The tears in her eyes reflected the unboxed man below.

One of Harrows's most likable men, Bowie was a very funny thinking-man who added to every affair he attended. His lively eyes often smiled behind his thick glasses, and his ceaseless appetite was welcomed by all who had spent an afternoon cooking for a party.

John Bowie was a good man.

John Bowie was a fun man.

John Bowie was also a homosexual who posed no threat to Dwight Evers, Bowie being the closest friend Carol had.

For this, Bowie was the only person outside her husband whom Carol had told of her lifelong condition.

It wasn't an easy thing for her to reveal.

And yet it had come out of her, so easily, one clear evening on the back porch of her and Dwight's home. John had been discussing books and magic tricks, two of his most profound interests, when Carol suddenly rose from the bench and told him.

I've died before, John. Many times.

Though famous for a healthy sense of humor, John wasn't one to take such a statement lightly. And Carol's green eyes often betrayed when she was serious.

Tell me, he'd said, his boots resting upon a wooden stool, his body hunched in a wicker chair. It was Carol's favorite posture he assumed. Perhaps that was what loosened her lips. *Tell me about every single time.*

And Carol did tell John Bowie about every time she'd died, every time she could remember. The doctors, she said, had no name for her condition. But she'd come up with one of her own many years ago.

Howltown, she'd said. *That's what I started calling it around age eight. I guess I was influenced by the names of the Trail-towns. The only places I knew of. And it is something of a town. To me. No sheriff, of course. No boardwalk, no bank, no booze. No nothing. But it's a place, here on the Trail, all the same. Even if I'm the only one who visits.* She'd paused. John noticed an odd combination of expressions on her face; Carol was both recalling her youth, when she named her coma, and despairing that it still existed. *To someone outside the coma,* she continued, *I appear . . . dead. Hardly a heartbeat. Far from fogging a mirror. And a pulse as slow as a slug. There's no light in there, John. I can hear the world around me, but I can't move. And the wind in there . . . it howls. So . . . Howltown. Pretty neat, huh?*

She told John how afraid she once was of the isolation of the coma. How her mother Hattie's constant tinkering in the workroom acted as an anchor to reality. *Without Hattie, I'd have broken in there. Gone mad.*

She told him of the hoarse breathing that acted as music in Howltown. And how Hattie said it must be Carol's own. She told John about the falling sensation, too.

From the second it starts, I'm falling. I fall into the coma and I don't touch ground until I wake.

John could see the relief in the face of his brilliant friend as she spoke. Carol, John knew, hadn't told anybody but Dwight. She was embarrassed over it, he surmised, convinced that her condition would be considered a burden and send most running. Carol had intimated that someone had run from her before. John listened closely and had ideas of his own. And as he spoke Carol realized why she had suddenly decided to confide in someone other than her husband. It wasn't only for safety's sake, though that played a major part, for what if Dwight were to die while Carol was inside the coma? Who would know that she still lived?

But telling John Bowie had just as much to do with Carol's desire to hear what he thought of it.

John had many things to say. John was as bright as Howltown was dark.

And now John Bowie was dead.

Lying barefoot in a gray suit on the bumpy dirt six feet beneath Carol's yellow shoes, John had been taken by the Illness, knew his death was afoot, and had asked for no box. Carol herself had seen to it that her naturalist friend, Harrows's resident pantheist, would decay the way he wanted to.

Directly into the dirt.

"He looks a bit like he . . . fell right into the hole," Dwight whis-

pered to Carol, the couple shoulder-to-shoulder. Carol's yellow dress
flapped in a breeze that didn't seem to reach her husband's black suit.

"It's what he wanted," Carol whispered. And her voice sounded
much older than the thirty-eight years she was.

The funeral director Robert Manders stood at a podium at the
head of Bowie's grave, telling the grievers what they already knew. "A
brilliant mind, an enthusiast, a thirst for knowledge in all subjects . . ."

Carol thought of John performing simple magic tricks at parties.
Making olives vanish. Pulling plums from the ears of drunk women.
She tried to smile but couldn't bring herself to do it.

"In the end," Dwight whispered, "no magic trick can save you."

"What?"

"It's sad," Dwight said. "That's all."

You two have as much in common as I do with a ladies' man, John once
told Carol. *You know he married you for your money, right?*

But Carol hadn't liked that joke and told him as much.

Dwight nodded across the grave to his colleague Lafayette. Carol
caught the gesture. Of all the people Dwight associated with, the
woman Lafayette was perhaps the least likable. Her gut hung proudly
over her black belt and tested the silver buttons of her white wool
shirt. A cemetery wind toyed with her long ponytail, sending it flapping across the deep wrinkles in her face. She'd always looked something like a witch to Carol, and Carol couldn't imagine a single
sentence that might've been exchanged between the pompous, dubi-
ous prig and the amazing man John Bowie who lay barefoot in his
gray suit on his back below.

Perhaps self-conscious of the unboxed man, conservative Manders
concluded his eulogy more quickly than Carol expected. Then again,
Bowie's entire life had concluded more quickly than Carol expected.
The Illness, she knew, was something to be scared of. Yet for a woman
who had died many times, Carol was perhaps less afraid than most.

"Hell's heaven," Dwight said. "I can hardly stomach this."

Carol brought her lips close to her husband's ear. "Dwight. Shut
up."

It was no secret Dwight had as little in common with John as did the witch Lafayette. Normally this bothered Carol deeply. How was it she'd married a man who didn't see the shine in her brilliant, favorite friend? How was it John couldn't make Dwight laugh? How was it—

But today was no day to be upset with Dwight.

And yet the couple were on hard times indeed.

It's because he doesn't ask questions like I do, John once said. Carol could almost hear his voice now. *He's more bull than man, and that's coming from a friend with a lot of turkey in him.*

John was always making jokes. But more important, always making Carol *laugh*.

She looked to his lips just as the gravediggers Lucas and Hank shoveled dirt upon his chest and chin. Then, with her mind's ear, Carol heard him say something he had never actually said while living. Something he would probably say now if he could.

Who else are you gonna tell now? Someone needs to know. What if you slipped into the coma right now and Dwight somehow died while you were in there? You need a safety valve, Carol. Security. I'm gone now. Do my ghost and the ghost of your mother a favor: Tell someone else.

"We need to tell someone else," Carol suddenly whispered. Dwight turned to face her.

"Tell someone else what?"

As Manders closed his book of notes, as Lucas and Hank covered Bowie's head completely, Carol closed her eyes and repeated herself. "We need to tell someone else."

"Come on, dear," Dwight said, tugging her elbow as the other grievers started to move from the graveside. "Let's discuss this at home."

But did Dwight know what she meant? She couldn't be sure. And why not? Her mother, Hattie, would've known. Hattie would already be sawing the pieces for her plan B. John would've known, too.

Dwight nodded a good day to Lafayette and led Carol to the cemetery grass. "What is it?" he asked.

Carol began walking toward their coach.

"What is it?" he repeated.

"What *is* it? A good friend has died. That's what it is."

"My heart is as heavy as yours," Dwight said, catching up.

Though Carol hated to hear it, John was often right about Dwight. And recently Dwight had changed. Ten, five, even three years ago he would be holding her hand, an arm draped over her shoulders, discussing the very topic she wanted him to address.

John Bowie was dead. Someone else needed to know about Howltown.

And yet talking about her condition was one of the hardest things for Carol Evers to do.

She had been spurned before.

Inside the coach she spoke her mind. And the argument began.

"Now nobody knows," she said, juggling the sorrow of losing John and the fear of being vulnerable once more.

"Knows what, dear?" Dwight looked as lost as a wolf cub with no pack.

"I'm talking about my condition."

Dwight nodded. But Carol couldn't tell what the nod meant.

"And now nobody knows," he said.

"Someone other than you needs to. If not . . . there's a very real risk of my being mishandled."

Dwight laughed.

Carol, stunned, sat up straighter. "Why are you laughing?"

"What are the chances, Carol? What are the chances that you'd slip into a coma right now, and that I would then drop dead while you were inside?"

The way he said it, Carol felt a little embarrassed for being so angry. And yet . . .

"If there's one thing Hattie taught me, it was not to waste a second when it comes to this. We need to tell someone. A doctor can't even detect a pulse when I'm in there. And hell's heaven, Dwight, you should have brought this up yourself."

"I'm sorry, Carol. Who do you want to tell?"

Carol heard the distant echo of hoarse breathing. Or perhaps it was the actual horses taking them home.

"Farrah."

"The maid girl?"

"Yes."

"I don't think I agree. You tell her and everybody's going to know."

"So what?"

"Well, it's you who keeps it secret. I'm just thinking of you, dear."

But he wasn't. Carol could tell.

"Farrah is perfect," Carol said. "She's bright. She's kind. And she's close."

"Her husband, Clyde, is a drunk. Loose lips."

"Well then, that's how it will be. And everybody will know."

"Are you . . . are you sure?"

"Yes." She thought of John Bowie. Whereas Hattie thought it wise to keep it a secret (*they'll take advantage of you, Carol, men from the Trail*), John encouraged her to let everyone in: *In the end, people are kinder than you think, Carol. Even the ones you thought were not.* "Yes. I'm absolutely sure."

But Dwight could tell she wasn't. Carol had suggested others before.

As the coach rolled rocky over stones in the road, Dwight adopted a more serious posture. He placed a hand upon hers.

"Do you . . . feel it coming on?"

Some of the steam of the argument was released. Dwight sounded concerned after all.

"I don't know."

They rode in silence with this between them: the knowledge that Dwight believed her comas were caused by stress. Her many adamant refutations that they were not.

She'd gone under when Hattie died, yes, but she'd also gone many times when, it appeared, life was fine.

Home, inside, the discussion picked up again.

"Do you plan on telling her yourself, tonight, on your walk through the garden?"

Dwight removed his suit coat and hung it in the foyer closet. Carol crossed her arms. Her eyes, damp with half-shed tears, reflected the lit candle on the credenza.

"How about this," she said. "If I haven't told Farrah by the next time I go under, I'd very much like *you* to tell her." She nodded. As if Dwight telling Farrah was easier than Carol doing it herself. Because, after all, it was. "You can bring her into the bedroom and show me to her in person. Have her feel my pulse. Show her how . . . dead I am. And yet . . . still living."

Dwight nodded. This was more like Carol. Unsure after all.

"I promise," he said. He wondered if Carol heard humoring in his voice.

"The next time it happens, let Farrah in."

"I promise."

Then, for Carol, the front door beyond her husband rippled. A slight rising wave from bottom to top.

She heard the hoarse breathing of Howltown.

Ripples didn't always mean the coma was coming, but no coma had ever come without them.

"Maybe you should take it easy tonight," Dwight said. "No walk."

Carol saw real concern on his face. She stepped to him and kissed his forehead.

"Don't plan so much, Dwight." She placed a fingertip between his eyes. "It's as if you've got an entire scene in there, the way things are supposed to play out, and you don't want anything to change that."

Dwight half smiled. "Just worried, dear."

Carol left the foyer and found Farrah in the parlor.

"I'm sorry," Farrah said. "About your friend." By the way Farrah was doing nothing in the parlor, not a strand of her brown hair out of place, Carol understood that she'd been listening to the discussion.

How much had she heard?

"Let's walk," Carol said, and her voice betrayed her sorrow. "The air will do us some good."

Outside, the sky was graying, but enough blue endured to show the pair the paths that wound through the perennials, the fruit-sprouting shrubs, the primary colors of the Evers estate. This, Carol knew well, was "the sweet time." For as wonderful as the flowers looked under the sun, there was no debating the beauty of the grounds by storm.

And a storm, Carol saw, was coming.

"Carol," Farrah said, and Carol knew what the girl was going to say. "I confess I overheard some of your conversation with Mister Evers."

Pebbles crunched under Farrah's plain shoes and Carol's boots.

"Yeah? And what did you hear?"

Carol wanted Farrah to have heard it all. Then, just as suddenly, she didn't.

"Only . . . a handful of words." Farrah stopped walking and breathed deep. "I heard you telling him that it was time you told me . . . something?"

Carol stared long into the girl's face. Her wide brown eyes spoke less of wonder and more of youth.

"Yes," Carol said. "But maybe . . . not just yet. Let's walk."

Carol then sensed the ripple coming strong and looked up, expecting to see it inches from her eyes.

"Carol?"

"I feel a little strange," she said as the pair reached the bottom of a limestone stairwell.

"Carol, we ought to bring you back inside if that's how you feel."

Carol raised a flat palm. "Not in peril, Farrah. Just . . . odd. Sad for my friend John."

Farrah looked to her lady's face, and Carol felt her looking. The girl was as sweet as a range rider brownie, Carol liked to say, and as much a friend as any in her life. Maybe, Carol weighed, it was time, the *perfect* time to tell her.

Not just yet, she thought, looking out over the flowers and plants, searching for evidence of that ripple. She wanted to tell Farrah, but it was not easy.

She'd been spurned once before.

A change of subject was in order.

"How is Clyde?" Carol asked, the sadness in her voice apparent.

At not quite twenty years old, the girl had a love life that seemed so much more tangible than Carol's own. In a peaceful yet longing way Carol guessed the majority of her own explosive life-moments had already happened. Arguments that lasted deep into the morning hours, love that shouldn't have been, great emotions, terrible emotions, words plucked from snowy peaks, conversations without end, and decisions that were made without the knowledge of their influence. But Farrah spoke of her problems with the endearing air of one who believed her trouble to be the trouble of the world, her decisions planetary, her disappointments red with imaginary bloodshed. Carol enjoyed very much hearing that the world was still on fire, every wave in the water a killer, every moon the shape of hysterics.

John liked the very same things.

"Clyde is . . . *Clyde.*"

Carol gasped as a ripple seemed to pass over the dirt at their feet. For a moment it looked as if her boot tips were underwater.

"Maybe we should head back," Farrah said, concerned.

But a second ripple came. Bigger than the first.

Carol stumbled and reached for Farrah's shoulder.

"Okay," Farrah said, the bits she'd heard of the conversation echoing in her head. "Time to take you inside."

She took Carol's hand and led her out of the garden.

"You know," Carol said, trying to ease the moment, seeing her young friend's worried profile as they walked back toward the house. "I had moments like you had with Clyde when I was your age."

"Really?" Farrah asked, happy Carol was talking, though her lady was breathing hard. "Tell me?"

"Have you heard of . . . James Moxie?"

"The outlaw? Maybe, but . . ."

"Yes," Carol said. "That's him."

Farrah stopped and turned to face her, her eyes and mouth perfect circles in her flushed face. Despite the funereal day, the news was flammable.

"You kissed an *outlaw*, Carol?"

"Well, he wasn't an outlaw back when I knew him. His 'glory' came years after. Hattie met him."

"What?"

"He came over one night."

"*What?* James Moxie was at your house? Met your mom?"

Carol pivoted, turning her face from Farrah. By talking about James Moxie she'd inadvertently reminded herself of something that felt very meaningful to her then.

There *was* someone else who knew about her condition.

Someone other than Dwight. Someone who had run from her, twenty years ago, unable to shoulder the burden of caring for a woman who died so often.

"There is someone else who knows." She said the words aloud to herself. But of course Farrah heard them.

"Who knows what, Carol?"

Carol shook her head, shooing the revelation away. Perhaps storing it.

"Well, it *was* something, I suppose. Our brief run. I believe he's down in Mackatoon now. I can't be sure."

"Do you mean it was more than a kiss?"

"That's not what I meant, digger, but yes, it was something."

"How much of something?"

Carol shook her head, shooing Farrah away. They were on the lawn now, nearing the house.

"One day, Carol, one day when you're not feeling so odd, you are going to tell me the whole story and I am going to listen. Oh, am I going to listen to that one!"

Carol smiled, and the heartbreak she felt for having lost John Bowie showed all the way through.

"Oh, Carol. I'm sorry."

Carol pulled open the creaky wooden back door, and the two stepped inside. Before shutting it, Carol looked to the garden, to the stone steps and the many paths beyond.

"Farrah," she said, "I would very much like to tell you something."

Farrah turned and saw her lady in the doorframe, still looking away from her. "What is it?"

Without turning to face her, Carol said, "I have a condition, Farrah. A sickness, you might say. It doesn't knock often, but when it does I've no power not to let it in."

As she spoke the words, she saw it.

The rise and fall of the horizon, the woods beyond the gardens, the gardens themselves.

She took hold of the wooden doorframe and braced herself for the wave.

The pond appeared to rise with it.

"Carol?"

The plants in the garden trembled, the bees dropped to the grass. Even the garden statues and the stone steps were made to move, stomping violence into the earth.

"Carol?"

It arrived at her boots, distorted the leather, rattled the hem of her dress.

"Hell's heaven, Farrah. It's here."

Then Carol collapsed. And Farrah's scream followed Carol into Howltown.

HOWLTOWN

F alling.
    Falling.
Falling.

And the winds came at her. And the darkness was absolute.

Carol retained a vivid image of the back door's threshold coming at her as she collapsed, felt the forever-sensation of falling. She knew it well. When she was a little girl the free fall was the scariest part. Now she'd try to heed her mother's three-decade-old advice:

Think of it as flying. More fun than falling.

And John Bowie's more abstract slant:

If you accept the falling as normal, it can become its own solid ground.

But John was drunk when he said it. And John had never been to Howltown.

Unless, Carol thought, *Howltown is like being dead and being dead is like Howltown.*

The feeling, the falling, would last until she woke, it always did, until her feet found solid ground in the form of opening her eyes, as her heart resumed its natural beat, as her lips parted and she could speak once again. But it was always a very long time till then.

Dwight's the only one who knows.

Thoughts were indistinguishable from speech in the coma. Thoughts were as loud as the voices of others. And this particular thought wasn't entirely true. James Moxie knew. It was why he'd run from her so long ago. And yet what good was it, Moxie knowing? How would he, a person glued firmly to her past, ever learn of her being in trouble, if into trouble she ever fell?

Stop worrying. Please. You'll land in a few days. Like always.

She heard the familiar labored breathing, the hoarse wheeze Hattie told her must be her own. Carol had heard it faintly all day. But it was more definitive now. Just as the color black itself was more complete than her memory of it; as if a child had colored a whole piece of paper, colored it . . .

All black . . .

Carol thought of Farrah's expression just as the last ripple hit, the anticipation of a secret about to be shared. Over the duration of Farrah's employ, Carol had gone under twice, and with each turn Dwight had asked for privacy as his lady had taken ill. But as good a man as any of the staff thought him to be, they also knew he was no doctor. Farrah and the other employees of the house had their questions as to what was wrong with Carol Evers. And the rumor mills never pumped so furiously as they did in the kitchens and gardens of finer homes.

The hoarse breathing continued steadily, and Carol thought of John Bowie. As if, in death, he had access to the coma. As if she could hear his lifeless lungs continuing to pump air to his lifeless body.

John!

John used to brainstorm solid surfaces Carol might be able to hang on to in the coma. *Reach out, if you can, as you fall. If you sense anything against your fingertips, anything at all . . . grab it.*

Over drinks in the parlor it was an exciting idea. And yet, once inside, once *falling,* Carol couldn't move at all. The only motion she felt came from the falling itself.

The cold wind against her.

Still, Carol tried. The image of the threshold still vivid in her memory and mind's eye.

The sound of breathing continued; the slow steady rumble that reminded Carol of her grandfather's wheezing. And just beyond it, between inhales and exhales, Carol heard familiar voices: the vague distant syllables of Dwight and Farrah talking.

Carol always heard the external world while inside the coma. But it was an unstable version of that world, as if the individual tones and timbres of the voices were amplified. The emotions behind them, too.

Dwight must be explaining her secret to Farrah, Carol thought. Calming the girl down.

Yet as the words sharpened, at times clearer, at others distorted, Carol heard Dwight speaking like the grievers at Bowie's funeral. His words came flat and final. There was resignation in his voice. As if Carol *had* in fact died this time.

Falling.

Falling.

Falling, Carol tried to listen harder, but the wind of falling wouldn't let her.

Hattie used to simulate this very thing by flapping papers close to Carol's ears as Carol sat in a chair in the workroom. Hattie would ask her to listen *past* the papers, to the other rooms of the house. At first it was difficult for an eight-year-old Carol to grasp. But one afternoon, through the crinkling, she heard the voice of a neighbor calling for the family dog, and Carol understood how it was done.

Three decades later Carol understood there were moments, while falling, that concentration could not penetrate. But there were also moments that it could.

John Bowie was long fascinated by the fact that Carol could hear while inside the coma. Once she had shared her secret, he'd sit beside her and read, talk, joke, as Carol fell blind through the coma. Dwight didn't like it. He said he was partial to her remaining calm and unbothered when she slipped into her deathlike trances. But Carol enjoyed it deeply when John's comforting singsongy voice danced throughout her personal darkness. As he did magic tricks for her that she could not see.

She longed for his voice now. The words of that wonderful man.

But it was Dwight whom she heard instead.

"We must carry her upstairs."

Carol imagined him kneeling beside her inert body, which must have been half in, half out of the house.

"Should I call a doctor?" Farrah asked, her voice bright, edged with hysteria.

"No," Dwight said and Carol believed the explanation was coming. The revelation of her condition. But what Dwight said instead, what Carol thought she heard, turned the winds in the coma to ice. "She's dead, Farrah."

The words were so wrong to Carol, so *untrue,* that she imagined she'd heard them wrong. After all, how often had she truly heard the world beyond those crinkling papers?

"Dead?" Farrah asked, the single syllable erupting like thunder in Howltown.

Is there a difference? John once mused, folded upon that wicker chair on the porch. *Between Howltown and Death? And if so, how would you know what it was?*

Falling, Carol tried to remain calm. She must have heard Dwight wrong. Must have. Must.

Maybe it's the space we all long for, John said. *Everyone wants to get away. You actually get the chance to do it.*

Dwight spoke. "It's a terrible thing. But Carol has—"

"She was just about to tell me something," Farrah said, her voice shaking.

Because both were breathing heavier (and in the coma their breathing sounded like gusts of dark wind), Carol believed they were carrying her now. They were most likely halfway up the stairs. Rising. And yet Carol continued to fall, deeper down.

"What did she tell you?" Dwight's words were sharp. Harsh. As if he was trying to read the maid's mind.

Have you read much about telekinesis? John once asked her. And his voice traveled through the gradations of darkness inside. An old question echoed. *Because the rules don't seem to apply in your coma. For starters, you appear dead when you're not. Perhaps inside you can do things you can't do out here? Like ... for example ... move objects with your mind.*

Desperately, still denying the truth of what she was hearing beyond the winds of falling, Carol wanted to prove John's theory true. If only she could move something. Anything. Let Dwight know she still lived.

"She hadn't ... told me yet ..." Farrah said, and now Carol was close to certain that the girl and Dwight stood on opposite sides of the bed Carol must lie upon. Their voices came to Carol in such a way as to give the bedroom dimensions, and the blankets and pillows muted the harsher echoes that thundered through Howltown.

Falling.

Falling.

Falling.

"But how much *did* she say?"

It was the way Dwight said this more than the words he chose. The way he sounded frightened that Farrah might know more than he wanted her to know.

If she could have moved, Carol would have shaken her head no. If she could have spoken, she would have cried, *Tell her, Dwight! TELL HER I'M ALIVE!*

But there was no parting of her lips, no cry for help.

"She said ... she said ..."

"Out with it!"

Carol felt as if she were falling through a cold patch, an area within the coma she had never been.

Fear was no stranger to Howltown, no traveler from the Trail, but the fear she felt now was shattering.

"She said she was feeling odd, Mister Evers!" Farrah blurted out. The horror in her voice, amplified in the coma, was deafening. "She said something about a ... a ... *ripple* coming. She—"

"She called it that?"

"Called what that?"

"A *ripple,* girl. She used that word?"

Carol tried hard to hear through the winds of the coma, through the papers Hattie used to crinkle by her ears.

"She used that word, yes. She told me she wanted to talk to me. Mister Evers . . . is she really dead?"

The hoarse breathing inhaled.

"Yes. She's dead."

Exhaled.

Then the wind grew louder, as if Carol were falling faster.

"It's very important that you tell me all you know, Farrah."

Dwight's voice was deeper and quieter than it was moments ago. Carol could imagine the expression he wore as he adopted this tone. It was the face Dwight made when he believed he could squeeze information out of someone he thought was less intelligent than himself.

But Farrah didn't respond.

Silence from the bedroom.

Carol listened close.

"Farrah?" Dwight said.

A thud. Something heavy falling to the floor.

Then, as it sometimes, mercifully, occurred within the coma, the next words that were spoken told Carol exactly what had happened in the world she'd fallen from.

"She's fainted," Dwight said aloud, disbelieving. "The maid has fainted."

Dwight's breathing came loud, near, and Carol wondered if perhaps he was going to cry. But the steadiness of his exhalations told Carol that he was exerting energy instead.

He was carrying her again.

Every few steps she heard the clack of his dress shoes against solid ground. The first floor again. In the kitchen, the echo was unmistakable.

Dwight grunted, and Carol heard a door opening, and she tried to deny what she was hearing. What she knew to be true.

Dwight was carrying her to the cellar.

She could smell it now, too, the stuffiness that entombed her half-way down the stairs, the bitter stench of stored root vegetables. The dust of a cellar used primarily for stowing, with suitcases from past travels upon the Trail, dresses that had lost some of their appeal, and suits Dwight no longer fit into.

Help.

There was an urgency to the sudden word. But Carol could not speak it.

He's hiding me, Carol thought, recalling their argument earlier this day. Could it be he was overreacting to her plea for further safety?

I don't think he's hiding you for your sake, angel. John's voice in Howl-town. *I think he's doing it for his own.*

The sound of Dwight's steps changed. He'd crossed from the solid concrete of the cellar to the gravelly floor of the storm room.

There, Carol knew, stood the morguelike slab she'd had installed herself, if ever she and Dwight had to dine below as a tornado tore through the Trail.

Dwight's breathing changed pace. No longer the grunts of hard work; now the long exhalations of having completed a task. Carol knew she was on the slab.

And yet . . . still falling.

The hoarse breathing continued.

"Do not wake, dear," Dwight said. And his voice was without reason. "You have no idea how dark it is, living in someone else's shadow."

Carol tried to understand, tried to process, but the singular idea that would not go away was simply too abhorrent to accept:

He wants you to stay this way.

"And for a man to go unseen, in the shadow of his wife . . . Oh, Carol. Do not wake. Do not deny me this triumph."

Falling.

Falling.

Falling.

Then Carol heard his shoes leaving the storm room, the creaking of the stairs leading up to the kitchen. Footfalls in the hallway, then foyer. The front door opened then closed.

The hooves of the horses came to fiery life in the drive.

Dwight!

The sound of the carriage evaporated into a night Carol could only imagine.

He wants you to stay this way.

But before Carol could ask another question, before she could attempt to make sense of the horrors upon her, the cellar door swung open again.

Through the wind, Carol heard.

Footsteps, again, on the creaking stairs.

Had she gotten it wrong? Was Dwight still here?

Bare feet on the stone floor and the quick shuffling of someone approaching.

A thief, perhaps. One of the many terrible men who stalked the Trail. Someone had been watching the house, waiting for the coach to leave.

As the bare feet reached the storm room, then entered, the many rough faces she'd seen on the Trail became one. It was a mask she'd known twenty years past, features not yet molded by life as an outlaw, and a name not yet legendary to those who heard it.

James Moxie.

For the duration of one slowed beating of her heart, she imagined Moxie entering the storm room and removing her, undoing what Dwight had begun.

Dwight wants you this way.

But *could* this be true?

"Carol!"

The shrieking sound of Farrah's voice so close to her ear echoed like a golden eagle's cracked call in Howltown.

"Carol! You look . . . you look . . ."

Farrah began sobbing again. Heavy rain in the coma. And to the beat of Farrah's falling tears, Carol tried hard to defy the only explanation she could find, the answer to where Dwight must have gone.

Dwight said she was dead.

Dwight drove off in the carriage.

Don't think it. Please don't think it.

But it was too late to stop it from coming. And when it arrived, it was whole.

He drove to the funeral home.

HELP!

But nobody could hear a silent plea sung from the storm room of a cellar in Harrows. Not even the girl who lamented beside her.

It's my worst fear, Hattie once told a nine-year-old Carol, as Mom hammered at wooden boards in the workroom. *My daughter buried alive.*

But Carol was not buried. She was falling.

Falling.

Falling.

And the voices that accompanied her were the voices of memory, with no volume to tell a funeral home director she was alive, no hand to stop the gravediggers from shoveling, no fingers to lift the lid of a casket that might be coming soon.

Closing soon, too.

Stop it! Carol scolded herself. *You're afraid. That's all. You heard him wrong.*

But she'd never misheard anything in Howltown. The opposite, in fact. For as long as Carol could remember, the things she'd heard as she fell were beyond even the truth of the words themselves. There was the truth of the person behind them.

What had Dwight begun?

"Oh, Carol!" Farrah suddenly cried, and her voice was a banshee shriek. "You look *alive!*"

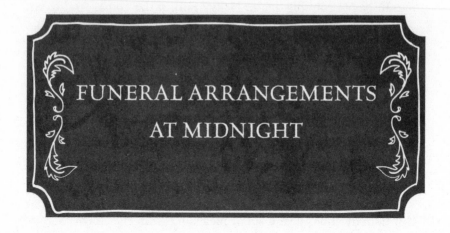

FUNERAL ARRANGEMENTS
AT MIDNIGHT

Dwight steered the gray steeds through downtown Harrows, passing Sheriff Opal's station halfway to the southern border. Nobody was out. The death of Carol's homosexual friend John Bowie had sent a shiver through town that Dwight could still feel clinging to the cool early-evening air. It bothered him.

Bowie was never a threat, not exactly. Because Bowie wasn't interested in women, Dwight felt just fine with all the time he and his wife had spent out on the porch, in the parlor, taking walks ... *talking*. There was no stopping the inevitable suggestion Carol made that they inform John Bowie of Carol's condition, and there was nothing Dwight could think of to refute it.

It was a very delicate business, planning a murder, and one had to be very careful with what one showed. And what one didn't.

Bowie's death was also inevitable, Dwight thought. Of course there was no predicting whom the Illness would suddenly take, and yet the way Bowie lived—the drinking and cavorting, the endless flirting and conversing, the idea that his mind and worldview might bring him to transcend the rituals most people had to endure—*that* was the end of John Bowie, and Dwight had spotted it the day he met him.

Perhaps John was a threat after all. A philosophical threat. A spiritual adversary. Someone more fun than Dwight.

But Dwight refused to admit it.

"To Lafayette's!" Dwight called, snapping the reins, guiding the gray horses past downtown Harrows to the wide-open wheat fields that always looked like ice drifts under the darkening sky. Lafayette lived here, in the border of dark willows that signified the start of the Trail.

Dwight thought and rehearsed. Rehearsed and thought.

He imagined himself standing before the funeral director Robert Manders.

"Manders," he said, his voice trembling. "She's gone!"

But as the words fell false from his lips, his mind remained focused on the incredible series of events that had led him to where he was. The Illness had taken Bowie in pieces (it always did, that's how it worked), and there had been plenty of time for Dwight to account for the fact that, with Bowie's eventual expiration, there would be nobody living who knew of Carol's condition.

But for Carol to go under on the very same night Bowie was buried?

Well, Dwight knew that was not exactly fortuitous luck. Carol was far too stubborn to recognize a correlation between her comas and the stresses life may or may not have placed upon her. Dwight had been keeping track of such things for close to five years. He'd even pointed it out to her, but Carol refuted this claim, insisting that if Hattie hadn't spotted it, it simply didn't exist.

And yet it did exist. Carol went under the very night Hattie died, too. Emotional duress almost always sent Carol to . . . to . . .

Howltown.

Carol's childish name for the comas.

He was about a mile away from Lafayette's shack. The pear-shaped ponytailed wrinkled witch of a Trail-watcher whose primary source of income was connecting civil men with uncivil monsters. Carol had never liked her. Dwight wasn't sure he liked her himself. But there was a lot of Carol's money to go around now. And Lafayette knew better than most what to do with a surplus.

"Manders," Dwight said, changing the timbre of his voice slightly. A tad less sad. "She's . . . *gone.*"

John Bowie wasn't the *only* one who knew of Carol's condition. But Carol certainly didn't need to know about Lafayette.

Dwight wanted to laugh with excitement, but couldn't. There were things to take care of before celebrating in any way. A quick conversation with Lafayette for starters. Funeral arrangements with Manders straight after.

And what of the girl, Farrah? How much *did* she know?

Dwight had carried her to the guest bedroom and placed her gently upon the mattress. Best to look gentlemanly at this stage of the game. And if she woke while he was away? She wouldn't think to check the cellar. She'd simply discover that her lady was no longer in the master bedroom and she'd rush into town, hysterical, claiming that her lady had died.

All good for Dwight.

"Manders . . . she's gone."

But now Dwight wasn't using a sad tone at all. Now he was blubbering with enthusiasm as the lone light in Lafayette's shack came aflame like a lightning bug: a solitary life living in the shadows.

She really does live like a witch, Dwight thought.

He parked the coach twenty feet from the lean-to and got down from the box quickly. Lafayette's door was open, as if this were only a summer night that had nothing to do with death. Nothing to do with murder at all.

"Evers?"

Lafayette's wrinkled face was in the window. Dwight hadn't seen it until he was inches from the open door.

"She's under."

Lafayette didn't look surprised. She didn't look like she'd heard Dwight at all. Dwight imagined that it was one of the many reasons the Trail-watcher was good at what she did.

"Come inside."

Dwight crossed the shack's threshold and thought of Carol collapsing upon the threshold of the back door at home. By the time he reached the small wooden table within, Lafayette was already seated.

"So we begin," Lafayette said.

"Manders," Dwight said, nodding. "Tonight."

Lafayette held up a fat open palm. Her eyes shone by candlelight. "Too rushed. Do it tomorrow."

"I want her buried now."

Lafayette laughed and with the laughter Dwight felt as if he were seeing the woman for the first time—how she truly was. It felt something like discovering the edicts of a club after the initiation had taken place.

"He's not gonna bury her *tonight*, Dwight. You can count on that. Let's stick to the plan."

"Plan? Carol has gone under. We bury her. That's the plan."

Lafayette looked over her shoulder, through the open front door. "Is she in the carriage?"

There was an uneasy, lustful curiosity in her voice. It made Dwight's stomach turn. "She's at home. Where she belongs, if Sheriff Opal were to ask."

Lafayette turned her emotionless eyes on Dwight. "So while you're with Manders . . . she could wake and . . . walk on out . . . maybe go to Manders, too . . . make a fool of you?"

"No. She won't wake tonight. She's never woken that quick."

"What's the quickest?"

"Two days. Since we've been married. Since she'd been under my watch."

"And before then?"

"*Two days!*" Dwight bellowed.

Even then Lafayette showed no impatience, no anger. "Then why rush?"

Dwight opened his mouth to speak. Closed it. Opened it again. "I want her buried now."

Lafayette rested her heavy hands upon her considerable gut. In the lantern shadows her ponytail looked something like a whip.

"It'll look like grief to Manders," Dwight said.

"Which it is, of course."

"Right. Which it is."

Lafayette seemed to consider this. "Anybody know she's died?"

"Yes."

Lafayette tilted her head. "Who?"

"Farrah Darrow. Our maid. Carol collapsed at her feet."

"Kill her," Lafayette said, without hesitation.

"No!"

"Why not?"

"I want no signs of foul play."

"You're right," Lafayette said. Then she belched. "If you killed her it would only raise suspicion. I still say you smother Carol."

"I won't do it."

"I could."

Dwight felt a wave of rage. Not because Lafayette had suggested killing his wife, but because Lafayette had emasculated him. And wasn't that exactly what Dwight was trying to bury?

"It could work," Lafayette suddenly said, dropping the current thread and picking up the former. "Going to Manders tonight could work. But you've got to play the celebrity angle."

"Celebrity?"

"Your wife would've wanted a private ceremony. She's so adored, after all, and perhaps a clandestine burial would suit her wishes best. Make it about her, Dwight. Not you."

"Yes. About her."

"Show me."

Many times Dwight had rehearsed for Lafayette. And yet, with the moment at hand, the pressure of getting Carol underground was enormous.

A clock ticked somewhere in Lafayette's shack.

"I'm going to go to Manders now and—"

Lafayette raised her hand, the implication clear.

So Dwight performed the lines he would deliver to Robert Manders. And as he did, Lafayette rose from the small table, her eyes bone white in the lantern light, as she modified Dwight's every word, coached him, even gripped him by the lapels of his jacket, slapped him, and roughed up his hair.

"There's a lot at stake here," Lafayette said. "And I can't be there with you when you do it. You gotta look the part, Dwight. You gotta *be* it."

Dwight went through his lines again, his many moods.

"No," Lafayette said. And *no* again. "Start over."

"Manders . . ."

"No."

"Manders . . ."

"No."

Their voices continued this way, echoes of themselves, for hours. Dwight rehearsed as Lafayette paced the shack.

Then without a hint Lafayette told Dwight she believed he was ready, and Dwight felt a flood of anxiety he'd never navigated before.

"It's time," Lafayette said, her voice like an unoiled tin joint, "for Dwight Evers to face the world for the first time as a grief-stricken, crestfallen widower."

But as Dwight fled Lafayette's shack, as the moon above told Dwight he'd been inside for longer than he'd realized, longer than he'd wanted, the Trail-watcher called out one last time.

"Hell's heaven, Evers, walk with less confidence. And *cry*."

Harrows's one funeral parlor was a large clean home overlooking the cemetery at the very northeastern border of town. Because the home was situated at the peak of a rather large hill, winter funerals were delicate, and more than one ceremony had included the creaking of coach wheels sliding. But come summer, the trees, the grass of the grounds, and even the graveyard itself spoke more of a well-tended garden than a place of final rest. Dwight had long considered the home one of the finest in Harrows and discussed with more than one local the shame of it being used for dressing bodies, burials, and meaningless final rites. Such potential, such austerity. And yet there was a gloom about the place. Despite the freshly painted green shutters, the manicured grounds, and the clouds reflected in the many clean windows, all Harrowsers had always known the home as the house of death, it being the only place in Harrows to be buried, a place each of them would one day be laid to rest.

Perhaps it was the wooden arch, the gateway to the graveyard, that gloomed it.

The sky was dark when Dwight rode up the hill to the front steps. The white lilies framing the front walk shone.

The girl Farrah may have heard something of his and Carol's conversation earlier. Dwight couldn't know. But he couldn't focus on that now. No no. That would have to come next. He'd already endured Lafayette. It was time for Manders.

How well rehearsed was he?

It was one thing to perform by Carol's sleeping body. It was certainly another to do so for Lafayette, even on the night of Carol's collapse. But as Dwight passed Sheriff Opal's station for the second time in less than three hours, and as the funeral home rose in relief against the moonlit sky, Dwight felt terribly unprepared.

The feeling did not go away as he left Harrows's Main Street and reached the spacious plots of the homes belonging to the richer men and women of the Trail. For the first time in his life, despite the anxiety, Dwight felt like he belonged up here. Thanks to Carol's "death," the money, of course, was his.

And some for Lafayette, he thought. But Lafayette didn't need to know the true numbers.

Dwight steered the gray horses and followed the circle dirt drive until he was flush with the walk and the front steps. In the moonlight his black suit appeared blue, and the gray strands in his hair glowed. He looked up to the big dark house and noted that not a single lantern flickered within. There was work to be done, Dwight imagined, what with the Illness that had come to Harrows, but even the grave-diggers, even the mortician, needed to sleep. Then he looked beyond the house, down the hill, and could see well the wooden arch and—beyond it—the stone and wood markers jutting up from the earth. Black shadows cut the moonlight, and lanterns flickered in the summer breeze on posts placed far apart at the wooded borders of the grounds.

John Bowie's grave still looked fresh. Even in the scant light. And the lumpy earth kept the knowledge in Bowie's brain silent.

Dwight knew there was no watchman. And yet ghouls were not uncommon in Harrows, or in any town on the Trail. Digging for buried treasure was easier than robbing banks. He also knew Robert Manders would be here. Aside from Sheriff Opal, nobody in Harrows was as married to his job as Manders.

Once he climbed down the black steps of the coach box, his boots connected hard with the gravel drive. Dwight crunched small stones and passed through the lilies before climbing the stone stairs leading to the oak front door.

Manders, Dwight knew, lived a floor above the office, and two floors above the stone cellar where Norm Guster dressed bodies as though painting portraits of rubber kings and queens. In his way Norm was Harrows's artist-in-residence, and not a funeral passed in which his work was not remarked upon.

There was a break in the sky, a flash, followed by the sound of far-off thunder as Dwight took hold of the brass knocker and sent a different kind of thunder through the funeral home.

Rain came quiet.

The girl. Farrah. What did she hear? What does she know?

But it wasn't time for that. Not yet.

An immediate shuffling came from within, followed by a flickering light. Dwight saw movement from behind the windows framing the door. Again, Dwight thought of the waste, the shame of such a brilliant edifice being used for such parochial, specific needs. Then the great door opened and Manders pulled his glasses from his sleep-shirt pocket.

"Mister Evers?"

Robert Manders was a small man, his thin hair always flattened to the contours of his head. His round cheeks rendered him eternally childish, despite his mature profession.

"I'm sorry to bother you, Robert. I didn't see a light in the window, but I have terribly sad news and need your assistance."

He thought of Lafayette pacing the shack, saying *no no no that's wrong* in her creaking voice.

Manders looked beyond Dwight, to the drive, and saw it was raining upon the coach.

"What is it, Mister Evers?"

Dwight breathed deep.

"Carol has died this evening."

How did it sound? True?

Manders, still able to feel sympathy despite a thousand meetings like this one, placed a soft hand on Dwight's damp shoulder.

"I'm so sorry. Please, come inside."

The foyer was black beyond the range of the funeral home director's lantern. Dwight followed him across the wood-floored foyer to the office. Manders stepped across a large green rug and patted the back of a small chair before rounding the desk and taking his seat behind it.

Rain anxiously fingertipped the windows.

"Was it the Illness?" Manders asked, his bespectacled eyes reflecting the one lantern in the room.

"No, Robert."

Manders studied the widower's face. "Has somebody seen her?"

"Seen her, Robert?"

Again, Lafayette saying no. Dwight felt a bump in the rhythm of the conversation.

"A doctor. It's very important to know what she died of before proceeding. Might've been the Illness."

Dwight reached his hand into his vest pocket and removed a folded piece of paper.

"Here is the determination," he said. He rose and handed Manders the note.

The funeral director read it slowly and looked up. "Who wrote this?"

He's gonna ask who wrote it, Lafayette had said many weeks ago.

"A very close friend of mine. A man I went to school with."

"You went to medical school?"

"No, but we shared some studies. His name is Alexander Wolfe. A magnificent practitioner from Charles. Is something wrong with it?"

Manders glanced at the paper again. "Not wrong, no, but contradictory. It says the cause of death is unknown. Is that right as you know it?"

Dwight nodded. The word *contradictory* rattled in his mind.

"But it also says she suffered from dizzy spells, bouts of weakness, shortness of breath, and a weak heart . . ."

Dwight looked to the paper and frowned. "Yes, that's all true. Where is the contradiction?"

"Well," Manders said, "I'm no doctor, and I don't mean to speak ill of your friend, but he clearly lists all the symptoms and signs of a heart attack, yet cites the cause as unknown."

"She died of a heart attack?"

Not wanting to be responsible for a diagnosis, Manders shook his head no.

"No. I mean . . . yes. Well, if this is correct, I believe she could have. When was she checked?"

"An hour ago. Possibly a bit more."

Manders looked at the letter again.

Dwight said, "I felt her pulse myself, Robert. I even held a mirror to her nose. I tell you it was too late when I heard the girl Farrah scream from seeing Carol fall."

"Carol fell?"

"Collapsed."

Manders's face softened. "I apologize if I seem a bit put out, Mister Evers, it's just that I like to see these things handled as efficiently and professionally as possible. It would surprise you the number of mishandled death certificates, misdiagnosed causes, and just plain fuddled details there are in these matters. I understand you are grieving. I do not mean to put you off."

"It seems to me the important part is that she's passed. I suppose, for me, it matters not why."

Manders saw Dwight's eyes were wet. "I understand."

There was a short silence between them. Thunder called from far away. Dwight thought of Farrah. Imagined her and Carol in the garden. Imagined Carol beginning to describe the coma. Then Manders said, "But with the Illness, it may be best to get a more thorough determination. It's important for all of us to know if the Illness has left Harrows or if it remains. Would you perhaps like Doctor Walker to look at her as well?"

He's gonna ask for a second look, Lafayette had said.

"Meaning no offense, Robert, but Alexander Wolfe's word is as good as any. No, I don't see any reason to study her again. Carol knew Alexander as well and in my shock I looked for someone close to us both." Now Dwight leaned forward and whispered, "I'd like it to be a small affair, Manders. Unpublicized."

"You've come here to arrange the funeral then."

"Yes. You see, Manders, I'd like Carol buried as soon as possible."

Manders breathed deep. Dwight didn't like the sound of it. Was he about to let Dwight down easy, in a professional manner? Or did he suspect something?

"I understand, Mister Evers. But as you know, there is something of a backlog right now, a line, so to speak. Thirteen deaths before her own. I haven't had to work Lucas and Hank so hard in quite some time. It's really a very frightening thing, the way the Illness has progressed. Rarely has Harrows experienced such tragedy. I'm glad Carol did not fall victim to it, though I realize that matters little now. How soon were you thinking?"

"Tomorrow morning."

Manders, well versed in the decorum of such moments, flashed Dwight a sympathetic face.

"Mister Evers. I'm sorry. But the soonest we can do this is two mornings from tomorrow's. As you know—"

Dwight rose from the chair with a flair and stepped to a bookshelf against a wall. The lantern light barely touched the bindings, and he read what words he could. After a moment of silence, his back to the funeral director, he said, "As you can see, Robert. I'm not handling this very well."

Manders was quiet.

Dwight turned to face him in the subtle flames. "If there's a way this can be done tomorrow morning . . ."

"I'm sorry, Mister Evers. It's just too soon."

Dwight reached his hand into his pocket, and for a moment Manders believed the man was going to bring forth money. Instead he removed a handkerchief and wiped sweat from his brow and neck.

"If only there was a way to expedite such moments, Robert. In the fog of my discontent I'm trying very hard to do the things I think she would have wanted done. It's a shame, isn't it, the way the grieving have to make decisions under such duress? It's almost cruel the way it works out. A man spends the bulk of his adult life caring for a lady, making certain she has what she desires, serving her in any way he can, and then she is stolen, the man is robbed, and at the precise moment that his spirit is shaken and his perspective stirred, he has to make . . . big decisions. It's no wonder there are so many examples of these matters being mishandled. Who can blame a man for how he reacts? I certainly can't. It's astonishing anything gets done at all. There ought to be a ledger kept, in which a person can jot down all that he wants done, kept out of sight so as to limit its 'realness' while living. And when that man passes, why, we'd just open the book and follow the notes. Unfortunately, there's no ledger. Too unsettling perhaps."

Manders looked to the window. As if the rain might advise him how to proceed.

"You can bring her here tomorrow morning," he said. "But the burial can be no sooner than two mornings following."

Dwight nodded. He turned again to the bookcase.

Manders asked quietly, "Where is she now?"

"Now?" Dwight turned to face him, his features gluey in the lantern light. "Now she is north of here."

Manders frowned. "What is north of here?"

Dwight held the director's eyes. He flashed a sympathetic expression of his own. "You've put me in a spot now, Manders. You see, I've decided to have someone else handle the dressing."

Manders looked surprised.

He's not going to like that, Lafayette said.

"I thought you might not like that," Dwight said. "But I have family in the same trade as you."

Manders shook his head. "I'm not worried about who does it, Mister Evers, as long as the job gets done. Do they plan on doing it there? In the house?"

"Yes," Dwight said suddenly.

Manders was quiet. The rain decreased then increased against the windows.

"What are their names?"

"Excuse me?"

"Your family. I don't mean to pry, but as I've said, I like to know things will be handled well."

Dwight stepped to the chair again and sat down. "The name is the same as mine. The Everses from Saskatine."

Manders was quiet for some time. In his pajama shirt he looked younger than his years, and again Dwight thought of Farrah.

"As you want it, Mister Evers. Will there be a showing?"

"No, Robert." Dwight could hear the nails of his plan being hammered into place. "Carol was, like most women, very protective of her image. I can't believe she'd want the town to see her this way. It's the same reason I'm asking for a quiet affair. Carol was . . . in her way . . . shy."

Manders nodded, though he'd never thought of Carol Evers as shy.

As they exited the office, the pair discussed Dwight bringing Carol the morning of the funeral. Manders carried the lantern, and as the director held open the front door Dwight placed a hand on his shoulder then immediately wished he hadn't.

It felt as though his insincerity might be transferred through touch.

"I appreciate you seeing me so late, Robert. And I apologize if things aren't entirely going through your hands. You see, Carol was a very loyal person. One of the many reasons why I loved her. Asking my family to handle things would have meant a great deal to her. As you can see, I'm struggling mightily with the loss. I do appreciate you seeing me. I am somewhat ashamed to say that the sooner this happens, the better for my constitution."

"Everything will be seen to," Manders said. "All will be handled the right way."

Dwight attempted a piteous smile. "Funny you using the word *right* like that, Robert. It all feels so completely *wrong* to me."

Then Dwight stepped into the dark and became one with the sky, the midnight, the black coach with its gray horses, and the flickering shadows beyond the wooden arch signifying the entrance to the cemetery. As Dwight rode away, along the length of the graveyard, Manders could not distinguish between his shape and that of the markers, stone and wood, sticking up from the earth.

It was dark.

But for Dwight, a nagging flicker of distant flame came to life in his mind's eye. It was birthed immediately following a thought he'd had:

Nobody knows.

The light seemed to warn him, to tell him that John Bowie might be dead and Lafayette certainly in on the deal, but Dwight might want to use that light, that distant flame, to check and make sure that nobody else knew, indeed.

MOXIE AND THE MESSENGER

When the message from Harrows came in, Mister Cadge knew exactly which of his employees should bring it to its destination. But the kid was near falling asleep on the bench outside.

"Got one for ya," Cadge said, lowering his head to block the sun with the brim of his visor. He tapped the kid on the shoulder.

The messenger looked up groggily, confused, before understanding what Mister Cadge meant.

Then he moved fast.

"Oh!" He grabbed his hat and leapt from the bench. "A delivery!"

"Best get on it," the old man said, handing the kid the folded paper.

"Thank you!" The messenger put on his hat now. He started to move from the porch, then paused. "Mister Cadge?"

"What is it?"

"I'm . . . I'm nervous to meet him."

Mister Cadge laughed the healthy drumroll of a sober man.

"I wouldn't be calling it a meeting, son. You're only a messenger after all." Cadge winked and the kid still did not move. Then Cadge said, "It's a fairly urgent telegram. Off with you now."

The messenger put the folded paper into the pocket of his vest and thanked Mister Cadge again. The old man had come through.

I won't tell you where the outlaw lives, boy, but I'll gladly hand you an envelope with his address upon it if an' when a message comes in.

The messenger leapt from the porch. He rushed across the small gravel lot to where an old brown mare stood hitched to a post. Mister Cadge looked out the window and saw that the kid was already on the horse, already heading north. It meant little to Cadge: James Moxie and outlawing and who was famous in Mackatoon and who had made a name for himself on the Trail. Whatever Moxie had done, he'd done it as a much younger man, and Cadge was just happy he didn't have to fear any gun-toting lunatic or hero-ruffian sulking about his town. James Moxie had stopped by the office and introduced himself when he first moved to Mackatoon. He was just as polite and cordial as President Coopersmith appeared to be, and maybe Mister Cadge did care a bit after all about who was famous and who wasn't because he did get something of a rise, a thrill, the moment the name James Moxie escaped the newcomer's lips and traveled over the cracked desk in the office. Sure, all that outlawing was for kids, stories to swap, big scary yarns all rolled up on one another and easy enough to carry from one fire to the next, but they *did* have their merit. The Trail was trashed with tales of the *underlaw*, the *overlaw*, the *beyondthelaw*, and Cadge had heard as many as the next old man: the wretched Trail, bordered by black birch and impenetrable walls of half-dead hickory; half dead half the year with snow at the roots and bone-glove ice suffocating the branches. The tunnel of tales, the Trail, dark enough to keep families at home at night.

Mister Cadge smiled. It wasn't easy being a pious man in these parts.

And hell's heaven if James Moxie's story didn't stick out just the littlest bit. Say hey to the high-hog if Moxie's feat in Abberstown wasn't just the tiniest bit more special than most.

They called it the Trick and though Cadge didn't know magic from music, it was one hell's heaven of a story.

Cadge went to the window again and saw that the messenger was gone, well out of view, probably a third of the way to the onetime outlaw's house by now. Again, he recalled the day Moxie came in, standing right here before his old cracked desk, his strong hand extended over the old wood, introducing himself like any man might, saying yes thank you in advance for any messages that may be sent my way and, look, here's where I live, right here is where one of the greatest outlaws who ever rode the Trail lives, *lives*, because he did not *die* out there in the impenetrable black mass of shadows and madness.

Unable to deny the thrill of it, Cadge laughed again. And the thought of the ebullient messenger on his way, the kid who sat slumped on the front porch for weeks at a time, waiting for the chance to meet Moxie—well, it made Cadge laugh even harder.

For the messenger, the feeling was near overwhelming. He was a young man who used to travel the Trail himself, before the horrors out there had him rethinking his life's path. He'd spent nights beneath the birch and maple and wondered if Moxie had done the same. He'd sometimes slept at the mossy lip of a green pond, sleeping through the celebratory sounds of the nearest town: gleeful revelry twanging through the tree-walls of the Trail as if the route were a tunnel . . . a wire . . . a tube by which messages and moods were sent by hoof and heel. But just as some kids went screaming back into the house when their parents told them scary stories out by the fire, the messenger had run from the Trail, unable to shoulder all the dark weight.

Yet what a wonderful feeling the messenger had now! He'd dodged the bigger trouble of the Trail, settled in Mackatoon, and was currently riding to *James Moxie's* house. A man he would've paid dearly to have met years ago.

Oh, how he wanted to know the contents of the telegram!

The horse's heavy hooves pounded the dirt, and the messenger's heart beat in sync. Yes, he was overwhelmed. His own personal imagining of the Trick in Abberstown played over and over in his frazzled head. Moxie on one end of the big pit. Daniel Prouds on the other. A high, blinding sun. The call for draw and Prouds's chest exploding red before Moxie even . . .

". . . before Moxie even pulled his gun."

The messenger howled delight into the morning sky.

Things were certainly hyperbolic now: The rays boring the summer clouds were alarmingly clean and bright; dirt motes came to living life by the hooves of the horse; the trees formed a presidential, a *regal* path to the outlaw. The fresh morning air filled his young lungs entire—air that blew over the roof and along the walls and windows of James Moxie's house; weaving serpentine through his garden of tomatoes and onions (or so the kid had heard); splitting the wood gate at the head of his property (or so the kid had heard); and traveling the small neat dirt walk to where he, the messenger, rode.

It was an exciting moment indeed, breathing the air James Moxie breathed, living the same day as him.

"I'm gonna ask him how he did it," the messenger said, bringing a hand to the folded telegram in his vest pocket. "It would be a pig-sin not to."

Then the messenger gasped as the trees split and a wood gate (it was true!) came into view. Then a garden followed (it, too, was true!), and finally . . .

"Hell's heaven," the messenger said. "It's his house."

This home, he thought, a bit disappointed, was no more magical than the one he himself was reared in.

And yet perhaps *some* magic.

James Moxie was standing against a wooden beam, sure as pig-shit, *right there,* drying his hands with a cloth, staring at the young rider approaching.

The messenger's body went cold rigid.

Did he know I was coming? Could he have?

The messenger gulped.

Magic, he thought.

It was a frightening ride to the gate, a tense one, and very different from how the messenger believed it would go. He'd always imagined he'd tie the horse to a hitching post and climb the mythic steps of a regal homestead adorned with gold knockers, mist, impossible unnamed creatures on the lawn.

But this was no different from delivering a telegram to Missus Henderson, Mackatoon's prized log-chopper.

The outlaw was as still as the post he leaned on. He wore no smile, gave no greeting, showed no expression at all. His red buttoned-up shirt had the messenger imagining the outlaw covered in blood, carrying so many years of it with him wherever he stood. His tan hat hid his eyes.

"Hello!" the messenger called without confidence. He raised a hand and waved. Moxie continued to dry his hands but did not respond.

At the wood gate the messenger stopped the horse and expected a reaction, a word. But nothing came.

Silent, he brought a hand to his vest pocket and removed the folded telegram. He held it up under the early-morning summer sun.

"I have a telegram for one James Moxie. Is that you, sir? I mean to say, of *course* it's you. I came as fast as I could."

"Not on that thing you didn't."

These were the first words the outlaw said to him, and at first the messenger didn't know what they meant. Then he looked down at the horse's back and smiled.

"Ha, yes, she's not in too good a shape."

Moxie stepped slowly from the beam.

The messenger dismounted and looped the harness to the farthest fence post. He lifted a small latch on the wood gate and let himself in. It was a powerful feeling, stepping foot on this man's property, simple and regular as it was. The garden came to life to his right. And the brim of the old man's hat shielded his face from the sun.

The messenger wanted to see those eyes. He knew well that James Moxie was close to forty years old, more than double his own age. What did forty years of burning fire look like, trapped in a man's eyes?

"Mister Cadge said it was pretty urgent."

As the messenger approached, the angles of the shadows changed and Moxie's face was revealed.

Hell's heaven, the messenger thought. *He doesn't look all that different from any man.*

A strong nose. A strong chin. Dark eyebrows floating above ... unexceptional eyes.

Moxie held out his hand.

The messenger handed the folded paper to him. Then said, "How'd you do it? How'd you do the Trick in Abberstown?"

Moxie took the telegram. He unfolded the paper.

The messenger laughed nervously.

"I'm sorry to have asked," the messenger said. "It's just ... you understand ... your story is the best ... the best the Trail has ever seen."

The outlaw glanced down at the message. Now, from this angle, he looked every bit the legend he was. His eyes seemed to generate heat as they read. His lips formed a perfect ruler across his face. The messenger was certainly satisfied with this. And beyond Moxie, inside the home, the messenger saw a blue owlfly in a yellowed jar resting on a small table.

Moxie, finished, set the telegram on the porch-fence rail and looked blankly beyond the garden, the horse, the town.

"You need I should return with a message then?"

Moxie did not respond. A small wind came and teetered the folded paper.

"The operator said it was something urgent, you need I—"

Moxie looked the kid in the face now and the kid saw something terrible there: the coming launch, perhaps, the legend about to perform.

"I'll need to get my things together," Moxie suddenly said. But not to the messenger. Not to anybody at all.

"Sure, sure. You need my help?"

Absently, it seemed, Moxie turned and stepped inside. His boots clacked hard against the porch, then the floorboards within.

The wind came again and rocked the folded paper. The messenger grabbed it and read:

```
James Moxie Sir
Carol Evers dead STOP Condition got the best of
her STOP As beautiful in death as in life STOP
Funeral in two days STOP Harrows STOP Understand
you knew her STOP
Missus Farrah Darrow
```

The messenger barely had time to read the last name before he saw a flash of the red shirt and Moxie was there, before him, above him.

"I'm sorry, Mister Moxie, I just—"

Moxie brought forth a new folded paper. "Send this back to the same address."

The messenger looked to the paper then back up at the outlaw then back to the paper before fully understanding that Moxie was answering the telegram.

"You read it," the outlaw said.

The messenger was frightened. "No . . . no . . . I . . . it . . . the wind—"

"It said two days. Two days from now. Not from yesterday?"

"No, sir. Two days from now."

Moxie leaned forward, his face as serious as any the kid ever saw. "Are you sure?"

"Yes. Yes, sir. I'm sure. The message came in just—"

Moxie stepped back inside.

The messenger watched him come out with a green sack.

"I'll be, James Moxie! Are you leaving then?"

Moxie didn't respond.

Condition got the best of her

"Maybe we're going the same way?"

Moxie vanished into the house again.

"I sure hope I didn't upset you! Hell's heaven, I didn't mean to do that!"

But talk as the messenger might, James Moxie didn't hear these anxious words; his mind was long elsewhere, twenty years elsewhere, in a time when Carol and he were safe from memories; before they had made them. Painfully, Moxie was inside those days again, walking with Carol through a white winter; Carol's fair brown hair pressed behind her ears, her teeth that showed in her smile, her smile that exposed a brilliant mind, a mind that worried, in those days, about a condition the doctors were telling her was getting worse.

Quickly he stepped outside. He crossed the yard, past the well, and reached the stables. Hanging inside was a full sack of feed, and Moxie brought it out. He held it above the trough and watched it spill, filling it entirely.

This was for the horses he wasn't going to ride.

Two days, Moxie thought. And just then two days felt like enough time.

Crossing the yard again, he was at the well and filled the bucket and carried it to the stables. He moved in a pattern; routine deeds performed by a body no longer tied to the mind. He opened the gate to the pen and took his best mare by the muzzle.

She was old, but she had what Moxie needed right now.

Endurance.

Moxie led the mare around the house, tied her to the front porch, and went in through the front door.

The blue owlfly was gone. Moxie noticed this without making a big show of it, and he understood the messenger had stolen it. With its oily, shining blue wings, it was the only thing with any color in the whole house. The first thing that would have caught the eye of a fool-messenger looking for a souvenir.

Thief.

Moxie went into the bedroom again and came forth with some bedding and a hoof pick. He carried the stuff outside, picked up the green sack, and brought it all to the mare.

Slung over the east post, the saddle looked worn but ready.

Pig-shit thief.

He rolled the bedding and tied it tight to the saddle, the saddle tight to the mare.

One last time he went inside.

Hog-swilling pig-shit thief.

Moxie grabbed some bread from the kitchen and filled a pouch with some water from the pitcher. He looked once more around his small home and left it.

Carol Evers dead STOP Condition got the best of her STOP As beautiful in death as in life STOP Funeral in two days STOP

Moxie crossed his porch and mounted the mare. It was too bad the messenger wasn't going north; on that horse he was riding Moxie could have caught up to him quick.

But Moxie didn't even have *quick* to spare.

Two days

Riding now, past his own gardens, heading for the Trail, Moxie felt the pressure of two days upon him, and thought, distantly, how time, like air, has a way of running out.

THE WAKE

E leanor, in her plain dress, stepped through the groups of two, three, and four, and poured lemonade and coffee while balancing a tray of peach cobbler and biscuit pie. She made small talk when called upon but mostly agreed . . . yes yes . . . a terrible thing . . . too young she was . . .

Dwight sat on a counter stool, a stuffed pheasant upon the table, and greeted those who came to grieve. His thick hair was combed back from his forehead, revealing a troubling display in place of his normally careless visage. Never clean-shaven, he had a thick graying mustache that hung above his strong five-o'clock beard, the tough skin stretched upon the masculine features of his face. The slight pouch of his belly was held tight by a black vest and a watch chain that was beginning to rust. His eyes were made extra cavernous by the low lighting in the parlor, the heavy black of his suit, and, as anybody would of course understand, the death of his wife.

"Eleanor," he said, getting her attention as she passed. "Let me know if you're in need of any supplies."

Eleanor nodded. There were guests in earshot, and for this Dwight looked good.

"Of course, Mister Evers. But don't worry about what needs us others have today. Just you worry 'bout your own."

Dwight held her free hand in both of his and nodded. Beside him was a man named Arthur, hired for the afternoon to shuffle the grievers along. Arthur, having worked in the Evers home many times, recognized many faces. The number of guests did not surprise him; Carol was a very popular woman in Harrows.

The Evers home was a big one, with twenty-inch stone walls, a lime green that matched Carol's garden. The gathering was in the parlor, where a clock ticked on the mantel of a fireplace that sat dark and unused. The sun came in through the high windows; the purple drapes were tied tightly aside. Some of the attendees had been in this room before, some had not, and Dwight could tell the difference: the way the virgins fingered the drapes, studied the photographs on the walls, or tilted their heads toward the ceiling. Even under the callous umbrella of death, the home elicited wonder.

Everybody stopped to examine the urn with the ashes of Carol's mother, Hattie, that stood upon the mantel beside the clock, as if she had something to do with time and timing yet.

And Carol, because of the way she'd lived her life, still cast a shadow in death. The house was, after all, hers. Paid for by her. Decorated by her. Spirited with twenty years of her bodily presence . . . no more.

But Dwight counted on that shadow fading.

He turned to see two strangers, a lady and a gentleman, standing beside him.

"We're certainly sorry to hear of your loss, Mister Evers," the man said, holding his hat by its brim to his chest. "It's never a nice thing."

Dwight nodded. "It's true, good man. Death is never a nice thing. Even for those old enough to deserve it."

The lady took Dwight's hand and gripped it. "If ever you need a lady to come through here . . . to make certain things are in order . . . you just call on us, Mister Evers."

"Barbara!" the man said, reddening.

Dwight smiled. "No need to blush, sir. You would be surprised how many women have offered to help. I guess it's fairly obvious the state I'm in. Look about you." He fanned his hand to the greater part of the room. "All this is her doing. From the chandelier and carpet to the very mood."

Barbara frowned.

"Well," Dwight said. "Not the mood today, but the one that usually existed in here. Carol had a manner of . . . illumination. It's a wonder we used lanterns at all. I thank you for your offer. I may even make you honest on it."

Arthur made a congenial gesture suggesting the widower was through speaking, and perhaps needed these exchanges of words to be brief. The couple passed.

The food and drink were going fast. The people talked at length about their affairs and death in general, and Carol's name broke through the word-tangle often, as though today her name was not to be whispered. Dwight heard it many times. Too many times. It wasn't unusual for her to steal a room, and he nodded slowly, guessing Carol's name had always come through other words to him, other voices, sharp and alone.

"Mister Evers, sir."

Another gentleman stood beside him, holding his hat.

"I'd like to express my deepest sympathy for you. Though I understand nothing I say can make it better, I feel it incumbent upon myself to point out that she is in a better place now."

Dwight hesitated before saying, "Well, sir, Carol and I were never what you'd call fastidious. If there be a heaven, as you allude to, I've no proof of it yet, and my findings yester eve only further confirm this for me."

He turned from the man, his eyes overcast, his lips tight to his face.

"I beg for your pardon, good sir, on such a day, but I did not mean to offend," the man said. "I can only tell you from those of us who are . . . fastidious . . . that she be in better hands now. Hands that I have no doubt will one day touch you and show this to be true."

Dwight nodded, but his expression did not change. Despite the edginess, there was some fun in this: playacting grief.

"No need for apologies, my good man. And I didn't hope to offend thee, either. Perhaps the best we can do, the compromise, is to say that the lady was too young, God or no God, and that dying is just the most awful thing we'll ever do."

The stranger closed his eyes and smiled sympathetically. Then Arthur shuffled him along. Dwight saw Patricia Johns waiting next in line.

"Patricia . . ."

She took the hand he held forth in both her own. "I'm so sorry, Dwight."

Dwight smiled sadly. "Would you believe," he said, "that earlier this morning a person told me no man ought to outlive his wife? That the man is supposed to go first?"

Patricia's eyes widened a bit. "Seems a strange thing to say on such a day."

"Yes, yes, but maybe also true. Your kind are given the gift of birthing . . . for that perhaps you are sentenced to endure death as penance."

Patricia clucked her tongue. "Morbid thoughts, Dwight Evers. But understandably so."

She knelt and kissed his cheek and touched his hand, too, for a moment before stepping into the crowd of people. Behind her stood another gentleman.

"Sir, Mister Evers, my name is Geoffrey Hughes. We have not met as of yet, and I regret that this is the time. But allow me to say that I am a great admirer of yours in matters of business, and I'd imagine a man of your stature can perhaps lean a bit on his place in life at a time like this."

Dwight frowned. Perhaps the man didn't know Dwight conducted no business of his own.

Dwight looked quickly to the urn. Hattie again. Carol's mother's money.

"Mister Hughes, I, too, regret seeing your face for the first time so soon after seeing my wife's go still. But as to your comment, you must not know the method of the heart, for a lifetime of good standing appears silly to me now, and all good deeds are rendered juvenile."

"Oh, I do not doubt that, Mister Evers. But perhaps in your darkest hour you can light the candle that shows you what you have remaining. Not many a man has had the success you have found."

At the mention of a candle, Dwight thought again of the nagging flickering he saw in his mind's eye the night before, leaving the Manders Funeral Home. The unwanted thought that he may have forgotten something. Something key.

"Mister Hughes, we are meeting, here, now, in my darkest hour, and I'm not aware of the candle of which you speak. The shadows you allude to have blocked me out completely from the sunny sidewalk where children play and men pass men with nods and good cheer. The sun went down yester eve and with it the clock-bell rang . . . a thunder-rush through the house . . . the glass rattled a bit . . . the furniture rattled a bit . . . and I had no illusion that the darkest hour was then upon me. The details of the very bedroom she lay in dissolved and met with the shadows . . . the things we had shared . . . the simple fringe on a throw pillow . . . the fabric of the drapes . . . and bigger things, too . . . less visible as they are . . . the sound of her slippers in the hall . . . the soothing sound of a comb through the knots in her hair . . . the atmosphere she created, erupting from her like clouds from the steam pipe . . . all this shook and then faded quickly into the shadows created by a clock telling me it was, in fact, the darkest hour. And in that moment, Mister Hughes, though I am aware your intentions are high, there was no candle. No. By definition of it being the darkest hour, there is no light to be seen."

Arthur nodded to Mister Hughes, gently asking him to move on.

Dwight saw a young man holding a folded piece of paper standing next in line.

"What's this?" Dwight asked, recognizing it as a messenger.

"Telegram for a girl who works in your house, Mister Evers. Come all the way from Mackatoon."

That flame again. The light in Dwight's mind swayed as if touched by the wind.

"Let's have it then."

The young man stepped forward and handed him the paper. Dwight unfolded it and, holding it close to his face, looking down the bridge of his nose, read:

```
Miss Farrah Darrow
Do not bury STOP Not dead STOP On my way STOP
James Moxie
```

It appeared to many visitors as though, after reading, Dwight went through the gamut of all bad emotions. That's how William Mooth, next in line, explained it later to his wife.

Ah, it was terrible, Martha. All in awful slow motion. The poor man twisted, made to rise, sat again, reread the telegram, looked about the room, made something of a fist, made to rise slowly, and sat again. Whatever it was he read, I feel awful bad the news had to be put on top of the news he'd already been sentenced to endure.

Then Dwight sat still half a minute, hands folded, composed.

"I think I'll remove myself from the gathering for a moment, Arthur," he finally said.

"Of course, sir."

Dwight took the tall man's hand and rose from the stool. He patted Arthur on the shoulder and asked him quietly if he wouldn't mind asking the messenger to wait a moment before leaving. Then Dwight walked through the gathered people as his wife's name popped out of conversation in sharp bright bursts. Ladies watched him pass and would later comment on how he appeared to have aged ten years since last they saw him. Others wiped tears from their eyes with their scarves. A man in his path stepped aside, and Dwight nodded absently before recognizing him as Sheriff Opal.

"Sheriff," he said, reaching forth his hand. "How wonderful of you to be here."

"Carol was one of the finest ladies in all of Harrows, Mister Evers."

"The finest, Sheriff."

"Yes, the finest."

Opal swallowed before saying, "Seems a lot of death going around these days, what with the Illness. If you don't mind my asking—"

"No, Sheriff Opal. A weak heart it was."

Opal held Dwight's gaze and nodded.

"Well, I don't mean to stop you, wherever you're headed." He stepped aside.

Dwight passed him and then others.

"The poor man is cracked," a lady whispered.

"Shaken to his bones," said another.

He exited the parlor and stepped quietly into the hall, his boots clacking a soft rhythm on the wood. Sounded a bit like the typing of a telegram. His black suit hugged his elbows as he reached for the kitchen door then slipped inside. More biscuit and bread and whiskey and lemonade were set out on the counter there, Eleanor's reserve, and Dwight stopped and poured himself a shot of the booze. In the same dream-daze the ladies of the parlor had noted, he continued, awkward but firm, through the breadth of the kitchen to the old cellar door. He did not look over his shoulder before turning the knob and taking from the inside wall a candlestick, lit, to guide him down the shoddy wooden stairs that creaked like braying dogs for his descent. He thought of all the faces he'd seen this morning . . . some of them familiar . . . many of them not. Replaying some of the conversation, he recalled Jonas Tom's pitying attempt at future company. He thought of the Walker girls, just eight and ten, daughters of the doctor, their hair done up for the visit. It was a parlor chock-full of condolences, a warm room turned cold with thoughts of mortality, the guests naturally contemplating their own delicate being, the fragility of their loved ones, calculating the day when they, too, would wear the face Dwight Evers wore today. Or even the face Carol wore. He could hear them now, above him, the cobwebbed support planks creaking with the shifting weight, the lamentation of voices muffled so well that not even the name of the deceased cut through like it had ...

Carol ...

... no more ...

Carol ...

... no more.

A path was created by the candle he held, but the corners of the basement remained in shadow. It was very cold, but Dwight did not bunch up, for he planned on his visit being brief, and the temperature was welcome in that it felt no colder than his blood.

Dwight stepped into the storm room Carol had long ago overseen being built, citing Harrows's fondness for windstorms and tornadoes. A stone cutaway room with walls as thick as the ones upstairs, a cold floor, and a great table-length slab in its center where they could put bread, food, wine, if ever they descended to avoid bad weather.

Dwight set the candlestick on the edge of the slab and lifted from it a small box of matches. He stepped to the wall and struck one against the stone, the length of the room coming to life behind him. He lit a second candle, its silver-plated sconce embedded deep into the wall, then stepped farther into the room, lit another, and another, until the three walls and the door were alight at last.

He now faced his wife, on her back upon the stone slab, her soft features mobile in the dancing candlelight. It appeared as if her eyes opened, the corners of her mouth turned up, as if the lines of her face were fluid, living lines where life might yet flow.

Then quite suddenly a second frightening thought occurred to Dwight, almost as alarming as the telegram from James Moxie.

Farrah isn't at the wake. Why?

He looked over his shoulder to the dark entrance of the storm room. It seemed possible then that either James Moxie or Farrah Darrow could come screaming out of that darkness, eyes like eggs, pistols in hand, firing upon the would-be widower. He thought of Sheriff Opal stepping quietly into the room.

Weak heart, huh, Evers? And yet ... it still beats?

Dwight stepped to Carol's side, his belt against the slab, his face very different now from the one he wore upstairs. He leaned over her and studied her before reaching into his suit coat's interior pocket and pulling forth a small hand mirror. He held it below her nose and counted how long it took to fog.

"Breathe," he said, quietly. "But do not wake." He lowered his face closer to her ear. He knew Carol heard voices in the coma. Knew she heard him now. "Can you fathom what little space you shall have upon waking? Can you fathom the loss of power? I am sorry for you, Carol. I truly am."

The words *buried alive* came to mind, and Dwight thought of Opal again.

Farrah had written James Moxie. And what did she tell him?

Dwight felt another jolt of horror peal through his blood and bones that was eventually squelched by the meaning inherent in Moxie's response.

Not dead.

As if Carol's long-ago lover, the insane outlaw of the Trail, felt compelled to tell Farrah that Carol was actually *not dead*. This, Dwight hoped, meant Farrah suggested Carol was.

How had Dwight overlooked James Moxie? When was the last time Carol had mentioned his name?

Looking down at her still face he remembered the time quite well. It was just after she'd told Dwight himself of her condition.

Now you'll go running from me, just like James Moxie did.

Moxie was the very reason Carol had kept her condition so secret. He'd scarred her by abandoning her. At the height of young love, first love, he'd chosen the Trail over her, over the care and attention he would have to pay a woman who often died.

Carol told Farrah about Moxie. Why?

Dwight thought of pinching his wife's nostrils shut.

It would be so simple, so quick, and then there would be no worry of when she woke, no concern about what Moxie would do if and when he arrived in Harrows.

Was he really coming? Now?

Dwight brought his fingers close to Carol's nose.

"No," he said. "Moxie will ask questions . . . ask to see if there are scratch marks inside the box. They'll dig her up . . . check her nose. *Not dead*, he said. But not going to know, says I."

Not dead.

The few words in Moxie's telegram chilled his blood to snow.

He studied Carol a moment longer before stepping to the walls again and blowing the candles out in the opposite order he had lit them. Breath by breath the room darkened; breath by breath fresh shadows fell upon Carol lying still. He walked the circumference of the room slowly, quietly, his shoes in rhythm with the unseen rats. He took hold of the candlestick and quietly left the storm room.

He would go upstairs again and take his seat beside Arthur who was managing things, making fluid work of the guests. But before he got there, Dwight would stop in the kitchen and pull from a drawer a clean sheet of paper then write the following few words:

Lafayette—
You are wanted.

And when he left the kitchen he would hand this paper to the waiting messenger and he'd give the young man an extra coin or two to make certain he got the message through soon, first, next. Dwight would then ask him to return with proof of its having been delivered.

On my way, Moxie had said. Boldly.

But Lafayette knew other people, other outlaws, other ways.

SMOKE

Smoke limped to the broke-down carriage blocking the Trail and pissed on it. He was far south, between Mackatoon and Baker, many miles from the colorful towns that offered the colorful thrills, but Smoke wasn't the sort of triggerman who sought women, whiskey, or wagers. To him the real adventure existed on the Trail itself, the miles and miles of dirt, dimmed to shadows by arching trees, some low enough that riders, even gentlemen, had to remove their hats. Smoke wore no hat. He never had. And his thinning blond hair gripped his skull like the small fingers of the many children he'd frightened along the way. He refused to wipe the sweat that traveled down his face. Let it be hot. Let himself burn. A broken carriage was fun. A bad accident was the very variety of excitement he longed for.

When he was done urinating, he fastened his pants and felt for the string loops in his pockets. These simple general-store-bought cords led down the length of both pant legs and into his dust-covered boots. There they were tied to small doors at his heels, hatches Smoke could easily open with a simple tug of the loops.

A popping sound. A quiet creaking of small tin hinges.

And the oil that sloshed in his tin-shins, his false lower legs, poured forth.

A unique triggerman, even for the Trail. One that even the Trail-watcher Edward Bunny didn't like to call on. Because the terrain was 80 percent shadowed at any time of day, there were plenty of places for bad men to hide.

And Smoke was a *bad* man. A mean man. Despite rumors of things worse than men on the Trail, Smoke was as monstrous as anything local folklore had invented.

The blue coach was on its side. Smoke's urine traveled the length of a crack in the expensive wood. Observing the puddle at his boots, he thought the shape of it looked something like President Cooper-smith. Coopersmith, like every president before her, had no good strategy for how to tame the Trail. So like every president before her, she did very little, ignoring the violence and horrors therein, leaving towns like Harrows and Mackatoon to hire lawmen and -women with enough mettle to do the protecting themselves.

Some were successful. Others were not. And Smoke, like most triggermen, knew that the spaces between these towns had no law at all.

This particular carriage was blocking Smoke's passage back north after wrapping up a job in Mackatoon. Wreckage barred the entire width of the Trail, and even the smallest bits of it were higher than he wanted to climb. His tin-shins, though secure, were not easy to navigate.

It was a lot to get over.

One of the white horses had been crushed by the front end of the coach. The other whinnied and jerked, held down hard by a wheel half wedged against a willow. This horse, wide-eyed and loud, looked to Smoke as if specifically asking for help; perhaps it understood somehow that it was dangerously close to ending up like the broken unmoving man beside him, facedown in the dirt. A second man had been thrown farther up the Trail, and though Smoke couldn't stand on his tiptoes (he had no toes, no physical legs below the knees) it was clear the man was dead. His head had caved in against another willow. The Trail was littered with splintered wood, torn white curtains, jewelry and gloves, luggage and clothes. Here . . . a rich accident.

"Hell's heaven," Smoke said. "Tough footing for a cripple to climb."

But Smoke was no stranger to ruin.

Adjusting his weight so that he was leaning on the left of his two tin-shins, the oil audibly sloshing inside, he bent at the waist, squinting at the cracked window of the coach's side door.

A bloodied palm appeared, sudden, flat against the glass.

There was someone stuck inside.

"Oh," Smoke said. "Life . . ."

Moments before, he'd been leaning against a willow counting cardinals in the sky. Having traveled the Trail as long as he had, Smoke knew all the names: the outlaws and triggermen, the well-to-dos and the ne'er-do-wells, the lawmen, the doctors, the dogs. He knew that if a man waited long enough on the side of the Trail, something entertaining would be delivered to him. So when he heard the carriage wheels, he wasn't surprised. Someone was always coming on the Trail. It was the only lifeline in the territory, here, shared by Ucatanani and Miskaloosa counties. Sometimes, hidden deep at the base of the shadows of the willows or pines, Smoke would remove his lower legs completely, roll up his dusty pant legs, and huff the rags that had absorbed much of that oil smell. Often this woke him up. The oil high was a good high. It was a great high today. And it wasn't long after he'd wedged the rags back into place and re-belted the tin-shins to his thighs that the blue carriage showed, propelled by two gorgeous white steeds.

Horses that couldn't know poor footing was near.

Smoke watched the legs of the steeds buckle together, their hooves caught in matching divots, as the carriage plunged forward, splintered to bits—in slow motion it seemed to Smoke—from front to middle to back. Smoke saw the looks on the drivers' faces as they were thrown. Heard the caterwauling terror of its passenger.

Then, just as suddenly, all was still.

Smoke watched the dust settle. He enjoyed the sound of rich wood cracking. Good kindling, he knew, for a good fire.

Now, eyeing the bloody hand against the glass, Smoke half sang to whomever it belonged to.

Lady trapped in a coach of clover,
I'm not going around you,
so I'll have to go over.

Smoke knew better than to chance the brush that bordered the Trail. False legs didn't do well with unknown footing. Once, his boots had sunk deep into jelly mud, so deep his tin-shins were buried. That day, as he decided to unfasten the shins, a lawman patrolling the Trail stopped to assist him. Smoke played the helpless cripple magnificently. But today, having just broiled a Mackatoon home to cinder, Smoke wasn't waiting for support.

"Help!"

The woman banged on the glass.

The leather belts that ran up Smoke's thighs, binding him to his tin-shins, had long doubled as leverage when he needed them to. Gripping one now, he lifted his right leg up and balanced one muddy boot heel on the cracked white window ledge. A faint slosh sounded as his foot connected. The boot stable, he reached high for the white trim, the cracked decorative molding wide enough for his fingers to grip. He pulled himself up.

"Help! I'm in here!"

Smoke reached level footing, the broad side of the blue coach. But the angle was not easy. And getting down was always harder than climbing.

He put his hands in his pockets. He slid his fingers into the loops.

He pulled on the strings.

Draw.

The popping sound always delighted him, the opening of the heels. The oil spread quick on the coach.

Smoke watched it travel that angle, divining toward the dead driver. The scant sunlight swirled in its stream and the oil cascaded over the body's edge, splashing the side of the coachman's nose below. Smoke inched farther up the wood and let his right leg hang over the broken back left wheel.

"Help! I'm in here!"

A red palm pounding on the glass.

The oil poured symmetrical down both sides of the circle wheel, and Smoke watched it drip to the dirt beneath it.

"Is that oil?" the woman cried. "I smell oil!"

Smoke let go of the strings in his pockets, and the soft clicks at his heels echoed their closing.

He limped carefully to the edge of the blue wood. He gauged the drop.

"Help me! I'm still inside! Can't you hear me?"

He closed his eyes. Held his breath. And stepped over the edge.

When he landed, dirt rose and pain exploded up his legs and back. Smoke howled. He cried out and he tried to keep quiet about it and then he cried out again.

"Who knows what shapes you'll see on the Trail!" he sang, limping, stiff-legged, north, as blood from his knee-stubs drooled down the tin-shins he balanced upon. "Who knows which way you'll turn!" He stuck two fingers into the chest pocket of his cream button-up country shirt and retrieved a small box. "Who knows how clever you are with the reins!" Opening the box, he wiped the sweat from his forehead with his sleeve at last. "Who knows how fast you'll burn."

The match head came quick to life.

He tossed it over his shoulder.

Whump

BOOM!

Behind him, the carriage went up, and Smoke knew it was a good one. He limped north, toward all the mad towns of the Trail, all mapped out in great detail in his memory and mind, from the boot smiths to the bawdy houses and all the bricks in the alleys between them. As if he were traveling a sheet of paper, an actual map, a series of playing cards like the ones Edward Bunny kept stitched into his brown coat to track all the outlaws and triggermen on the Trail. As if the crinkling he heard was not the sound of wood catching behind him, not the sound of somebody clamoring for escape, not even the sound of her skin, heated, hot, then flaking, but rather like Smoke was leaving boot prints on the maps he'd seen in so many sheriffs' offices in every town on the Trail.

From the same chest pocket that held his matches, Smoke removed a folded piece of paper and read the name printed there.

JAMES MOXIE

He whistled a single syllable, as though part of the song the flames sang behind him.

Moxie was the biggest name Smoke had ever been hired for.

And the legendary outlaw wasn't far away.

Smoke limped on. Burning for hire was a way of life. But burning for no reason at all was *living*.

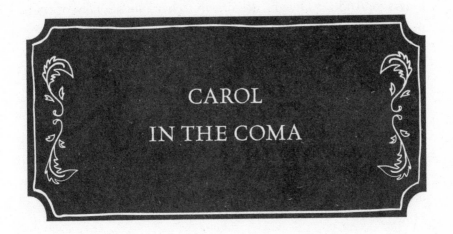

CAROL
IN THE COMA

The name *Moxie*, spoken by Dwight, resounded so heavily that it nearly blotted out the words that followed. As if words with more emotional meaning echoed louder in Howltown.

There was no doubt now that Dwight wanted her dead. And while Carol wanted desperately to tell herself that there had been no signs of this, no indication of Dwight's horrific unhappiness, she had to admit that there were.

And the knowledge increased the darkness she fell through. And the horrific anxiety that came with it was blue, untamable lightning through her body. Even at eight years old, with no understanding of what she was enduring, Carol had never been so scared in the coma.

Nor so alone.

Among her memories and her mind's eye, bad connections were made. Dwight's behavior *had* been changing: He'd become mean like a dog becomes mean; the clipped manner in which he spoke, and the inordinate amount of time he'd begun sharing with the woman Lafayette. The wrinkled Trail-watcher was known for her shady dealings, her dismissal of all things polite and kind. Carol, in charge of all the Evers business affairs, had sworn off working with the woman long ago. And yet Dwight was drawn to her. Not sexually, of course not, Lafayette was about as appealing as a mother pig, and yet ... drawn to *something*. Carol, falling, understood that she should have paid more attention to this, should have wondered at the things, and people, that had begun to attract her husband's attention and time.

Moxie.

The name returned with a deafening clap but did nothing to calm Carol's electrified nerves. For the deeper she fell, the farther she felt from being able to do anything about any of this at all. And the name of an old lover only added to the confusion, the warped shadows, of Howltown.

Dwight.

Lafayette.

Burial.

Moxie.

The way Dwight spoke, it was as if James was on his way. As if he knew she was not dead.

Carol, scared as she was, was still intuitive enough to know that Dwight must have received a telegram. But the question that burned white among so much black was: *How* had James heard of her "death"?

Carol imagined she fell past posters that described her "sudden" death. Posters hanging in every business in Harrows.

CAROL EVERS—DEAD

An announcement must have been made. Perhaps funeral plans as well. James got word that way, through the uncontainable spreading of bad news, and then ...

... then what?

In the complete darkness, falling, black wind by her ears, Carol recalled James as he was, before he took to the Trail. Before he made the cruel decision to leave her behind, to leave *love* behind, too afraid to face the work of it.

Pigs, Carol thought. It felt good to think it. And while she had put these bad feelings behind her many years ago, the past had a way of slithering into Howltown.

No sheriff in here. No laws, either.

Again, Hattie's voice:

You can't rely on anybody else, Carol. Not when you're inside a place nobody else can go. You must find peace in there. Or rage. Either way, your own. And then? Then maybe you can act on it.

Her husband was trying to kill her and an old dismissive lover was riding to check up on her too late. If ever she could be excused for lack of peace, this was that time.

Moxie.

She'd heard more than just Dwight's voice, too. The ceiling had been creaking for many minutes—though time was difficult to track in the coma. How many people were upstairs? And did anybody, any one of them, wonder as to where she was?

This is your wake. John Bowie's voice. The truth.

This resonated. Huge. A volcanic eruption of more shadows.

Was anybody up there who might help her? Anybody prone to suspicion?

Sheriff Opal! Carol called but her lips did not part.

Possibly Harrows's beloved sheriff was standing a floor above her, kindly paying his respects for a woman who was not dead.

The anger Carol felt at this thought was strong enough to momentarily dull the nerves.

Hattie would've been proud.

Hattie, she thought, her thoughts like muffled voices. *John. Help me. Tell me how to move. Tell me how to stop falling. Give me a hundred more theories to go with the hundred you already gave me. Maybe one will work . . . one must work!*

Oh, how Carol wanted to crawl out of Howltown! How she wanted to climb the steps to the kitchen, take the hall to the parlor, present herself, as the darkness of the coma clung to her in pieces like mud to the body of the unearthed dead.

Not dead! she would say, just as James had written to Dwight. Not dead. And the expressions of grief would fall from the faces of the grievers, and Sheriff Opal would quietly take Dwight's wrist in his hand.

Of the many experiments Hattie conducted on an adolescent Carol was one she called the Object Light. When Carol went under, Hattie would light a solitary candle and stand in one corner of the room for five minutes, then stand in another. Then she'd bring it a step closer. Five minutes spent at each spot in the room, as Carol lay deadlike on the floor. When Carol woke, Hattie would ask her if she'd seen it, the light, at any point in the fall. If she had, Hattie theorized, if there was a certain angle, perhaps a spot, that showed in the darkness, they could build upon that knowledge.

But there was no light in Howltown.

Never.

John Bowie had ideas, too.

Since Howltown is an abstract place, have you considered simply . . . imagining a door?

This way of thinking best defined the difference between Hattie's hard-nosed *we can build you stairs in there* and John's spiritual "kinesis." And while both were trying to help—always, always—neither worked any better than the other.

Yet Carol tried.

She tried to remember a time when she and James Moxie were very young, teenagers off the Trail, when it felt as if, together, they could keep the comas at bay.

James, she believed, lived in Mackatoon these days. And as she fell deeper into the darkness, as the winds whispered of silence and death so close to her ears, Carol understood that whether or not he was coming, Mackatoon was a two-day ride.

How soon would Dwight get her into the earth?

Sheriff Opal!

But her lips did not part. As she felt rage rush through her still body, as she fought against ascribing any hope to a man who once deserted her, her lips did not part.

And the labored breathing, the hoarse rhythm that acted as a clock in Howltown inhaled.

Exhaled.

Again.

And between these thunderous respirations, the bitter music by which she worked, Carol tried.

Tried to move.

MOXIE ON THE TRAIL

Nine years . . .

The words came quickly, and they hurt. It'd been nine years since Moxie quit the Trail. Nine years since he'd last left Mackatoon under the morning sun. And in those years—even in the years before those—Carol's condition hadn't entirely left his mind. Her sudden comas, the state she fell into, the death-trance, where not even the finest instruments could detect a heartbeat.

Oh, the *appearance* of death, the limp body of the woman he desired, was not something a young James Moxie could handle. It was enough to send him running, directionless, toward the Trail. And it was on the Trail, *this* Trail, that he became legend—a myth he foolishly believed had ended nine years ago but that he had taken up again this morning.

Do you have another magic trick in you?

Thoughts were always shinier, wider, more difficult to corral on the Trail.

Fifteen years . . .

Because that's how long it was since Moxie had been to Harrows. The well-to-do town's name brought with it many memories, most of which were peaceful. Harrows was where he and his longtime riding partner Jefferson slept under the stars, out there in the wheat fields at the town's southern border. The pair had fun in those sleepy willow trees, dancing with women from town, drowning in wild youth, drunk and free.

Yet not entirely free. Never free of the guilt for having left a lover because she was sick.

At the word *lover* Moxie felt a familiar tugging on his heart.

Was it possible he had never fallen out of love with Carol? Could a man sustain such a feeling, twenty years since seeing her?

Harrows was also the name of the place where Carol got married to a man named Dwight Evers, and long ago this news tore holes in Moxie's soul. For a long time Moxie believed he was past all this, had grown bigger than these memories. But now that they had returned, it was clear they'd always been close.

He spit in the dirt, barely missing his boot and the body of the mare. Of course Harrows was the farthest town on the Trail; all things Carol, for him, were as trying, as cumbersome, as out of reach.

Twenty years . . .

Had it really been over two decades since last he saw her? And could she, as she was now, replace the vision he'd held for all those years? Looking into the dark shadows of the Trail, Moxie didn't believe she could. Carol would always come cleaner than he, younger than he, smarter than he, and *better.* Carol, whether or not she had grown bitter, could never shake the perfect temperament his memory afforded her. What was she like now? Free? Happy? Anxious? These were not romantic notions, but rather the refined and whittled forms of once true, literal images, forms reshaped from years of the guilt-squeeze, the scalpel of regret, as it came again and again from a distance Moxie could never quite locate. Every line in Carol's face, every fold in a skirt she once wore, even the dust at the tip of her boots— any and all of it were the rendering of this guilt, this good-promise destroyed, by him, two decades past, before his name was known on the Trail, before he assumed the life of the outlaw for having broken his own inner codes, the laws *within,* without the knowledge of course of how to fix them.

Moxie was only half a mile outside of Mackatoon, and already the sunless borders were shifting in the spectral darkness of the Trail. At all points wide enough to allow a carriage passage, and at many points two, the solid earth of the Trail reached sudden walls of heavy vegetation, the towers of plant life, the very greens that brought so much claustrophobia to those who rode. Today, for all the memories these walls stirred and for all the movement within the shadows, the Trail was certainly quiet. Moxie wondered if it had always been so, the early hours, the sun not yet high enough to expose all that traveled, crawled, or pulled itself along the packed earth and dry mud, in those rare places where the sun bore down in full. Perhaps, this time, this journey, he was finally seeing it for what it was.

He thought of all the men who once wanted to ride with him, long ago, having heard of his Trick at Abberstown.

He felt the false glory of that now.

The mare was steady, breathing hard but breathing well. Moxie looked ahead, where the black borders seemed to meet, to close up, to swallow.

It was on this stretch that Moxie and Jefferson raced drunk on horseback, each fueled by individual bad moods, trying to beat them, trying to feel good again. *Reborn!* Jefferson kept calling. *Reborn!* Moxie recalled closing his eyes, the horse then leading him blind as dirt pelted the skin of his face. The hooves were thunder that day but an actual storm enveloped the Trail by night, and he and Jefferson were small dry islands beneath an oak under the inevitable black wave of rain.

Reborn!

The false freedom of the Trail. The impossibility of living a life with no rules.

It hurt, these memories, seeing it all, himself, so clearly now. Who had he fooled?

Certainly not Carol.

The guilt was and always had been tremendous.

Something big moved in the brush to Moxie's right, and the old outlaw did not make a sudden move. He looked slowly from under the tan brim of his hat. It'd been a long time since Moxie had to distinguish between animal and man, but he would never unlearn the lesson of the Trail.

A man, he thought. *An outlaw.*

A deer materialized in the graying shadows. Had he no *feel* for this place anymore?

This stretch of Trail was the very length he came south down, nine years ago, heading for Mackatoon, done with the Trail at last. Mackatoon was hardly more than a name to him then, a peaceful place, far enough from the towns that called him legend. He was thirty years old then, had years then, years he would tend to his garden, his library of books, and the better side of three aging horses in an uneasy but deserved solitude. And yet . . . *was* any of it deserved?

Carol, he suddenly thought.

And the town of Harrows felt very far away.

The few words delivered in Farrah Darrow's telegram were enough to suggest volumes of memory in great detail, a floating diary of heart-pounding episodes. His mind was with Carol, but Carol was only the start, the spark that flamed the years to follow: his years alone, breathing the air of the Trail he no longer wanted to be famous on. It was enough to puncture his spirit, enough to drive Moxie a little mad, with memory, with morality, with whether or not the years had been wasted. He'd made a name here, the letters of that name constituting as much a myth as any to have raised hell's heaven through these woods, these waters, this dirt. It was enough to confuse him, too, to mock him, to arouse in him warring conclusions.

The Trail did this to troubled men. Tangled them like unseen strings on a magician's stage.

Two days of riding could kill him.

Movement from the brush to his left. Moxie turned slow.

Moxie had heard more than his share of Trail myths, yarns rolled down steep hillsides, unraveling until they shape-shifted from fiction to fact. Chilling tales that lent the long, winding, and often isolated path a shade of something darker. A color deeper than midnight blue, more blinding than black.

Some rumors were worse, Moxie thought, than robbery, rape, and murder.

These stories dressed the Trail in a cloak, gave it claws. These stories gave the Trail its horror.

For who that rode so far from reason could deny the possibility of hysteria?

Movement again. Moxie eyed it.

There was a man in the brush. Standing. Facing the Trail.

Moxie slowed the horse.

He placed his right hand on his right holster. It wasn't uncommon for strangers to draw guns without a warning on the Trail. Moxie had done it himself many times. Nobody walked the Trail alone with good intentions, and a man half hidden by the branches of a hackleberry tree certainly was hiding.

Drawing first was wise, and the dance that followed was often an ugly one.

Draw, Jefferson used to say. *Before you even know they're there.*

But Moxie did not draw.

And as he passed it, the shape in the shadows became only the bulging of a tree's trunk, as if the tree itself were trying to fool him.

Moxie nudged the mare along. The fabled outlaw, famous for his duel in Abberstown, continued.

Not a man, Moxie thought.

And yet . . . behind him now . . . the shape laughed. A sound Moxie could not hear.

As the mare entered deeper shadows still, the shape emerged from the tree trunk and followed. The shadows came with it, as if flowing from the figure, a cloak, an afterimage, a blackened second being. The figure had features, details buried in the body of its silhouette, but these were no more than gradations of black ... lips only a bat could see ... unseen wrinkles in a face that rippled without wind.

It laughed again, a subtle ripple in the leaves of the birch, a wave in the bark, too. The borders of the Trail shook with it.

Moxie noticed and so did the mare.

"You saw me," the shape whispered. *"Perhaps you recognized me, too. We once cheered whiskey in Portsoothe. How long till you admit you know me? Not long."*

Moxie, sensing a whisper on the wind, pulled gently on the reins, cocked his head to one side.

"You carry me all the way to Harrows," Moxie told the mare, "and I'll let you sleep in the house."

There existed maps that declared the boundaries of these woods. Maps in the souvenir shops, the welcome posts, on the very wall behind which Sheriff Opal of Harrows sat back in his chair and thought nothing of James Moxie or Carol Evers at all, not yet. Yellowed paper maps like a monocle on the black beady eye of a bird, a photo, a moment, a view. But there was no accounting for the scope of experiencing the Trail firsthand. The Trail, it seemed, was bigger in person than it was on paper. The legends were off. The space immeasurable.

And within that space ... trickery.

More laughter now, a sliver of it heard, a piece, the unfolding of a triangular corner of a memory.

Moxie rode steady, quiet, listening. His red shirt a nosebleed on the dark lips of the Trail.

A definitive path of sunlight appeared as the trees overhead parted at last. No longer early morning, day was nearly at hand.

Moxie recalled a night at a tavern in Portsoothe twenty years past, seated at a wet wood bar, a stranger suddenly beside him.

It's love, Moxie drunkenly declared that night, speaking to the stranger with no introduction. *But it's more ... too much more ...*

The stranger was somehow featureless. Moxie attributed this to the whiskey.

Leave her then.

A voice sharp as the barber's blade. The meaning even sharper.

Moxie, then, in love for the first time, turned to the man he couldn't place, could not entirely define.

Leave her? What do you mean by that?

I mean a great deal, the stranger said. *More than we have time to discuss.*

Please, tell me what you mean.

Because Moxie needed to know. Moxie needed to make a decision.

Then the stranger said something that Moxie would never forget no matter how many fresh memories were made.

Your mind is already made up.

He had to say something in return. Had to refute this. But even then Moxie knew it was true.

You know the workings of my mind?

Here the stranger laughed. Things rippled then in the bar not unlike the way they would ripple twenty years later on the Trail.

Carol, the stranger said. *Do you hear her name? Carol. I've said it again. And how does it make you feel? What's not the feeling that settles, but the feeling that comes first?*

Moxie, ambushed by this direct talk, stared blankly into the bottles behind the bar. The stranger went on.

You can't care for her, Moxie. No man can. This woman asks too much . . . she is too much . . .

The words felt heavy, ugly, mean.

It's not her fault.

No, it never is.

It's not her—

In your more lucid moments, Moxie, fault means nothing to you. She exists, James Moxie, and she exists for you in this way . . . this terribly demanding, clumsy way . . .

Moxie looked up suddenly to the barkeep.

Get another, the stranger said. *Get two.*

Moxie, drunk, scared, young, ordered two more.

The drinks came quick, and he slowly slid one toward the stranger. Moxie raised his glass and saw a wrinkled hand raise the other.

Now, the stranger said, *we cheer.*

Beyond them, outside them, loud voices cried, women cackled, glasses came down upon wood.

Moxie felt his glass touch the stranger's and in that moment, in the briefest illumination, a break in the shadows and smoke showed him the man's face.

Moxie gasped.

Who are you? Moxie, not yet legend, was scared.

The stranger laughed. It seemed to come from every booth, every corner of the tavern.

Drink. Drink and I'll show you.

Moxie closed his eyes. The whiskey went down harsh. His chest burned. When he opened his eyes, the stranger was closer.

I'm the guilty thought you have of leaving the one you love. I'm the twisting in your heart. I'm the sour end of things, the brittle finish when all hope of recovery has been swallowed by the snouts of the pigs.

The tavern door opened to allow another patron in, and Moxie saw rain falling from the darkened sky. He slurred as he spoke.

I don't understand.

A glass broke in a corner booth and Moxie looked, and when he looked back he saw the stranger was closer yet.

I am present when things fall apart.

The stranger's lips weren't moving. Moxie tried to tell himself it was the whiskey. Despite the proximity, he couldn't get a read on the man's face. As if the man had many faces at once.

I am the stranger at the funeral. The one all mourners say belongs to someone else.

He held Moxie's blurred gaze. His own was still as the face in a dark oil portrait. His lips did not move.

I am Rot, James Moxie. I am the moment after you've decided to leave the one you love. I'm a step beyond guilt. After the feeling has turned black. Once the mold sets in.

Laughter. All throughout the tavern.

Moxie felt a gust of cold air as another man stumbled through the door, arm over the shoulders of a thin woman.

Moxie, breathing hard, did not want to look back at the face of the stranger.

Were it not for death, I would hardly exist.

The stranger laughed again. Then laughter erupted forth from every booth, every shadow. Even the barkeep broke free with it. And still the stranger's face remained expressionless. An oil portrait, yes, an uneasy rendering, the sort of painting children stepped quickly past in the second-story halls of their homes.

A gray cloud appeared behind the stranger as smoke rose from the open laughing mouths of the other patrons.

Moxie suddenly felt very young. Too young. How old was this stranger? It was true that Moxie had come to Portsoothe to get far from Carol, from her condition. It had become too much: the regularity with which she collapsed, falling into her death-trance slumber; no pulse, no beat, no breath. And here this stranger knew the workings of his heart. He called himself Rot. In Moxie's blurriness he wondered if his love was, indeed, rotting. This man . . . this thing . . . this—

You're a monster, he said.

Hearing it, he believed it.

James Moxie! the stranger said, his mouth moving at last. *What a mean thing to say!*

Now, riding the Trail for the first time in nine years, Moxie did not attribute these memories to the shape he'd seen against the tree in the shadows. No connection was made there at all. Yet Moxie knew well the shudders. The guilt he felt for his decision in Portsoothe was a bigger picture than the shadowed portrait he vaguely remembered and could not describe: the face that seemed not to talk when it talked . . . the mouth that seemed not to laugh when it did.

What was it we cheered? he thought, glancing up now at the wider breadth of sunlight descending. But he wasn't sure they had cheered anything at all.

James Moxie! the stranger had said. *What a mean thing to say!*

Yet Moxie remembered the words that followed the hazy toast.

I'm no more a monster than a fox is . . . let loose in the chicken pen . . . its snout red with fowl blood . . . its feet wet with eggshells and the smashed bodies of baby chicks yet to see the moon. I'm no more a monster than the man who finds the fox and holds him by his neck to the tree stump where he wields his ax and severs the snout that robbed him. I'm no more a monster than the hiccup in the same man's chest as he bends to lift a box from the cellar stairs, a box to carry the dead chickens. And I'm no more a monster than the water pooled at the bottom of the same cellar stairs down which the man falls . . . his final face wet and distorted with hate, with pain, and with surprise. In truth, I'm much more like the wife who finds him there and cleans the tragic mess. You see . . . there are worse things on the Trail than the men and women who steal, punish, and brutalize. And I'm not the only one.

The words came rippling to Moxie now, folds in the memory of a man who hadn't taken this path in close to a decade. Oh, the many meanings of the Trail.

"Harrows," he said.

In Portsoothe he had decided, finally, to turn his back on Carol.

But he was going to her now.

Love, he thought, and the word came with strength but no color. The confusion in his heart was manifold. The guilt was direct.

Moxie and the mare continued. The shape kept pace. And soon the figure slipped into Moxie's own shadow, vanishing, as the sun broke through again, rose even higher, as the day commenced and the light played tricks with the Trail.

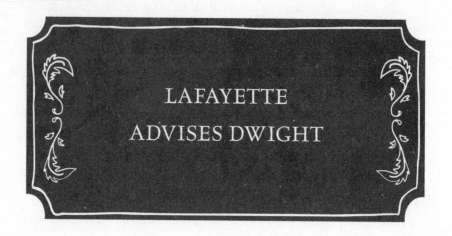

LAFAYETTE
ADVISES DWIGHT

Dwight stood in the parlor and peered through the drapes of its biggest window. The last of the grievers were walking toward their carriages, farther, toward their homes. The sky was gray though it was still very early in the day. It might rain. Or possibly, it was an illusion, an afterimage created by the black and gray dress of the men and women who departed, holding hands, arms over shoulders, having experienced the closeness to death that shatters most social walls.

Couples climbed the steps to their respective coaches and Dwight heard their muffled voices instructing their drivers, *Home, Go west, Take us to town.* Dwight scanned them, men and women of funereal colors, as if Carol were already buried.

It brought Dwight great pleasure, the success of the wake.

The burial must be no different.

As the coaches drove away, dust from the drive rose knee-high in a cloud. And deep within the cloud Dwight saw Lafayette's form approaching.

Every town on the Trail harbored someone capable of culling any and all resources from the others. In affluent Harrows, Lafayette was that woman.

Dwight heard the knocking at the door. Lafayette, who wore the same clothing she'd worn the evening before, was professional enough to have knocked quietly. No obvious urgency in a woman who got things done as quickly as possible. And Dwight did not answer straightaway, watching as he did the last of the leavers, making a small game of the meeting-to-be, reminding his partner who wielded the power in this house.

As the last coach vanished, Dwight responded. Quietly, without speaking, he walked Lafayette into the kitchen, where the sink was stuffed with dishes and the table still loaded with desserts.

"Let me tell you a story, Evers. You wanna hear a story?"

Her voice was too loud for Dwight. The early-afternoon dew glistened off the toes of Lafayette's boots. Her long chin bobbed as she spoke, in step with her considerable ponytail against her upper back, and the words seemed to cascade down the buttons of her white business blouse. Lafayette was a true two inches taller than Dwight, and her size had long assisted her in these matters.

"A young man out of Friar came to see me once. Said he had spent the whole of his life working toward becoming an oilman. Said he got himself on Mossman's team digging holes and worked himself up to some kind of supervisor. I told the kid I didn't give a pig's shit how well he was doing. He was real nervous, asking me if this mister or that mister could hear us and whispering when whispering wasn't necessary. Told me his family was getting in the way of his being an oilman. Had a wife and three daughters. I told him that sounded nice. He told me it would be if they didn't get in the way. I told him whatever family he had was his own decision and his own fault and he looked over his shoulder and asked me to keep it down. Said he needed to get rid of the family. I told him he should get a divorce. Even cited a lawyer he should see. 'I didn't come to you for legal advice,' he says. I said, 'But yes you did.' He told me the wife was demanding he be home for this or that, making life real hard for him when he made to leave for the day's work. I told him that's what families do. But he was serious and he had the money and I suggested to him the same man I'm suggesting to you right now. He said fine, that would be fine. I don't know if he had something on the side, and a pig could shit and I'd care more about that, but he paid me right then and I told him to go to work tomorrow just like he did every day and by the time he got home it'd be done. He shuddered like all men shudder after things are determined, and we parted ways. He came to me a week after, shaking, boiling, fumed. I don't like public scenes, Evers, and I took him by his shirt and pulled him into an alley and told him he better get his head together. He told me he came home from work to find his wife charred, her bones in an odd way on the front lawn, the spine and arms and skull set up as though she were crawling up and out of the earth. I told him the man I'd suggested sounded like an artist. He said that wasn't the worst of it. Said he found the bones of his three girls sitting on the porch in a circle. Black bones. Said they were set up so they were pointing at the bones of their mother, as though acknowledging her emerging from the ground. Said they were screaming, 'screaming skulls.' I told him any skull can look like it's screaming. He was mad, Evers, red-mad. He said he hadn't asked for the children to be involved. I told him he'd asked for the family. He said he meant it different, meant it like his wife was the family and don't I know that kids can't stop a man from moving up in the oil world? I told him to be more specific next time. He started shaking again and he told me that around the knee bones of the kids was a small pile of snuff, as if momma was coming up from the dirt to get her some and like the kids didn't want her to have it. Told me the 'animal' had to've set it up that way, that while he was at work, a true-blue psycho was chuckling on his lawn, setting up his daughters' bones like they were little fiends. I asked him if he had more time now . . . for the oil gig. He said yes he did."

"You see," Dwight said. "That story scares me."

"I should hope it does."

"I don't want a loose bird on my dollar."

Lafayette's wrinkled face stretched into a smile. Her eyes had never looked so deep-set to Dwight. "Whoever you hire, he's going to be a little bit mad," she said.

"You told me he was a cripple."

"So he is."

Dwight shook his head.

Lafayette went on, "The man's good, Evers."

"I want someone who can get to him fast."

"He'll catch him. He'll get to him before he reaches Harrows. I can guarantee that."

"What's my insurance?"

"You hire Smoke. He does it."

"That's not good enough."

"Isn't it? You don't want to hire someone to watch this guy."

Dwight looked as though he might.

"Evers," Lafayette said. "This man doesn't count the same sheep that we do."

"It's my dollar."

Lafayette's smile fell from her eyes. "You hire someone to watch Smoke and Smoke might start watching you."

"He sounds more than a little mad."

"He is. And he's in the area."

Dwight looked out the window, quickly. "What area?"

"Mackatoon."

"Another job?"

"Another job."

Then Dwight looked Lafayette in the eye and nodded and it was sealed.

Lafayette studied him. "I'm curious," she said. "What'd James Moxie do to you?"

Dwight looked surprised. As if Lafayette was suggesting Moxie could or would do something to him.

"Nothing."

"But you want him killed."

He didn't want to tell Lafayette that Moxie knew Carol's secret. A revelation like that would send cracks through the foundation of their plan.

What else did you overlook, Evers? Maybe I should get out now, Evers? Maybe you brought me in on a sour deal?

"Nothing yet," Dwight said.

"And this has nothing to do with your wife?"

"No," Dwight said. "Nothing at all."

Lafayette laughed. It was the sound of one who doesn't want to know where someone else buries their dirt. She started for the door.

"And you don't want a loose bird!"

But Dwight wouldn't let her have the last word. He cried out to her as she exited his home, yelling as the front door closed.

"This is *my* idea! This is what *I* want to do! Don't forget, Lafayette, I brought you in on this deal! I'm making the big decisions here!"

But Lafayette, having her hands in every conceivable channel of communication, her ears to every telegram office on the Trail, had already known about Farrah Darrow's telegram to James Moxie. For this, Lafayette had hired Smoke on her own. Smoke to follow Moxie. The loose bird and the legend. Let Dwight Evers think he was making big decisions. Let him believe he was emerging, born again, from the shadow of his wife. And let him suffer, too, under the weight of that new sun.

FRESH OIL

It once was he rode into town and people blanched. Men avoided his eyes and women turned their backs, hoping not to be seen. It once was the domesticated dogs of the Trail-towns barked at him from afar. It once was he was whole, he was awesome, he was dread.

And while he was certainly still noticed, Smoke spotted the benign curiosity in the eyes of the Mackatooners now. Things hadn't been like they used to be in a long time. Old men nudged each other on front porches and kids stopped to look up at the rider whose legs hung limply by the horse's side. He was a rare sight, indeed: the gangly limp-legged hatless man arriving on Blandon Street. Even the traditionally disinterested had to watch him, and anybody who saw him held his image a breath or two longer than they would an ordinary stranger.

His thinning hair added years to him that he had not earned; his yellow shirt, rolled to the elbows, gifted him levity that he did not deserve; and the fact that he carried no gun squelched the uneasiness his image inspired.

He was not feared. Not yet.

Smoke halted the horse at the post office where a series of hitching posts stood crooked in the dirt. Only one was unused and Smoke knew it was going to be difficult getting off the gelding without much room to maneuver.

He gripped his right thigh and lifted the whole of his leg up and over the horse's head. The scant oil sloshed within. He'd used most of it on this Mackatoon job and the broken carriage that followed.

A small lady, watching, felt pity for him and crossed the street, her eyes sympathetic behind thick glasses.

It didn't used to be like this.

"Do you need some help?" she said, looking up at him.

Others on the street grew silent, sensing what the woman had not.

While the stranger was certainly crippled, it didn't mean he wasn't dangerous. The Trail delivered tricks all the time.

Smoke faced the lady, seated as he was, both legs on the same side of the horse.

"That I do," he said, his voice a singsong. But some in earshot knew better than to sing along. "Know where to get good oil around here?"

The lady smiled, seeing the man didn't catch her meaning.

"Yes. In fact—" She turned and pointed up the planked porches of the Blandon Street shops beneath their wood awnings. "—if you just . . . uh . . ."

"Walk?" Smoke asked, helping her sound out the word.

"Why, yes. If you just walk on up the boardwalk there, beyond the blacksmith you'll find Kirk's General. He sells oil out the back."

"Is it the good stuff?" Smoke asked, pointing at the lady and raising his eyebrows high. "It better be the good stuff or it just won't do."

The lady considered.

"Yes," she said. "I'm not sure, of course, of what you're used to. But I think it works fine. Many people get their oil at Kirk's."

"Kirk's!"

"Yes."

Smoke braced himself as he pushed off the horse's back and slid to the ground. He landed hard; the oil sloshed and the tin cut through the old rags and into the flesh of his stubs. He suppressed a howl and forced a smile instead.

"Oh, my," the lady said. "Are you sure I can't help you? I can maybe run and get some for you. And there's a very good doctor in town as well."

Smoke held her eyes as he hitched the horse and removed a small hip-satchel of rags. "What would I need with a doctor, ma'am?"

And his voice was not singsong anymore. His voice was the pain of stolen legs.

The lady blushed, understanding at last that she had broached an offensive topic.

"I didn't mean anything by it, young man. I just saw you were struggling some . . ."

"How so struggling?"

The lady smiled nervously. She looked to Blandon Street for someone who might explain it better than she. "I can't say exactly . . . I—"

"Show me."

But others on the street backed away. A man gripped a pistol in its holster.

The lady stammered.

"Tell me." Smoke limped toward her. "Was I crying?"

"Well, no, of course not . . ."

"Was I hanging from my horse, like I might fall?"

"Pardon?"

Smoke limped closer yet, and the lady arched back.

"Let me know," Smoke said. "Please, I need to know. Was I slobbering? Was I slobbering all over myself?"

The lady turned her face from him, trying to locate a smile but not finding it.

"Let me know," he whispered now, his lips touching her ear. "Is it that obvious I've got a problem with ma legs?"

The lady stammered. Someone cocked a gun.

Smoke's face burst into a smile. He thrust his hands toward the sky, and the lady screamed.

"Of course there's a problem with my legs, ma'am!"

He laughed and the lady, staring at his outstretched fingers, laughed nervously with him. Smoke planted a palm flat on her shoulder. He eyed the man who had cocked the gun.

"Shudders," he said, speaking to the lady. "Thanks an awful lot for the oil tip. I'll go check it out for myself. Walk there, even."

The lady breathed relief. *Fear,* Smoke thought. *Like it used to be.*

"Kirk's," she repeated, still shaking.

"But if it's not the good stuff," Smoke said, his lips curling down again, "I'll have no choice but to find you, ask you what made you think it was."

The lady stammered, but Smoke was already limping past her. Blandon Street was silent as he stepped awkwardly up onto the boardwalk and struggled toward the general store. He stuck his tongue out at a man standing just inside a tavern. He passed the open door of the blacksmith and chuckled at the sight of the fat man forging a pistol.

A gentleman exited Kirk's General and saw Smoke and held the door for him. Smoke stared at him blankly and the man, confused, let it close and passed him. Smoke opened the door himself and limped inside.

"I hear you've got the good stuff," he bellowed. "Oil!"

"I'll be with you in just a moment."

It was an old man, his face bunched, reviewing a ledger through glasses on the end of his nose. Behind him was a towering oak shelf of glass jars. The counter displayed boxes of candy for children. The dark wood floors and walls made something of a shadowed box out of the space, and Smoke thought of the road magician he'd seen who made a donkey disappear.

He stepped to the counter and eyed the ledger with the shopkeeper.

The old man, seeing he hadn't gotten through to the customer, set the ledger down.

"Yes, and how can I help you, sir?"

Smoke spoke slowly, deliberately. The oil, of course, was very important to him. "A real nice lady told me you got the good stuff here. The best oil in town."

"I've got oil."

"Is it the good stuff?"

"Well, I'm not sure I know the difference."

Smoke frowned. "Does it burn easy, man?"

The proprietor eyeballed Smoke long before answering, "As well as oil burns, I gather."

Smoke nodded. "Sounds like the good stuff. Where do you keep it?"

The man wiped his hands on his blue apron and walked Smoke the length of the store to a back door made of pine.

"Barrels are in there. Check it out for yourself. Might not be the oil you're looking for."

"You need the money now?" Smoke asked.

"Nope. Bring out whatever you need and I'll count it from there. Too many folk come in saying they need a thimble and come out with a mug. Fuddles up my paperwork, it does."

Then the man left him.

Smoke slipped behind the wood door and saw six big barrels in the dim light. From where he stood it looked like standard fare, maybe something a bit better, and he knew it would do. He grabbed a handful of rags from a shelf, limped across the dark room to a stool, and sat down, quickly rolling up his pant legs then unfastening the belts holding the tin-shins to his legs. It always felt good to do this. Big relief. Like removing a hat on a hot summer day. He removed both shins, sensing the trigger-strings as they tickled his thighs on the way down his pants.

Yes, it always felt good to take the legs off.

He turned them over, letting the old stuff spill out on Kirk's dirty floor. His naked thighs were pocked with sores, spots where the flesh was discolored, unhealthy, and maybe would never get good again.

He brought one of the shins to his lap and quietly removed the boot. The toe was packed with cloth, and Smoke pulled it out then jammed a fresh one from his satchel back in. Things were already feeling cleaner. He did the same with the other boot and then set to funneling the oil into the tin-cylinders, holding the heels closed with his thumbs, blocking any spillage. Out of the barrels, the oil looked smoother than he'd guessed it would.

When both shins were full Smoke set one down, picked up a boot, and replugged it with the tin stump at its end. He held the string now with his thumb to make sure he didn't have to fish it out of the boot later. He centered the shin, then set it all on the floor to make double sure. Then he removed the dirty cloth lining the top of the tin and replaced it with a rag from the shelf. He tore it in half, not wanting the whole thing; it was difficult walking with too much padding under the stub. Once the shin was ready, he set to doing the same for the other.

The old man never came back and Smoke guessed he was lost in his ledger. Maybe he was having a good day. Smoke sure was.

James Moxie, he thought.

It was just another job. Always. But he couldn't deny the luster, the way the outlaw's name was lit up on fire in his mind. James Moxie was a legend of the Trail. In fact, he'd become so just about the time Smoke lost his legs. Felt damn close to an eclipse, the way Moxie suddenly rose up and blocked Smoke's own legend on the way.

Moxie Moxie Moxie my,
A drop of oil in your eye . . .

After wrapping his job here in Mackatoon, Smoke found a paper jutting out from under his saddle. Sometimes the Trail-watchers operated this way: hidden notes, secret papers. It was just a job, of course, but James Moxie could be trickier than most.

He was certainly tricky at Abberstown.

Smoke was no stranger to magic. He'd watched many shows, clamoring with the crowds as the traveling magicians came through with their caravans. He'd watched enough sleight of hand to consider his own trick, false shins, to be something of an illusion, too. The Reappearing Legs. And yet there was an edge to what Moxie did in Abberstown. Smoke knew that some men were levitating women these days. Some made elephants disappear. But what exactly had Moxie done to win that duel? Without so much as removing his gun?

Moxie Moxie Moxie myth,
Fibs and fiction, pomp and piss.

The two shins were set upright on the ground and he slid his knees directly above them. He threaded the strings up his pant legs, as far as they would reach, barely poking out the holes he'd cut long ago in his pockets. Then, using his arms, he lowered himself from the stool. He shifted the stubs of his knees against the rags covering the tin until he had it right. Then, finally, he began the laborious task of strapping the belts to the existing sore spots on his thighs.

Finished, he rolled his pant legs back down.

He looked at his legs in the dim light.

Presto.

Jamming his hands in his pockets, he thumbed the string loops and tugged, allowing the heels of his boots to open, spreading a small amount of Kirk's own fresh oil on the floor.

He let go of the strings.

He could sing all he wanted about James Moxie, but Smoke knew there was something to that Abberstown story. Maybe it was the fact he hadn't heard a theory that explained it. Or maybe Smoke's interest rose in relief from the ashes of his own fallen name.

Sweating, Smoke leaned side-to-side, testing his balance. It'd be a bad thing to walk back into the store, take a fall, and spill all this fresh oil in front of the proprietor himself.

It had happened before.

He held his arms out. Leaned forward. Leaned back. Things felt good. Things felt *great*.

He brought one of the dirty rags to his nose and huffed the remaining fumes.

James Moxie, he thought again, and this time a wave of infallible confidence washed over him. *I'm a man of magic, too.*

Reloaded, Smoke limped through the wood door and back into the shop.

"How much you get?" the old man asked as Smoke appeared.

Smoke shook his head.

"It wasn't the good stuff."

The man eyeballed him, looked him over from head to boot tip.

"Eh? Sure were back there long enough."

"That's how I do it," Smoke said, stopping before the counter. "I take my oil very seriously. Your stuff is good. Just not the *good stuff.*"

Kirk stared as the strange, hatless man limped out of his store empty-handed.

Back on the planked walk, Smoke entered a tavern. Inside, the locals watched him walk.

"Got any matches here?"

"Sure we do. You wanna get a beer with them, though."

"Can't just get a box?"

"Gotta get a beer with it."

"Let me think about that."

The bartender addressed someone else and Smoke turned and limped back to the door. Two men talking at a table paused to watch him pass. Maybe they'd heard of him. A lot of people had.

It wasn't until Smoke was upon his horse again and riding, heading north, that the bartender noted the missing matches from their container.

By then Smoke was gone, his voice a singsong rhyme.

Moxie Moxie Moxie moo,
I'm coming, coming, after you . . .

CLYDE AND
THE GRAVEDIGGERS

While Farrah was returning home from mailing her telegram to James Moxie (a thing she could hardly believe she did and a thing she wasn't sure *why* she did, except for a feeling that he should know), her husband, Clyde, was battling a hangover the enthusiastic way: He was already drinking at the Lamb's Wool. But despite the liquor, and what he hoped it might do for himself, all he could think of was the story Farrah had told him late last night: finding her lady's body in the cellar of the Evers home. It was unsettling, of course, though Clyde guessed most of that was because of the manner in which it was told. He'd never known someone to cry as much as his wife had the night before.

Clyde, lifting a glass from the wood bar, sipped.

"It's a bit early, even for you, Clyde," the bartender, Bill, said.

Clyde looked over his shoulder to the otherwise empty tavern, as if expecting backup and finding none.

"I had something of a long night. Long morning, too."

As Clyde set his glass back upon the bar, the saloon doors swung in and Hank James and Lucas Morgan entered. Clyde knew they were gravediggers at the Manders Funeral Home, and he'd spoken

with both more than once; drunk nights, as music played, brief conversations about death in dim lighting. Today, though, their figures
reminded him only of Farrah, for Farrah's lady died and Farrah's lady
would be buried no doubt in a grave dug by these men.

"Hello, Bill," Lucas said, sitting a stool away from Clyde. He turned
and tipped his hat to Clyde, and Clyde nodded in return. Hank followed his fellow digger. The pair did not order, but Bill provided them
with glasses of whiskey anyway.

"You've had a workload, I'd say," Bill said, folding his arms. "Enough
graves for a season, I'd say."

Hank nodded.

"That we have. The Illness. More digging these past two weeks
than my shoulders care to tell you."

"Could have dug a hole to Albert's Port!" Lucas said, and the three
men smiled.

Soon their conversation became meaningless sounds and syllables
for Clyde, and his thoughts returned once again to Farrah and her
story. The events she described came coupled with a bad low feeling
in his chest and belly, but he couldn't pinpoint exactly why. Was there
anything exactly wrong with a man keeping his wife in the cellar after
finding her dead? Would Farrah have preferred the bedroom?

She was glowing, Clyde. She shone.

Farrah kept saying that. All night she kept saying that.

"Bill," he called.

Bill refilled his glass.

"This is your third already, Clyde," Bill said, meaning no harm by it.

Hank and Lucas turned to look at Clyde and Lucas said, "By good-
ness, there's a real drinker there. Three already and we haven't even
made it to work yet."

They raised their glasses and Clyde did, too, and the three cheered.
Hank called what it was they cheered—*to the end of the Illness*—and
as their glasses touched Clyde thought of the empty bottle of whiskey
on the counter in the kitchen at home. He thought of Farrah drink-

ing from it and Farrah using it to punctuate the story that bothered her so.

After a sip from the fresh drink, Clyde wiped his mouth with the back of his hand and felt at peace for the first time all day. Sure, Farrah was upset, but not because there was something foul about Carol's being in the cellar; Farrah was grieving and nothing more.

"Have you heard, Bill, that Carol Evers passed?"

Clyde looked up to Lucas after the gravedigger spoke, and he listened as the three men talked about how young she was and whether or not it was the Illness that got her. Bill had heard the news from a man who'd been in even earlier than Clyde. Bill also said he thought the Illness had left Harrows and Lucas and Hank said they'd hoped the same thing, but thirty-eight years only did seem a little young for so vibrant a woman as Carol Evers. So maybe. Then Clyde told them. He didn't think there was anything wrong in telling them. The gravediggers were talking about her death and how Mister Evers must feel and without waiting for a right place to insert what he wanted to say, Clyde just told them.

"He's keeping her in the cellar."

The gravediggers turned to him. Bill stopped drying a glass.

"It's what I heard. Yeah. Her body is in the cellar. Waiting to be buried, I suppose."

He waited for a response. In that moment, drunk as he was, he understood that he wanted to know what these two men thought of what he'd told them. He wanted to know if two professional gravediggers thought it was as strange as Farrah did.

"Well," Lucas said, shrugging, "I suppose she's got to be somewhere."

Bill refilled their glasses and Clyde felt relief. Not many men in Harrows had been as close to death as Lucas and Hank. Farrah, he believed, was grieving. Nothing more.

Natural.

"You fellas know my wife, Farrah?" he asked.

They did.

"She works for Mister and Missus Evers," Clyde went on, blabbering now. "She's taking her lady's death very hard. She saw her, she did. Last night. In the cellar."

Then Clyde downed most of his drink. He thought of the wake Farrah had missed.

"If you guys see her, make her feel better. Say something nice. She's taking her lady's death very hard."

He set the glass on the bar and Bill refilled it. Clyde sipped, feeling some relief for having verified, really, that there was nothing odd about what Mister Evers was doing. But he had no way of knowing that his loose lips, wet still with whiskey, had allowed powerful words to escape, words that would travel, mostly innocently, all the way to Sheriff Opal, who would consider it very odd indeed that someone with as many bedrooms as Dwight Evers would keep his dead bride in a cold, drafty storm room in a cellar.

MOXIE IN
THE BARBERSHOP

Moxie was stepping toward a saloon when he saw the ghost of Molly.

It was a small town, Baker, and he'd hooked the mare's reins to a hitching post by a trough, twenty paces from the boardwalk. People walked the planks of Nero Street in summer dresses and dusty vests, and among them Moxie saw her looking at him from behind a glass door as it was opened, but she was gone by the time the door swung back to.

The name *Molly* crossed his mind, and it was a dark strange feeling because the only Molly he knew who looked anything like that did so some twenty years ago. The look of her wouldn't have bothered him as much had she not been gesturing. Yes, when Moxie saw her, the girl behind the glass was beckoning him, asking him to come to her, just as Molly had in a tavern two decades past. A band was playing then, and she was asking him to come meet her friend Carol.

Moxie knew he had Carol on the mind. He was nearly strangled with memories of her on the Trail. The mare had done the walking while Moxie swam with Carol in the mossy lake down the hill from the courthouse, stood in the grassy backyard and tossed bugle nuts up at Carol's window, and waited with her in a crowd of sweaty folk eager to see a boxing match. Yes, he'd been drunk, sober, asleep, upset, in love, and ashamed on this ride, reliving the entirety of his and Carol's youthful tryst. Mistaking a young girl for Molly was understandable, even likely.

But Moxie didn't like the gesture. The gesture was too real.

The lithe girl had bent forward, eyes wide, beckoning . . . waving him this way . . . this way . . .

You've gotta meet my friend Carol . . . Carol . . . come on . . .

Moxie stepped onto the boardwalk and passed the tavern, trembling inside, twisted with guilt. Ah, that face, the face of Molly, the girl who connected him to Carol in the first place, as if she'd lit a flame that hadn't flickered in two-decades-plus but hadn't gone out all the same. Coming to the glass door in which he'd seen the apparition, Moxie found it belonged to a barbershop. She was not on the other side of the glass; not even a girl who looked like her. None that he could see. Mostly, the glass reflected the street behind him: the storefronts across the way, a haberdashery with a painted blue sign, horses carting barrows of feed and produce, the people of Baker on their way.

Moxie entered the barbershop. A bell chimed above him.

"You can take a seat if you're expecting a shave."

Two men were seated, bibs across their chests. Two bald men shaved them. And beyond the quartet, in a chair against the back wall, a body under a white slipcover reclined, its head cocked back, its face draped in towels.

"Sir?"

Moxie turned to the closer barber doing the shaving.

"A younger girl," Moxie said. "About twenty. Dark hair. Bright-green eyes. Was she just in here?"

The barbers shook their heads.

"You lost one?" the heavier one asked.

"Thought I recognized a face."

The thinner barber pointed at him with his razor. "But you *could* use a shave as well, if I may be so bold."

Moxie passed them both, heading to the sink in back. The reclining man covered in towels was still as he approached.

"How about you?" Moxie asked him. "You see a young girl come through here? Dark hair? Green eyes?"

Something shifted beneath the slip. As if the man's chin had moved on its own without the rest of his face.

"How young, would you say?"

And the voice was a snake's belly upon wet leaves. Moxie gripped his gun.

"Young enough."

"Young enough, you say? Young enough to live without fear, you'd say?"

Moxie looked to the barbers. They were busy with their shaves. Neither seemed to hear.

"I don't have time to banter," Moxie said, trying to remain calm. But the voice . . . familiar . . .

"Young enough to crawl through the swamps if she lost her favorite bow, you'd say?"

Moxie fingered the gun at his hip. "What do you know about her?"

"Young enough to believe life is a gift, you'd say?"

What face, Moxie thought, could such a voice belong to?

"I've known young, sir," the hidden man said. "I've known so young that they do not yet exist."

Moxie looked to the man's fat fingers upon the chair's armrests. The towels across his face appeared to tighten, and features emerged beneath them. The cheekbones rose, tenting the fabric as it valleyed smoothly into wide lips. And where there should be eyes, two bumps trained on Moxie's own.

In the shadow by the neck of the slip, Moxie saw a worm's-skin throat.

Moxie removed his gun from its holster.

"Why, I've known so young it's tragic. I've known young enough to be just a kernel . . . a guilt-addled thing floating at the surface of an old man's watery mind."

The throat moved, sluglike, and Moxie believed, momentarily, that a great asp writhed beneath the towels.

And the cloth grew tighter to the suggestion of a face.

"If it's young you're looking for," the hidden man said, "I suggest the womb. It's the furthest young can be from old and you can still see it. Swimming in there . . . feeding off the blood of the mother. Dark hair did you say? Yes, I may have seen her, strung up as she was in a tree . . . her young blood dripping on the old earth . . . pooling like a mirror there . . . reflecting the bottom of her feet . . . the length of her legs . . . and up her filthy loose skirt."

Moxie saw the fingers were thin and gray now, rice paper, flaking with the wind of Moxie's own question.

"Who are you?"

The towel was still, but the voice continued.

"I'm a young girl hanging from a tree. I'm a goat starved with no master to feed it. My ribs poke the flesh of my flank. I'm the hollow of the trunk where the big spiders live and lay their eggs. I'm a thing old enough to know that old was once young and that because young becomes old there is no love of life, only a fear of decay. There is no favorite bow, nothing to keep it all from coming unwrapped. There are only bright flashes that hide the shape of me curled in the corner . . . reaching. I am a young girl's reflection in her own blood. I am one step beyond decay, sir. I am *Rot*."

Moxie spun from the figure. From the memory, too. But the thunder of his boots on the barbershop floorboards was interrupted by the thunder of the voice.

"Go home, James Moxie. You passed on your chance to help her."

Moxie whirled back and rushed the shape beneath the slip. He was upon it before the barbers could stop him.

"WHO ARE YOU?"

Moxie tore the towels aside. A fat man with eyes bloodshot from sleep sat up in the seat, raging.

"What in God's name are you doing, man?"

A new voice. A different man. The other was gone.

Rot. Moxie recalled a blurred evening in Portsoothe. Advice to leave the woman he loved.

As the fat man continued to shout, as the barbers rushed to pull Moxie aside, the possibility that the thing, Rot, had been here, scared Moxie deep. Was he losing his mind? Only a few hours upon the Trail . . . was he *losing his mind?*

The details of Portsoothe were filled in: a man whose face he could barely see; whose mouth seemed not to move as he spoke; whose dark expression seemed painted with greasepaint for the stage.

Moxie pulled himself from the hands of the barbers and stumbled toward the door.

Through the glass he saw Molly again.

But Molly as she was now, dead twelve years.

"Molly!" Moxie yelled.

The girl's eyes, once green, were now a watery white. Her dark hair now flowed with ash.

Moxie exploded out the door, reaching for Molly on the boardwalk, but his hands found nothing solid, no girl, dead or alive.

As the door swung shut behind him, he heard the fat man carrying on.

"You should be ashamed of such behavior! I've never heard of such a thing! Accosting a man as he gets a shave! You ought to be put away! I was attacked! That man attacked me, did he not? It's an outrage! Accosting a man as he gets a shave!"

Moxie looked up and down the boardwalk, searching for the corpse of Molly. It struck him, insanely, that he'd take Molly as he'd seen her now, rotting, if it meant she'd repeat the past, the part she'd played in his life.

You gotta meet my friend Carol . . .

If it meant she would deliver him to Carol.

Seeing no girl, Moxie looked to the people of Baker for a false face, one so unnatural as to be greasepaint upon the idiot smoothness of a mannequin.

But no Rot.

No Molly.

Moxie hurried back to the mare, to the Trail, to a funeral he needed to end before it began. To the woman he needed to save from being buried alive, no matter how many memories tried to stop him.

Deep within, this idea comforted him. Despite the horrors he'd seen, the dark feelings he felt. For he had no doubt the memories *were* trying to stop him. Yet what need would there be to stop Moxie, if Carol were already dead?

"Ride!" Moxie called to the mare.

And the mare rode.

DESPAIR IN HOWLTOWN

She could hear him pacing before she heard him speak. Dress shoes on the gravel storm room floor. Did he have a candle lit? That had always been the worst of it for her, the lack of light. Not in Howltown—Carol didn't expect any in there—but in the cellar itself. Just because she couldn't see didn't mean she didn't know the darkness of the unlit cellar. Black within black. As if the darkness below the house were pressurizing that of the coma, stuffing Carol deeper down. At first, she thought Dwight's scuffling was rats. Farrah claimed to have seen one *as big as a badger* and it was difficult, now, to write that off as the hysterics of a young woman. Who knew what was down here when the lights were off, when the air was still, when no human posed a threat to their dwelling? But through the dark winds of her perpetual fall, Carol was able to determine they were shoes after all, for no animal moved with the neurotic regularity that this sound betrayed. A pendulum, it seemed, swinging beside her inert body on the slab.

And yet Dwight's labored breathing was no match for the hoarse wheezing she heard inside the coma.

"You had to tell James Moxie? What'd you tell him for? Attention? Were you flirting? Did you want him to feel bad for you?"

His words pelleted the coma like globs of black tar. Angry rain in Howltown.

"Hell's heaven, Carol." Pacing. Pacing. Breathing hard. "He's on his way here! An outlaw! Hell's heaven, Carol. What can I do? What *should* I do?"

Even now Dwight was asking for her help.

Even in his plan to murder her, Carol had to do the dying first.

Again she felt the blue electricity through her nerves: anger, terror, shock, and a leviathan sadness she hadn't imagined possible. Dwight had always argued that Carol went under following stressful events; was it possible that now, given what she was forced to accept, this betrayal, that she would fall farther, deeper than she'd ever been before?

How long would Carol stay under this time?

No!

She screamed the word without parting her lips, but the two letters were swallowed fast by the impenetrable darkness that propelled her.

And yet, *no* was certainly better than *yes.*

Oh, to open her eyes right now.

Right now!

You say it takes two to four days, John Bowie once said. *That means some falls are twice as long as others. That means you're not going to the same place every time. Does this mean something? Is there a finish line, a landing, after all?*

Carol couldn't help but imagine him as she'd last seen him, barefoot and unboxed at the bottom of a grave. Yet this dead version of John still sat in that wicker chair on the Everses' front porch, folded in on himself, running a coin along the knuckles of his hand as he thought of ways to help her.

"He's coming," Dwight said, and his voice was much closer now, the syllables grotesque. "Will he kill me? *Will he?* Oh, Carol." Closer yet. As if he was kneeling beside her. Carol heard tears in his voice. "Please don't let him kill me. Please don't. *Carol!*" She heard a flat dull thud and hoped he'd hit the slab and not her defenseless body. Then Dwight started laughing. And the sound of it, in the coma, was the sound of a dying hyena, an animal left to starve. "I've hired someone, Carol. Yes. I've hired someone to stop him from coming."

More of the blue electricity that she only felt but could not see. The flaming nerves that did nothing to illuminate the darkness she fell through.

Moxie is going to get killed, she thought. Then, as if she had to think it whether or not she wanted to: *For you.*

John Bowie spoke up again, his dead throat spouting philosophy still.

I'm close, he'd once said, with a glass of whiskey in one hand, a playing card in the other. *There's a solution to this and I'm close to figuring it out.*

But he never did figure it out. Not exactly. And Carol couldn't fault him.

Even Hattie couldn't help.

What if I actually dropped you from a great height as you're falling . . . a safety net far below. Maybe the two falls would somehow cancel each other out . . .

So many wild theories. So many times Carol's mother and her best friend tried to help.

Help! Carol tried to yell, but she knew that any help would have to come from within the coma. Any help would have to come from herself.

As Dwight paced, he continued to speak, revealing everything. Carol understood that, if she were to wake, if she were to open her eyes right now, Dwight would have no choice but to kill her with his own hands. As his shoes kept anxious rhythm on the storm room floor, Carol could hear Hattie at work, too. Her mother's perpetual tinkering. The time she built the back-mattress so that Carol would never fall flat to the floor. The time she constructed the helmet out of birch. To the rain of her husband's selfish tears, Carol heard Hattie working.

Then, as Dwight inhaled and exhaled the fear of an outlaw on his way, John spoke up as he did the day he thought he figured it out.

He'd sat up fast in the wicker chair and snapped his fingers.

Hey, hey, he said. *If you feel the wind against your face, it's obviously blowing . . . up. And yet . . . you're falling . . . down.* There was a sparkle in his beautiful eyes that day, magnified by his glasses. *Might this mean you're not moving at all? Might you be . . . sitting still? And if so . . . doesn't that sound more manageable? A falling woman is in a much worse predicament than one sitting still. Think about it, Carol. What* can *you do in there?*

Carol remembered how they walked through the gardens and talked about that until the sun rose above Harrows. She remembered, too, how they reached no conclusion, how John felt defeated for having, as he said, *come so close to figuring it out.*

But now, as Dwight continued to pace, as deep-blue volts continued to course through her blood and body, Carol thought maybe she and John had figured it out after all.

What *can* a woman do who is stuck, facedown, neither falling nor rising after all?

Roll over, Carol thought. Then, incredibly, she laughed. Despite the horrors, the betrayal, the knowledge of a heinous husband and a former lover at a disadvantage, Moxie, not knowing he was being tracked, Carol found space enough to laugh.

Roll over.

Of all the words she and John Bowie exchanged, never had they mentioned these two.

Her brief laughter was condors taking flight, vanishing into the folds of Howltown, where, Carol knew, they would find no food and starve.

But as her laughter died, it was replaced with something much more useful to her.

Hope.

RINALDO

Rinaldo was in Abberstown when Moxie performed the Trick. In those days he was sweeping peanut shells, broken glass, and a wide assortment of disgust from the floor of Lady Hennessey's bawdy house. He did other things, too, other duties, like *cleaning the sheets* (just the thought of it now made him rush to the bucket), knocking on the doors when *time was up*, restocking the liquor shelves, and often dunking a whore's head in cold bathwater if Lady Hennessey thought her unable to perform. Dark days, yes, but Rinaldo now counted them as penance paid to bear witness to a miracle.

James Moxie in Abberstown. A duel. Moxie the victor without removing his gun from its holster. As if the outlaw had sent a bullet his foe's way with his mind alone.

Today, to his absolute astonishment, he had in his possession an official piece of paper with James Moxie's name on it.

A piece of paper he should not have.

Now nearing his fiftieth year, married with two lovely children, and living in a comfortable and clean home in Griggsville, Rinaldo kissed his wife on the forehead and went in to do the same to the little ones. The family took afternoon naps, and he often took this opportunity to muse alone in the big shed in the backyard. After tucking the sheets to his son's and daughter's little chins, he quietly closed the door behind him.

Stepping outside, the afternoon air felt calming. He needed that. Calming. Summer sunlight washed the grass path and painted his boots a deep yellow. He came to the shed and whispered, "Who goes there?"

Because today he was nervous; today he'd been a part of something he didn't want to be a part of. Shouldn't have been a part of. Had no business with.

Today he'd delivered his hero's death sentence.

He entered the shed and stepped toward a pile of thick blankets stacked beside a brown wooden chest. On the chest was a small purple box: Rinaldo's own box of magic. After seeing James Moxie's feat in Abberstown, Rinaldo took quickly to the craft.

He plopped onto the blankets and reached for a box of matches beside the box of tricks. The small shed and all its clutter showed when he lit one: boxes of newspaper clippings, JAMES MOXIE wanted posters, and the tall wooden cabinet his wife, Liliana, refused to step inside of so that he might cut her in half.

He reached his small hand under the blankets and removed a pipe.

He leaned back into the blankets and smoked.

The fabric seemed to soften beneath him and soon he was sprawled, almost completely lying down. His mind swam with anecdotes and sometimes he laughed and other times he stared seriously at the ceiling. Thirty minutes into this haphazard meditation, he bent forward and slipped his boots off, his feet naked upon the cold earth before he found them too cold and brought them up onto the blankets where it was warmer. He sat this way for a long time, the candlelight dancing on the ceiling.

A wolf or dog howled outside and Rinaldo sat up fast, ripped from his splendor. The noise lent some urgency to the real reason he'd come to the shed.

Removing the piece of paper from his pocket, Rinaldo held it where he could read it and, squinting, read it again for the seventh time this day.

```
James Moxie STOP Mackatoon STOP On his way to
Harrows STOP Send the Cripple STOP Urgent
```

He felt no less guilty about it for having smoked.

His time at Lady Hennessey's, long ago, had exposed him to every variety of outlaw and triggerman that traveled the Trail. For reasons he was unsure of, Rinaldo had become a confidant for these men. Usually the bad ones.

At the time this gave him strange comfort—accepted as he was at all, even by men who leered, cheated, and murdered. Many nights he sat at the bawdy house bar, listening to the woes and wonders of real life on the Trail. The men and women seemed to think he was safe. Perhaps it was his kind face. Perhaps it was the fact that he didn't speak much. For whatever the reason, Rinaldo was told things, too many things. Most outlaws, it seemed, experienced something like confession when talking to him. Soon, for this, his role in the bawdy house ballooned, a natural progression: His being a friendly ear became his being an ideal middleman, a nondescript nobody who could deliver their messages, telegrams, and (often) illegal notes. Many an evening at Lady Hennessey's ended with Rinaldo holding a piece of paper, similar to the one he held now, a word or two from the rapscallion who had written it, a message for someone equally beastly.

See to it Johansen gets this? She'll be stopping in soon.

Do me a favor, huh? And don't be showing this off . . .

Eh, little Rinaldo, do me a favor . . .

Tell Lafayette I says hello.

For this, Rinaldo, too, became famous on the Trail. But to his distress, not for the same reasons James Moxie had.

Not famous for magic.

Rinaldo in Abberstown. He's the one to go through.

Did you leave it with Rinaldo? Abberstown? Lady Hennessey's . . . you know the man.

Rinaldo, simple as he was, received these papers with the same expression he wore when he mopped. Much younger then, he thought little of the consequences of the words he delivered. He knew the men and women were bad and could guess their correspondences were no better, yet he had felt free from responsibility.

After all, what was he doing but taking a sheet of paper from one hand and placing it in another?

Lady Hennessey's had a way of pulling even the cleanest men into the mud, and Rinaldo, now very happy in Griggsville, called himself lucky for not having gotten dirtier, stuck there for longer than he was.

Rinaldo reached for the pipe again.

Today those questionable relations were renewed.

How did this happen? he mused, flummoxed, smoke rising from his lips.

The ceiling of the shed gave him no concrete response.

Rinaldo had no doubt that what James Moxie did in Abberstown was real magic. Of course, by now he'd heard the same theories everyone had. Men loved to talk about it over cards, at the bar, waiting for a coach. Most tried to dissect the moment; toothless drunks called it sleight of hand; lawmen claimed another shooter; young outlaws couldn't guess how to practice it. But hardly a man saw it happen like Rinaldo had.

James Moxie faced Daniel Prouds over a ditch on Dunkle Street and Prouds's chest exploded in deep rose before Moxie moved his hand. The blood bursting from Prouds's pink shirt would forever remain fixed in Rinaldo's memory: a sudden flight of red ravens; a rising cardinal corpse.

Oh, how many times had Liliana listened to Rinaldo blabber, stoned, about Abberstown! His wife rolled her eyes at him so often he was surprised they weren't loose. Smoking now, he remembered well the early years. When he and Liliana first moved to Griggsville, when he bought the Disappearing Box and Liliana agreed to step inside. But try as he might, he could not make her vanish until she explained it to him.

Mirrors, she'd taught him.

And so did Moxie use mirrors? Under a sun so bright? In front of a crowd of so many? Rinaldo learned many tricks in those days, trying hard to emulate the great James Moxie. And as the years passed he accumulated many toys, many cards, the games and tricks that gave him infinite pleasure in the large shed, smoking from his pipe, often re-creating Moxie's stance in Abberstown. Yes, there was a marginal flash, a gun fired, and yet . . . none drawn?

Rinaldo pondered this once again. But the good cheer he usually felt was difficult to find.

"Guilt," Rinaldo said, watching the smoke dissolve into the candlelit ceiling.

Because guilt was indeed what he was wrestling now. The ugly back-and-forth swinging of the heavy pendulum.

"Guilt."

Today Rinaldo had delivered a message. Today he had taken a piece of paper to the post office and seen to it that the words he now saw by the shed's candlelight were sent far south, to Mackatoon, where James Moxie called home.

"Moxie!" he suddenly screamed.

How did this happen?

Earlier, Rinaldo had been walking the streets of Griggsville when he saw the man named Mutton gesturing to him from across the road. Mutton, a snow-cold man whom Rinaldo never liked even when he himself was in the loving throes of booze, gestured with a gloved hand. And winked.

Hell's heaven, Rinaldo thought, already the old familiar sensation of his youthful tryst at the bawdy house returning. *Don't go to him.*

But cross the road he did, unable to feign the ignorance he now so wished he had.

"Thought you didn't recognize me there for a second, Rinaldo."

Mutton looked worse than Rinaldo remembered. The skin of his face like orange rinds.

"Of course I recognized you," Rinaldo responded. Always wanting to be accepted. Always wanting to be liked.

They exchanged false pleasantries before Mutton eyed Rinaldo a second longer than was comfortable and said, "Look here, Rinaldo. I'm in something of a bind. It seems I'm wanted yonder." He fanned a gloved hand to a saloon door, where a heavy woman was looking their way. "Yet I have some work to do." Rinaldo felt suddenly as if he was at a place he shouldn't have come. "You remember the old days, don't ya, 'Naldo? You remember how it used to be . . ." Mutton pulled from his vest pocket a folded piece of paper. Rinaldo observed but did not speak. "What say you deliver this message for me? It's an easy gig, really, all's you got to do is step into the post office and send these six or seven words. I'd very much appreciate it . . . seeing as I'm wanted yonder."

Rinaldo looked at the paper and thought of Liliana. He thought of the children.

"Of course," the bad man continued, "there's a coin or two in it for you." Then he leaned forward and Rinaldo smelled rat on the man's breath. "Just like we used to do."

Rinaldo continued to stare at the paper as if it were an invitation to his past, to a time before he met Liliana. To the days before love and family and his shed of magic.

"Now, you haven't changed, have you, 'Naldo?"

Rinaldo felt trapped by Mutton's gaze. And yet what harm could it do, to do something he'd done so many times before?

Abberstown was, after all, magic for Rinaldo. Reliving a sliver couldn't hurt . . . too badly?

"No, of course not. I'll deliver your telegram."

The people-pleaser. The yes-man. Still.

Rinaldo took the paper. Mutton smiled, his gums black with smoke. "Thatta boy, 'Naldo. Just like we used to do."

After delivering the message, unable to shake a vision of Liliana wagging a finger at him, and halfway home, Rinaldo stopped walking and decided to do something he'd never done before.

He pulled the folded paper from his pocket and read the message he'd delivered.

Then he read it again.

And again.

"Hell's heaven," Rinaldo said. And his voice sounded like it did twenty years ago, as he naïvely fluffed pillows.

The few words on the paper dug fast. Little knives. Big wounds.

His first inclination was to race back to the post office and tell them there had been a mistake. It was impossible these were the words he'd played a part in sending.

```
James Moxie STOP Mackatoon STOP On his way to
Harrows STOP Send the Cripple STOP Urgent
```

There in the road the sun felt uncomfortably hot. He sweat as though under the stage lights of a magic show of his own.

One in which he had failed to fool anybody.

Now, in the shed, reclining in a cloud of smoke, Rinaldo leaned forward and stuck his short arms into the box of tricks on the chest at his bare feet. He removed a pack of cards and shuffled them, laying some out upon the dirt.

He cried.

"Pick any card in the deck!" Rinaldo said, loud, to the empty shed. "Any card in the deck and I'll show you which card you have chosen." Then he removed a card and looked at it. "Don't tell me what it is, though I must admit that it doesn't matter for this trick whether or not I know what it is." The word *trick* made him ill and Rinaldo looked about the shed, suddenly feeling cold, strange, and very alone. "Now slide it back into the deck and I'll show you which it was!" But there was no thrill, no sleight of hand deft enough to conceal the ugliness he felt.

The guilt.

He slid the card back in the deck.

He exhaled until he felt empty of air.

Rinaldo, so long a stranger to guilt, set the cards back in the box and blew out the candle.

He exited the shed, tiptoed quickly across the sunny yard, and entered his home by the back door.

Passing his son and daughter's bedroom he stopped, thinking he would slip inside and tell them hello. Perhaps their warmth would make him feel better.

```
James Moxie STOP Mackatoon STOP On his way to
Harrows STOP Send the Cripple STOP Urgent
```

But in the hallways of his home, his hand upon the children's bedroom door, he thought he knew who *the Cripple* was.

He thought of a hatless man on stilts. Tin legs. A limping cowboy. The cruelest man Rinaldo had ever encountered on the Trail.

Smoke.

As if by opening the door he would be exposing his children to this madman, Rinaldo went instead to the master bedroom, where Liliana still slept.

He knelt beside the bed.

"I did something terrible today, Liliana!"

He shook her.

At first she did not stir, and Rinaldo saw that man again, as if he had already been here, to Rinaldo's very home, had already stolen the life from Liliana.

"Liliana!"

His wife shot up in bed. Eyes wide.

"What? What is it, Rinaldo?"

"I killed James Moxie!"

Rinaldo couldn't see his wife well but heard her grunt and knew she had rolled her eyes.

"You smoke too much, Rinaldo! You smoke too much!"

SMOKE GETS A HAIRCUT

Holding the razor to the hatless man's neck, Quint couldn't quit thinking about his client's legs. There was something too fitting about it. Like all Quint had to do was move quick and then the crazy-talking man (a triggerman, possibly) would be symmetrical. No legs and no head. And if the man thought he was fooling anyone by covering them with his pants, he was surely mistaken. Quint had a peg leg of his own. But even he marveled at the fact that this man must have two.

"I heard word that the magic man was in town a bit earlier," Smoke suddenly said, pivoting from the subject he was on quickly. The heavyset barber hardly heard it happen. Quint's partner, the thinner Franklin, was busy washing hair in the back tub.

"And who would that be?" Quint asked, setting the razor on the counter and picking up the scissors again. The limper had asked for "only a little bit" and Quint wondered if that was because he had "only a little bit" of money. Hard to tell these days.

Smoke smiled. In the glass, the smile looked genuine.

"An outlaw," Smoke said. "Heard he was in this very place of business."

Quint frowned. Began cutting.

"Just a little bit," Smoke said. His eyes were fixed on Quint's in the glass.

"I don't know of any magic man coming in here," he said. Then he called out to his partner. "Franklin! You know of any magic outlaw who came in here earlier today?"

"Magic outlaw?" Franklin repeated. Smoke watched him in the glass, too. Saw the way he stroked his chin with one hand. Thinking. "You mean James Moxie?"

Smoke turned his head to face Franklin, and Quint cut off more than he'd meant to.

"I'm sorry, mister—"

But Smoke didn't care about the hair.

"That's him all right. Heard it on Nero Street a moment ago. Someone said James Moxie himself had been here in Baker. Here in this shop."

Observing him in the glass, Quint felt suddenly uneasy at the sight of him. Surely this limper was a triggerman. And yet . . . no guns.

"Quint?" Franklin asked. "You think that . . . was him?"

Smoke's eyes traveled from one bald barber to the other.

Quint considered.

"I don't think so, Franklin. That man was in a huff."

"A huff, you say?" Smoke asked. "What was he huffing about, then?"

"Started shoutin' at a customer," Franklin said. "Damn near scared the hog-piss out of him."

"How'd he do that?"

"Charged him," Quint said. "Ran straight at him and tore the towels off his face."

"But James Moxie," Franklin said. "Would he have to use his hands to do such a thing?"

Smoke laughed.

"I wouldn't laugh at a man like James Moxie," Quint said. "Might be able to hear you still."

"He still here, you mean?"

"No," Quint said. "Only, he's able to do things us ordinary folk aren't."

Then the two barbers and the man getting a wash in the back began the inevitable exchange of myths.

"Man has to use his hands."

"Didn't in Abberstown."

"Stage show."

"Magic."

"Mind power, huh?"

"Something like it, yes."

"Sure would hate to face him on Nero Street."

"You seen the fire in his eyes? Enough to burn this place down."

Smoke, his hair only half cut, gripped the sides of the chair and pulled himself up to standing.

"You know my name, too?" he said.

Quint and Franklin exchanged glances across the shop. It had been a lively afternoon, indeed.

"Well, I might," Quint said, "but what I do know is that we're not quite finished here. If you'll sit back—"

"You know why they call me Smoke?"

Quint tried not to look down to those legs again.

"I don't know any Smoke," Franklin said.

Smoke stared at Quint, saw the fear in his eyes. Held it.

"You do, though, don't you, heavyset?"

Quint stepped back and nodded. "I've heard of a man named Smoke. Yes. A bad man, indeed."

Smoke smiled. His hair, half done, made the look in his eyes even more unbalanced than when he'd walked in. "Did the magic outlaw say what made him so mad?"

"No, sir. He didn't."

"Did he say anything at all?"

Quint shook his head. Smoke took the razor from the counter.

"Hey now," Franklin said.

Smoke held out an open palm. "Let me tell you why they call me Smoke."

Then Smoke stepped toward the barber, razor neck-high. Franklin and the customer in back sat still. Smoke brought the razor to Quint's neck.

"It's because I got a trick of my own."

"Okay, son."

"I can vanish."

"Okay. Watch it now."

"Without ..." Smoke suddenly turned the razor around, gave it handle-first to the trembling barber. "Without paying for a haircut."

Then Smoke smiled. He limped past the heavy bald barber and stepped back out onto the Nero Street boardwalk. He looked up and down the road once, as if some evidence of the man he followed might remain.

He saw potential information in the eyes of everyone who passed, and decided, finally, that when you were chasing someone, not stopping was always better than stopping.

Moxie was no more magic than a mouse.

"An old one," Smoke said. "Who will, sooner than later, need to stop."

Then Smoke limped across the uneven planks on his way to the castrated gelding, hitched to a sun-bleached post.

Behind him, the barbers watched him through the glass of their front door. Both held tight to the images of the crazed James Moxie and the curt triggerman Smoke.

Without talking about it, they both imagined the two of them vanishing farther up the Trail where, eventually, their respective bedlams must meet.

MOXIE AND RINALDO

Griggsville wasn't easily seen from deeper south on the Trail, but one had to pass through it to continue. The town was surrounded by pine-and-spruce-covered hills, a natural barrier, a great wooden barrel from which poured forth the sounds of human lust and vice, violence and ecstasy, fear, hatred, and joy. For those arriving after dark, whether from north or south, the lantern lights and great bonfires would give the town away, if the sound of the carousal hadn't already. But during the day, as Moxie rode now, it wasn't until the last breadth of hills that he could see the very height of Hog's Hotel. Its fabled plaster snout pointed up to hell's heaven. The town gates, two tall wood posts wrapped tight with ivy, supported giant wire letters spelling GRIGGSVILLE, and Moxie passed under, the shadow of the letters upon his face, then his back, then the back of the mare.

There were more taverns in Griggsville than in any other town on the Trail. It was a place to celebrate, a place to drink and to dance, a place to be young. But as wild as Griggsville was, most men did not remove their guns at cards, the house madams ran clean homes, and the streets were free of debris. Big shows were scheduled at the theaters; people from as far as Harrows and Mackatoon came to experience the mammoth curtains dividing. The friendly lawmen made sure it all ran well, and that the money the tourists brought in was not wasted.

James Moxie looked the part that he was: a man passing through on a mare.

No lawman stopped him upon entering, and he felt no eyes upon him.

But he should have.

A small man carrying lumber absently dropped a loose board when he saw the outlaw and did not apologize to the lady who had to step over the wood on her way. James Moxie missed him, distracted by the town's good cheer, the sun high in the sky, the bright signs and polished steel hitching posts, the fabulous dresses the ladies wore, the hats, too, floating above the streets, seemingly independent of the heads they shadowed.

He didn't see the wide-eyed man who now followed the mare, step for step, bumping into people on the boardwalk, knocking one man's papers to the planks.

Is it him? Rinaldo thought. *Is it possible he's here?*

It had been over a decade since he'd seen him. But a hero is always recognizable to those who adore him. Rinaldo saw the face from Abberstown hovering above the blood-red shirt Moxie wore.

Moxie continued, slow for the traffic of bodies, multicolored coaches parked in front of the saloons and hotels, and other riders, heading south, having already had their fun. The sounds of the townsfolk were soothing, the loneliness of the ride exposed therein, and Moxie allowed his mind to be carried by it, hidden inside, as the mare took his body through the revelry. He didn't hear it, then, when the little man called to him from the dust rising from the hooves and boots in the road.

"James Moxie!"

The outlaw rode slowly through the gay streets. If anybody other than Rinaldo cared to study them, Moxie and the mare might look out of place after all . . . a tiny one-man cortège, gray and dusty brown, the farthest point of an unseen procession.

"James Moxie!"

Now Moxie did hear the excited voice but did not address the man who it belonged to. Griggsville was too easy a place to get stuck in.

"Mister Moxie! James Moxie!"

The outlaw felt tugging at his boot and he looked down, his eyes blazing. Rinaldo removed his hand fast.

The awe he felt was paralyzing. But he found motion with his mouth.

"My name is Rinaldo! I need to speak with you! It is very urgent we speak!"

"I'm only passing through," Moxie said. And his voice was saloon doors creaking closed.

"You must! We must speak for a moment! I have news for you!"

Moxie kept his eyes on the road ahead.

"It's about you!" Rinaldo thought of Liliana, shooing him and his fancies away. "It's about you and the men who are after you!"

"No men are after me."

"Yes . . . yes they are! I delivered the telegram myself!"

Moxie, his idol, looked down at him again and stopped the mare. The Griggsville bustle went on, people passed, voices tangled in bliss.

"Tell me more, Rinaldo."

Rinaldo breathed heavily. James Moxie had just spoken his name.

"Please," Rinaldo said, his lungs burning. "Let's not talk in the middle of the road."

"I've no time to waste."

"I won't waste your time."

Moxie, feeling the dirt road and flow of traffic continuing now without him, feeling the pinch of time lost, the clock that ticked beside a sleeping Carol, followed Rinaldo to the side of the road.

"I didn't realize the message I was delivering," Rinaldo said, speaking fast, wiping his forehead dry with a handkerchief from his pocket. "A bad man gave it to me."

An old couple stepped to the side, avoiding the pair. Moxie, still upon his horse, asked, "What did the telegram say?"

Rinaldo swallowed.

"It said you were in Mackatoon. On your way to Harrows I believe. It said to *Send the Cripple.*"

Moxie looked back to the road, his eyes distant, considering.

Animated, Rinaldo continued, "The man who gave me the telegram, he was no good, James Moxie. You must believe me."

The street felt too crowded for Moxie then. The sun too hot. Hotter than when he passed under the great wire letters. And within this sudden disorientation, Moxie understood that what the little man was telling him had much bigger implications than he knew.

If someone was tracking him, someone had *hired* the man to do so. Who?

"Who gave you this telegram, Rinaldo?"

"A man named Mutton. He—"

"Where did it come from? What town? Harrows?"

The Griggsville heat came down hard. Sweat fell from the outlaw's face. The brim of Moxie's hat blocked the sun above, and in his silhouette Rinaldo saw two burning white eyes, teeth clenched.

He felt he must answer this question.

But he couldn't. He didn't know where the telegram came from.

"I'm sorry—"

Moxie was long quiet, then said, "Thank you for your help, Rinaldo."

Rinaldo, relieved, slapped the mare on her side.

"You are welcome, James Moxie! Man of magic!"

Moxie, lost in the future, the past, and the present, too, responded quietly, "There was no magic, Rinaldo."

Rinaldo did not hesitate to respond.

"Oh, that isn't true. I saw it. I was there."

"There was no magic."

"I wish you could stay. You could take lodging with my family and me. You could show me how the Trick was done?"

"I thank you again, Rinaldo."

Then he kicked the mare and guided her back into traffic.

Rinaldo, overwhelmed, watched him go.

"Be safe, Moxie!"

Then as Moxie fell from view, as he was too far for Rinaldo to reach, Rinaldo felt a sudden pang of terror.

"Oh, no! I didn't tell him that the triggerman's name is Smoke!"

He imagined Liliana again, wagging a finger. Maybe Moxie knew Smoke. Could spot him if he knew who was coming.

Moxie, nearing the north side of town, imagined Carol plucking finite breaths from a glass jar at her bedside. He felt he had wasted time indeed. Whoever was following him had surely gained. And the rush to Harrows was heightened; the guilt for Carol increased.

Send the Cripple . . .

Moxie studied Rinaldo's words.

As the rage within him swelled, the guilt grew, too.

And the sun began to go down on Griggsville.

MANDERS PREPARES
A GRAVE

The office at the funeral home was closed, it being close to dark, but Robert Manders would have answered the door had anyone knocked. The Illness that had come to Harrows, an illness that Doctor Walker believed was either contained or gone, brought the home much work to do, and Manders couldn't rule out the possibility of more coming. It was a delicate business, being the director of a vibrant town's one death depot, and Manders never forgot the cardinal rule of his profession: No matter how many bodies came through his front doors, each was the only for those who carried it.

His father took over the home when Robert was ten years old. Until then Dad was a gravedigger, a job that stained his clothes with grass and earth and gave him a distinct odor, a cloud of something not quite antique but not fresh, either, a smell young Robert detected in the house before seeing the old man was home. Dad worked with a digger named Hubert, and the pair discussed much over the empty plots they dug. A favorite topic was the idea of one day owning their own funeral home, hiring gravediggers instead. The sudden death of Howard Lauren, the home's owner at the time, made this a surprising possibility. After a brief meeting with town officials, the two young gravediggers got permission to purchase the place on loan and begin to run it themselves. Who else was so eager to handle the dead? So ready? Robert and his mother moved into the home with Dad, taking residency on the second floor. And thus began the young Manders's long desensitization to death, dead bodies, and the crude process of preservation. By the time he was fifteen he could do the work himself. And by the time Robert was twenty, Hubert sold Allan Manders his share of the place and suddenly Robert was next in line, his future secured.

"Robert?"

Manders had been looking out the window, dazed, mechanically watching the men dig a fresh plot. The name *Alexander Wolfe* played and replayed in his head. Dwight Evers's doctor of choice. Manders was leaning back in his chair, his fingers to his chin, half storing the image of the silhouettes against the darkening sky. He turned slowly to the door.

"Yes, Norman, come in."

Norman was wearing his white apron and smelled of the stuffy basement. "I'm finished."

Robert nodded. "Very well. How did it go?"

"It's good work."

Robert smiled. "I'm sure it is."

When the diggers arrived this afternoon, Manders talked to them about Carol Evers. He discovered the pair had already learned of her death. He walked them to the plot listings on the wood square outside the cemetery gates. There he explained where she was to be buried. The men had other graves to dig, but they assured the director they would get to Carol's before the sun went down. Manders turned to leave when Lucas said, "Plot Twenty will be an improvement on where she rests now."

Often the talk between the gravediggers was nonsense to the director, but this bit caught Manders's attention.

"What was that, Lucas?"

"I said—"

"And where does she rest now?"

"In the cellar of the Evers home, Mister Manders. Heard it from the husband of Missus Farrah Darrow. Girl saw Carol Evers there herself yester eve."

Behind his glasses, Manders's eyes grew distant. Then he reminded the men they had much work to do, excused himself, and crossed the gravel drive to the front stone steps of the home.

Much of the rest of his day was spent looking absently out the window.

At one point he left the office and took the stone stairs to the basement where Norman was preparing the body of Wilhelm Boyd, the seventy-seven-year-old former attorney. Though it was Manders's job to ensure things were done right, the director had given the deceased only a cursory glance. Norman was truly the best at what he did. In his lifetime at the home, Robert had never known a man who performed his part more fastidiously.

"How are we on supplies?" Manders asked, then in the basement. But his voice was distant, his mind someplace else.

"Eh?"

Manders didn't repeat himself and Norman didn't ask him to.

The director circled the table supporting Wilhelm Boyd's body and sat upon a stool at the far wall. Norman worked as if no one was there, and in a way no one was. Manders watched but did not register the steadfast makeup artist. Instead he took in the vague shades of movement, the process he had borne witness to a thousand times, and did not fight to keep his mind from wandering.

Now, both in the office, Norman was through.

"I'll be going home now, Mister Manders."

The director nodded. As Norman removed his apron, Manders said, "Carol Evers won't be coming here."

The body-dresser bunched his thick brow. Often, under the basement lights, Norman's face looked theatrical, leathery, and hard. Now it looked downright vaudevillian.

"How's that?"

"Seems Mister Evers has hired family to take care of it."

Norman seemed to consider this, then said, "I'll be going home, Mister Manders. Mister Boyd is ready."

"Very well. And thank you. Good evening to you."

Norman left and Manders resumed his long stare out the office window.

Plot Twenty will be an improvement on where she rests now.

Through the glass he saw the diggers were shin-deep and the sky much darker beyond them. Manders rose and exited the office, then the home itself. Crossing the yard, passing the podium of plot locations, he came to the diggers.

"I told you two it was going to be a Benson?"

His voice carried across the quiet graveyard.

"Yes you did, sir. This'll work for a Benson."

"Oh," Manders said, "I'm sure it will. Just wanted to make sure you knew."

Hugh Benson was a carpenter in town. As coffin makers went, he was not Manders's preferred craftsman.

"We're gonna have to make sure the bearers hold tight, sir."

Manders nodded.

"Yes we are, Lucas. It wouldn't be the first time a Benson split on us."

If you asked Robert Manders, Hugh Benson's coffins weren't much more than six pieces of wood and a few picture-framing nails. In fact, he wondered if Benson didn't cut his wood with a dinner knife.

Certainly not the right box for a woman like Carol Evers.

"You expecting a big showing, sir?"

"No. Private ceremony. Perhaps Mister Evers alone."

Lucas looked at Manders.

"I'd have thought the whole town would be out for this one. Missus Evers was liked by all, I reckon."

"Indeed she was," Manders said.

Manders watched the men work for a minute or more. Lucas's boots and shins vanished in the shadows of the hole with the shovel-head.

Manders looked to John Bowie's grave. Still looked fresh. Not quite one with the rest of the graveyard. And here one of Bowie's best friends would be joining him already.

"I have some matters to attend to, gentlemen."

It was true, but back in his office he didn't acknowledge them.

He sat in the dark instead, the last vestige of sunlight creeping behind a horizon wide enough to distort it, sending a purple wash through the window and across his desk. He tapped his fingers upon the chair's armrest and made to get up but stayed put. He leaned back in his chair again and then leaned forward and sighed and tapped his fingers on the desk instead. From a drawer he removed a sheet of paper, and in the waning light made notes he didn't need to make. Things he would do without a reminder.

See Marcy Donaldson about flowers.

Talk to August Marbles; what will the weather be like?

Make sure Lucas reinforces the coffin.

Get bell from town.

He glanced out the window. The gravediggers weren't visible now. All Manders could see were the tallest of the headstones, spiking above the tangle of crosses and stones. But the director didn't need to see the men to know their actions in detail. By memory and imagination he watched them patting the sides of the deep hole with their shovel-heads, checking the height against their own.

Manders rose from his chair at last and crossed the office. His boots clucked against the wood floor then got quiet as he stepped on the rug before the bookshelf. He lit a candle and took the stick from the lower shelf, lifting it up and up until it was just above his head. With his other hand he reached and pulled down a heavy leather volume and returned with it to his desk.

HARROWS AND SURROUNDING AREAS: LEDGER OF REGISTRY

The black letters went deep into the thick auburn leather. Manders adjusted his glasses and opened it.

He was still reading, the candlelight dancing about the office, when the gravediggers finished and went home for the night. He was alone now, both in the parlor and on the grounds. And he was still reading when the purple wash of sky gave way to gray, then a deep blue marking another night's arrival.

And where does she rest now?

In the cellar of the Evers home, Mister Manders. Girl saw her there herself.

Manders flipped the pages. The fine paper sounded hollow, like it wasn't strong enough to deliver him what he desired. But still he flipped ... and flipped ... leaning closer and closer to the text ... the words ... the names ...

The name *Alexander Wolfe* continued to sound off in his head, and Manders searched for him, searching for Dwight Evers's doctor of choice.

Was it possible Robert Manders hadn't heard of a doctor who lived near?

His fingers passed over the thin white pages. Looking ... searching ... hoping ...

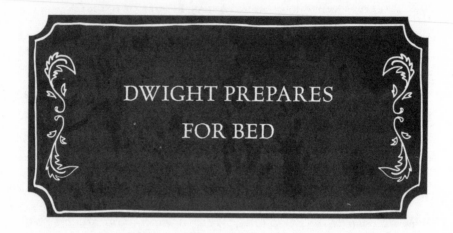

DWIGHT PREPARES
FOR BED

Dwight hung his suit coat on the chair at the vanity. He caught his reflection, thought he looked reasonably grieved, but still messed up his hair in the glass. There was no one to perform for in this room, but Dwight wanted desperately to stay in character. As if the wallpaper might tattle.

His tie hung loose around his neck, and his boots were already at the foot of the bed. Unbuttoning his white shirt as he walked, he hung it and the tie on the hook inside the boudoir door. At the sink in the washroom he washed his face and cleaned his teeth and ran his wet hands over his lips.

The morning after tomorrow, he thought, *Carol will be buried.*

The thought was not comforting. The date was not soon enough. What if she were to wake before then?

What if she were to wake . . . right now?

James Moxie hadn't left his mind since the moment Dwight read that he was coming. Lafayette had told him not to worry; the freak Smoke would do the job. But there would be hell's heaven to pay if he didn't.

Moxie would talk about Carol's condition. Moxie would tell Sheriff Opal. Opal would tell Manders. Together they'd exhume Carol, check, find scratch marks inside the coffin, ask Dwight why he hadn't mentioned her condition, surely he knew of it, didn't he think it might apply?

Stepping to the bed, Dwight held an image of the two men, the outlaw and the triggerman, lost somewhere in the darkness of the Trail. Where was Smoke now? Where was Moxie? For all Dwight knew the Cripple was drinking his own blood on a riverbed, possibly facedown in pig-shit, full of holes. Maybe James Moxie was plunging a knife in Smoke's back this minute as he, Dwight, sat on the edge of his large hard mattress.

It was foolishness, placing a thing of such importance in the hands of a risky stranger.

You're trafficking in madmen now, Lafayette had said in their meeting. Dwight's hands shook with the memory.

He pulled off his socks and tossed them onto the bearskin rug.

It was possible that Moxie was holding the Cripple's head underwater now, an old rusty tub in some woeful hotel washroom. It wasn't difficult for Dwight to imagine water splashing over the sides of that tub, the name of he who'd sent him already out of the triggerman's mouth and into the mind of the outlaw.

. . . who would then come for you, Dwight ol' boy . . .

Another flat reality of Lafayette's. And Dwight knew the sow wasn't exaggerating.

But did Smoke know who'd hired him? Had Dwight overlooked that aspect? Should he have told Lafayette to leave his, Dwight's, name out of it?

And more important right now . . . *could* a crippled man defeat a legend like Moxie?

The chaos frightened him deeply.

Dwight was out of his element.

Way out.

Ninety-five percent of the couple's money came from Carol and her family. The house, the company, the clothes: All were either bought by or initially funded by Carol's side over the course of their seventeen-year marriage. That Hattie; always lurking, always present, long after her own death. Not only had Dwight never hired a man to murder before . . . he hadn't paid for laundry in almost two decades.

Where was Smoke now? *Right now?*

Lafayette had assured him there was no question the Cripple had enough time to get to the outlaw. Yet these things had a way of happening, former lovers coming together, old love, people connected by the dust traces of a past bond, something to do with fate or the way things were and the way they still are.

Anxious, he got up off the bed and removed his pants. He blew out the candle on the small table where Carol used to set her handbag, her hat, her mirrors. The bedroom was now lit by a single candle on the other side of the bed, his side, and early moonlight slipped in through the open drapes. He crossed the room and peered outside, through the glass, to the front yard below.

Was Moxie out there, crouched in the shadows beneath the sill?

Dwight inched back from the glass. Maybe there was a gun pointed at him. A gun in the hand of a legend, a legend whose name struck fear into the hearts of heartless men and women like Lafayette. Dwight could feel it: the cold tunnel a bullet might pass before shattering the glass, shattering the bones of his ribs, splintering his bones against the green stone wall above the bed. He could smell it, he thought, the smoke rising from a hot gun . . . a gun that was always hot . . . a gun that was boiling the moment it was drawn. He could hear it, too. A click out there. The swoosh of the steel against the leather holster, the horse hoof clacking, and the explosion of a pure shot, all just before his skull cracked, a dropped soup bowl, his bones held twiglike together by baggy skin.

Dwight physically shuddered.

Where was James Moxie . . . *right now?*

Dwight got into bed, leaned across the mattress, and blew out the remaining candle. The bedroom went dark and he stared into the blackness beyond his feet. The moonlight did not reach that darkness.

But it did touch some of the furniture along the window's wall, distorting it, changing the chair into a crouched crippled man, the highboy into a legendary outlaw without remorse.

"He walked out on her twenty years ago," Dwight spoke into the darkness. "Why would he come back now?"

The unfairness of it squeezed him.

A vision again of Smoke, his head in a trough, Moxie above him, soot-faced, howling, *Who sent you? WHO SENT YOU?*

But *did* Smoke know?

Dwight's lack of knowledge of the ways of the Trail scared him deeply.

Soon the night birds called beyond the window glass. The frogs and grasshoppers followed.

Dwight lay on his back, his hair soft upon the pillow. He pulled the blanket up to his chest and closed his eyes.

Moxie's telegram appeared like blood-red letters typed into the ceiling:

DO NOT BURY

NOT DEAD

ON MY WAY

The unseen threads of former lovers.

Dwight stared long enough for his eyes to get used to the dark; long enough to feel confident that the shape in the corner was Carol's vanity, the shape beside that the door. Breathing heavy, he fell asleep . . . images of the crippled madman roving a featureless landscape outside all time and detail. And the outlaw, too . . . as Dwight dreamed . . . James Moxie was out there, too.

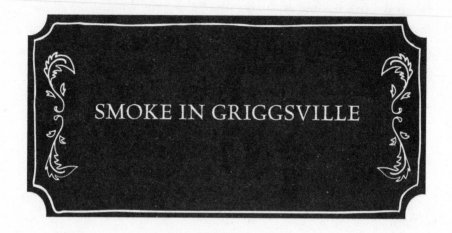

SMOKE IN GRIGGSVILLE

S moke was sitting on a stool at the bar and Rinaldo came to him.
He'd beckoned the local from across the saloon, an exaggerated twirling of a finger, as though expressing that he, too, had an
affinity for the magic outlaw Moxie. Rinaldo had been shouting about
the Trick at Abberstown and, much more important, about how the
"magician" had been in Griggsville this very afternoon.

"I'd just been thinking of the man. I was telling Liliana how much
he's meant to me . . ."

He had a few listeners but none as keen as Smoke. The hired man
sat alone at the bar, his elbows on the wood, and smiled as the small
loudmouth paraded from table to table, drunkenly boasting of his
encounter. Hardly any of the patrons believed Rinaldo, and those
who did smiled politely. Smoke waited for another dip in interest, for
the saloon to quiet, then signaled him over.

Rinaldo, happy for the willing audience, went to him quickly. "Do
I know you?"

"Not . . . quite . . . yet. But I sure as pig-shit want to hear more of
your story."

"You appreciate James Moxie then?"

"Me? I sure do, I do. One of the classiest outlaws the Trail has ever known. You say you saw him today?"

Rinaldo put his right hand in the air. "Not only do I say it . . . but I swear it."

"Is that right?"

Rinaldo smiled. He took the open stool beside Smoke. "I actually helped him a great deal."

"Is that so? And what would a legend need from a man such as yourself?"

Rinaldo smiled, proud. "I did nothing less than tell him he was in danger."

"Fascinating."

Smoke ordered a beer for Rinaldo. Water for himself. "Tell me more. What was James Moxie like?"

Rinaldo's eyes widened. "James Moxie is a generous man."

"How so?"

"He didn't have to honor me by speaking with me, but that's just what he did."

"He stopped and carried on a whole conversation with you?"

"I had real information for him."

"Like what?"

Rinaldo considered. "I'm not so sure I should tell you that much, stranger."

The two men sipped their drinks.

"Well, I sure wish I'd had a chance to see him," Smoke said, shaking his head for the missed opportunity. "When'd you see him?"

"This after!"

"What time?"

Rinaldo considered. "Three hours past. A few minutes less."

Smoke exaggeratedly snapped his fingers. Just missed him.

Rinaldo leaned forward, wobbled, and almost fell off the stool. "I'll tell you a secret, sir. I'll tell you something very special to me."

Smoke set his water upon the bar and waited.

"I was there," Rinaldo whispered, loud. "In Abberstown."

"Really . . ."

"Yes. Indeed I was. I'm old enough to have been working at the time."

Smoke placed a hand upon Rinaldo's wrist. "Describe it for me."

Rinaldo was very willing to talk. "Just two men, sir, facing each other on Dunkle Street. James Moxie stood on one side, Daniel Prouds the other. Draw was called. A *single* shot was fired. Prouds's chest blew open. But James Moxie never drew. I watched him close. And I wasn't the only one. He did not draw."

Smoke feigned disbelief. "Impossible."

"Some say so. But those some are wrong."

"What was the Trick?"

"I don't know."

"Surely you've got a theory."

"I do."

"And surely you asked. Today . . ."

"I did."

"But he didn't tell you, did he."

"No. He did not."

"What's your theory, then?"

Rinaldo breathed deep. "His magic . . . is *real*."

"I see."

Rinaldo looked to the other patrons then back to the stranger beside him. By the time Smoke's face was in focus again, Rinaldo started, for the friendly demeanor was gone. And in its stead was a seriousness Rinaldo did not like.

"Why don't you just tell me what you told him today."

Rinaldo, blurry, attempted to end the conversation. "The important thing is—"

"Why don't you just tell me what you told him today."

Rinaldo quickly took a sip of his beer. He knew bad men. He'd run letters for bad men for many years. There was a lack of depth in the eyes of bad men, as if they observed the world from well within their head, far from being able to feel for others.

Smoke's face lit up with a smile. The friendliness was back.

"Well, it would sure make for a better story," Smoke said. "You see, James Moxie has always been something of a hero of mine. That man Prouds you mention was none other than the brother of a man who'd done awful things to my family and me. This is the true and truly. I've long meant to travel to Mackatoon and thank the outlaw myself."

Rinaldo smiled. Smoke, it seemed, had spoken magic words. A fellow Moxie enthusiast, indeed.

"You know he lives in Mackatoon, then."

"But of course."

Rinaldo looked around to make certain no one else could hear.

"Not many people do. That's where they sent the assassin, you see."

"The assassin?"

"*Yes.* There is a bad man after our friend Moxie. A man with a black heart and broken legs."

"I see." Smoke sipped his water. "And that's what you done told him today. That he's got a triggerman on his trail."

Rinaldo belched. "I might have saved his life. One could say."

"You might've. You just might've."

Then flat silence between them. Rinaldo breathed heavy with booze. Smoke sat still as a spider.

"If you'll excuse me, sir," Rinaldo said. "I've drunk more than my share celebrating and I need to step outside."

In the glass behind the bar, Smoke watched Rinaldo exit the saloon.

Giving Rinaldo enough time to enter the outhouse, Smoke rose and limped, navigating the web of Griggsville drunkards. Outside, the moon seemed to outline his body, trace the contours, stopping where the stubs of his knees met the cloth at the top of his tin-shins.

A drunkard in the shadows thought Smoke might be the angel of death, floating toward Rinaldo in the outhouse.

"Everybody's gotta use the shitter," he called. "Everybody's gotta
go."

The black sky seemed to extend from Smoke's very mind. Anger
wide enough to dome the Trail.

"It's a nasty shame to go this way," he called, not worried about
witnesses. He'd burn them, too.

For as slowly as he moved, Smoke acted fast. He took hold of a
wood board from a pile beside the outhouse and jammed it hard
under the black handle.

He slipped his pointer fingers into the string loops in his pockets.
Draw.

A magic all Smoke's own.

He felt the string pull along his thighs, heard the soft click of his
boot heels opening.

The oil came next.

No windows on the box, the door secured, there was no exit for
Rinaldo.

Smoke sang.

> *Oh, it's a pity it's a patter it's a pitter!*
> *To lose thy life on the shitter!*
> *Oh, it's a queer it's a quail it's a quitter!*
> *Who falls down dead on the shitter!*

The tavern's back door opened and a man stumbled out and Smoke
turned to him and the man saw him and stumbled back inside.

Smoke pulled a matchbook from the chest pocket of his shirt. A
flame quickly came to life between his dirty fingers.

He limped to the door, a silhouette on half stilts, and pressed his
forehead against the wood.

"You think it smells bad in there now, hog-sucker? Just wait. You're
gonna be your own legend after this one. Just like your man. A hog-
blessed legend of the Trail."

He pushed off from the door. He dropped the match.

The outhouse went up fast.

Smoke did not wait to watch it ash. But he watched for as long as he could. Knowing that sometimes the pride one takes in one's work is better for the job than any pace or progress can ever be.

Halfway through the burning Smoke limped toward the saloon, his horse, and the outlaw who now knew he was not alone on the Trail.

MOXIE BY THE FIRE

Night of the first day had come. Moxie knew he was exactly half the distance to Harrows. He didn't want to stop. He didn't want to have to stop but the horse was breathing heavy and Moxie knew that, in the end, a rested horse would get him there faster.

The sky was already black, and the stars were uncountable. The pines had gone from green to gray, and now even their tops were difficult to see. Many years had passed since Moxie last watched the sun go down so slowly, in this way, the gradation in step with his travel north, the Trail turned black. The horse moved slowly during the summer sun's descent and when Moxie saw the first vestige of illumination ahead, moonlight at last, he felt relief, the rest somehow indicating that the ride tomorrow had already begun.

He jerked the reins, and the mare pulled up lethargic. Moxie dismounted, untied the bedding, and laid out a blanket for himself. He walked the horse to a solid pine near the blanket's edge and soothed her, rubbing her mane. There was still plenty of water and feed. After caring for her, he set to finding himself some wood.

In the dark, he thought. Carol, a day closer now, felt infinitely far.

The reality of her was something from his youth; riding to her was something like riding to the breakfast table he shared with his mother and father as a child. Gathering wood in the dark, Moxie questioned what he was truly doing.

Can a man set right his past?

With these questions came the possible futility of the ride and the hopelessness of absolution.

The guilt was unbearable.

With an armful of sticks and smaller logs, he stomped through the dark back to camp. He made a small fire near the blanket, and the horse stood silent. It was a good fire and it felt good and Moxie hadn't realized how cold he had gotten until he was sitting, warming his hands. He studied the mare, the way the flames altered her features, changing her eyes from white to black and back again. The way she looked into the darkness beyond the fire.

Moxie thought of Carol. Carol on her back, arms folded, sleeping. Decades ago, Moxie was plagued with nightmares that resembled these thoughts. Horrible visions of her death recurring: Carol, young, floating in the bathtub, her skin pruned by the time he found her, her body bloated, waterlogged, stiff. In those days he worried about leaving her for even an hour, lest he return to find she had collapsed into a fire like this one. But the worst was the dream in which Carol was already buried ... muffled screams from the earth ... the scratching of her nails against the wood ... her grave-bell echoing through the graveyard. Moxie would rush in these dreams, breaking apart the dirt with his hands, an unfair race with the oxygen left in her box. Even now, looking into the fire, he could hear her voice, pleading, getting weaker as he dug three feet, six feet, nine feet, twenty feet ... until the sun was blocked by the height of the grave and the sky was a pale-blue square at the end of a tunnel going up ... up ... a square from which insane laughter escaped ... a tiny impossible place to be ... Carol's salvation out of reach ... out of air ...

The horse neighed and Moxie looked up into the darkness. Fires were good for the warmth but fires also created black worlds beyond the range of the flames. Moxie rubbed his hands together and saw the shape of Carol in the rising smoke, sleeping . . . not dead.

"We have another long ride tomorrow," he said. The horse looked to him and then into the darkness of the woods again.

Moxie spread the corners of the blanket and lay down. He slept, briefly, and when he woke he saw a man seated on the other side of the fire.

It was very dark but the fire was still burning. Brighter, Moxie realized, than it had been when he'd fallen asleep. A foreign crackling sound, as though something not from the Trail was burning in there. He did not rise. He stared at the figure, seated, a pair of wide eyes focused on the fire and a face seen in pieces, as the flames would let him.

"I know that you are awake," the man said. Moxie knew it was the voice from the barbershop. The voice from a tavern in Portsoothe many years ago.

He made to rise but the voice stopped him.

"You don't want to see me. Not yet."

It breathed, an audible wheeze, black wind across a gravel sky.

"Who are you?" Moxie asked.

The flames split for the duration of a heartbeat, a fraction of that, and Moxie saw the eyes again, large and unfocused, darting from the fire to the ground beside it.

"You must really want to know this. You ask every time . . ."

Then the eyes connected with Moxie's own and the flames came together to block the view once more.

But Moxie had seen enough of the face. The rippling features. The exchange of faces, as if one had been painted upon another with grease.

"I want you to turn back," the thing said.

Moxie was silent.

"There was a time, the right time, for you to be doing what you're doing. But that time has passed."

Moxie was silent.

"There's no reason to let it propel you," it said. "All men have regrets."

"She's not dead," Moxie finally said.

Fingers of flame suddenly reached for him and Moxie hurried back in the dirt. He heard a hissing, water boiling, an egg under the sun.

"She's *dead*."

Moxie got up and the fire rose with him, blocking the face on the other side. The mare breathed heavy but did not wake.

"You don't want to see this face. Not yet."

Clouds obscured the moon and the fire crackled sharp. A wind came then, whirling the embers up in a circle around the fire and making the flames rise even higher. In them Moxie saw the eyes again, the form, seated, but suspended, perhaps, above the dirt.

"Have you considered that she does not want you to come?"

"No." But he had.

"Have you considered that she is already rotting?"

"No." But he had.

"Have you considered that the people in her life now will laugh at you when you arrive? That they will turn you back as I do now, sending you on your chivalrous way?"

"I'm not interested in her people."

"No. You're not."

Moxie heard movement to his right and turned quick. A man emerged from the blackness. Moxie recognized him at once.

"I told you she was dead once already, James."

Moxie remembered this man. His face, his voice, even the clothes he wore: the derby hat, the necktie, the rolled-up blue sleeves, the leather case in one hand. This man was a doctor once, lifetimes ago: the man he'd brought Carol to the first time he thought she'd died.

"She's . . . not . . ." Moxie said.

"I told you she was dead once already."

Deep breathing from across the fire. The doctor's eyes swelled, grew, until they popped, and the flaked pieces of his eyeballs sizzled in the flames.

Moxie backed up fast.

"You were wrong, Doctor!"

"Was I?" The doctor, eyeless, gripped his bag. "Dead to you anyway, the way you left her."

Moxie stared into the caverns above the doctor's nose. Saw Carol on her back in the wrinkles of one. Himself walking away from her in the other.

"As I recall," the doctor continued "you had little difficulty ignoring her once. Why the change of heart?"

Another flame reached for Moxie's boot. He stepped aside.

"She's not dead."

"Yes," the doctor said. "She is. It doesn't take a medicine man to smell her now."

The doctor's mouth swung open; a tongue unraveled, fell hard to the dirt, and rolled toward Moxie.

Moxie steeled himself.

Then it was only the doctor again. The doctor as he'd looked some twenty years ago. His eyes were intact again, the same eyes that had looked into Moxie's own, long ago, explaining Carol's condition.

"Let me show you something," he said now.

"I don't want to see it."

"Yes, you do."

The shape on the other side of the fire continued to breathe, hoarse, steady, slow.

The doctor knelt in the dirt and opened his black bag. From it he removed something large, shapeless, dripping.

"This, James, is her stomach. I've removed it to determine her cause of death. And here . . ." He knelt again and came up with more of her. "These are her lungs. Now, James, you know a lady can't breathe without her lungs, don't you?"

Moxie fingered the pistol in his right holster.

"You were wrong, Doctor."

The doctor stepped forward, his face changing again, a ram's head upon his shoulders.

"You will suffer like her if you continue to ride!"

Moxie drew his gun and fired. Through the smoke of the shot the doctor appeared, whole, himself again.

"You see," the doctor said. "You've made me mad."

The breathing from the other side of the fire became wind and the doctor blew apart, his pieces floating as the embers had moments ago.

Moxie turned to face the thing from the tavern in Portsoothe. The impossibility whose face was not fixed.

"Please, sit."

"I'll stand."

"You'll sit."

Against his will, Moxie fell to the dirt.

"I will tell you this once more, James Moxie. Turn back now. Go home. Blood no longer flows through the veins of the woman. You ride for a corpse, James Moxie. There is no meaning in your journey, there is no journey. You cannot rid yourself of the guilt for having left her once, for having turned your back on her then. All you can do now is repeat your choices, reenact the spineless steps of your youth. Do you remember them? Here . . . I have given you the footprints to follow." Moxie saw fresh prints appear in the dirt by the fire. "Your boots have not changed since then. You will recognize the shape of your own steps walking away from the very thing you rush to now. Here . . . I have given you the same weather." Moxie shuddered as the wind turned to ice. "The same air that coddled a mind that once de- cided wisely. Do you sense it? Can you feel the same day upon you? Your face has changed, but the bones beneath it have not. Here . . . I give you the same food in your belly. Do you feel it? Yes. I can see you do. Nothing has changed, but the skin upon your body is slack. Noth- ing has changed, but the color in your eyes has gone gray. Here . . . I give you the footprints, the air, the food, and the *sounds,* too. Do you hear? Can you hear her sobbing for your exit?"

Shivering, Moxie felt the sudden food in his belly, and as he shook his head no, the water in his eyes began to freeze.

"Can you hear the woman weeping for the man who turned his

back once and will do so again? The thing you try to change is not the noble thing you think it is. The thing you seek is immovable, unchangeable, dead. Guilt cannot be overcome, only endured. Turn back now and you will make worthy your decision then, for it will still be true. The woman is dead. Do you see the path? Do you see the prints? Yes . . . you know the steps well. I imagine they look different from the ones you remember . . . the ones that replay in your sleepless slumber. They look different from the ones you try to avoid when you walk the dirt roads of your memory. They look different not because they are, but because you remember them wrong. You remember them as smaller than they were . . . someone else's steps . . . the decision of a younger man. But that younger man is you and these are your prints. You have altered them to fit the bottom of boots you can live with . . . a size you no longer recognize . . . *someone else's choice.* Here . . . I give you the boots . . . try them on . . . tell me they do not fit. They do . . . James Moxie . . . they do . . ."

The fire rose higher than the trees, melting the ice in the sky.

Moxie saw old boots in the flames. Red boots, wet with snow.

"The only choice you have," Rot said, "is to convince yourself there was never anything to feel guilty for to begin with."

Moxie, still on his back, looked to the prints in the dirt by the fire's edge and felt too much of everything. All of it at once. His bones ached. His body was bloated. The voice continued, twisting his mind in braids.

But Moxie rose to his knees. Rot laughed: black wings taking flight, the rhythm of hammers driving nails into a casket. Moxie tried but could not stand. Rot laughed and the cachinnation dug into Moxie's ears as the worms would soon dig into Carol's.

Soon.

Soon.

Soon.

On his knees beside the fire, Moxie believed he was going to die. His day's ride was a journey to death, to die alone, here in these Trail woods. With Carol, she of so many deaths, on his mind.

He closed his eyes and he cried. And when he opened them again the feeling was gone. His body was not bloated. He did not shiver from cold.

Slowly, Moxie rose and looked through the flames and saw no one was there. The shape, the thing, Rot was gone.

He stepped cautiously around the fire, guns drawn, and saw only sticks, no trace of the fiend, the voice that exhumed his mistakes, the words that burned bold in his brain.

But the prints of his past remained.

Moxie eased himself carefully down to the ground and lay back on the blanket, still gripping both guns, his eyes fixed on the stars. His body hurt from riding. His body hurt from the guilt.

He lay this way a long time, thinking of Carol, ignoring every cracked stick in the dark wood, every fallen leaf on this side of the Trail. He thought of Carol and of the black-haired, green-eyed girl Molly, too . . . as she beckoned him . . . asked him to come . . . come on . . . come meet my friend Carol . . . Molly's gesture as innocent then as it was today in the glass of a barbershop in Baker . . . come meet my friend Carol . . . you're going to love her . . . my friend . . . you're going to love . . .

Carol

CAROL AND MOXIE

Memories more like nightmares and dreams like true visions, scattered, fallen from a shelf, out of order, or maybe proof that the order never mattered to begin with . . .

It's its own condition, the second doctor said. *It's very different from a coma.*

This doctor knew better than the first.

But Carol already knew all this. Only she was in a coma and couldn't tell James what she should have told him already.

When she woke, she did.

I die. Many times, I die.

She was on a cot in the doctor's home. Moxie sat in a chair beside her.

How often does it happen?

There is no pattern. But I heard you in there, James. Heard you carrying me to the first doctor's and now here.

I was scared, Carol.

I know.

Eventually the doctor joined them.

In the coma, Carol, your pulse beats slow enough that had I not held my finger longer than I normally would, I wouldn't have known it existed. Your flesh has color but you do not stir, and even your breathing was very difficult to detect. I don't entirely blame the last doctor for what he told James. I might have thought you were dead myself.

Carol took Moxie's hand.

I should've told you.

Why didn't you?

I was worried it would scare you away . . .

. . . Come on, the girl was saying, *come meet my friend . . . meet my friend Carol . . .*

Moxie was a young man, but this wasn't the first tavern he'd been in. It was just the most *fun.*

Come on . . . she's over here . . . her name is Carol . . . you're going to fall in love with her . . .

He'd been standing against the wall, holding his glass, grinning with the other young men and women, listening to the musicians playing on stage. He'd already had enough whiskey to know he was drunk and the dark-haired girl, beckoning him, made him nervous.

What are you saying?

But she couldn't hear him over the music and Moxie pointed at himself, questioning.

Me?

Come on, she said, waving, smiling, *come on . . .*

Moxie adjusted his hat and followed the girl through the bodies. She crossed the bar to the other side where the boys played guitars or piano, beat hand drums, and screamed rather than sang. Moxie spilled some of his drink on his shirt on the walk, and by the time he caught up he was wiping it down with his hand.

The dark-haired girl turned her full face to him and pointed to another girl standing against the wall, light-brown hair, smart eyes, sweating there, too, like the rest of them . . .

. . . *Not like this,* Moxie said, answering whether or not he'd experienced such a kiss before.

Carol smiled. There was something extra innocent about this man. It was as if he couldn't help but speak what he thought.

Well I'm glad to hear it, she said, running her fingers through his black hair. She kissed him again and Moxie, moving on instinct and doing what he wanted to do, took her face in his hands and kissed her back. They sat this way, the blue moonlight coming through the crack in the barn doors washing them, a long time . . .

. . . *Mother doesn't like the name Howltown, never has,* she said. *She just calls it "that place." But that title frightens me more. It's too close to the truth. For that place is certainly not this one . . .*

. . . *Don't worry,* Carol said, smiling, turning to him as the snow fell on her hair. *Hattie's going to like you. Why wouldn't she? I do.*

Moxie followed her out of the coach and walked with her up the long drive to her mother's house. Hattie, Carol said, was something of an inventor. Spent all her time tinkering. Always planning, always building.

You're bound to see gears and levers all over the workroom floor. Ignore them if you want to. Or don't. Ask her about them. Maybe she'll even tell you about the Box.

The Box?

Carol smiled.

Like I said, she's always tinkering with something new.

The ground was frosted but the air was warm, the snowfall having broken the spell. He held the gate for Carol and didn't see as her mother peered out through the front window. When they reached the door, Hattie opened it and Moxie was introduced. They stepped inside and Hattie said,

Why, you look like a gentleman outlaw if ever I saw one.

But she didn't show James the workroom. Asked Carol not to bring it up again . . .

. . . *Silas!* Moxie screamed, pounding the door again. *Silas! Open the door! She's dead, Silas! Carol's dead!* . . .

. . . They were buying her a hat the first time she collapsed in front of him. Carol was at the mirror, angling her head, and Moxie was telling her they all looked good because they did. She made him try on ladies' hats and laughed as he imitated her mother. The salesman shooed him away and brought Carol a pile of fresh ones. She said, *Ooh, that one looks good!* Then she fell . . .

. . . *Not like this,* Moxie said, answering Silas, who had asked him if he'd ever felt this way before.

Well, you're in for a lifetime of work, I'm afraid. Love isn't easy.

Love?

The pair sat behind a barn, their backs to the wood.

Do you like her smell?

I do.

Do you like her walk?

Moxie blushed.

I do.

Does she look as soft as the lamb's wool to you?

She does, Silas.
You love her then.
I love her . . .

. . . She's dead, the first doctor said, setting her wrist back on the table.

Moxie, sweating, raging, looked like the man he would one day become.

You're wrong, Doctor. I felt her heart beating. As I carried her here I felt . . . a beat.

The doctor, his face serious beneath a derby hat, removed his glasses and hooked them in his vest pocket. His blue shirtsleeves were rolled up to the elbows.

A beat? Just one?

Isn't one enough?

The doctor frowned. *Maybe you did feel a beat,* he said. *But it isn't beating anymore.*

Where else can I take her? Moxie asked.

I'm afraid any professional is going to tell you the same thing. When a person is dead . . . they're dead no matter who looks at her.

On the table Carol looked like someone had stolen something from her while she was sleeping. But not everything.

You're wrong, Doctor.

He put Silas's coat over her and slid his arms under her neck and knees and carried her out the door . . .

. . . Silas ran to the door and saw his friend soaked outside. Carol was limp, leaning against him.

What is it, James?

She's dead, Silas! She just . . . suddenly fell!

Silas told him the name of a doctor. Told him how to get to his house.

Wait, Silas said as Moxie turned to go. He ran back inside and came out with a coat he laid over her body, supported there in Moxie's arms . . .

. . . *My name is Carol,* Carol said, extending her hand. *I see my friend dragged you to me.*

Moxie smiled and reached his hand out and then pulled it back and wiped it on his pants, realizing there was whiskey on it . . .

. . . *I love you,* Carol said.

I love you, Carol.

You do.

I do.

Carol rose from the kitchen table.

If we're going to do this, you're going to have to live with my dying.

Moxie swallowed hard. *I get it . . . I will . . . you understand.*

But she could tell he was scared . . .

. . . *It's its own condition,* the second doctor said, standing over Carol's stiff body. *It's something like a seizure, but very different. I've read of it but I hadn't expected I'd ever run into it.*

She's alive then?

Oh, no question. Her heart beats. You felt it yourself.

Moxie was dripping water on the examination room floor. Silas's coat hung on the back of a chair. The doctor rubbed his eyes, and Moxie could tell the man was a good man.

How long will she sleep?

The doctor thought about it.

I honestly don't know. Like I said, I've never seen it in person before. I don't imagine many of us have. My worry is that she will not receive the proper nourishment for the duration of her spell. How long can a person exist under such circumstances? I've no idea. We need to watch her. We need to feed her through needles . . . tubes . . . and I cannot guarantee her current position will improve any.

But it did. Carol woke the next day . . .

. . . *Can you imagine if they would've buried you?*

But Carol had stopped thinking about burials long ago.

They walked in silence. Then James said, *You know this makes you special . . . like a ghost.*

Carol had heard something like that before. Another doctor called her *reborn* when she was just a girl. Hattie got angry when the doctor said that. Told the doctor that nobody could be reborn unless they died first.

But didn't I? Carol had asked.

Hattie turned on her, eyes cold as river water. *Not on my watch, Carol . . .*

. . . *Do this,* she said, turning to him in the kitchen. *Catch me a blue owlfly. I know, I know. You're a big man. But do it. Catch me an owlfly and bring it to my door and I'll know you're ready. I'll know what it means. Catch a blue owlfly, put her in a jar, and leave it at my door if you want to . . . you don't even have to knock . . . just set it on the sill. I'll see it. And I'll know you're ready . . .*

. . . *I suppose it is a lot to handle,* Silas said, leaning back against the barn. *But not much more than a man has to handle anyway.*

Moxie was quiet.

Think of it this way, Silas said, *you've already gone through it three times.*

Moxie nodded but did not speak. The vacancy in his friend's eyes frightened Silas.

Have you considered, Silas said, *that the only reason you'd walk away is that you care about her? Have you? Because that's what it is, James. You don't want to have to see her that way again . . .*

. . . *My name is Moxie.*

Moxie? That's a queer one.

Well. He blushed and removed his hat. *My name is James Moxie.*

I like it. Do you like this song, James Moxie?

Moxie looked over his shoulder at the band. He smiled.

I do.

It went like this:

Oh we'll have fun when our folks hit the Trail,
When our horses sleep, from the beer and the bale,
When our enemies die, and the grudges they carried,
And we'll keep on dancing, long after they're buried . . .

. . . *Physically, she's very close to dead. But her mind continues. She says she's not thirsty or hungry in there and also, I find this fascinating, she described it as one continuous fall. I told her that sounded frightening. She told me that depended on how often you fall.*

The doctor, clearly charged by the events, spoke as Carol rested, awake, in another room.

Moxie just wanted to know when it would happen again.

I can't say. And because of that it's important you take very good care of her. It's important you watch her. Say she was crossing the road, a coach approaches . . . it would be a terrible thing if she were alone, say, if she were to fall . . .

. . . Moxie carried the package under one arm. He walked steady but his heart beat hard. Silas was right. The doctors were right. Carol was right.

But he couldn't do it.

Carol's house was just a fence-length away but there he turned back. The air was icy, winter on the Trail. Moxie's red boots left heavy prints in the snowy dirt. He felt something like an entirely open life before him. A life in which he didn't have to worry that his lady might slip into false death with every syllable of laughter that escaped her lips. A life without keeping watch of Carol every minute, every hour, every day. Had he seen her house it would have been the last time he saw it. But he didn't walk quite that far. Years later, he wouldn't be able to remember exactly when it was, the last time he'd seen her house.

Or her person.

His boots dug into the snowy gravel of the Trail, and the package felt oily and snakelike under his arm. He ought to drop it, he thought. He ought to drop it on a rock. Or maybe he should just tuck it behind a tree and cover it with leaves and if she ever chanced upon it she might smile; something to warm the cold he was going to leave her with.

He did neither, carrying the jarred owlfly home with him instead.

How many times had she died now? How many times had he believed it was real death . . . this time?

Five? Six? And with each one Moxie held his own breath lest this be the time she slipped too far . . . slept too long . . . her false cadaver just a room away . . . him there at the window, looking out at all the infinity of a wide-open, carefree life.

He entered his home and set the jar on the table. He took the paper off it, and when he did the dying sunlight came through the oily wings of the blue owlfly within, painting the other side of the glass with its color.

Moxie covered it again and began packing.

The decision to leave Carol had shaken his reality, his identity, in many ways. Staying put was now impossible.

When a man turns his back on one thing, he must then be facing another.

The Trail waited.

Moxie, a single green sack packed with his scant belongings, took to it . . .

. . . *I'd have thought she was dead myself,* the second doctor said. *Could have fooled a coroner, I'd say. Could've fooled a coroner, a funeral director, and a coffin maker all at once. Could've fooled a whole town. A whole town . . . unable to hear the bell because she couldn't ring it . . . a whole town grieving the loss of a living woman . . . that bell positioned useless above her grave . . . the string an inch from a hand that just didn't have the power to pull it . . .*

MANDERS VISITS
SHERIFF OPAL

Opal was sleeping deep when the knocking came.

The sheriff of Harrows lived a rather routine life: He left the office every day when the sun went down and he returned just as it came up. Sometimes it was necessary he stick around, and so he might. Sometimes he wanted to keep his eye on things. But most commonly Opal tipped his hat to the ladies he passed, minding the men and the boys. And no matter what time he left he stopped off in Eleanor Roberts's kitchen in the Corey Hotel and took with him a sack full of steak, to eat on his horse ride home. If you lived in Harrows and did nothing wrong, you might not know the law existed. The sheriff was one for keeping the peace and had no mind to meddle, no mind to push himself on the people who elected him.

But if you did do something wrong . . .

It wasn't the first time he woke in the middle of the night to the sound of knocking. Often it was Deputy Cole, asking advice, informing Opal of a fight that had ended badly. Usually Opal would be kind with the deputy, either instructing him how to fix things or telling him he needn't really have come all this way for the matter.

"Shudders," he said, sitting up in bed. "I'm coming."

The knock came again. It was light, too graceful to be Cole with urgent news. Opal didn't like to guess, but he thought it might be a newcomer looking for protection, a harmless beef to do with new neighbors.

The sheriff grabbed his gun off his night table and headed up the hall. He walked slow, having heard enough horror stories of fool sheriffs gunned down at the threshold of their own front doors.

"Who goes there?" Opal called, one hand on the knob, the other holding the gun chest-high.

"It's Robert Manders, Sheriff Opal."

Opal frowned. A funeral director knocking at night was a curious thing, indeed.

He lowered his gun and opened the door. "What's the matter, Manders? You got ghouls?"

The director tried to be cordial, but Opal could tell he was concerned.

"Come in," Opal said, stepping aside. "We'll talk in the kitchen."

Manders followed the sheriff to a small white table adorned with a single candle. Opal lit it and sat down, fanning his hand to the other seat, asking the director to do the same.

Manders did. "I feel strange having come here."

"I'd think so. If it was anything other than strange that you came here for I might think you strange myself."

"It's true. I wouldn't wake you without something worth waking you for."

"What is it, Manders?"

"It's Carol Evers, Sheriff."

"All right. What about her?"

"She passed yester eve."

"I was at the wake."

"And Mister Evers visited with me."

"To set things up."

"Well, not everything. Mister Evers has hired someone else to dress the body."

"Someone from out of town? Family?"

"That's what he said. Family. Do you know them?"

"I do not."

Manders hesitated before asking, "How about a Doctor Alexander Wolfe. Have you heard of him?"

"I have not."

"It's the name of the doctor who determined Carol Evers's cause of death."

"All right."

"Well, Sheriff Opal, that's the part that concerns me. I'm most likely out of line in saying so, but I couldn't help feeling things were out of sorts when I talked to Mister Evers."

"How's that?"

"I couldn't get a clean line on what he was telling me, and the note he gave me from this Doctor Wolfe was, truth be told, suspicious."

"That's a big word in my dictionary, Manders."

"I imagine it is."

"Go on."

"I checked the ledger of registry tonight in my office and found absolutely no trace of any doctor named Alexander Wolfe."

Opal studied Manders closely. In the flickering candle the funeral director looked like a child's drawing of "concerned."

"How reliable is this book?"

"The registry?"

"The registry."

"Well, it's important I'm up to date on these matters. I have the current edition. I think it goes back no later than a year."

"He could have gotten cleared in that year?"

"Yes."

"And what area does the book cover?"

"A fair-sized stretch of land. I'd gather almost every town you've ever been to is in this book. Most of the Trail."

"Where'd Evers say he was from? Did he?"

"Yes. He said he was from Charles."

"Is that it?"

"Well, there's that and the note."

"The doctor's note."

"The doctor's note."

"From an Alexander Wolfe."

"I don't think in my entire life I've read a less professional account."

"Do you have that note on you?"

"I do not. I gave it back to Mister Evers."

"And what did it say, then?"

"Oh, it employed correct language, I suppose, but there was really no conclusion and it lacked any sense of studied jargon."

Opal didn't like what he was hearing. Manders was a man he took seriously.

"Are you suggesting he made him up?"

"Yes. I think I am."

Opal sat silent half a minute.

"Don't hold hands with your thoughts yet, Manders. Not thoughts like those. Way too many possibilities to start thinking yours is the right one. Could be the doctor isn't legit. Hell's heaven, I've got friends who prefer witch doctors. Things get real drafty when you start opening windows on a person's preferences."

"But the doctor couldn't be from too far out of town."

"That's right."

"Because he saw her soon after she died."

"That's right. But just because he has to be from around here and isn't in your book doesn't mean he doesn't exist. You ever known Mister Evers to get sick?"

"I'm sure he has."

"Me, too. But I don't know who he saw to get his runny nose plugged and I don't know who he'd go to for his wife's passing."

"I understand."

"Is that it?"

"Yes, Sheriff. I think that's it. Though I might add, Mister Evers seemed desirous of getting Carol into the ground as soon as possible."

"How's that?"

"He asked that the burial take place this very morning. I told him it could not. Not with the Illness probably just leaving Harrows now."

"But the wake was today."

"I suppose he meant directly following."

Opal studied Manders's eyes specifically. No one in Harrows handled as much death as the funeral director, and information from Manders had helped solve more than one case. Yet Dwight Evers never struck Opal as someone to worry about.

"So then, is that it?"

"Well, Lucas and Hank tell me Mister Evers is keeping Carol in the cellar."

"What does that mean?"

"I don't know. But it seems a curious place to keep a lady."

"How do they know this?"

"They heard it from Clyde Darrow, Sheriff, who heard it from his wife, Carol's girl Farrah."

Opal exhaled long and looked into the flame.

"The funeral is the next morning after?"

"Yes it is."

"At your place?"

"Yes. I had the plot dug this evening."

"Okay."

Opal ran his fingers through his hair once and got up.

"You understand by your coming here tonight you're accusing a man of suspicious behavior?"

"I do. Though I hope nobody has to hear of my coming."

"I just might need you later is all. I'll look into it, I will. But it's almost too bright to be anything foul. Those sorts of things usually hide themselves better. My advice to you is to carry on with your business as you would and let me do the looking."

Opal saw Manders out and thanked him for coming. He locked the door and walked back to his bedroom. In bed, he closed his eyes and thought it was a strange thing for a man with so many bedrooms to keep his dead wife in the cellar. Even if only for a short spell. It was weird, is what it was. Like maybe the only reason a man would do such a thing was because he didn't want anybody to see her the way she was.

He's hiding her.

But Opal knew better than to jump to conclusions.

He considered getting back out of bed and riding over to the Evers home. A lot of adjusting could be carried out in one night. He didn't like that the funeral director felt compelled to come out. Got dressed and rode all the way out here.

Opal sat up once and then lay down again.

Tomorrow, he told himself. *Tomorrow.*

But it wasn't a confident directive, and the three syllables troubled him as he slept.

SMOKE SLEEPS, TOO

When he limped, stiff-legged, into the bawdy house, the girl thought she'd just tell him it was too late at night for a customer. The last thing on earth she wanted to deal with was a pity case, and she knew the girls didn't love doing the cripples. There was something extra pathetic about this one, like the man was too broken even for a place this foul. But it was that late hour when the place still rollicked, the moment just before the fun would crack in half, and she silently cursed the man for not showing twenty minutes later. Then it would have been easy. Then she could have fanned her hand out to the two dozen men and women passed out on the couches, the floors, the piano, and he would have seen for himself the night was over. But he hadn't. And here he was. And he didn't look like he could even make it up the stairs let alone climb atop one of the girls. But the closer he got, the more the girl guessed this wasn't his first time in a house of ill repute.

Something unnerving about this one.

Maybe it was the lack of a hat. Or the fact that only half his hair was cut.

"Kind of a late-night decision, eh?"

Smoke, who had been observing the jolly rancor, looked at her now. "It's always late at night in a place like this."

She didn't like the way he spoke. The way he looked at her as he spoke. She reacted fast, attempting to establish a tough veneer. A thing she was used to.

"Did it take a while to get up the nerve or did you just find yourself bored?"

He didn't answer. Only looked around a little more.

The girl decided no, she didn't feel good about him at all.

But she didn't show it.

"You'd like to see the girls, then?"

Smoke put his elbows on the counter. "No."

"No?"

"No, ma'am."

"You want a drink?"

"I'm working right now."

"If you're just looking for a place to sleep . . ."

Smoke lit up. A smile. Ghastly as a smashed plum.

"That's it," he said, and the girl thought she smelled oil on his breath. "A place to sleep. Here's what I'd like: I'd like a room, one of the rooms you'd give a man with a girl but I don't want the girl. All right?"

The girl tried to remain polite. She knew what to do with the rough ones. But this one hadn't gotten rough yet.

"There's a hotel," she said. "Just up Howard Street."

Smoke looked at her without expression.

"Understand," she said, "it'd be . . . unusual for me to just rent out a room."

"Then let's be unusual. Let's be downright weird."

Wild piano chords clanged from the adjacent room. Girls giggled.

"You mind my asking why you'd pick a place like this to get some peaceful sleep?"

"I never said I was looking for peace."

The girl felt a strong urge to fetch the madam and almost did, but recently she'd been scolded for calling when she could've handled the situation herself. *You get my attention when it's an emergency, Susan, and you do it yourself when it's not.* Was this an emergency? Hardly. *Not yet,* she thought. But the man talked crazier than he walked.

"I'm not sure there are any rooms available." Her voice betrayed her blossoming unease.

Smoke looked at the girl for a long time. She could tell he was thinking, and all she could think was that he was thinking whether or not to kill her.

And he smelled, yes, he definitely smelled of oil.

"Hell's heaven," he finally said, his face calm, too calm. "Here's what we'll do. You'll go and set me up a room where I'm alone for the night and I won't burn this pig-shit palace down. You go and clear a room out for me and I won't torch you. You like your face? Sure you do. I do, too. I like your face. It's a fine face! Do your fine face a favor and go along . . . make room for me . . . get me the dirtiest mattress in this place if needs be, but be quick about it. My legs hurt. My legs always hurt. But they hurt more than usual now. And if you go and get me that room, I'll let you all continue to make merry. Hell, I'll let you *live.* You wanna live, doncha?"

He glowered. "Get me a room, girl, and I won't sear the flesh from your bones."

Smoke snapped his fingers and a small flame appeared at the head of a match and the girl let out a little scream.

An hour later, the sounds from below considerably quieter, Smoke sat on a fold-out wooden chair and stared into the darkness of a rotten room. He thought of the lawman who'd stopped him at the head of town. He thought of how the officer didn't laugh when he told him his name was James Moxie but then told him he wasn't the first. Not the first what? Smoke had asked him. Not even the first one today. Smoke smiled. I tell you what, Smoke said suddenly, taking the lawman by surprise. I'm gonna go to that there cathouse right there and spend the night. I may bed one of the girls and I may not, but either way that's where I'll be and that's the only place I'll be. The officer said something about himself being the one to make the rules here and Smoke said go on, then, make the rules. Then the lawman told him that he better go straight to that cathouse and do whatever he was going to do and get out by sunup. Smoke smiled. He hated towns like this one. He thanked the officer and passed and the officer asked him what was wrong with his legs and Smoke told him he done broke his knees fishing. Straight to the cathouse, the man said. Smoke thought about pulling the strings. He even had his fingers in the little holes and was set to drop oil all the way to the pig-shit northern exit from town. And if he did that, and then passed the cathouse and the law came running to ask why he hadn't stopped like he said he would, Smoke would toss a match and the whole sour town would go up at once. He liked this idea. It was a good idea. A town with so many troughs burning too fast for the buckets. The sound of the storefronts splintering. The crack of an entire town square. The crush would be magnificent. He would enjoy watching it burn, the good wood turned to dust, ash in the sky, sailing upward before coming back down like a gray rain . . . pieces of the general store settling in the street . . . bits of the tavern mixed with ashes from the church.

Suddenly Smoke wished for an urn of oil as big as the bat-black sky. He had his fingers in the loops, but his legs told him to rest. They demanded it.

Now he stared into the darkness of his room and listened as the hullabaloo diminished below. The sound of the girls gave way to the sound of the women and the sound of the women gave way to the sound of the glasses being gathered, the doors locked, and the women again, dulcet tones now, reviewing the night they'd had.

He leaned forward in the chair and removed his shins, setting them beside the mattress on the floor. Then he lowered himself down. The stubs of his knees throbbed and the sores on his thighs were hot, then cold, then he was partially free of the pain. One of the sores had split open, and Smoke touched it and grimaced. He could never quite get rid of the sensation of wearing the legs altogether. Like a man with a hand just cut off. Still thinks it's there. Only Smoke felt it double. Old legs, new legs. Still there. On his back he could smell the oil and the oil smelled good. He fell asleep that way . . . the scent of the oil giving him strange dreams . . . dreams of himself dripping with it . . . swimming in it . . . a full tin-man with enough oil in him to burn all the pig-shit towns on the Trail.

In one dream he caught up to James Moxie and invited him into a tavern for a drink and the outlaw went with him and Smoke gave him a glass full of the good stuff. Moxie thanked him and drank it and Smoke laughed and told him to open his mouth and then he tossed a match down the outlaw's throat and red flames came rushing out of Moxie's mouth. But Smoke recoiled when this happened, for the flames came out too fast, too strong, and reached for him instead. Stay back, outlaw, Smoke said and the outlaw breathed fire and the fire caught on Smoke's shirt and pants and his shins, too, and then the whole place went *whump boom!* and beyond the flames, beyond the fire he saw the outlaw staring at him, not burning, and Smoke howled as the fire caught the hair on his arms, the hair on his head, and his flesh smelled like rotting mice and his bones blackened and the flames scurried up his neck over his teeth across his paperlike tongue down his ashen throat.

But his eyes remained. His eyes were the last to go and with them Smoke saw Moxie through the blaze.

The outlaw wasn't laughing. Wasn't talking, wasn't anything.

Wasn't burning, neither.

LIGHT

It's your own breathing, Hattie said. She said it once and she said it with such flat finality that a very young Carol never forgot it. Hattie had a way of talking like that when she wanted to. Her maternal face would become something of a static rendering, a face that neither frowned nor smiled. The truth, Carol came to understand it, as Hattie saw it.

For years the theory helped Carol. At eight years old, hearing hoarse breathing inside the coma was enough to scare her silly. Was someone else in there with her? Did something live in Howltown?

It's your own breathing.

No further explanation. No saying that Carol's body was slowed down and if her heart beat at one-sixtieth of its normal rate her breathing must change as well. Hattie must not have felt the need to explain her take. *It's your own breathing* it was and *it's your own breathing* it would be.

And yet John Bowie opened the door on this one, sitting across from Carol at Finn's, Harrows's finer seafood saloon.

At risk of sounding morbid, Carol, I'd at least consider that the coma could be a new place, indeed. Have you considered that the coma is a plane of its own? A sort of nonreligious purgatory? Perhaps the coma is between life and death. And the breathing you hear is . . . not of this world.

As interesting as it was to discuss over dinner, these words were much more frightening when falling through the darkness. And sometimes Carol wished John had never spoken them.

Like now. Falling, still able to see the threshold she fell toward, still able to see the ripple roll across the garden toward her. And yet what if John Bowie was right? What if the dead she heard breathing was dead John himself?

Carol quickly, forcibly shoved these thoughts aside. Right now she needed to do more than *remember.* She needed to do more than weigh the words of two incredible people she loved.

She needed to act.

Roll over.

But how? She didn't know exactly. She'd never tried before. It seemed simple, in theory: If a wind was pressing against her, wouldn't a slight tilt to the right or left roll her over completely?

Carol felt the electricity, the burning nerves of anxiety. She imagined herself rolling, unable to stop, spinning like John Bowie's toy top forever.

And the steady hoarse rhythm was getting louder.

It's your own breathing. This time it was Carol herself who said this. Of course it was her own breathing. And it made perfect sense. She was exerting herself, trying to rotate in the darkness, to feel the wind against her back for the first time ever in the coma.

To fall *up*, perhaps, instead.

She was working. It was *something.*

Long ago, Hattie built a pulley contraption that rolled on wheels, followed Carol wherever she went. And the moment Carol fell, limp, it held her up in a standing position. Carol experienced one coma that way, standing. But there was no change within. Still the sensation of falling.

Still . . .

So how to beat it? How to . . . climb out?

Roll over.

She tried. Oh, how she tried. Such a natural movement, a tilt to either the right or the left, a simple inch would do. And yet ... she couldn't.

Heavier wheezing from the darkness and Carol continued to tell herself it was her own. Her body was slowed down in the coma. It wasn't labored breathing she was hearing but the grains-of-sand details of a regularly expelled exhalation, amplified in Howltown. Inhale. Exhale. All her own.

Carol concentrated on the roll. Rolling over.

Once, as a young girl, Hattie helped Carol up the wood ladder of a metal slide. From the top, it looked like a hundred-foot drop. Scared but exhilarated, Carol let go of Hattie's hand and came softly to the dirt at the slide's end. For this, Carol would call out for Hattie when the collapse came, when the free fall toward an impossible distance occurred ... this slide with no wood ladder, no reality from which to discharge ... not even the convincing cold metal of the slide beneath her ... and, most frightening of all, no lip, no dirt, no end. Yet the sensation was always *toward the earth*. Often Carol imagined the fall carried her *into* the earth, cracking its crust like a child's piñata, falling farther ... deeper ... never into a variety of muted light, but into the black *solid black* that dizzied her with misdirection, unease, confusion, lest a stone wall wait at the end there to greet her.

Or, here, a stone slab.

If you know you're on your back in the workroom, Hattie once said, *then maybe you can plant your hands against it, whether it exists in the coma or not. Maybe you can still sit up without waking.*

Now, trying so hard to focus on the slab, to roll, it felt to Carol as if every coma previous to this one constituted one continuous fall.

The breathing. Closer now.

In her mind's eye Carol saw her friend John Bowie sitting up in his grave. Barefoot and unboxed, he raised his right hand as if about to suggest something.

Then Carol felt a hand upon her shoulder.

John!

But this was not the hand of John Bowie. This was no friend. The burn she felt from its subfreezing temperature told her so.

Carol tried to look, tried to see who had touched her, if such a thing was possible at all. But turning her head was just as impossible as turning her body, and so Carol only stared into the darkness through which she fell.

Someone's in here with you. Someone's in here with you. SOMEONE'S IN HERE WITH YOU, CAROL!

Carol had never felt another person in the darkness. Not a moment's contact with Hattie ever translated into the coma itself. Even as Dwight and Farrah carried her body upstairs, Carol felt nothing.

But now . . . fingertips . . . a palm . . . a hand rolling her over.

Roll over.

Carol felt herself rolling. Rolling onto her back.

ROLL OVER

Was she doing this? Was she responsible for the roll?

NO

And the two letters, thought by her, exploded across the everywhere sky of Howltown.

Rolling now (*rolling!*), she heard shuffling. Feet upon stone.

Rats, she told herself. Because if it wasn't rats, then how about that?

She was sideways now, yes, there was no question she had rolled (*been rolled, Carol, BEEN rolled, someone did this, someone NOT YOU*) to her side, a woman falling through black tar infinity on her side, her dress no doubt flapping in a different way, her hair now wholly off to one side, as though pulled.

Still rolling.

Rolling over.

Until Carol felt the momentum of her roll, felt herself moving quicker, unable to influence the speed of the spin at all.

You're going to keep rolling, spinning, twirling into nothingness, CAN'T STOP forever CAN'T STOP forever CAN'T—

She stopped.

The roll was complete. And for the first time ever in her life, Carol Evers was on her back in Howltown.

She looked up.

And saw all the darkness she'd fallen through.

She heard the hoarse wheezing. She recalled the cold hand. And just as she attempted to shove these frightening aspects from her mind, Carol saw.

Carol *saw*.

Light.

And the anxiety she'd felt at discovering her husband's betrayal was laughable compared with the sensation of sight in the coma.

She was no longer falling. And yet not awake. She lay on her back on a stone slab in a storm room she could see. A storm room she had assisted in building herself.

And the light . . .

It appeared to be a sconce, yes, one of the candles aflame upon the left stone wall. And at the very distant arc of the candle's range, she saw (*saw!*) the open dark space of the storm room entrance.

Carol could hardly comprehend the sight of it. It was the storm room, yes. Not in a dream. Not in her mind's eye. And whoever had helped her onto her back had also given her this light.

Right?

Near fifty times now she had climbed the wood ladder with her mother and called Hattie's name as she fell through the earth's crust, to the inner core where, only Carol knew, there was no heat, no fire, no *light*.

She was not awake. Yet . . . what had become of Howltown?

You've reached the end, she thought. And with this thought came an even deeper plunging of fear.

For what could be considered the finish of a place with no lines?

But Carol knew this was no end. Whoever had rolled her over was only beginning.

She heard the shuffling of bare skin on a pebbled floor.

This, Carol now recognized, was not the patter of rodent feet within a dusty cellar.

"John?"

Her voice. Her lips had moved. Movement and light. The shock of it was so great that she hardly had time to reprimand herself for calling her friend's name.

Wherever she was, this was no place John Bowie would be. In life or death. For while it looked like the storm room and smelled like her cellar in Harrows, Carol was very aware that, light or no light, she was still deep in the darkness.

She stared at the entrance to the storm room because she couldn't bring herself to look anywhere else. She held her breath, the sour air growing even more stale within her.

She steeled herself for the sight of whoever had rolled her over.

The candle flickered but no wind came and Carol heard the hoarse breathing more clearly than she ever had before.

A face peered in at the storm room door.

It was not Dwight. Not Hattie in death. Nor John.

The face looked painted. Or as if *several* faces had been painted upon the same flat canvas, stored so deep in the shadows that Carol couldn't see its frame.

Carol expelled the sour air with a cry for help.

This fear was deeper than any grave.

She heard a baying from far away, echoes off a stone passage. Madly, she imagined she *was* buried but buried *beneath* the graves of the graveyard. Even ghouls did not dig this deep. The howl she'd heard did not resemble lament, but celebration, as if the creature who cried did not scratch its coffin lid but rather the wood beneath, until the splinters might give way to dirt, and the dirt give way to Carol.

"Carol."

It was the watcher who spoke. The one peering in the doorway like a voyeur. The head whose many faces she could see.

"*Carol, Carol, Carol . . .*"

The lines of its face were fluid, one painted face becoming another. Its mouth did not move.

Despite knowing she couldn't, Carol tried to move.

The watcher entered and Carol saw its mouth was a blur, its nose too small for its eyes, its skin a shade of horse urine.

Then his features changed, entirely, occupying only the top right corner of his face before flowing like blood back down to their proper positions.

"I've watched you," it said, as though what it spoke of could somehow be considered sane. It pressed its back to the wall, sliding away from Carol now, deeper into the storm room. "I've watched you fall for a long time now . . ."

Sliding along the wall, its chin drooped like candle wax to its chest.

"Do you hear that?" it said. "This is the sound of Rot's approach, Carol. The rot that follows death. Deserved or not."

A second face sprang from the blackness to Carol's right. Its skin stretched back to from where it came, breath as foul as a mole's den.

Once again, despite knowing she couldn't, Carol tried to move.

The face beside her broke into clumps of dirt. The pieces fell to the storm room floor.

"*That,*" Rot said, still coming, sliding against the right wall now, advancing parallel to the length of her still body, "is something you'll have to get used to. You will not be waking this time."

Suddenly it was beside her, its face a finger-length from her own.

Its breathing was the hoarse music of Howltown.

"You've heard tales of babes left to starve in the brush, men strung up by their toes, hearts removed and hearts never found. But there are worse things on the Trail than outlaws . . ."

Carol closed her eyes. But the world, her world, went dark for only a breath, as, her eyes still closed, the dimensions of the cellar returned, lit anew by the same candle in its sconce coming to life. The man peered once again from across the storm room, wild eyes in the entrance, watching her on the slab.

But his voice continued beside her.

"Rot, Carol. Rot."

She opened her eyes and saw he was still against the wall. Still coming. He wore a childish smile, his lips blurred, and Carol was afraid to close her eyes again, to open them, to close them, to—

"Sleep, Carol," he said, fingering the wall. And his fingertips sounded like the pattering of rats. "You do not want to be awake for all that comes your way."

Carol watched as he became the cracks in the stone walls, as the candlelight flickered but did not dissolve.

Then it was gone.

Carol heard her mother hammering. Heard James Moxie crying out that she was dead. Heard Dwight, too, whimpering in the shadows of this impossible cellar.

She closed her eyes and this time did find darkness. But when she opened them again, the room was still lit. As if her visitor wanted her to see all that was coming her way.

She heard, too, the cries of those in their graves who did not desire to dig up, but rather down, burrowing deeper, to where Carol lay, to where they could already smell the possibility of rot, reaching for a woman who would soon be buried alive, and whose rot was ordained, was assured, was coming.

Then the wind returned. And Carol didn't know which way she fell.

But up or down, down or up, the light remained, and through the rippling storm room walls, through the flickering flame, she saw all the nightmares of her youth, life in Howltown, coming.

And yet there *was* hope. For Carol had learned that both monsters and madmen make mistakes. Dwight had overlooked her former lover, a man on the Trail who knew of her condition. And the thing that just left her, that had killed the electricity in her veins, leaving her in the cold empty country beyond anxiety and fear, that thing had made a mistake of his own.

For all he wanted to frighten her, and for all he had, he'd also changed her lot.

He'd rolled her over.

And Carol, never having been on her back before in the coma, discovered immediately, alone, that things were different now.

She moved.

It was slight. Hardly anything at all, but movement all the same.

Using every pound of inner strength she possessed, Carol lifted her chin toward her chest, then allowed her head to travel the quarter inch back down to the stone slab.

It was a start. An astonishing one. And it gave her the strength to try again. And again, until, as the sun rose outside Harrows, a sun that did not penetrate the storm room, Carol could conceive of actually sitting up, of actually rising, of actually taking action, in Howltown.

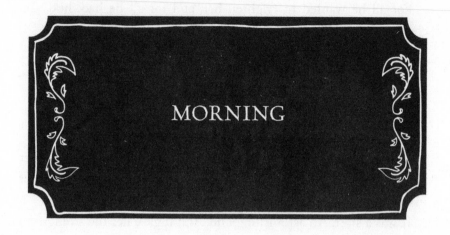

MORNING

Moxie opened his eyes to see the mare walking, unhitched, about the ashes of the fire. He woke to the sound of wood crushed to dust beneath a hoof. Someone had unhitched her overnight. And yet she had not left him.

Moxie rose.

Probably it was the horror from Portsoothe, the face he'd seen through the fire, floating above the dirt.

But maybe not.

Moxie put his hat on and quickly hitched the mare. Then, pausing to think, he unhitched her again.

He brought his face close to hers.

"Thank you, old girl."

Leaving her free, he rolled the bedding. He got water from the pouch and let the mare drink. She lapped it up readily and Moxie wondered if in some way the unnatural fire, the occurrences of the night before, had added to her thirst.

Had the mare taken off, curious or otherwise, Moxie would've had little chance of making it to Harrows. The telegram from Farrah Darrow told him that Carol's funeral was set for tomorrow morning.

Moxie had made it half the Trail in one day. If he could maintain this pace, he could get there in time. And yet ... whoever hired the triggerman, the man Rinaldo spoke of, whoever wanted Moxie dead no doubt wanted Carol dead, too.

Perhaps that's who unhitched the horse. Perhaps not.

And then there was the horror from Portsoothe. Rot.

Moxie understood clearly that, in the state Carol was in, it would only take a modicum of pressure on a pillow to kill her. Pinching her nostrils would do the trick.

Why hadn't whoever hired the triggerman done so already? And who was to say he hadn't?

Moxie fed the mare. He looked up to the sky. The sun was not visible, though something of it showed. A thin purple beam washed across the landscape, the treetops, the ashes of the fire, the extra boot prints still present in the dirt.

"Are you good now, old girl?" He patted the mare on the muzzle and put the feed away.

He remembered Carol telling the second doctor she was conscious of what was going on while inside the coma, but that voices were strange: familiar but changed. This meant she was most likely somewhat conscious now.

Moxie mounted the mare.

Again, he imagined Carol plucking one breath after another from a jar.

At some point she'd run out.

The outlaw looked down to the ashes of the fire.

I am Rot.

A wave of steady rage flowed through him.

He closed his eyes, and the purple morning passed over the stoic features of his face.

"Let's go, old girl."

On the Trail again, the very top of the sun showing now, the mare, rested, moved with strength, and with the will and haste of her master ...

... Smoke brought a hand to his nose as he limped through the lobby. The place smelled like pig-shit. Whiskey, beef, beer, and sex. Men snored on worn couches, their heads on the armrests, their mouths slack, open like torn water pouches. The smell of the morning ghosts of the tramps assaulted him; a dozen stale perfumes jostling for air; the scents left behind of the beasts who wore them.

Smoke limped.

Beneath his boots he saw the carpet was stained, fresh blots of spilled drinks and piss. The place was a kennel, all pissing hog's hell for territory and mounting each other for sport.

By the front door, on the floor, he spotted a half-eaten waterlogged piece of bread. He pinched it between his fingers, limped back to one of the sleeping men, and dropped it into his open mouth. Then he grabbed a stool from the bar and limped out of the cathouse.

Outside, Smoke counted three horses tied to posts beside his own. He untied the strongest and set the stool beside it. Gripping his thigh, he swung his right leg over its back and pulled himself up by the mane. Some oil spilled out between the rags and spotted the chestnut back of the animal. The beast felt strong beneath his weak and warped legs.

Goodbye to the castrated gelding. This horse was a stallion.

"Wherever you were headed before," Smoke told the animal, "we're going north now."

He pulled the reins and the horse responded. Pulling away from the post, Smoke looked to the dirt and saw a set of fast fresh tracks crossing town. Someone in a hurry this morning. Before Smoke woke.

Smoke studied the tracks. It wasn't the outlaw—Moxie was ahead of him, of this Smoke was sure. So who?

"A lot of pig-shit travels the Trail," he half sang. "From hell's heaven to heaven's hell."

He smacked the stallion on the side of its strong body. He dismissed the fresh tracks and focused instead on an impossible legend: a man duel-triumphant without drawing his gun.

"Oh, he's an outlaw!" Smoke sang in full, his voice growing stronger under the purple band of dawn. "And he knows how to hide!" The horse crossed the town's northern border. "Oh . . . he's an outlaw!" Smoke bellowed to the empty Trail ahead. "But today's his last ride! Oh, today's his last ride!" The horse neighed. "You like that, horse-fella? Oh, but you do! You must! Today's his last ride!" . . .

. . . Dwight took hold of the gun beneath his pillow and sat up in bed. There was a man in his bedroom.

"Wake," the stranger said.

Dwight fired once into the corner. But the shape remained.

Dwight fired again. A hole exploded in the plaster and the shape remained.

"Did the outlaw kill me last night?" Dwight cried.

The stranger moved, slightly, and Dwight saw one face morph into another.

"Who are you?" Dwight asked.

"You need to hide your lady."

His voice was skin peeling, his voice was breaking bones.

"What do you know about my lady? My lady is dead."

The stranger's face spread wide on the bones of its face before dissolving into the shadows behind it.

"You need to hide your lady now."

When Dwight responded, his voice shook along with his hands.

"You need to leave my business to me. My lady is dead. Leave now, whoever you are, or I'll shoot again!"

The stranger stepped away from the wall, closer to the bed.

Was this James Moxie, then? Was this the end?

"People are coming for you," the stranger said. A new face. A new mouth. "They've already set out for your home."

"People? What people? I've nothing to hide! My lady is—"

The shape came closer. Dwight recoiled, blinked, and when he opened his eyes again the form was sliding along the contours of the wall, changing with the shape of the vanity as it passed into the unlit hall beyond.

Dwight leapt from bed. He shouted to the open door.

"I will not hide anything! I will not hide her! You know nothing of my lady! You know nothing of me!"

But he was fearful the stranger did.

Unsure what to do first, where to go, who to trust, Dwight stood motionless in the center of the bedroom. Then he rushed to the window.

He saw nobody. Heard no more.

You've got to hide your lady.

People are coming for you.

They've already set out for your home.

Sleep still in his eyes, Dwight looked long at the bedroom doorway.

Then he moved quickly, toward the hall, the first floor, the cellar, and the first place he could think to hide her . . .

. . . "It's most likely nothing, Cole," Opal said, leaning back in his chair.

"But you think it might be?"

"Enough to ask you to come with me. Sure."

The deputy rubbed his red eyes.

"Mister Evers, though? And Carol Evers? I just never would have guessed anything foul going on."

"And don't guess it now. We don't know a thing. All we got is the idea of a mortician who might be hot he didn't get the job to dress her."

Cole nodded. "Sheesh, Opal, that would be an ugly reason to go tattling."

"Have you seen uglier?"

"I suppose I have."

"Yes you have."

Opal rose now and glanced through the blinds of the window. But for a purpling sky, it was still dark yet; hardly a person could be seen on the street.

"When are we going to head out?" Cole asked, scratching his head.

"We're gonna go right now."

Cole nodded. He'd figured as much.

"Let me get my things, Sheriff."

As Cole vanished, Opal looked to Deputy Kern, seated across the station at Opal's wooden desk.

"We shouldn't be gone long."

"Sheriff, you really think Mister Evers might have done something?" Kern asked.

"I don't think anything. And you and Deputy Cole better stop thinking I'm thinking something just because I'm thinking out loud."

"Sure I will, Sheriff."

Opal stepped to his desk, picked up a plate of steak and eggs, and shoveled some of it into his mouth. He held the plate out to Kern. "You eat yet?"

"No, Sheriff, I haven't."

"You want the rest of these?"

"No thank you, Sheriff, I surely don't."

"Well, you better eat something. I don't want to come back in a few hours and find you're off getting fed somewhere."

"I'll be here, Sheriff. You can count on that."

"I can't count on anything, Kern."

Cole came back into the room, wearing a coat, his gun at his hip.

"I'm ready when you say, Sheriff."

The deputy followed Opal out the door. The men mounted their horses and started toward the Evers home.

"It's about half an hour's ride," Opal said. "And if you feel like talking any, try talking about something nice. I don't want my mind all cluttered with your worrying and asking questions."

"Sure thing, Sheriff. How about Marcy Reynolds? You hear she had her baby?"

"I sure did," Opal answered, squinting into the purple-and-orange sunrise at the end of the road. "And that's nice . . . little baby Lucy . . . seven pounds I heard. A good healthy baby . . . that's nice . . ."

DWIGHT VISITS
LAFAYETTE AGAIN

The two stood in the alley behind the tavern. The alley smelled of garbage. The sun was up and Dwight removed his coat, draping it over one arm. The day was far too warm, he felt; suffocating. He couldn't shake the nightmare image of the stranger in the corner of his bedroom. A ghoul, perhaps. A crazed man. Way Dwight saw it, nobody's ghost stories ought to be trusted when experienced upon waking. Whatever he saw, it couldn't have been as bad as he thought it was.

Damn Manders! If only Carol was already buried, there'd be no better place to hide her. All this madcap anxiety would be behind him. His worrying about what Farrah Darrow knew—and now what this . . . *stranger* . . . knew—all of it would be put to rest. Beneath him. Buried. Instead, today Carol could wake, tonight she could wake. Right now, as he spoke with Lafayette, Carol could rise and walk straight to Sheriff Opal's station armed with everything she'd heard in the coma.

Dwight wasn't even sure of what he'd said in her presence and what he hadn't.

Damn Manders! Shouldn't a man, a *grieving* man, be permitted to bury his wife where and when he deemed fit? Hell's heaven, Carol was dead!

But the stranger who woke him knew she wasn't.

Someone knows, someone knows, someone knows . . .

Dwight needed to put out the fire in his blood.

"It's a bad thing to get nervous in this business, Evers."

"I don't like not knowing is what it is," Dwight said.

Lafayette eyeballed him. Her hair hung loose about her face, no longer in a ponytail, and Dwight thought she appeared unhinged. He wondered if everything looked unhinged to a frightened man.

"You can hire as many people as you like, Evers. You can hire everybody. But then everybody knows."

A bluebird settled on a chicken-wire garbage box. It made a belching sound, as though it'd just eaten.

"You don't expect me to believe that the men you work with are part of *everybody*, do you?"

"These men know people, Evers. They talk."

"Lafayette," Dwight whispered, "I need to know Moxie is dead."

"You hired a professional. You should act the same. Wait."

"I want to hire someone for Smoke."

"It's just not smart thinking, Evers."

"Can you do it?"

"Of course I can do it. But I'm in on this deal. And I don't like this." A second bluebird landed on the wire box. Lafayette said, "The Cripple will be back before your second man has time to leave. My advice is you go home. You keep crawling into the daylight like this, hiring more men, and presto, people you don't want around will be knocking on your door. People you thought you had nothing to do with."

"What does that mean?"

"What do you think that means?"

Dwight looked over his shoulder. To the mouth of the alley. The birds looked nervous, he thought.

Hide your lady.

"I need to know Moxie's dead."

"Just tell me what you want to do."

"I want you to get someone to watch the Cripple."

Lafayette exhaled. "I'll tell you what I think you should do and then you tell me what you want me to do. I think you should go home and grieve. I think you should go home and make sure things are set right with the funeral and grieve with friends and family and forget about the outlaw and the Cripple. I think you should bury your wife, like any good man would, and I think you should wait. Moxie makes it here safe? Then we can talk about hiring someone else. You don't understand the character you're paying. He might have finished the job and done another for no money at all. Or he could be at the gates of Harrows now, the blood of your outlaw on his hands as proof. You send someone else out and you'll upset the man. You don't want that loose bird landing on your shoulder. Men like this don't like to be babysat. You send someone, he'll know it. And when he comes back to let you know the job is done he might do one more for himself."

"Don't threaten me, Lafayette."

"This is no threat, Evers. This is the Trail."

A third bird settled on the wire box and nipped at the first two. Dwight yelled, "Pig-shit *birds!*"

Lafayette laughed. Dwight said, "I want someone to follow Smoke."

Lafayette nodded. "Consider it done."

"Who do you have in mind?"

"I've got a man."

"Who is it?"

"I've got a man, Evers. He'll check on him. He'll report back. What more do you need me to tell you?"

Chilled now, Dwight slipped his coat back on. Lafayette said, "Just remember I warned you. Remember I said Smoke won't like it."

"I don't care what the freak likes. He works for *me.*"

Then Dwight knelt and picked up a stone and threw it at the birds. But he missed badly and the bluebirds only watched it clip the alley's brick wall before falling to the dirt. They continued pecking at the wire.

Dwight surely expected Lafayette to say something—*nice aim*—that implied he was misfiring and making bad choices but when he turned around to face the Trail-watcher, he only saw Lafayette's unkempt hair slipping out of view, out the mouth of the alley.

"Good," Dwight said. As if Lafayette's absence somehow validated his decision after all. The wheels were in motion now. Someone would watch Smoke. And Smoke would catch Moxie. And Moxie would die.

A simple chain, Dwight thought. Easy pieces. One after the other.

"Moxie will die," he said, stepping from the alley. He paused for a woman and the woman looked at him as if maybe she'd heard what he just said. He watched her walk away, imagining his own deeds formulating in her head, as if, just by seeing him, she'd been able to determine all he had in mind.

She looked nervous to Dwight. Hell's heaven, the whole world was nervous.

But not Lafayette. Lafayette had predicted Dwight would want someone to watch Smoke. Let Dwight think he was calling the shots. Let him believe he was born again. Either way, Lafayette wasn't going to hire someone as crazed as Smoke to follow Smoke. No. In fact, she'd already sent word down the pipe, the Trail, the unseen channel of communication that Lafayette knew as well as witches knew the contents of their brews. She'd hired someone, yes. But rather than hire another man who might need to be watched, she'd sent for the man who does the watching.

MOXIE AT
THE HERMIT HOUSE

Moxie hadn't seen his longtime riding partner in nine years but knew that didn't matter. Jefferson was just about as stuck in time as nobody deserved to be, and Moxie wouldn't be surprised if he hadn't noticed any time pass at all.

The horse was tired. She had endurance, but she was old. Hadn't been ridden this much over two days since before Moxie settled. It was hard terrain, and more than one tricky incline brought the beast to gasping. At times Moxie thought little of it, a sacrifice, let the horse die if she must, but the horse had done well by him and the brief stop at Jefferson's would do them both some good.

In truth, Moxie needed to pick something up.

Rinaldo's news was worrisome. Moxie didn't know of any crippled triggerman. The guy could be good; some hit men were.

It'd been a long time since Moxie knew the names of the Trail.

"We're gonna take a break here, old girl."

He led the horse onto a path overgrown with ferns and moss-coated logs. Off the Trail the dirt was more like clay, and the horse stopped. Moxie patted her hide gently, encouraging, and the pair set across it. The beast's hooves crushed black leaves and snapped dead branches. The sun came through fractured, unwelcome in this dying landscape. He could see Jefferson's home, a brick rectangle between the withered trees; an old one-room schoolhouse Jefferson found soon after the pair stopped riding together.

Moxie could use some help. The sight of Jefferson's home was a good one.

He guided the mare through a yard covered in junk. Barrels, wagon parts, broken chairs stuck into the earth. Bales of hay, too. Beside a moss-grown cabinet, he dismounted and looped the horse to an old hitching post half covered in mushrooms, once used by the teachers. Above the house he saw the blackened top of a chimney, soot that reached down the length of brick like black oil oozing.

Someone was moving inside.

Moxie saw the shape of a man behind a blanket covering a cracked window. The place, the setting, felt funereal. Moxie thought of holes in the earth. The trees surrounding the home were dying. The grass was yellowed. Dishes were piled on the front stone step. And the shape within did not move well.

A cripple, Moxie thought.

Cautiously, his eyes on the window, he removed the gun from his right holster. Rinaldo's warning burned hot.

Was the triggerman ahead of him? Here?

He cocked the gun.

The shape within crossed the breadth of the window and stopped.

The thin blanket was pulled aside and Moxie saw the face of his old friend and he exhaled, lowering his gun.

It'd been a long time since Moxie had experienced that type of rush. But the sight of his friend trumped the rising nostalgia.

Jefferson had taken a turn for the worse.

The door opened and Jefferson came out hunched forward. One hand was on his lower back, the other already extended to shake Moxie's.

"Hello, friend," Moxie said, smiling for the first time since the telegram told him Carol would be buried.

"Jimmy! Jimmy ... I tell you it's been too long, boy. Too long. Why ... it's been a decade or more!"

"Almost," Moxie said.

They embraced.

Jefferson's back was in bad shape. He could hardly stand. His clothes were ragged, and he smelled of sweat and urine. He smelled of meat, too.

"You been cooking?" Moxie asked.

"Oh, yes I have, Jimmy. You want some?"

Moxie considered. "I do, Jefferson. Come on over and meet my horse."

Jefferson leaned farther forward, one hand craned to his back, and followed Moxie to the looped mare. "That's a good horse, Jimmy. She sure is."

"I know it, Jefferson. Rode all the way from Mackatoon yester morn'."

"Shudders, Jimmy! Mackatoon yesterday?"

"Got to be in Harrows by nightfall."

"You'll make it. You'll make it."

Jefferson stroked the mare's neck. "What's her name, Jimmy?"

Moxie gave the horse water and considered. "Never named my horses, Jefferson. I think Old Girl will do."

Jefferson's face lit up. Moxie liked to see that.

"*Old Girl* is a fine name, Jimmy! Just fine! Let's get her fed."

Moxie made to help him but Jefferson stepped to an open bale with a pitchfork beside it and brought some hay to the horse. A goat watched before walking deeper into the tall weeds of the yard.

"There you go, Old Girl," Jefferson said, wincing.

Then Jefferson asked Moxie if he'd like to see his place. Moxie said of course he would. Moxie untied the green sack from the saddle, and they crossed the yard and entered the schoolhouse.

The first word Moxie thought upon entering, before the words *filth* or *disarray*, was *books*. The schoolhouse was stuffed with them. Stacks of books from floor to mid-wall, shelves too high for Moxie to read the spines, certainly too high for Jefferson to get to now. Loose pages covered the floor like carpet and crunched beneath his dirty boots. Tabletops barely supported the weight of biblio-pyramids: towers from countertop to stone ceiling. Still, nothing matched the spectacle on the walls. Handwritten words covered the bricks, grease marks from a greasy hand. Words everywhere, some bigger than others, titles, chapter titles, footnotes, some sloping at the corners, finding room. Moxie bent to read a passage.

"Are these your words?" he asked.

Jefferson nodded. "That's right, they are, Jimmy. Been writin' my own book."

On the walls, Moxie thought.

Moxie smiled again. But Jefferson did not look good. For Moxie, this was hard to see, and yet the help he needed from Jefferson was not in the form of Jefferson's person.

There was no separation of rooms in the house. It was one long rectangle where once a teacher lectured. A well-dressed small Trail-towner, Moxie imagined; a man or woman certainly no better read than Jefferson. A child's desk remained from those days, and Moxie saw that Jefferson still used it: Papers were piled upon it, some written by Jefferson, some torn from other books. Difficult, long words were carved into the wood of it, too. A map of Ucatanani and Miskaloosa counties hung from the wall, and string connected town to town on the Trail.

With his trigger finger, Moxie followed the string from Macka-toon to Harrows.

Looking around, he saw there was a lot of string. Stacks of books were held together with string; candles were secured to their sticks with it; coats hung from the string between bookshelves; balls of string stood precariously piled in the corners; string for the pictures, string for the tools.

Enough of it to cocoon the schoolhouse twice over.

Moxie sat in a small chair once used by a young student. Set the green sack on a second chair beside him.

"You taking care of your back?" he asked, his voice quiet in the padded house. "I'm worried."

"*You're* worried? It's all I can think 'bout!" Jefferson laughed and walked uneasily to a table. "I like your red shirt, Jimmy. Makes you look young. Like you stepped straight outta the past." He paused. Moxie imagined he was recalling that past. "Want that meat now, Jimmy?"

Moxie looked out through the cracked window and saw the mare was still eating.

"Thank you," Moxie said. "That'd be fine."

Jefferson scooped some beef onto a plate as Moxie eyed an old fish tank, now used to store more books. Through the glass he read titles he'd never heard of before. String held the covers closed.

"You rob a library, Jefferson?"

Jefferson came with two plates, handed one to Moxie, and had a hard time setting himself down on a rocker. "That's a dream of mine, you know," he said. "Imagine all them bindings. Could make a bed of 'em."

"Surprised you don't sleep on a bed of books as it stands."

"Ha! Well, sometimes I do!" Jefferson struggled to lift his fork. "What leads you to Harrows, Jimmy?"

It was hard to reconcile the sight of Jefferson now with the lightning-rod riding partner Moxie had discovered the Trail with.

"Going to break apart a funeral."

"You don't say?"

"I do."

Moxie ate.

Jefferson cackled, his half-toothless mouth a black hole of joy.

"We done some things, Jimmy. We have. But a funeral? That'd be a Trail-topper to be sure."

"I brought you something," Moxie said, patting the sack beside him.

Jefferson bunched his brow and looked down at it. "No presents, Jimmy. You being here is more'n enough."

"Take them," Moxie said. "I don't need them." He knelt and removed a new pair of boots. A shirt he'd worn but once, gardening. A fresh pair of pants.

Jefferson smiled. "Well, Jimmy. I could sure use me some clothes."

"It feels good, Jefferson. It feels good to be riding again."

Jefferson's head bobbed slowly in the dull light. "I'd join you but I got no horse. Sure as shudders none as nice as yours."

But both knew Jefferson could ride no more.

Moxie felt a longing for the past. The nights. The people. The legends.

"I'd like that," Moxie said. "Might've brought another had I known you'd come. Things are tricky out there."

"How's that, Jimmy?"

"Might have some bad men on my tail."

"You always have. We both have."

"You're right, Jefferson. But it's been some time. I been planting rosebushes for near a decade."

"A triggerman?"

"Yes. And . . . something else."

Jefferson's eyes clouded. "There are worse things than men on the Trail, Jimmy." A Trail mantra. A phrase both had heard a thousand times and more. A truth both saw for themselves.

"Yes. There are."

"Hurts ya, don't it . . ."

"Riding?"

"Riding and not riding, too."

"Yes, it does. Yester eve I slept about as sore as any man ever slept."

"I believe you." Jefferson cackled again. Quieter. Now he was sitting up and pointing. "Jimmy, Jimmy, you remember the time we hid in that hole for all of two days? Shudders, Jimmy. We must've heard those men pass o'er us a dozen times. They talked 'bout where we were, theorized all the livelong day! We was right under 'em, Jimmy! Right there under 'em!"

He fell back into his seat again and laughed, bringing his hands to his chest.

Moxie smiled and looked to the window and saw the mare still eating.

"You writing about those days?" Moxie asked.

"Some," Jefferson said. "I'm writing 'bout the burden o' thinking hard on things for so many years."

Moxie nodded. "I'd read that book."

"I'm writing about riding, too, 'cause I can't separate the two. Thinking and riding. Rides and thoughts."

Moxie looked up and saw more writing on the ceiling. "You hurt your back doing this?"

"That I did."

"You thinking of taking a photo, Jefferson?"

"Sure I do. I met a man with a camera one time. Wouldn't mind stealing something like that."

Moxie smiled again. "Used to be we could take it while they watched."

"Used to be!"

The men laughed. Jefferson coughed.

Then Moxie said, "I've got to get riding, Jefferson."

"I expect you could use something from me, Jimmy."

"I could," Moxie said, glad Jefferson had brought it up.

"Well, you done seen for yourself I got enough."

"I did."

With difficulty, Jefferson got up and crossed the room. Moxie heard him rummaging behind a stack of leather-bound books.

"You want something to drink, Jimmy?"

"I thank you, but no, Jefferson. On the return I'll say yes."

Moxie rose. Jefferson handed him a yellow canvas bag.

"You look good, Jimmy. Don' worry 'bout who's tailing you. He's the one to worry."

Moxie nodded. "Use the clothes I brought you, Jefferson. It's good to see you, old friend."

Jefferson took his hand. "I'm just upset I ain't going with you!"

Moxie saw longing in his friend's eyes, as if every bone in Jefferson's body was fiending for the Trail.

Then Jefferson walked Moxie to the door.

"I'm gonna take another look at your four-legger . . ."

Outside on the front step, Moxie said, "Jefferson, if a crippled man comes through here, you don't need to be talking to him. Any man with a physical problem or anything like one. You got it?"

"Sure, Jimmy, I got it."

"A one-armed man, a limping man, even a man with just one eye, anybody like that comes knocking at your door and I'd like to be sure you won't answer is what I'm asking."

"Sure, Jimmy."

Moxie patted his good friend on the shoulder.

"If the good old days were as good as we believe them to have been, then you should see me soon, on the return. I'll bring you any books I find."

"That'd be fine, Jimmy."

"Thanks for the meat, Jefferson."

Moxie crossed the lawn gripping the bag Jefferson gave him. He tied it to where the green sack had been and unhitched the mare. In that moment it was very clear to him how far Harrows was. As if he could count the pebbles of dirt between himself and Carol.

The length of the Trail.

"That's a good girl," Moxie said, patting the mare and mounting her.

"That's a fine girl, all right, Jimmy! Old Girl!" Jefferson called from the front step. "And she's gonna get you there by nightfall, no worries."

Moxie tipped his hat goodbye and turned the horse around.

The pair were rested, fed, and ready for the remainder.

Jefferson's brick schoolhouse behind him, Moxie knew there would be no more friends along the way. Just Carol at rest, and those who didn't want him to wake her.

OPAL AT THE EVERS HOME

The sheriff knocked twice before he tried the handle. The deputy made a noise like he was about to say something but Opal looked at him and he didn't. The door was locked and so Opal knocked again.

He called Dwight's name and his voice boomed across the quiet yard. It was full morning now—the ride over had taken longer than Opal said it would—and the sun was up and showing. Cole looked to the sky and saw it above the house and for a minute couldn't believe anything foul whatsoever could take place within such a home.

"I suppose we ought to go around back then," Opal said. Cole nodded but didn't make to move and the sheriff looked at him sternly and Cole understood that he was the one who was supposed to go around back then.

He left the sheriff standing at the door and took the stone steps Carol had put in herself across the grassy yard. Yellowed spots showed in the sunlight and Cole thought them dead. Squirrels scurried up the big willow trees. He heard the sheriff call Evers's name again as he turned the corner of the house; there he saw the top of the gardens, down the hill he was now ascending, and the stone path that must lead to the back door. He, too, called Evers's name, not wanting to chance upon the man relaxing, working, or, worse, grieving.

"Mister Evers! It's Deputy Cole and Sheriff Opal! We're here to see you're doing all right!"

There was no answer, and Cole wondered if the quiet was what Opal called the "loaded" kind.

"Mister Evers! Deputy Cole here!"

He knocked on the back door and heard the empty echo follow. He thought of Opal trying the front door and knew that if he didn't try this one here he would get a talking-to when he came back around. He called out one last time and tried the handle and found it was locked and blew out a sigh of relief.

He's not home.

Cole stepped away from the door and then thought he hadn't tried hard enough. He thought of Opal saying as much.

He turned and tried the handle again and the door opened. Cole peered into the darkness.

"Mister Evers? Deputy Cole here. Sheriff Opal is out front. We've been trying to get your attention. Opal wants to talk to you some."

No answer came, no movement from within. Cole stepped in and closed the door behind him but then opened it again to give him some light. He crossed the room and found himself in the family kitchen. It was strange, uninvited as he was, seeing dishes that weren't his, a glass on the counter, a bowl of something on the table. He took the hall to the front door, unlocked it, and found Opal still standing there.

"Just let yourself right in, did you?"

Cole raised his brows. "I thought that's what you wanted—"

Opal stepped past him, already looking about the home. "It's cold in here, Cole. Am I right?"

"Sure is, Sheriff."

Opal took a cursory glance into the parlor and then the dining room, too. Cole followed him as he stepped through the house, his boots clunking against the wood floors, stopping to examine things that interested him.

"I suppose we better go downstairs," Opal said.

"Sheriff?"

"Yes, Cole?"

"What do we do if she's down there?"

"What do we do? We give her a once-over and hope Dwight Evers can explain who Alexander Wolfe is."

"Give her a once-over."

"That's right."

"For bruises or whatnot."

Opal was looking at the chandelier hanging in the foyer but now he turned to his deputy. "That's right, Cole. We're looking for foul play. Not their taste in drapes."

Cole nodded and followed Opal deeper into the house.

The sheriff checked the office. He looked at some papers on the desk and thought, yes, he had seen something like fear in Manders's eyes. Fear in the eyes of a man who handled dead bodies all day. A man who oversaw the makeup applied to dead eyelids, dressing up the fleshy faces of bloated ladies who no longer breathed. Manders buried children. Jane Flurry was just five when she caught the cough that sent her down into the earth. And Doris Mickey's kid must have been something to look at after he fell from the roof of their house like he did. If there was a man in Harrows who ought to be immune to the shudders of finality, it was Robert Manders.

"Sheriff!"

Cole was calling from the kitchen. Opal went to him.

"This here's the door to the cellar."

Opal came into the kitchen and stuck his head in the frame. He took the candlestick from the wall and asked Cole if he had a match. The deputy lit it.

"Well," Opal said. "Let's hope for the best."

"What's the best?"

"Nothing," Opal said. "Nothing is best."

Cole followed him down the creaking stairs.

Once they reached the cellar floor, Opal didn't speak anymore, didn't call out to Evers, and Cole understood he shouldn't, either. The sheriff stopped and brought the candle to the wall, checking some luggage he found there. The cases were empty and Cole guessed he was looking to see if Dwight Evers had planned on going somewhere fast.

Opal turned and trained the light on the doorway of a storm room. The more affluent citizens of Harrows had these types of rooms in their basements. Shelter. Some citizens had numerous subterranean rooms. Opal had found some bad things in the cellars of Harrows.

His shoes scuffled the concrete floor as he stepped to the entrance and stopped. He held the candle far out before him.

"Nothing," he whispered.

Cole leaned over his shoulder and saw the same nothing. A cold empty room with a stone slab of a table. More morgue than anything else. Opal stepped farther into the room and brought the candle low, illuminating the ground on the other side of the slab. Whatever he was searching for, Cole was certain he hadn't found it.

And yet there were some breaks in the dust on the slab. Two spots for shoulder blades, perhaps, a clean circle made by the back of a head.

Then Opal motioned for Cole to follow him out of the room, and the two walked the rest of the damp basement. At the far end were some crates filled with traditional home items: books, papers, tools.

Opal turned to Cole. "Where is she then?"

He was talking now, not whispering, and his voice echoed off the stone.

"Getting made up, Sheriff?"

Opal nodded. Wondered if he should have come last night. "Sounds about right."

The sheriff waited another moment, studying the dimensions the light gave him, and then crossed back to the stairs.

In the kitchen again, Opal told Cole they ought to check the bedrooms. Cole followed him up the stairs, the dark wood creaking. The sheriff tried the first door and decided it looked like the master bedroom. He walked the dimensions of the room once, stopped to look out through the drapes, then paused at a series of gunshots in the plaster wall.

"Well well."

"No blood," Cole said, squatting beside the sheriff. It wasn't uncommon to find bullet holes in even the finest homes in Harrows.

The lawmen checked all four rooms upstairs.

"She's not here," Cole said.

"No. She's not."

They returned to the first floor. They locked the front door from the inside and went out the back. Cole asked him, "You think anything untoward is going on, Sheriff?"

"I want to say there isn't, Cole, but I just don't know."

Manders came to mind again. Manders who had shaken the rubber hand of every person to die in Harrows for two decades running. The local authority, death-desensitized. It ought to take a monster to rattle Robert Manders.

But Dwight Evers?

"Let's get back," Opal said. "Kern's probably thin as a toothpick from starving."

The deputy didn't talk on the ride back into town. He knew better than to bother the sheriff when Opal was thinking like this. It wasn't even the right time to bring up something nice.

It was time to let Sheriff Opal work.

CAROL CARRIED

Dwight had carried her to the coach. Carol heard every grunt, every heavy step, every creak on the way.

But more important, she *saw* it.

The light had not been put out.

As Dwight took her from the slab, Carol wasn't sure which she feared more: losing the light, or it somehow coming with her. Dwight was taking her somewhere new.

Where?

The graveyard?

Was this it? Her burial?

She did not cry for help. Instead, she did something she had never done.

Carol sat up in Howltown.

Whether or not this action was replicable, possible, in the real world, Carol did not yet know. But the act of rising, even half rising, was a triumph.

Oh, how she wanted to tell John Bowie! Oh, how she wanted Hattie to know!

Mom! Mom! I sat up! By no accident or lucky mistake, I sat up!

And yet ... the monster *had* made a mistake. The monster had rolled her over, turning her wholly toward the direction from which she'd fallen. And for the first time ever inside the coma, Carol held out hope that she might have some control in the coma.

Sitting up proved as much.

It happened as the image of the storm room was strangely replaced with the image of the cellar at large, as if Carol were looking through a photo album, a book of pictures too fine for even the most affluent Harrowsers. Yes, in the light that still shone inside the coma (the light the monster no doubt left for her) the storm room became the cellar, then the cellar the cellar stairs. From there Carol saw still images of the kitchen, a hall, the dining room, the parlor, the foyer, the front door. All flipped, it seemed, by unseen hands. She did not see Dwight, who carried her, and so the moments played out as if Carol were a ghost, floating through the very house she owned.

Dwight's voice came from far away, deep within the clacking of his shoes upon the kitchen floor, steps like falling rocks in Howltown.

"Hide your lady, he said! Hide her I am!"

By the time he'd carried her out the front door, he was breathing hard. Carol saw a still image of the coach in the drive. Then a similar image but with the coach door open. Then she was inside it. Sitting up. On the floor. And yet *not* sitting up, too.

The Carol whom Dwight hid lay as deathlike upon her back as she had in the storm room.

But while the sense of unfathomable progress (*Sitting up! In Howltown!*) waged war with the horrors of betrayal and electrified nerves, Carol's senses of place and time were confused even more so by the image she saw inside the coach.

The image of herself, still on her back.

She saw her own eyes closed, her hair splayed across her forehead. The same yellow dress and brown boots she'd worn while walking with Farrah in the garden. Carol stared long at her own image as Dwight snapped the reins and the horse hooves erupted like a stone avalanche in Howltown.

A mirror, she thought.

Dwight had placed a mirror inside the coach with her. He'd set it on the floor, facing her, as if he'd wanted her to see that, despite her incredible achievement, she was actually no better off than she was before the monster made his mistake in the storm room.

But Dwight couldn't have known about that. And the mirror frightened her, not only because of what it showed her, but because it meant Dwight had plans. And what might they be?

"Hide your lady!" Dwight called. And his voice was the muddy crest of a freshly dug grave. "And hide her I am!"

Carol looked to her sleeping form in the mirror. She recognized it as a mirror John Bowie had brought to the house one evening, what he studiously described as *the kind of mirror you set up in the middle of the room. It reflects on both sides. That way you can see yourself, no matter where you are. And if you were to fall in its presence . . . who knows . . . maybe watching yourself fall might help.*

Dwight didn't know John had gotten it for her. Nor would he have cared. Yet despite the helpful gift John had presented it as, Dwight was now using it for some means Carol could not guess at. And the anger she felt at her husband, for using anything John Bowie had given her at all, gave her a deeper strength. One she badly needed.

She looked to her hands in the glass. She concentrated on her fingers.

The Carol who was sitting up watched the Carol inert on the floor of the coach.

And as she tried to move her fingers, as Dwight directed the horses toward the unknown, Carol's unknown, she succeeded in lifting her fingers, her *physical* fingers, slightly, from the coach floor, then, momentarily defeated, let them fall limp again.

Then she heard the crazed sound of many hoarse voices, many throats erupting into laughter, like the many faces that appeared and then vanished in the impossible candlelight of the storm room.

Light or no light, Carol was still in Howltown. And no glimpse of herself in the real world was going to get her out.

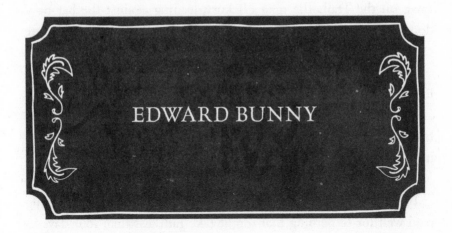

EDWARD BUNNY

E dward Bunny was playing cards in a saloon in Portsoothe when the man named Hickory came through the swivel doors. Edward knew his face well: Hickory was an outlaw-liaison, a man with news, and when he showed up it meant he had something to tell you.

Edward Bunny himself was a Trail-watcher. Triggermen were hired every day. Outlaws ran rampant. Bunny kept track of them all. To some men, it was very important to know where the killers on the Trail were at any given point in time. None of the guns had permanent homes. Hardly any of them went by real names. Bunny's job was to track them, report where they were, hire them out, then report on the status of their job.

A common hiring of Edward Bunny went as so: Bunny would receive a telegram asking "who is near" and Bunny would respond with a couple of names. Another telegram would come asking, "Who is best for the job?"—not meaning that Bunny knew the details of the hit, but rather that he knew which assassins were sober, stable, and capable at the time of the communication. It was an important job, the hub of a dark wheel. Bunny had no boss but was contacted often by Lafayette up in Harrows, and men and women like her in every town on the Trail. The man Hickory, leaning against the bar now, doing a bad job feigning indifference, meant that it was Lafayette calling, indeed.

None of the hit men particularly liked Edward Bunny. Nobody liked to be followed, and who knew how he picked who was sober and who wasn't. For this, Bunny often faced death: a barrel between his eyes, a tavern full of mad, drunk crooks. Even the whores disliked him.

And yet Bunny put real money in their pockets.

If Bunny contacted a triggerman, the man knew he was getting paid well for something that might take him less than four days to carry out. Most lawmen knew who Bunny was, but there was nothing in the county laws to lynch a man for speaking with another and Bunny had no blood on his hands. In fact, Edward Bunny had never killed a man in his life. But he'd orchestrated the deaths of a hundred. His intricate system of Trail-watching consisted of a deck of playing cards sewn into his brown jacket pocket: The cards represented the individual hit men and outlaws of the Trail. Sam Jordan was the Jack of Knives. Howard "Bone Ax" Freely the Nine of Darts. Paula Hughes from Kellytown the Six of Bullets. And so on. The way the cards were stacked corresponded with the towns on the Trail: If Freely was in, say, Mackatoon, his card would be on the very bottom of the deck, Mackatoon being the southernmost Trail-town. If Marla Morgan was in Harrows, hers would be on the top, Harrows being the Trail's northern peak. There were no names on these cards. No faces. No notes. But Bunny knew them very well. And the clever lawmen who cut open the secret pocket in his jacket found nothing but a shuffled deck of cards, a meaningless possession, and certainly nothing to lock a man up over.

Today Bunny was making a couple of outlaws some money in a different way. He was terrible at playing cards.

"Bunny," Otis Parlance said, his voice rough with smoke. "You gotta practice."

Bunny, shaking his head, his thin hair barely covering his round skull, did not respond. Behind his small, thick glasses he glared once at Parlance and motioned for another hand.

As Bernie Garland shuffled, Bunny watched Hickory at the bar. His eyes were on the cards on the table, but he paid attention to the leaning shape, doing his customary awful job of trying to hide the fact he was here for business. In all his life Bunny had never known a more obvious informant.

"Bunny!" Lawrence Buchanan said, raising his glass. "A drink. On me. With your money!"

The outlaws broke into laughter, and the bartender looked over to the quartet with concern. For a moment Bunny and Hickory locked eyes. Then Bunny took hold of his cards.

"Lawrence," Bunny said, thinking of the Seven of Darts that represented Buchanan in his pocket. "I don't drink."

There was a moment of bad silence. It was just another reason to dislike Edward Bunny. The man never drank, never got drunk.

The hand went around and Bunny raised, and all the outlaws met him because Edward Bunny hardly ever won. Behind his glasses, Bunny's eyes sparkled and his round face broke into a slight child's smile.

At the bar Hickory looked to Bunny and then pretended he hadn't, shoving a handful of peanuts into his mouth. The bartender watched him and shook his head, knowing well what Hickory was doing in his tavern and who he was here to see.

"Bunny!" Parlance said. "You wouldn't be holding something good, now would you? You look like you done got asked to the ball!"

Bunny, sweating beneath his vest, glanced at Otis but did not respond.

Then Bunny raised again, and now the three crooks could feel the growing pile of money in their own pockets. When Edward Bunny asked you to play cards, you took him up on it. No other man on the Trail had such a delusional image of himself as a card player.

"High stakes, Bunny."

"Getting serious, Bunny."

"Must have all fifty-two in that hand, Bunny."

Bunny started tapping a small black shoe on the tavern's wood floor. The men had seen him this way before. Drinks or no drinks, Bunny played like a drunk.

"We're all still in, Bunny," Buchanan said. "What are you going to do?"

Bunny stared at his hand in silence. Then he reached into his vest, pulled forth more money, and set it on the table. The men joked but Bunny could hear in their voices they were starting to believe him. Parlance said, "You're a hard man to read, Bunny," and set his cards down.

"That's a pretty pile of coin," Bernie Garland said. "It's going to look very nice in my vest."

At the bar Hickory ordered another drink and then coughed for Bunny to hear. Without looking at him, Bunny shook his head. Hickory was about as well hidden as a sheriff's badge.

"How about a drink?" Garland asked Bunny, smiling.

"I don't drink, Bernie."

Bunny raised again and Buchanan folded without comment. Bunny looked to Garland, who looked down at his cards. Hickory tapped his fingers on the wood bar and it sounded like a clock, ticking.

"Now, Bunny," Garland said, wiping his forehead with the back of his hand. "You've got me thinking."

Bunny laughed. A single high-pitched clap, and the bartender turned his head.

At the bar Hickory made a slight moaning sound.

Bunny raised once more and then so did Garland and the men put their cards down. Bunny turned his over like an excited child, his thin hair wet on his head, his glasses reflecting the cards on the table.

His mouth smiled but his eyes did not and Garland shook his head as Bunny made sense of the cards.

"Bunny," Garland said. "I done told you that pile was gonna look nice on my mantel."

There was a moment of silence before Bunny slammed his fist hard on the table and pointed a finger at Garland and shook it. His face was tomato red. Then Hickory coughed again and Bunny, breathing hard, flattened his hair to his head, adjusted his glasses, and said, "Nice playing with you, gentlemen."

He took his brown suit jacket from the back of his chair and walked to the bar.

Hickory stood half a foot taller than the Trail-watcher.

"What is it?" Bunny asked.

"Smoke."

Bunny did not respond.

"You want a drink, Bunny?"

"I don't drink."

"He's following James Moxie."

"I know that, you idiot."

"Hey, Bunny. I'm just—"

"When we do this, Hickory, when you come in here and I come over here and we get to talking about the things we talk about, just give me the facts and move on. Understand? You think I don't know where Smoke and Moxie are?"

"No, sir, Bunny, I—"

"None of this chitchat. No explanations. Understand?"

"Hey, ease up, Bunny."

The bartender approached and Bunny glared at him and he turned away again.

"She just wants a report, Bunny. Lafayette just wants—"

But Hickory stopped talking because Bunny was staring at him like he was gonna slap him.

"You know what to do, Bunny," Hickory said. Then he downed his whiskey and nodded and left the tavern.

Bunny sat at the bar. The bartender brought him a lemonade.

Smoke.

Bunny knew Smoke was the craziest pig-shitter on the Trail. Most hit men were afraid of him. Nobody liked talking to him. It was im-

possible to have anything like a conversation with the man. In his
deck, Smoke was the Two of Storms. Two for the two tin legs, Storms
for the darkness surrounding the crazed hatless triggerman. James
Moxie was the King of Bullets. Bunny liked the irony—a man becoming King of Bullets for not firing his gun. The picture cards were
reserved for the big names, and though it'd been nine years since
James Moxie rode the Trail, his was a hard name to lessen. But while
the Trick in Abberstown might have been the greatest feat the Trail
had ever known, James Moxie didn't have the teeth some of the others did. There was something . . . soft about him to Bunny. And yet his
name still chilled.

Mystery. Or mysticism.

Magic.

That King of Bullets had sat on the bottom of his deck for a very
long time. Lately it'd been moving up, toward Harrows. And the Two
of Storms had been following. Some ten cards away still, but certainly
closing in.

Bunny laughed and downed the lemonade.

In a way he was the boss of these terrible men. All of them knew
him. All of them . . . so *tough*. Yet not one would like the job of following Smoke on the Trail.

Smoke had some stories. And Bunny had heard them all.

He wiped his mouth with a napkin from the bar. He felt for the
deck of cards in the pocket of his brown jacket, then slipped the jacket
on and walked to the table where the three outlaws still drank.

"Bunny," Bernie Garland said. "You look like you got something
funny on your mind."

Bunny glared at them. These three.

Sometimes outlaws didn't like being watched. Smoke surely
wouldn't. But these bastards needed babysitting. Why, if a man like
Edward Bunny wasn't around, the Trail would be mad carnage chaos
and only the law would see any of the money.

"What is it, Bunny?"

Bunny just stared at them, sweat dripping down his cheeks. Then his mouth smiled and his eyes did not, and his black shoes clacked on the tavern's wood floor as he exited through the saloon doors.

The sun was out in Portsoothe, but not very high. Smoke was near. Bunny knew this because Bunny knew more about these pig-shitters than any of them wanted him to.

He headed up Portsoothe Street, thinking of the gradual climbing of the slow-moving Two of Storms and that long-slumbering King of Bullets.

As the sun made waxy his sweating face, Bunny could practically feel the pair moving in his pocket. Lafayette wasn't the only one who wanted to see to it that they collided.

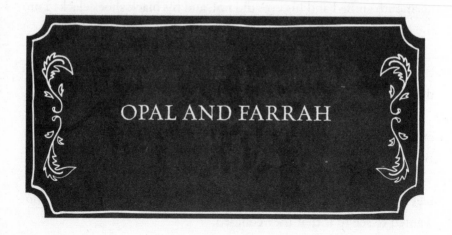

OPAL AND FARRAH

Farrah hadn't stopped drinking since finding Carol on the slab in the cellar. Clyde was doing all he could to calm her, to help her, but the only thing that was making any progress was a series of bottles. And yet she wasn't drunk. Not entirely. As if the horror of seeing her lady die, and the confusion of seeing her so lifelike in the storm room, refused to be washed away.

She stepped out of the general store, a fresh bottle of whiskey in hand, and saw Sheriff Opal rise from a bench along the boardwalk.

"Evening, Missus Darrow."

Farrah acknowledged the lawman and stepped by him. The name *Dwight Evers* burst in her mind and fizzled. She wondered if Opal had somehow kept tabs on how much she'd drunk. But there was no law against drowning yourself.

"Missus Darrow, you mind having a word with me?"

Farrah turned clumsily. Seeing her now, the sun full upon her features, the sheriff could tell the girl had been drinking indeed. But more than that, she'd been crying. A lot.

"I'd no idea you were wanting to talk to me, Sheriff Opal. I do apologize."

Harrowsers passed on the planks of the boardwalks. As if Carol Evers had never died. As if everybody was kept cold in the cellar of a home with warm rooms.

Opal removed his hat.

"Let's find ourselves some privacy, Farrah."

She walked with the lawman to the end of the boardwalk and turned down a quiet, wooded side road. Opal was careful to present himself gently.

"I understand you had quite a relationship with Missus Evers, Farrah, and I'm awful sorry things have come to pass as they have."

Farrah stared long into the sheriff's eyes. A small flame sparked inside her. A flicker, it seemed, of hope.

Sheriff Opal wanted to talk about Carol.

"I'm not sure what I want to ask you, young lady. There are a number of questions on my mind."

"Ask me anything. Please."

He watched the girl a moment before continuing.

"Did you see Missus Evers the night she died?"

"I was with her when she collapsed."

"That right?"

"That it is. We'd been walking through the garden. She didn't seem well."

"Didn't seem well how?"

"She said she didn't feel well."

Opal nodded. "Did she explain that any further?"

"I think she was about to, Sheriff. She wanted to tell me something just before she fell. She hinted at a preexisting condition."

"What'd she say? How'd she put it?"

Farrah sighed. Her eyes were wet with more tears to come. She shivered at the thought of Dwight asking her the same questions.

"She told me she had a sickness. Said it didn't come often and that she could see it when it did."

Opal frowned. "Do you know what she was referring to?"

"No, sir. I'm sorry. But I don't."

Opal nodded. He studied Farrah's face and felt sorry for her. He'd seen her many times in town, and this version of her was the wrong one.

"Farrah, I only ask you these questions because it's my job around town to understand what's happened to anyone living in Harrows. It's about safety. Protection."

"Of course. But surely you feel something is wrong for you to be asking questions."

Opal paused. There was hope in her voice. "Do you think something's wrong, Farrah?"

"I don't know. Maybe."

"You see, that answer frightens me."

Now the tears did come. Quietly, falling gently down her face. Then Opal said, "I've never been very good at hiding where I'm going. Used to be people told me I'd never make it in the law business 'cause I wasn't clever enough. I'm interested to know about you finding Missus Evers in the storm room."

Farrah's eyes widened.

"How did you know about that?"

Opal did not smile when he answered. "I'm not sure myself. But I heard it, I did."

Farrah imagined Clyde, drunk, running his mouth at a tavern. She would have words with him later. Or maybe not. Maybe this time Clyde had given her a gift.

Then she told Opal the same story she'd told Clyde the morning after she found Carol. That Dwight was very serious about discovering what Missus Evers told her before dying. How she fainted, woke up alone in the house, and found her lady in the cellar. Opal listened closely.

"How long were you asleep for?"

"I don't know."

"Can you try to figure it out for me? It might mean a lot."

Farrah brought a hand to her forehead. The phrase *a lot* frightened her. She worked through it with the sheriff. The sun was not yet fully down when she fainted. "When I came to it was dark, but the sun was showing by the time I got home."

Opal nodded. *Girl's got a bad feeling, too,* he thought. *First the minister of death, now the dead lady's girl . . .*

"Any idea where she is now, Farrah?"

"Carol?"

"Yes."

"I don't know. The cellar still. I don't know."

Opal nodded. He didn't want to tell he'd been down there.

"Let's talk a moment more. A couple more questions, if I may."

"Of course."

She gripped the whiskey bottle tight. A man passed and tipped his cap to Opal. Opal waited for him to be gone.

"How did Mister Evers look to you when he learned the reason you screamed?"

Farrah held his eyes and answered, "He wanted to know what she almost told me, Sheriff."

"Sure. His wife collapsed, after all. But what I mean to ask is, did you notice anything beyond grief?"

Farrah looked confused. And yet eager. "I'm not sure I understand."

"Sure. I wouldn't expect you to."

"But . . ."

"But what, now?"

Farrah breathed deep. "Before she fell, before our walk in the garden, I overheard the two of them arguing."

"Uh-huh. Arguing."

"And Carol was telling Mister Evers something about . . . *the next time it happens* and *someone else needs to know.* Something like that."

"The next time what happens?"

"I don't know."

"Is that all?"

"No."

"Uh-huh."

"She also told Mister Evers that it was time to let me in."

"Let who in?"

"Me."

"Into what? Any idea?"

"None, sir."

Opal nodded. He made to speak but Farrah cut him off.

"I don't mean to accuse, but ... but Mister Evers really was intent on ... finding something out." Farrah's eyes were red with it. "I don't know what it means. I'm sorry. I shouldn't have said as much."

Opal nodded, studying the girl's face. Noting how dry her face looked despite her tears. As if her skin was flaking with her lady's. As if she'd cried and dried up six times today already.

"I'm not asking you to accuse, Farrah. But the way I like to work is to get a feel for things. You see, once I had a man come to me and tell me his brother had a terrible accident with a shovel. I listened to him but then I got to thinking that the words he used to describe his brother weren't the kindest words a man ever used. I egged this side of him on a bit, you see, and sure enough, turned out the man had done his own brother in and was looking to cover it up. You, here, just sort of said something that caught my ear is all. You worrying about accusing someone makes me think you had the thought yourself. And you never can tell when one of those silly old thoughts ends up being nothing other than the truth. They're worth checking, I'd say."

Farrah looked up and down the street now. "I'm not sure what I meant." But not defeated. She had hope yet.

"Sure, sure," Opal said, reassuring her. "The cellar."

"I'm sorry?"

"You were in the cellar. And I apologize in advance for making you do this once more. But you saw your lady there in the storm room. You touched her, you asked her to wake, and ..."

"And? I've already told you. I—"

"And something crossed your mind."

Farrah shook her head. The gesture of a woman who'd discovered she was going to do something she wasn't sure she wanted to.

"I thought Mister Evers might have done something to her."

Opal nodded, his eyes on hers. "I imagine their cellar is as cold as any."

"Colder, sir."

Farrah looked to the dirt at their feet.

"Well, look now," Opal said, planting both his big hands on his hips. Farrah noticed how close his hands were to his guns. As if, because of what she'd told him, danger was coming. "You and I have had ourselves a real hog of a conversation here. Don't think I missed it that it's been suggested Mister Evers might have done something terrible, suggested by someone who spends more time with him than I do. But truth is, we don't know that he has, and chances are very high he hasn't. In all my years in law I've only encountered a couple of men who did something as wrong as killing their own wife. Thing is, too many edges aren't squaring off.

"And maybe I shouldn't be saying as much to a young lady like yourself, but as it goes I got a feeling, and my feeling about you is that you could help me. Maybe you already have, maybe you're about to. But let's not part ways today with worry on our minds. Most likely we should be grieving the loss of a wonderful lady. Sometimes, in such matters, someone does something a bit out of the ordinary and everyone gets uneasy, pointing fingers and saying this or that can't be right because this or that was done wrong. Mister Evers is most likely dealing with the loss of his wife. Can we blame him if he acts any different than he normally would? I'd say not. And I say it's a much more suspicious thing if he did. But you and me ... we ought to keep our heads and let me look further into things and hopefully I come knocking on your door and tell you that it was just plain old justified sadness that got the better of us today and made us think such wretched thoughts."

Farrah thought, *We've gotta do something.* Then she thought of the telegram she sent to James Moxie. The news of Carol's death. She wiped her face with her arm.

"All right, Sheriff."

"Let me ask you something before I let you go. You ever meet an Alexander Wolfe? Friend of Mister Evers?"

Farrah tried to remember.

"There've been many people to the house since I started there."

"For parties and such?"

"Yes, gatherings."

"Uh-huh. But no Alexander Wolfe? Alex, maybe? From west of Harrows? From Charles?"

Farrah shook her head like she'd disappointed the sheriff.

"That's all right," he said. "How about Mister Evers's family . . . you ever meet anybody in the same line of work as Mister Manders over there?"

"Is that what he said?"

"Is that what who said?"

"Mister Evers." Farrah reddened. "Did he say he'd gotten his family to take care of her?"

"He did, indeed."

Farrah shook her head no. A definitive no. She'd never met anybody else in her life in Manders's line of work.

"Well, all right," Opal said. He put his hat back upon his head and smiled in a fatherly way. "I thank you and I thank you again for taking the time with me. And if you remember anything else—"

"Of course."

"But don't sit around trying to remember things all day, neither. That'll just rip you in half. You can trust me there." He studied her sad face a moment longer and said, "If anything funny is going on, I'll find out what it is. You can rest with that as a pillow."

SMOKE CLOSE

Jefferson had just finished writing when the knocking came. At first he thought it was his old friend again, come back for one more memory, but Jefferson was no fool to the ways of the chase. He peered out the window. Through the blanket he couldn't tell if the hatless man was crippled or not. He was standing still, his hands in his pockets, looking down at the dirt, and there was no horse looped in the yard.

"I know you're home," the stranger called, and Jefferson could tell a bad man when he saw one.

Worse. This man, whoever he was, crippled or not, was crazy. You could see it clear as canvas in his eyes.

Jefferson watched for a long time before slinking back along the wall. Hunched, he hurried to where a shotgun hung by string above a bookshelf. He untied it and took it down.

"I can hear you in there."

Jefferson gripped the barrel and hunched to the kitchen table. Above it was another shelf, stabilized by string, and on it were the shells. He set the gun on the table and grimaced as he tried, unable, to reach them.

"I've had a bit of an accident," Smoke called. "My coach fell to bits from that hole out on the Trail. I could sure use some assistance."

Jefferson pulled a chair over to the shelf. Taking hold of the chair-back, he lifted himself up.

"I won't be long. You just let me know if you can help and where I can get help if you can't."

Up on the chair Jefferson took hold of the shells and had difficulty getting back down.

Smoke continued, "You don't need to open the door. Just let me know where I can get some help . . ."

Jefferson opened the chamber and thumbed the shells inside.

"I know you're in there. Don't make it so I come in on my own."

Jefferson braced himself with the nearest chair and hunched past the table. He limped across the room, lifted the gun, and shot a hole through the door. Wood splinters exploded.

"Ain't coming in on your own now!" Jefferson yelled.

He hunched to the door and looked through the break. It was hard to see whether or not the man lay dead on his stoop. Jefferson, sweating, hunched to the window and pulled back the blankets and saw the man wasn't there at all.

"Hell's heaven . . ."

No body, no blood.

Jefferson limped to the other side of the old schoolhouse, kicking yellowed pages out of the way. He looked out the window.

The man was in the backyard. Making a pile of his things. Jefferson didn't need the confirmation now, but he saw the man was crippled.

"Tell me what you gave him," Smoke yelled, tossing another book on the pile.

Jefferson hunched back to the kitchen table and reloaded. Sweat dripped from his chin. It felt incredible, in its way . . . *action*. He held the gun tight, as if gripping his own entire history on the Trail. At the window again, he used the barrel to push aside the drapes and knocked on the glass with it. "You 'bout ready for hell's heaven, kid?"

Smoke kept his eyes on the pile when he responded. "I know he didn't stop by for supper."

"Nobody stopped by at all, Cripple."

"What'd he need, hermit. Just tell me what he took."

Smoke took a birdhouse from a maple tree and tossed it onto the heap. The wood split when it landed. Cracked eggs half rolled forth.

Jefferson knocked on the window again. Smoke looked up. Jefferson fired through the glass.

When the smoke and glass cleared he saw the man had been hit. He'd shot him in the shin. "I'm aiming for your chest next, kid."

Smoke looked down. Oil spilled fast. His pant leg and boot were black with it. He'd been hit high, just under the knee. The serrated tin already dug into his flesh.

"Come on out here and shoot a cripple to his face, hermit!"

Jefferson howled with delight. Moxie was right. It felt *good*.

He slunk back against the wall out of view and reloaded the gun. When he came back Smoke was adding to the pile.

"You're a thirsty one, Cripple. Ready to drink your own blood, you are!"

He fired again. A tree to Smoke's right cracked thunder.

Smoke pulled a small box from his pocket and removed a match. It came to life between his fingers, and he let it fall to the oil below.

Whump . . .

The pile took flight. Jefferson howled as he watched his things go aflame. He reloaded the gun quickly and limped to the door. He could hear his things burning, crackling, the horror of all hoarders. His shoulder against the front door, he staggered out of the schoolhouse.

"You be about ready to die, Cripple! It's coming now . . ."

Fresh pain gripped his back; pincers along the spine. When he rounded the schoolhouse, gun held high, he saw the Cripple was facing him.

The cockiness that graced the triggerman's face was no longer there. In its stead was rage.

Jefferson was only twenty feet from him but Smoke didn't move. Jefferson saw a second match come to life.

He watched it fall.

whump

BOOM!

Moxie's old riding partner saw it coming but didn't understand what it was. He hadn't seen Smoke's hands in his pockets when he rounded the house himself. He hadn't seen when Smoke laid bare a path of oil thick enough to trap a horse.

The flames rose like a living wall and got to Jefferson before his debilitating back would let him get out of the way.

Smoke watched him burn.

Jefferson's body contorted strangely as he fell to his knees. As if, in death, the old outlaw was more mobile after all. The flames rendered him like the blackened yard tools on the burnt grass. Smoke didn't move. He didn't speak. He watched.

When it was over, Smoke limped around the schoolhouse and kicked in the front door. Oil splashed against the open cut on his knee. He looked inside.

All he saw was books.

And all he saw was paper.

All he saw was a burn to be.

The hermit had shot him in the shin. The hermit was ashes on the grass.

"*All you had to do was tell me!*" Smoke screamed, knocking things from the table. "*All you had to do was tell me what the old man stopped by for!*"

Sweating, he turned around and saw the writings on the walls. He grabbed a mug from a counter.

"*I'm gonna burn it all, hermit! Burn every pig-shitting word!*"

Books . . . papers . . . pages . . .

Smoke burned it all. The hermit was dead and the outlaw was getting closer to Harrows but for one magnificent moment Smoke just needed to burn.

By the time he was done, the words on the walls had melted into unintelligible marks, symbols, nonsense. Black smudges like the writings of a blind madman.

And all the hermit had to do was tell him what the outlaw came for.

"Could've saved your life, pig-shitter."

But all Smoke had to do was look up and he would've seen what gift Moxie had received.

Jefferson had just finished writing about Abberstown when Smoke knocked on the door . . .

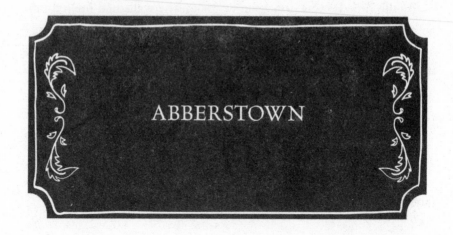

ABBERSTOWN

... *The people in West Franklinville don't tell it right. The people in Juni-per don't tell it right. The people in Mackatoon don't really know the truth about it and the ones who do don't tell it right, neither. Some say James Moxie dropped six men with one shot. Others say he breathed fire. Even the ones who was there, the crowd that started all the talking in the first place, even they don't get it right. 'Cause that's how easy it is once a legend begins. Moxie done his thing with mayhaps two dozen watchers but a story like his travels quick. It's got to, 'cause it done pop up so much in their memories that they gotta tell the nearest person or they're liable to implode. What's more interesting anyway? Men talk fishing. Men talk women. Men talk cards. But shudders aplenty if bearing witness to a magnificent move don't trump them all.*

Imagine yourself, sitting on a stool, drinking good beer, and the fella next to you starts off 'bout how his crop ain't coming up like it ought to and how it'd sure be nice if some rain would drop and how fertile and wonder-ful his dirt usually is. And here you are, listening, but bubbling over with that story of your own; not so much wanting to beat his but wanting to hear something better than this and you know the scene you witnessed is just about as exciting as it gets. Why, after some time, you'd tell it. You'd have to. 'Cause in the landscape we all live in, the outlaw can be artist. The outlaw can be entertainment. Lest he be the black-soul kind that kills for sport, the outlaw is the man men can get together o'er.

The outlaw is the man made of stories.

Some people say it was a trick. I know Moxie would say the same himself but you can't go on the word of the man who done it. I've heard people call it cheap *and I've argued with those people.* It's not a fair fight, *some* say. No matter what he done. *I ask them what was unfair about it? Some answer they don't know and others say,* Well, if magic were used and both men don' know magic, then it ain't a fair fight. *I laugh and say,* What if guns are used and one of the men don' know how to use guns? *The outlaw's object isn't always fairness. In fact, the outlaw's object is usually whatever he came there to get. Frank Tilly robbed a bank in Bully by dressing up as the manager after noticing he looked an awful lot like the man. Some people say that's not a fair fight. They say Tilly ought to've come in and held the place up and made the tellers put the coin in a bag and seen if he could outrun the law through the streets of Bully. As it stood, Tilly left at lunchtime through a back door, a sleeping sack loaded with coin. He was discovered in Harrows living like a prince. People don't like that no chase was involved. People don't like that no guns were drawn. But I say that's as clean a pile of pig-shit as any I ever stepped in. Tilly used his brain. And hell's heaven if his story ain't a good one to tell.*

Now, Moxie was something different altogether. Moxie's story scared some. People don't like magic when it's black and nobody could figure out any other way to title what he done. I rode out of Abberstown with Moxie after he did it and it was the last ride he took as an anonymous. Next time we saw others after, people inched their way to ask him how he done it, and when Moxie turned to face them you saw fear fill their own. What if he does it to me, *they were thinking.* What if he drops me right now without drawing a gun?

What people don't know is why Moxie was facing Daniel Prouds in the first place. And don't you know that's the least interesting color of the yarn. But it helps shed light 'cause once you get the idea that Prouds was a sack of pig-shit you don't care about fair fights or the rules of engagement and all you wanna hear is how someone like Moxie came in and skinned the swine. Down in Pruetville a man tells me James Moxie wasn't a good outlaw 'cause he didn't kill enough to count. I told him I was under the impression Moxie done lived off his outlawing for some eleven years and if that ain't good work, you've got your facts twisted. He said I was right, but then he said magic doesn't count. I laughed then and I laugh now. Magic most certainly counts. And in the case of James Moxie and Daniel Prouds, magic happened, though I know it weren't the type that man and most men imply.

The magic is in Moxie's brain. 'Cause the idea to do what he done didn't exist until it did. Presto. And how do you explain that?

Moxie and I were on a cross-country crime spree when our horses stepped over the Abberstown border. Ignorant as it was, we saw ourselves as vigilantes, spirit-riders on the Trail who put it good to the pig-shitters of the world. I'm not saying we were the good guys, but there's no questioning whether or not James Moxie and myself were on the opposite side of the coin as that throat-slitter shitter Daniel Prouds.

Nobody knew our names yet in them days and we used them freely. Down the road Moxie would have to pretend to be someone he wasn't and I think all that got to him 'cause he stopped wanting to talk about it. But when we first crossed into Abberstown I introduced myself as Jefferson and James introduced himself as James. The town was even more alive then than it is now and we rode Main Street with fire in our hearts for we knew we weren't getting out of there without some fun. You can tell with the bigger towns. Albert's Port and Donner ain't no fun. Neither is Kelly-town. Never had no fun in any of them places. But Griggsville . . . Harrows, too . . . and most definitely Abberstown . . . now, these are the places a man beneath the law can scoop something up nobody else noticed 'cause everybody else was busy scooping their own. I laugh now remembering Moxie tipping his hat to a lawman who passed us upon entering. He done tipped his hat and said, 'Afternoon, Officer,' before muttering 'You're gonna come looking for us later' under his breath.

We were an exciting duo, the sort of fellows outlaws could recognize at a glance. Not because we were wanted, though we were, but because like kind recognizes like kind. Like vampires, understand, or drunks: An out-law can see himself reflected in the eyes of another, no matter how black or gray his heart may be. We seen a couple upon entering and they seen us. Men outside the tavern. Men at the hitching post out front of the bawdy house.

But neither of us saw Daniel Prouds until we started to drinking at a place they used to call Leonard's Barnburner 'cause his theme was fire and his ladies set drinks aflame. Back then I brought some books with me on the Trail. There were a heap of lonely nights by the fire, understand, and I defy anyone to name a man I rode with who didn't eventually ask me what went on inside them. Now, I don't recall the exact volumes I had on me, but I carried them with me into Leonard's lest a rapscallion come nab 'em from my horse.

I'd no way of knowing that a routine gesture like that, just bringing in my books, would spark the single most interesting moment in outlawing history thus far.

Moxie and I done drank three beers apiece 'fore I mentioned to him we had no way of paying for what we drunk. He shrugged and reminded me we done drank many times without knowing who was paying. So we or-dered another and watched as the ladies set our neighbors' drinks aflame. It was like a wedding in there, people were having so much fun. 'We gotta come to Abberstown more often,' Moxie said. But we never went back through there again.

Another round and Moxie suggested we see what else the town had going for it. I told him we'd be in trouble if we didn't pay and then planned on staying in town. Moxie thought I was right but gave me no good plan. I told him we could trade in my books for the beer. He told me I liked my books and shouldn't have to part with them. I told him I done read them all three and wouldn't mind and I'd just as soon get some more in Kellytown. He shrugged and said it was my decision but he'd like to help sell 'em. We were young, understand, not so young that we were stupid but young enough to think trading books for beer was equal and fair.

Moxie took my stack and crossed the room and stood next to a table of well-dressed gentlemen and asked if they'd like three leather-bound good books if they'd buy us our beers. The men laughed and Moxie did, too, and then he brought the stack to another table and soon the place was all shouting out about the men with the books but no money for beer. Moxie was pure then, not yet tarnished by his own name, and he went to just about every table in the joint and by the last couple was plopping himself in chairs along with the Abberstowners and going into a routine that had us all laughing. I could tell we were gonna get our drinks paid for and Moxie gave me a wink, letting me know I'd come up with a good plan. And it worked. Sort of it did. An elderly man seated at the bar called out, 'Hear hear, I'd like a look at them books.' Moxie got to his feet and carried them o'er to him and the man brought out his specs and examined their spines. 'These are good titles,' he said, and I answered, 'I know they are.' 'Haven't seen this one in some five years,' he said. 'I got her in Ecksburg,' I told him. He looked me over like I might have taken it as opposed to having read it. I told him my favorite scene and why and he said, 'Gentlemen, let's go out back and take a closer look at these and if I like them I'll buy your beers indeed.' 'Why don' we take a look out front,' Moxie said. The man smiled and said, ''Cause I'd rather do so in private.' Moxie and I followed him through the back door of Leonard's in Abberstown and into the sun-soaked alley behind the bulk of Main Street's storefronts. It was in that alley that we done met Daniel Prouds.

The old man asked for the books and Moxie removed the considerable string that kept them together in a stack and put the string in his pocket. I said the books looked fine in the sunlight but before the man had a chance to agree all three of us done heard a lady hollering down the alley. We turned and saw she was on the ground, and a man was above her, kicking her in her neck. He had other men with him and they stood and watched and Moxie and I could tell it was a whore there on the ground and something clicked in Moxie and I still don' know exactly what it was.

I said, 'Hold on there, Jimmy,' but he was already crossing the dirt alley, calling for them to get off the lady. The men turned and one said, 'This ain't your business,' and Moxie done knocked him out. Now, I seen some hits and I seen some poor hits thrown by Moxie himself, but this one was square. This one broke teeth. I was beside Moxie now as the other men turned and

I took him by the arm, telling him we oughtta get, that we didn't know nothing about these men. Like I done said before, the outlaw recognizes the outlaw, and I had little doubts these were the blackhearted sort.

The one who had been kicking the lady came forth and told Moxie he was gonna kill him right here if he didn't get gone and Moxie asked him to do it. The man smiled and I guess he had some real trouble on his hands 'cause he told Moxie there'd be a duel, in an hour, at the far empty end of Dunkle Street, instead of shooting Jimmy as he said he would. Moxie said Dunkle Street was a long street. The man told Jimmy there was work being done, a great rectangle of a hole in the road, men putting in a pipe. He told Jimmy they could stand at either end. 'It looks something like a grave,' he said, 'which ought to make your trip all the faster.' 'That's very kind of you,' Moxie said. 'I try to be kind,' the man answered. 'And let me introduce myself,' the man said, 'I'm Daniel Prouds, I think it important you know the name of the man who kills you.' Moxie held his gaze cold and said 'My name is James Moxie' in return.

Oh, this man Prouds was the classic pig-shit-eating gentleman-outlaw. He wore the watch chain and purple vest and fine pressed pink shirt beneath. He had a black mustache and black hair that came out from under his old white hat. White gloves stained with the struggle he'd had with the lady. Black boots that shone in the sunlight. A finer-dressed outlaw would've been hard to find and almost always them type's the pig-shitters.

'We best be going,' I told Moxie as we left the old man with the loose books and stepped back into the bar. But Moxie wasn't having it. Not that day. I done told him he done never been in a duel and he said I was right. I asked him ain't you worried and he answered yes. But he weren't having us leaving town and I started thinking of life alone on the Trail. It was a long hour I say.

And in that hour people talked. Word traveled that two men were gonna have a shootout and one of them was Daniel Prouds and one of them was an out-of-towner who done stuck his nose in Prouds's business. Moxie told me he needed some time to think. I told him he needed some time to practice. He got up and left me there at the bar and I guess it was either on the walk he took or right then before it that the idea hit him.

The idea that would transcend the Trail.

I don' know who the locals were rooting for 'cause Prouds wasn't a liked man about town but Moxie was in the wrong as far as they could tell. A few knew I'd been riding with the dead-man-to-be and treated me as such. A small cathouse custodian named Rinaldo asked if I thought Jimmy had a chance and I told him I'd be shocked if Moxie didn't win it. And that's how I handled it. I did my part, pretending Moxie was the best un-known gun they'd never seen. But I was full of shudders by then, truth be told, and no longer worried myself o'er how to pay for the beers we'd drank.

Moxie returned just before the hour was up and sat beside me at the bar.

'People are talking,' I said.

'Uh-huh.'

'They say he's good, Jimmy.'

'Uh-huh.'

We waited without talking the last ten minutes of that hour and I swear it that the place went respectfully silent when the two of us rose and walked through the tables. It was funereal, it was. And funereal is a word that ought to only be used near death.

I asked a man which direction the work was being done on the road. Jimmy told me he knew where it was. 'You went and saw it?' I asked him. 'Sure I did,' he said. Well, I figured that wasn't gonna help us any and we walked the long boardwalk like we would the plank. My heart was ticklish it was beating so irregular and I asked Jimmy a couple more times if he was certain before I just shut up, not wanting to mess him up. 'Make sure I get the side with sun in my eyes,' he said. Hell's heaven, I thought, that sure didn't sound like a man who shot a duel before. But Jimmy insisted.

There was already a good crowd when we showed up and I saw some of the people looking at Jimmy and sizing him up, saying So this is him. *I can' tell you if anybody else could see it but I knew my good friend was scared. I don't think I ever seen him exactly like it before. His eyes were polar white and he talked in clipped, half words. I seen sweat coming down the brim of his hat. He was looking out at that hole in the road . . . that rectangle that did look like an exaggerated grave after all.*

Oh, the ominous stuff was out that day.

A man that was neither Prouds nor Moxie suddenly called for the men to come forward and so they did.

I weren't in the huddle when the men chose sides but I can only guess Moxie asked for the side with the sun in his eyes. Much later he'd tell me it was 'cause it was the only side he could ask for and expect to get it. A third party informed the crowd that since the men would be shooting o'er a hole in the earth, there would be no pacing. My heart nearly failed me when they took their places, Prouds on the near side and Moxie on the far with, yes, the sun in his eyes. The well-dressed pig-shitter's back was to me and his suit looked blood purple in the sunlight. Moxie knelt to the dirt and it appeared that he cleared a stone from under his boot and when he came up his face was lit up strong by the sky. I felt sorry his last expression would be so witnessed.

But I had something akin to hope. Maybe just the H of it.

Anybody could see by their stances that Prouds had done it before. And Jimmy looked like a child, a young fool about to spread a lady's legs for the first time. Prouds was stiff as stone.

The moderator stepped to the center edge of the pipe hole. He looked from Moxie to Prouds and announced that all was ready. Both men held their hands at their sides, fingers out, slightly bent forward. Jimmy's hands looked too far from his holster.

I made to say something, to scream it, but the moderator's arm was in the air and he called it

Draw

before I said it.

Prouds moved snakelike but Moxie only made a fist.

There was a shot, a single shot so loud that me and everybody else winced and when I opened my eyes I saw Prouds stumbling . . . his guns still resting useless in his belt . . . his hands at his chest, red blood spilling out and over his fingers. He turned for a moment, still wobbling, and I got one good look at his face, his eyes like rolling marbles, before he fell forward at last, and fell into the hole at his feet.

The crowd was startled silent. To a man, and that includes me, everybody turned their heads to Jimmy who stood there breathing heavy and rocking lightly on the heels of his boots. The moderator didn't know what to say. Nobody did. Jimmy'd performed some kind of magic. Already a rumor'd spread that Jimmy's hand was so fast it was like he hadn't drawn at all. It was the only way to relate to what they'd seen. When they replayed the memory and talked to others who did the same, the idea that Moxie actually didn't draw was galvanized by the power of communal witness. And once they refused the idea of his hand being like lightning, it only left magic as an explanation.

The right one, it seemed.

Suddenly people were talking a lot and I seen the moderator step toward Moxie and I ran out there to be sure Jimmy weren't going to jail, but when I got there the man was only shaking his head, looking at the hand that didn't draw, looking at the cold gun in the holster, and no doubt trying to reconcile it with Prouds's chest exploding deep red all over the pipe. Jimmy didn't say a word. I'd never seen him as cold as I saw him in that moment. 'What you say we skip town?' I asked him. 'You got your books?' he asked. 'My books, Jimmy? Don' you worry none about my books. Let's us wipe the pig-shit from our boots and get the hell's heaven out of Abberstown.'

Already I noted how people were treating him like a legend. Whatever they seen, they never seen it before. We left the witnesses gaping on the street. By nightfall all of Abberstown would know Moxie's name. By week's end most of the Trail.

And by the next time Jimmy and I took to the Trail, everybody in every city was talking about James Moxie and the magic he done sent into Daniel Prouds's good suit.

On the ride out I asked Jimmy how he done it. He shook his head slowly side-to-side and it was the first time I seen him look himself since agreeing to the duel.

'It wasn't magic, Jefferson,' he said.

'I know it weren't. So what was it?'

Jimmy asked me if I remembered the old man looking at my books out back, I said of course I did, he said, 'Yeah, well . . .'

Here the words were already smudged to black by Smoke's oil and flames.

AT THE MANDERS FUNERAL HOME

Manders sat at his desk and frowned.

The diggers were complaining of a figure lurking about the grounds. Manders had just received a delivery he was happy for when the diggers came in and told him they'd seen a man in and out of the tree trunks bordering the cemetery. Lucas said he might have seen the man up in one of the trees. Manders said that sounded like they were seeing things. No, boss, Lucas said, someone's been around. Manders reminded him it wouldn't be the first time a prowler lurked and Lucas agreed.

But Hank was a bit more shaken. Said he'd heard something fuddling beneath the dirt he was digging for a Missus Winifred Jones's casket. Hank said it got to where he stepped out of the hole he was digging, certain as he was that something was about to break free of the dirt. I thought it was worms at first, he told Manders, but it'd have to've been a hundred thousand worms to make the noise it made. Manders said it sounded like they were hearing things, too, but promised to have the grounds checked for groundhogs and prairie dogs later.

Even Norman was flustered. The unflappable makeup artist came to Manders after the diggers left and told him he'd heard someone talking in the basement. He was working on Missus Jones's lips when he'd heard it. I don't mean to bother you, Norm said, but I don't much appreciate the diggers lurking about the basement while I'm workin'. Of course, Manders told him, you just get back to work and let me know if anyone comes bothering you again. When Norm left, the director wondered. Either his staff was going cuckoo or they had some variation of ghouls. Manders had been hit by ghouls before. No doubt every graveyard along the Trail had. There was nothing a director could do but hire two or three corpse-sitters to watch the grounds all night, and that just didn't make fiscal sense what with the low rate at which something like that happened.

Once, three years back, at six in the morning, Lucas had thought the grass covering one of the graves to be out of sorts (*I knew it wasn't no job me or Hank did, boss*) and Manders gave him the okay to dig. By six thirty he and Hank had uncovered a plot full of old clothing. The body? Manders didn't know. Lucas and Hank sure didn't know. And Manders believed the family didn't really need to, either. Of course Opal was told and Opal put a little time into it, but the truth was it wasn't an easy thing to do, locating the sort of person who would do that. Why do you think they buried the old clothing? Hank asked then. I don't know, Hank, maybe they found better clothes on the body.

As funeral director, Manders heard all sorts of stories. The director in Kellytown woke to find the corpses of four children piled on his roof. The man from Griggsville had eight robberies in one evening, all right out from under his watchman's nose. Manders understood it was part of the trade. Things could get uneasy in any line of work. When yours was death and dying, *uneasy* could look downright deranged.

Lurkers in trees. A hundred thousand worms. Voices in the dressing room.

But the delivery . . . the delivery put Manders's mind at ease.

He was doing the paperwork for Winifred Jones's funeral when he spotted Donald Herricks's boy wheeling something big up the front steps. Manders pulled the drapes aside but couldn't make out what it was. He met the Herricks boy at the front door and the young man told him he'd been sent this way with this box and that's all he knew. Who is it from? Manders asked. I really don't know. Nobody told you? Nobody, sir. All right, Manders said, holding open the door, wheel it on in. Once Herricks had the thing in the main lobby Manders pulled off the blanket and was surprised to find a Bellafonte. A gorgeous Bellafonte, Manders would say, the oak painted a rich yellow and a fine orange, and the longer he looked at it the more he felt it might actually be the nicest casket he'd ever seen in his career. Young man, he said, not looking at the delivery boy, are you positive no letter was attached? The kid Herricks reached into his pockets and pulled out a sheet of paper and handed it over to Manders. I'm sorry, he said, slipped my mind. I thought so, Manders said. Something this nice doesn't come from nowhere.

But after reading the letter it turned out it had. Three words, FOR CAROL EVERS, was all the paper boasted. No sender. No signer. No condolences and no words of explanation.

Manders asked if maybe there wasn't another piece of paper and the boy checked his pockets and said, no, I remember now, that really was the only piece. Manders found the arrival of this Bellafonte just about the most curious thing he'd ever encountered. But as he ran his fingers along the wonderfully smooth edges, the beautifully finished wood, he realized the casket made him happy. Happy because it lent the first bit of class to Carol Evers's funeral since he'd found out she'd died. It was nice to see *someone* was giving the ceremony some thought. Could it have been sent by Dwight? Manders didn't think so. In fact, the question survived less time in his musings than whether the staff outhouse needed a lock.

He circled the massive casket, looking at it from all angles. Hank and Lucas came in covered in grass and Lucas asked if that wasn't a

Bellafonte. Manders smiled and said it sure was and that it was for Carol Evers. Lucas said them things are built to last. Manders said it'd take a mother draft horse robbed of her baby to break free of that thing. Hank said they might need some extra hands carrying it and Manders said he was happy the Manders Funeral Home would no longer be responsible for putting a lady like Carol Evers into the ground in a Benson.

JOHN'S TWO-SIDED MIRROR

She saw her fingers lift. In the glass. Saw them move. The real her. Not the her that, until today, could do nothing in Howltown, never could. It was the other her, the physical her that Hattie so longed to assist, the her that, had Hattie seen her fingers move, would've leapt out of her skin, considering it the single most important breakthrough in either of their lives.

Yes, the sleeping Carol, the one the town would bury, *that* Carol moved her fingers in the glass. And after that, with the incredible enthusiasm of having broken through, even at all, Carol focused her attention on her head.

And as her head turned slowly toward the glass, as the woman reflected did the same, Carol heard the hoarse wheezing, the monster who had lit her coma, the monster who wanted, no doubt, for her to see all that came her way. She heard it approaching fast, as though upon horseback, a sickly wheezing that did not necessarily indicate poor lungs, but spoke rather of no lungs at all; a thing beyond life and death.

A thing called Rot.

And by the time Rot arrived at the carriage, Carol heard no hooves, and she knew the creature had flown, soared, floated to where she lay, trying so hard to conquer Howltown.

When Rot opened the coach door, Carol's head was not facing the mirror. She was looking up, as she had been on the stone slab in the cellar. And the look upon the fiend's face, the one she could barely see, suggested he knew something unacceptable was afoot in the coach. The one thing he simply could not allow.

Progress.

He stared long at the glass Dwight had put in the coach.

Then, with the same cold palm that had rolled her over, Rot touched Carol once more. And out of the corner of her eye, in the glass, she saw the same hand emerging from the shadows of the coach, settling upon her flesh. Somehow the reflection was worse. It was one thing—a nightmare—to be touched in the coma, but the horror of knowing it was happening in a world in which she could not wake was leviathan.

Carol did not move.

Soon she heard the unmistakable exhale of a satisfied man. And she believed that whatever she had done to alert him, to bring him to the coach, was no longer his sole concern.

Then he was off again, as though needing to address much more than Carol herself.

Or as if he understood that, no matter how hard Carol tried to move, to wake, to live, she would not succeed.

And the moment he was gone, Carol tried to do all three again.

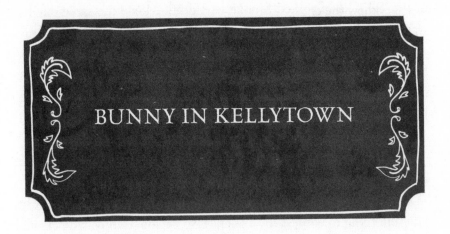

BUNNY IN KELLYTOWN

It was evening, not dark yet, and the Kellytowners were either leaving their homes for the taverns or eating dinner as families inside. Kellytown, like Harrows, was one of the wealthier towns on the Trail. Bankers, tradesmen, and horse owners called the fancy nook home, but the thing Kellytown was best known for was oil.

Edward Bunny witnessed the destruction Smoke wreaked at the schoolhouse. He'd heard many stories about the hit man's anger, but seeing it in person was something different. Watching from the woods near the junk-littered yard of the man who used to run with James Moxie, Bunny thought the triggerman was more demon than madman. The killing of the hermit was ghastly, but Bunny had seen a lot of gore in the towns on the Trail. The fire, though, the flames curling out the schoolhouse windows, black smoke coming out the chimney and doors, and Smoke standing before it like an insane child: Bunny couldn't stop the hairs on his arms from rising.

He knew Smoke hadn't caught up to James Moxie yet, and that's really what Lafayette wanted to know. Bunny guessed that whoever hired the hit man was worried lest Moxie make it all the way to Harrows. When Bunny first heard the story, through the greasy grapevine of the Trail, he imagined Smoke would kill Moxie the same day he was hired. Moxie hadn't ridden in a long time and, no matter the myth, the man's bones had to be tired, his body slower, his mind a little loose. But Lafayette, or whoever Lafayette was asking for, was right to worry. From where Edward Bunny watched, it looked like James Moxie's lead on Smoke might not lessen. At least not before the legendary outlaw reached Harrows.

Too many stops, Bunny thought, sitting by a window in a tavern in Kellytown. *Too many distractions. Too crazy.*

He frowned and sipped from a glass of lemonade. Yes, it was a very different thing to witness the Trail tales in person. Bunny had personally seen more than one average occurrence rendered big myth by word of mouth. He thought most outlaws had names they didn't deserve, and most triggermen were less dangerous than the lawmen. The Trail needed a man like himself. A smart man who saw the truth of the Trail. If not for Edward Bunny, every baby-faced pig-shitter would be a legend and all men entering saloons would do so with the cocky stride of an epic.

But Smoke at the schoolhouse. This was the real thing.

He sipped his lemonade and watched quietly out the window as the tavern grew louder behind him. He didn't recognize any outlaws and he thought that was good. Tracking a man on the Trail was easy work, and he wasn't in the mood for excess chatter. The rich Kellytowners didn't know who he was. If they were told he was a man of the Trail, he would probably be asked to leave. Bunny, like the outlaws and hit men he despised, was not without his own hyperbolic history.

Smoke needed to stop in Kellytown because Smoke was low on oil. This, Bunny thought, was silly. The Cripple could have made ground on the outlaw had he not stopped to burn the schoolhouse down. And now he had to stop twice because of it.

Bunny tailed him to a Kellytown depot and decided to wait in the tavern until Smoke was done. He was interested to know how those legs were refilled, but the safety of a cool glass of lemonade in a slightly distant saloon won out.

And now Bunny was restless. It'd been near twenty minutes and he looked about the tavern for a game he could get into. He knew the Kellytowners were high rollers compared with most residents of Trail-towns, and he saw it as a chance to make a lot of money. Sipping his drink, he observed some games and decided on the one he'd join. As he rose from his seat, planning to introduce himself with a false name to the pig-shit bankers seated at a four-top, he saw Smoke limp by the front window at last. He finished his lemonade and set it on the wood counter. The bartender asked if he'd like another and Bunny didn't answer, already slipping through the saloon doors.

Outside he did not see Smoke. He couldn't be far, Bunny knew, not with those legs, and the hit man's powerful horse—no doubt stolen—was hitched near the entrance to town. Yet the pebbled road was empty.

He continued in the direction he'd seen Smoke going. He glanced casually into storefronts and taverns, looked long down side streets and alleys. When he got to the edge of Kellytown's Orchard Road he smelled something that made him stop.

Burning oil.

Bunny looked up and saw a thin column of black smoke rising above the green treetops. He wiped his forehead with his brown jacket sleeve and shook his head. Smoke was a little mad, yes, but he was just like all the other pig-shit toughers who let every little distraction stop him on the way to doing a job. What was he burning now? These men were dumb, Bunny thought, and their dumbness made them easy to track. He would tell Lafayette that Smoke was too busy torching meaningless trifles to catch James Moxie, no matter how long it'd been for the legend. Lafayette could tell whoever'd hired him he had every right to worry. James Moxie might be rusty, but hell's heaven he was more mobile than Smoke.

More focused, too.

Shaking his head, Bunny took a small road running alongside the heavy foliage that hid the source of the fire. A strong wind passed, and Bunny could smell that he was closer. He stepped to the border of trees and split the branches with his bare hands. He couldn't see for the shadows and the black smoke, but this was certainly where it was. Good at hiding, Bunny walked a little farther ahead and slipped into the woods.

All these triggermen were the same. Pig pellets for brains.

When he was close enough to see the source, a small pile of bricks in a clearing, he did not see Smoke anywhere near it. Bunny stepped lightly through the woods.

Hiding behind the trunk of a big tree, Bunny waited. Smoke would return. Whatever he was doing here didn't make any sense and so he'd return and make sense of it. Sweat fell from Bunny's thin hair. He scanned the woods surrounding the small fire and then saw something *inside* the fire that made him look closer. Smoke, it looked like, was burning something after all. Whatever it was, Bunny wanted to see it. It wasn't even a matter of informing Lafayette. Bunny just wanted to know. He stepped quietly from around the trunk and thought he saw it was a playing card, the Two of Storms, when he tripped, his black boot connecting with something that sounded like tin.

He grunted as he fell. A stick jabbed him in the nose and his knee hit a rock but none of this registered as quickly as the slick boot heel upon his throat, threatening to crush him.

In the soft sunlight and shadows, Bunny saw Smoke above him.

"You following me, Bunny?"

Bunny couldn't talk. He gagged and his face was red and with his hands he tried to move Smoke's heel but couldn't. He kicked and flailed and Smoke pressed harder.

"Stay still, Bunny."

The smell of burning oil choked him and Smoke's boot choked him and Bunny's face was changing from red to purple quick.

"You want a drink, Bunny?"

Smoke slid his boot along Bunny's throat until the tip was pressing hard on the apple. Saliva sloshed out the sides of Bunny's mouth.

"You *do* wanna drink, don't you."

Smoke turned until the boot heel was over Bunny's mouth. Then he fingered the string in his pocket and pulled.

The fresh oil came fast, thick, and filled Bunny's open mouth.

The Trail-watcher writhed and gurgled beneath it, trying to scream. His small hands gripped the tin-shin. Oil pooled on the ground surrounding his head.

"I need your help on a couple of things, Bunny," Smoke said.

Choking, Bunny spit as much out as he could.

Smoke slid his boot again, and now the heel was back on Bunny's throat. Bunny looked up at the triggerman through glasses wet with oil. Despite his desperation, he couldn't help but notice Smoke's hair, half cut.

"I've been seeing two sets of tracks," Smoke said, "when there should only be one. You with the outlaw?" Then Smoke looked up, to the sky, as if thinking. "But that don't make sense, does it. You're right here with me. Any idea who those second tracks belong to?"

Bunny struggled but Smoke eased the pressure enough to let him speak.

"There's a hundred set of tracks on the Trail!" Bunny blurted. "You *pig-shit fool!*"

Smoke reapplied the pressure. "A pig-shitter? Me? Might be. Might be so. You think I'm . . . overthinking, Bunny?"

Bunny gargled a bundle of throaty syllables.

"Might be," Smoke said. "Might be so."

"Get offa me!" Bunny was able to say.

Smoke shook his head no. "I told you I needed your help on a couple of things. That means I got one more request. That okay, Bunny?"

Bunny struggled to nod.

"Do this pig-shitter fool a favor, Edward, will you?"

Flame came to life between Smoke's fingers, and Bunny's eyes grew wide.

"Will you?"

Bunny wiped oil from his face with his hands.

"Tell me which cards represent the men who took my legs."

Garbled syllables came forth in answer, and Smoke eased the pressure on Bunny's neck.

"Say it again, Bunny."

The woods were quiet save the struggle. Smoke listened very close. "And?"

Again, leaning closer, bending at the waist, Smoke only listened. "And? And?"

After Bunny was through, Smoke did not smile. He did not sing or howl or rhyme. With his boot still hard on Bunny's throat, he bent forward and took hold of the deck of cards in the secret pocket of Edward Bunny's brown jacket. Bunny struggled but Smoke had no trouble tearing it loose. Then he rose to standing again and held the cards before him, leafing through the yellowed deck, stopping at the four cards Bunny had struggled to name. They were all four of them the same suit, Knives, and they were all four of them together in a row.

"You don't drink," Smoke said, looking again at the red face beneath his boot.

Bunny couldn't respond. He couldn't do anything but look up at one of the dozens of pig-shitters who needed someone like him to watch over them.

"Let me buy you one, anyhow."

A fresh match came to life between Smoke's fingertips. Bunny tried to scream.

The oil glistened on Bunny's lips and teeth. Smoke removed his boot heel at last.

As the blessed gust of oxygen entered Bunny's throat, Smoke let the match fall.

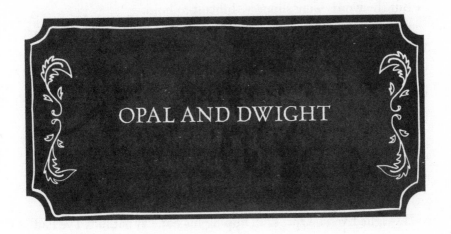

OPAL AND DWIGHT

Dwight saw the silhouette in the distance but couldn't tell who it was. A conclave of cardinals rose from in front of the horse's hooves, a red curtain appearing then pulled aside as the birds settled on the thick branches of the willows lining the Trail.

The silhouette remained upon its horse.

Dwight was at the helm of the family's curtained coach, the gray steeds moving strong and steady. The cardinals sang as he snapped the reins.

Then, enough light, the right angle, and Dwight saw it was the sheriff.

Carol was still in the coach.

There may come a convergence, Lafayette had said, *where what you're doing crosses paths with the inquisitive law. And when it does . . . you are a grieving man and nothing more.*

Dwight, trembling, suddenly cold, saw Lafayette's wrinkled face in his mind's eye; saw her ponytail swinging with the winds of always being right.

Dwight gripped the reins and told himself, *You are a grieving man and nothing more, a grieving man and nothing more, a grieving man . . .*

But the words were slippery, difficult to hold.

Evening was at hand and Opal sat patiently on his still horse. Dwight slowed the coach down a pace and ran a hand through his hair, matting it down as best he could. The shadows of the overhanging willows played tricks with the shape, but there was no questioning the stance of a lawman armed with questions.

Despite the nerves, Dwight had rehearsed this moment many times.

He slowed the coach gracefully to a stop beside the waiting sheriff. "Evening, Sheriff Opal."

"Dwight Evers," Opal said, tipping his hat. "What luck I've had."

"Were you looking for me? Out here on the Trail?"

"Indeed I was. Done exhausted all the finer restaurants already."

Dwight smiled. "You flatter me, Opal. Nor do you know me that well. I've been eating beef brisket all my life."

Opal smiled, too. "You mind coming down from up there so's you and I can have a little chat?"

Dwight set the reins upon the black cushion and climbed down. Opal dismounted at the same time and the men faced each other at the northernmost tip of the Trail.

"What is it that has you searching Harrows for its newest widower, Sheriff?"

"Well, that's just it, isn't it? I have some questions about the passing of your wife."

Dwight feigned surprise. "Is that right? Go on, then. I should like to know what mystery beguiles you."

Opal removed his hat and wiped his forehead with the sleeve of his shirt. "I understand you must be broken up and I'd like to apologize in advance for anything I say that might offend."

"Go ahead, Sheriff. I'm a man as much as any. Surely I can assist the law no matter what spell of grief I may be under."

"That's fine. Very nice. I'd like to know what it is your wife died of."

Dwight breathed deep. "I'm not sure. The doctor told me it was a combination of things. A weak heart it seems."

"And which doctor was this?"

"This was my good friend Alexander Wolfe."

"Wolfe. I don't recognize the name. Where does Doctor Wolfe usually practice?"

"In Charles. Alexander and I go far back. I used to visit him when he was still in medical school."

"Is that right?"

"That it is."

"Well, the reason I ask, and don't go thinking me jumping to any conclusions here, is because Alexander Wolfe didn't show up in any registry I could get my hands on and I'm concerned maybe he isn't the best man to tell you how it happened."

"I thought you said you didn't know the name of the doctor I brought her to?"

"I misspoke."

Silence. Momentary.

"You looked him up?" Dwight asked.

Opal nodded.

"That sounds something like you're checking up on me, Sheriff Opal."

"Does it?"

"I'd say so."

"Well?"

Dwight tried to look confused. "Well what, Sheriff?"

"Can you tell me why Wolfe isn't listed?"

Dwight brought a hand to his chin and feigned consideration. "No, I don't think I can. Unless he's pulled one over on half of Charles and his good friends like me. Alexander Wolfe is a recommended specialist. I've known him since he was back in medical school."

Opal studied Dwight's face. The way the man's lips moved. His darting eyes.

"You said as much. But a doctor you personally thought capable of determining the cause of your wife's passing, surely such a man is registered. Official, as they say."

"I'm not sure I agree with you there. My being his friend might have kept me ignorant of any lack of credentials. But I'm not concerned with that. I believe in Alexander Wolfe."

"If I ride on out to Charles I'm bound to find the man myself?"

"Well, of course."

"I just might do as much. Maybe he can tell me himself why I'm having the trouble I am verifying him."

"May I ask what the need is?"

"Well, a lady passes in my town and I like to know the reason. Maybe it was something she drank. Maybe it was in the beef. A man in my line of work doesn't love unverifiable ends."

"No, I imagine you wouldn't. But I'm telling you I know the man and saw him check my wife myself."

"I understand all that. Just want to make sure you were with the best man for the job."

"I see. For a moment it sounded as though you were wondering whether or not he exists."

Opal watched Dwight closely.

"When did he check her, Mister Evers?"

"When?"

"That's right."

"The evening she collapsed."

"Charles is a bit of a ride. You do all that in the dark?"

"It wasn't quite nightfall. I carried lanterns, if you must have these details to complete your picture."

"There are plenty of doctors here in Harrows. Doctor Walker is excellent. And he knows the Illness inside out."

"I do think you're overstepping here. A man can go to any doctor he chooses."

"Of course. But seeing the urgency of your wife's state . . ."

"There was no urgency."

"No?"

"No. She was beyond assistance."

"I see."

"Do you?"

"How's that?"

"I can't help but get the feeling you're not believing me."

Opal smiled. "Like I said, I'm not a big fan of the unknown."

"Remember that I am a grieving man."

And nothing more, Dwight thought.

"I do."

The men were quiet again. Leaves blew over their boots on the trail.

"Look, I can tell you're upset by my questions here, but if you'd just stomach through a couple more, I can walk away feeling as peaceful as an old pig."

"That would be fine."

"Your family will be dressing the body."

"Indeed. My sister and her husband."

"And where is she now?"

"Carol?"

"Yes, sir. I'm sorry to ask."

Suddenly, horrifically, Dwight thought maybe Opal had already been to his house. He weighed what to say next with delicacy.

"She's with them now. I'm returning from there myself."

Opal nodded. It was the answer he was hoping for. If Dwight had said she was at home, he would be lying. And a man lying about the whereabouts of his deceased wife was nothing but a bad thing.

"Your sister a mortician?"

"Her husband is, yes. She knows something of it, too."

"Whereabouts?"

Dwight pointed beyond the Trail.

"An hour in that direction, Sheriff."

"An hour? By coach, I bet."

"Yes, by coach."

Opal put his hat back on his head.

"Let me ask you one more thing, Mister Evers. You hear your house girl shriek and go and find your wife on the floor, not breathing . . .

terrible thing to discover. You drive your coach to a good friend of yours, hoping he could tell you what went wrong. Then what?"

"I drove back to Harrows. I went to see Manders."

It was not lost on Dwight that Opal knew of Farrah's having been present when Carol collapsed. Had he spoken with her? Dwight suddenly felt empowered for not having smothered Carol or pinching her nostrils shut. Not all of Lafayette's suggestions were wise. Dwight knew right from wrong, too. Farrah could be pointing a finger at him already, and the line it made would go directly to any marks upon Carol's body, any sign of a struggle at all.

"And where was Carol throughout?"

"While I saw Manders?"

"That's right. Usually a man delivers the body to someone like Manders right away."

"I put Carol upstairs," Dwight said. He felt sure he was revealing something. Treading close to getting caught in a small lie. And small lies had a tendency to grow big. "But I couldn't bear to look upon her there in our bed. So, I am somewhat bothered to say, I carried her to the cellar. We have a storm room down there and I suppose I thought the table in there as good a spot as any to keep her before my brother-in-law had a chance to dress her."

Opal nodded. The story lined up with what Farrah told him. Opal just didn't like the story.

"Well, I'll tell you, I wouldn't mind a chance at talking to that Alexander Wolfe. If you can make that happen, I'd be much obliged. Again, it's my duty to keep Harrows safe. Who knows what he doesn't even know he discovered. Something even a registered doctor might not."

Dwight nodded.

"I'll get him for you. I trust that after you've met him you will feel the same as I do; that is, it doesn't matter whether or not he's in one of your books."

Opal thought of Manders knocking on his door at midnight. He thought of Farrah in the cellar.

"Here's what I'd like, Mister Evers. I'd like to meet this Alexander Wolfe as soon as you can get him, which, according to your story, you being so close, shouldn't be difficult."

"My story?"

"Let me put it to you this way. If you don't produce the doctor, there'll be some trouble. I'll have questions and more questions until you do. And who knows what sort of thoughts I'll start thinking regarding who determined your wife's death and whether she was seen at all."

Dwight looked crazed into Opal's eyes. "That's a *terrible* thing to say . . ."

"Do you understand me, Dwight?"

"I do."

"And?"

"And . . . and I will."

"That's good. That'll do just fine. Now let me see inside the coach."

Dwight froze.

The command. So sudden.

Opal waited.

"You want to see inside the coach? This coach?"

Opal looked to the black wood of the black door.

"That very."

"Of course."

Dwight headed for the coach. His heart beat heavy and he wondered if Opal might not hear it. At the door, he placed his hand upon the handle and faced Opal once more.

"You'll excuse me, but nothing makes me sadder than looking upon the very bench I once shared with Carol."

He opened the door.

Opal looked inside.

It was a fine two-bencher, the seats facing each other, adorned with identical purple cushions.

"Thank you, Mister Evers."

"Surely you weren't expecting to find—"

"I wasn't expecting to find anything. I apologize for the intrusion."
Dwight shut the door.

In that moment, he looked like a grieving man to Opal.

"Is that all, Sheriff?"

"Thank you. That's it. Please understand that as sheriff—"

"No need to explain yourself. I understand. What with the Illness so close."

Opal nodded. Then he left Dwight alone with the coach.

He mounted his horse and headed south along the Trail to Harrows. Things still bothered him. Greatly. Heading into the meeting with Dwight, he had no real intention of going so hard at him. But between Manders's uncertainty, Farrah's testimony, and the perfect series of answers Mister Evers gave him, his instincts told him not to hold back. The thing a man like Dwight Evers didn't know was that men who told the truth had holes in their stories. More so than the liars. There were holes in reality, Opal mused, but none in a good cover story. Carol Evers was set to be buried tomorrow morning. Whether or not Dwight produced the doctor, he'd have Manders and Norm give her a closer look. It'd be a good thing to have her body on hand.

Dwight just didn't seem . . . *angry* enough for having been questioned.

As Opal rode out of sight, Dwight waited. Then he waited some more. Then he opened the door to the coach once again.

The stranger in his bedroom this morning had been right. The shroud who woke him had helped.

Hide your lady.

Opal had been in the cellar, Dwight had no doubt.

Reaching into the coach, he removed the angled mirror that hid Carol's sleeping body. Dwight smiled. To think that Opal must have assumed there were two benches. Two pillows.

Seeing his wife upon the floor was a particular delight for Dwight. So moneyed in life, so poor in death.

He placed the mirror back where it was, where Opal had been

fooled by it, and closed the coach door. He climbed back up to the driver's box and snapped the reins hard. The cardinals took flight, perhaps aware that a man had escaped a hanging, perhaps simply searching the field for mice.

The lawman needed more . . . the doctor . . . proof. There wouldn't be time to produce Alexander Wolfe before the burial. That was okay. For now. But Dwight would have to think of something soon.

Riding again, Dwight thought of Opal. The clever sheriff who was only a few feet from the body he longed to examine.

"I thank you for not waking," Dwight called over his shoulder. "Would've been very bad for me."

What had Farrah told Opal? What did she know?

Anger wrangled his heart but there was patience in there, too.

After all, things were falling into place.

He had help, though he didn't want to think too hard on who it was that was helping him.

The shifting faces. The voice like a casket creaking closed.

Carol would be in the ground tomorrow morning.

Hell's heaven, Dwight was close.

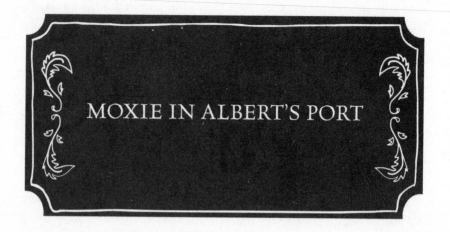

MOXIE IN ALBERT'S PORT

Albert's Port was a midsized Trail-town that was 93 percent surrounded by the Ossiwak River. People who lived close called the river the O not only for the first letter of its name but because of the nearly complete circle it made. For this, the only entrance into Albert's Port was over a lengthy wooden bridge. From there, a passer-through took Manage Street straight to another, wider, bridge at the north side of town. As Moxie rode Old Girl into Albert's Port, her hooves clacked loud against the boards and the sun was lowering, purple in the sky once again, the day's bookends, and the outlaw was required to introduce himself to a lawman stationed on the town side of the bridge.

"James Moxie," he said, patting Old Girl gently on the back.

The officer spat on the ground.

"I may do my living here in the middle of nowhere, sir, but that don't make me lost."

"Officer?"

"You arnt James Moxie any more than I am."

"Am I not?"

"You don't look like him."

"Have you ever seen him?"

"No, sir. I sure haven't. But he don't look like you."

Moxie stared cold into the lawman's eyes. Such a small obstacle, it seemed to Moxie, this man, taking up so little of the space between himself and Carol.

"What if I told you my name was John?" Moxie said.

"I'd think it was more like your real name."

"My name is John, then. I'm heading to Harrows. I'll be passing through. Nothing more."

"If you're James Moxie," the officer said, crossing his arms, "tell me how you did it and maybe I'll let you through."

"That was long ago, Officer. I don't recall the details."

"You arnt James Moxie."

"Do I need to convince you?"

"You can start by telling me how you did it in Abberstown. I'm sure Harrows can wait. It'll be there whenever it is you arrive."

"Harrows can't wait."

"Is that right?"

Moxie's eyes flashed white in the darkening sky. "This is how it's going to go, lawman. I'm going to say good day to you now, and pass straight through your town on my way to Harrows."

"You can pass all you want. I arnt allowed to stop you. But I'll sure as pig-shit keep my eye on you every half second you're here."

"That's fine."

"Is it fine? I wonder."

The officer stepped aside, and Moxie rode by him on the mare.

Dark-red letters on a wooden stake welcomed the outlaw to Albert's Port. Beyond it he could see the canopies and storefronts, the masts for small boats on the river, the horses tied to hitching posts, and the people upon the planked boardwalks. From a shadowed awning, two more lawmen on horseback emerged.

Moxie watched them come.

"Our boy up front flashed his badge. That's a bad sign. Means we got to quit doing what we're doing and watch you."

Moxie didn't respond. The men flanked him as he rode.

"What do you suppose the reason was for us coming out to meet you?"

"Don't know, Officers."

"Sure. Don't know. Frank didn't say nothing? Didn't mention why he didn't like you?"

"I didn't note whether he liked me or not."

"We arnt children, now," the other officer said, chuckling. "Surely he said something."

Moxie kept his eyes on the road.

"He didn't believe I am who I say I am."

"Is that right? That's suspicious now. What name you give him?"

Moxie breathed deep.

"Mine."

"Uh-huh. And what name is that?"

"James Moxie."

The lawmen laughed. One spat in the dirt.

"You arnt James Moxie, fella. And if you were we'd put you away on your name alone."

"That's right, I am," Moxie said.

"Bill," the second officer said. "Bill ... what was it Moxie did? What did he do again?"

"He done outdueled a man without ever drawing is what he did."

"How's that?"

"That's it all right."

Moxie saw the bridge at the north side of town now.

"Tell me, James Moxie," Bill said. "How does a man draw blood without ever drawing the gun?"

Moxie answered, "He doesn't."

Bill laughed without humor.

"But I wanna know," he said. "How does a man do a thing like that?"

"He doesn't."

"No. He sure doesn't."

Citizens of Albert's Port came out of the storefronts. The colorful evening sky reflected in the glass of the doors they opened. Moxie saw faces behind windows, men holding the reins of their horses, little boys and girls whose play could wait.

"I'll give you once more," Bill said, cutting Moxie's mare off with his own. "What's your business here?"

Moxie stopped the mare.

"My business is up in Harrows. My horse needs water and I could use some myself. Albert's Port has more water than you can bottle. Otherwise, I have no business here."

"And your name?"

"My name is still James Moxie."

"All right," Bill said. Moxie knew what would happen next before it did. "We're gonna bring you inside for a minute is what we're gonna do."

Moxie looked to the northern bridge. So close to the continuation of the Trail.

"Take me inside then."

Bill dismounted and took the reins of both horses. He guided them up Manage Street to the Albert's Port jail. People whispered and the lawmen told them there was nothing to see, no excitement. At the jail, Moxie dismounted. He stuck his arm into the bag he'd gotten from Jefferson's schoolhouse.

Bill quickly put his hand on Moxie's shoulder. "What do you got in there?"

Moxie looked at him. "Water for Old Girl."

The lawman shook his head no. "Let me see."

Moxie removed his hand and Bill looked inside the bag. He saw there a pouch of water.

"The mare's not lying about her name," he said. "And she could really use some."

Bill studied Moxie's face and turned to the other officer.

"Wesley, get the horse some water."

Then he led Moxie inside.

The station was like others the outlaw knew from his riding days.
Jefferson and Moxie had seen many. Six barred cells made a hall beyond two wooden desks. The place was clean, the desks clear of clutter, indicating to Moxie that the sheriff reclining in her chair would
be a tough one. The prisoners came to the bars to see who had been
brought in.

"Looks like another fool!" someone cackled.

The sheriff, fanning herself with a folded wanted poster, removed
her boots from the desk and stood up.

"Who we got here?" she asked, her eyebrows arched like the hands
of a clock. Time ticking away.

"Man gave a false name," Wesley said.

"That right? What name he give?"

"James Moxie."

The two lawmen snorted laughter but the sheriff eyed Moxie as if
they'd brought in something poisonous to the touch.

Moxie said, "I need to be in Harrows."

"What's that again?"

"Ordinarily I'd oblige you, but I have business in Harrows."

The sheriff cleared her throat. "That's very sweet of you, stranger,
but it doesn't work that way."

"On what grounds are you locking me up?"

She fanned a hand to the hall of cells. "You see these cells? These
are men who claimed they'd be passing through for a night. Albert's
Port is a nice town, you see, and I'm something of the janitor. Call me
Sheriff Marge and I'll call you by your rightful name the moment you
give it to us."

An old man gripped the bars of his cell and snarled at Moxie.

"Did he lie about his name, too?" Moxie asked.

The sheriff's face grew grave. Then graver. "No, sir. He drowned a
woman in the O is what he done."

Sheriff Marge pulled from her belt a ring of keys. The deputy came
in behind Moxie and the sheriff said, "Take his gun, Dep Bill. He's
been fingering it since entering."

The deputy took Moxie's gun.

Sheriff Marge unlocked the cell opposite the old killer and looked at the outlaw.

"Consider this a free hotel," she said. "On us."

Moxie stepped inside. A vision of the sun going down on Harrows dimmed his mind's eye.

"Sheriff," Moxie said. "Please. I don't have time."

She locked the cell door.

"Nobody does, stranger. Or shall we call you . . . No Name."

Then she walked back to her desk. Her boots hard against the clean wood floor. The deputy, still holding Moxie's gun, stood before the outlaw's cell.

"James Moxie, huh."

Moxie didn't respond. He was thinking of dirt piled so high it obscured the moon in Harrows.

The deputy talked about the Trick at Abberstown. The way he told it, James Moxie had hired a second shooter, a comrade in the crowd.

"All those toughers had friends in those days. Yessir. Nowadays it's every man for himself on the Trail. But back then—"

As he spoke, Moxie heard a whisper from the shadows of the empty cell beside his. It was clear the deputy hadn't heard it and Moxie turned and saw the silhouette of a man lying down on a bunk.

"What kind of man turns his back on a sick woman? What kind of man leaves her that way?"

The whisper was steady, the syllables like small bullets fired.

The deputy went on. "James Moxie might be the most frightening outlaw the Trail has ever known because he's the only one who's been able to keep his secret. You hear what I'm saying, No Name? You know he was never properly put away?" The deputy shook his head, studied Moxie's gun in his palm. "You sure picked a poor name to give."

The man in the cell beside Moxie's sat up and Moxie recognized his face.

Silas Hite, he thought. The man whose house he'd carried Carol's limp body to the first time he'd feared she'd died.

"I told you that night behind the barn," Silas said, his voice like stirring milk. *"I told you a man can't quit someone he loves because he's scared. I told you so . . . but you did . . . didn't you? You broke her heart 'cause she was sick, James."*

"Hey, Wesley!" the deputy called. "What do you think James Moxie looks like? You think he looks like this man here? Red shirt and tired?"

Wesley laughed from his desk.

Silas Hite stepped to the bars adjoining Moxie's cell. *"Look at you . . . here . . . in jail . . . just when you're trying to do right."*

"Bad men feared him," Deputy Bill went on. *"Good* men feared him, the law wanted him—"

Sheriff Marge got up again and joined the deputy in the hall of cells. "He's still a wanted man," she said.

"This long after?" Bill asked.

Sheriff Marge looked at Moxie with a mix of sarcasm and suspicion. As if she hadn't quite ruled out that it was him. "Just because we're on the side of the law, Dep Bill, don't make us any less curious how it was done. Not to mention a man *did* die that day."

The deputy carried on from there, studying the gun as he spoke: the fine woodwork, the shine of the old steel. Behind him, the old crook who'd drowned the woman in the O told what he knew about James Moxie, the stories he'd heard. And Silas Hite went on.

"You let her rot, James. You broke her heart and a better man came and held her 'cause she was sick . . . sick, James . . ."

"Leave me alone," Moxie said through clenched teeth.

The sheriff looked at him quick and hard. "What's that?"

Moxie kept quiet and Deputy Bill continued. Sheriff Marge started telling all that she'd heard other sheriffs say about Moxie. The old killer giggled and crowed and Moxie kept still, the town of Harrows diminishing, Carol's burial coming at him too soon, too fast.

Silas hissed profanities. Sheriff Marge spoke of Abberstown. The crook sang a Trail song until the sheriff shut him up.

Moxie watched his gun closely, resting in the deputy's hand.

"I heard James Moxie killed seven men in Kellytown while playing a hand of cards. Both his hands were occupied with the cards ... never touched his gun ..."

"... James Moxie used to live in the trees on the Trail ... he hid bodies up there ..."

"... heard maybe he kept them alive ... kept them scared ... never used a gun ... people didn't know if and when they'd get shot because he never touched his gun ..."

"... children ... women ... families on the Trail ... a ghost ... a demon ..."

Silas's fingers stretched through the bars and touched Moxie's arm.

"Turn back," Hite whispered. *"Let her rot like you did before. But this time let her rot in the earth. Let her rot, James. It's all you know how to do. It's all you've ever done—"*

Sheriff Marge described yellowing wanted posters, paper that grew old for how long James Moxie rode free on the Trail.

"I tell you what," the old killer said. "I met him once!"

"Did you?" Deputy Bill asked.

"In Baker, I met him once! He was *tall* ... tall as the trees! And his hands were as big as my head! Hell's heaven what I could do with hands like those ..."

Deputy Bill turned toward the old man and the station exploded with smoke and sound and the old killer's chest blew apart, splattering Sheriff Marge's shirt with blood, skin, and bone.

Then, silence in the station.

Sheriff Marge and Deputy Bill stood very still. Their eyes as wide as those of the trout that swam in the O. The gun smoked, proving to both what had happened.

But not the *how* of it.

"Hog-shit, Bill," Sheriff Marge suddenly said. "You shot the man."

But her voice betrayed her doubts.

"I didn't do it, Marge!"

"I saw you shoot him."

But her voice betrayed her doubts.

"I didn't touch the trigger, Marge! I didn't *touch* it!"

The two locked eyes, then slowly turned to face Moxie alone in his cell.

"My name is James Moxie," Moxie said. "And I need to be in Harrows. Now."

Sheriff Marge stared long.

"Holy hell's heaven," she said. "It's him. It's pig-shitting him."

She took the keys quick from her belt.

"Marge, you just gonna . . . let him . . ."

"Give him his gun, Bill."

The gun was still hot. Marge unlocked the cell.

"Give him his *gun*, Bill."

Moxie stepped slow out of the cell. The deputy held out the gun. Moxie took it.

"Now you just . . . just . . ." Sheriff Marge stammered, ". . . you just . . . get on . . . now . . . just . . ."

At the jail door, Moxie heard Silas Hite calling to him, mocking still.

"Let her rot, James . . . it's already begun . . . let the pig-shit earth seep into her pores . . . into her nose . . . into her mouth that once asked you for help . . . that once cried out when you didn't . . ."

Moxie felt the guilt.

The loss of time, too.

"My horse," he said to the trembling officers, both still washed in the gore of the old man killer, "thanks you for the water."

Then he left the jail and, by the wide northern bridge, all of Albert's Port, too.

CAROL IN THE COMA
IN THE COACH

Dwight sat alone on a blanket on Harper's Hill.

The coach and horses stood twenty paces from the idyllic scene: a man in a suit, the blue blanket from the driver's box spread upon the tall grass, a glass of wine. Though a closer look would reveal there was no actual glass, and that the man spoke to someone who was not there.

He did not speak to Carol. Rather, he spoke to the wife he'd always wished he had.

A meek wife. A simple wife. A wife who needed him, a dependent soul who flattered Dwight with all she asked for and who exalted his status in Harrows with all she received.

"Martha, dear, a glass of wine. It's good for you."

Because Dwight would know what was good for her. His wife. A persuadable wife. A wife who cast no shadow.

"We've got a funeral tomorrow, Martha. Burying an old friend. But what I'd like to know is . . . what do you feel like doing after?"

Despite his performance, his voice trembled with having just met Opal on the Trail.

The wind lifted the opposite side of the blanket, and for a moment

Dwight believed a woman named Martha had risen to take in the view.

"Here's what I propose," Dwight said, wiping imaginary wine from his lips. He'd gotten very good at rehearsing. Pretending. Playacting. "I'd like to take you to Griggsville for the afternoon. They've always got such good shows. What do you say, dear? Burial in the morning, theater at night?"

Many years ago, Dwight and Carol took in a magic show in Griggsville. John Bowie had been with them then, and the sexually exotic snot had gotten so drunk he passed out in the theater restroom. Dwight found him in there, lying on his back, and splashed cold toilet water on his face to revive him.

Sipping his imaginary wine, Dwight smiled at how much John Bowie in the washroom looked like John Bowie in the grave.

Unboxed.

"If anybody finds it odd that we've taken in a show on the same day of the funeral, I'll simply explain to them the power of art for the grieving."

Dwight rose and tossed his unseen glass over the ledge of Harper's Hill. North of Harrows, Harper's was as north as many Trail folk had ever been. It was usually barren of people, there being no business to conduct or friends to see; the hill wasn't on the way to anyplace else.

"Martha? What is it? Do you need something? Need something . . . from me?"

It was a good feeling. Being needed. Surely Dwight would find a woman just like Martha. Perhaps there was one at the wake yesterday afternoon. Perhaps a woman felt sympathy for the widower and the hidden machinations behind all romantic convergences had already begun to tick.

Like a clock.

Dwight looked to the coach.

Sheriff Opal had questioned him good on the Trail. Scared him something fierce. But that mirror . . . he wondered if Carol would have realized that he'd gotten the mirror trick from the very show they'd seen in Griggsville. The man on stage made a donkey disappear. John Bowie was so delighted he howled and stood up and an usher had to ask him to settle down.

But poor John Bowie was dead now. Didn't get to see Dwight's trick. A simple slanted mirror. Good enough to fool a lawman.

"Maybe we should ride farther south than Griggsville, Martha," Dwight said, still eyeing the coach. "Maybe we should leave the Trail altogether."

He knelt and rolled up the blanket and when he looked up to the edge of Harper's Hill he imagined himself leaping. He could end this now. Squeeze himself out of this vise-grip of anxiety by running off the edge of the Trail's highest peak. Carol would wake when she woke and life in Harrows would go on without him.

"Martha?"

But there was no Martha, no dutiful wife. Only the independent, brilliant, and beautiful one who'd long made him feel small every time he saw her reflected large in someone else's eyes.

Carol.

Carol's shadow.

Hide your lady.

The stranger in his bedroom. The shape he'd shot.

As he laid the blanket upon the driver's seat, Dwight saw many faces appear then disappear on the skull of the stranger he woke to.

There was Opal demanding to meet Alexander Wolfe, that figment-doctor, invented by Dwight and Lafayette in Lafayette's shack in south Harrows.

Lafayette herself, demanding Dwight rehearse his lines again. Advising against hiring someone to follow Smoke.

Smoke, whom Dwight had never seen before but whom he imagined as having black eyes, leather skin, teeth as hard as tombstones.

Hardly recognizing that he was driving now, that the gray steeds were carrying him back toward his home, more faces came. And with each one, anxiety rekindled.

Farrah Darrow. How much did she know? Anything at all? Surely not enough to send Dwight to the hang-rope, but ... enough to worry Opal?

The messenger boy who had brought him the news that Moxie was coming.

Opal again.

Dwight shook at the thought of returning home to find Opal in the parlor.

Sorry, Evers. I, too, was at that show in Griggsville. John Bowie nearly threw up on my badge.

Another face. Another Dwight had never seen.

James Moxie.

James Moxie knew magic. Had to know it better than John Bowie and certainly knew it better than Dwight.

Perhaps he had mirrors of his own? How could Dwight be sure that the willows he rode past weren't the reflections of the willows across the Trail? That James Moxie wasn't set to leap out from behind a false setting, gun already firing?

Dwight searched the base of the trees. Scanned the shadows.

"Relax," Dwight told himself. "Dammit! *Relax!*"

What did Moxie look like? It was easy to imagine a solid brick of a face. Chips in the mortar from duels on the Trail. A thin line of a mouth that barely spoke. Cavernous eyes from which black winds erupted. And a mind behind those eyes capable of firing guns without drawing them.

"STOP IT!"

Dwight's voice sounded limp among the clatter of the horses' hooves. The creaking of the coach.

And the coach door swinging open and closed. Open and closed behind him.

"What?"

Dwight pulled up hard on the reins. The steeds came to an unnatural stop, both whinnying as they adjusted, the dust rising muzzle-high.

Dwight leaned over, peered around the coach's side.

The door slowly swung closed, connected with the coach, then swung open again.

Dwight looked back down the Trail.

Carol's body? Was it there in the dirt?

"Oh," he moaned and quickly, rabbitlike, got down from the driver's box.

The coach door was swinging closed again and Dwight grabbed its handle and opened it.

Carol was sitting up, eyes open, both hands raised as if reaching for him.

"Oh, no!"

Dwight leapt back from the coach and the door swung closed again. Carol vanished behind the black wood and Dwight stared long at the window.

But the window only reflected the willows behind him.

"Carol?"

Dwight wondered if perhaps he'd snapped. All those faces, all those plans.

"Carol . . . dear?"

He reached for the door and gripped the handle. Surely she would be lying on her back. Surely his anxiety had gotten the best of him. Surely no reality could match the paranoid fantasies of his worried mind.

He opened the door.

Carol was still sitting up, eyes open, hands out and up.

Her expression hadn't changed.

Dwight's did.

"Carol? *Carol!* Oh my . . . oh hell's heaven . . . Carol!"

He stepped toward her, as though to embrace her. Then he stopped.

"Carol?"

She wasn't moving. She did not blink.

"Carol, I thought you were . . ."

He waved a hand close to her face. Her eyes did not follow his fingers.

"Carol," Dwight said, exhaling so deeply it felt as if he'd escaped his own body. "You . . . you're still in Howltown, aren't you?"

He pulled from his pocket a mirror and held it under her nose. Looking from her eyes to the glass, he counted.

The mirror fogged up at second twenty-two.

"Still alive," he said. "Still in that dark city of your own."

He pocketed the mirror.

"I wonder, Carol, how difficult it was for you to reach a sitting position? I wonder what I look like to you right now." He smiled for her. Snapped his teeth. "You've never moved before . . . why now?"

Why now, indeed. Why now when Dwight needed less stress than ever?

He placed a fingertip against her chest.

He pushed.

Carol fell back to the coach's floor. But her fingernail scratched Dwight's face on the way.

"Hey!"

Dwight brought a hand to his cheek and saw, yes, a thin trickle of blood.

They're gonna know. It's a sign of a struggle. THEY'RE GONNA KNOW!

"Stop it!"

His voice, chastising himself, echoed across the open Trail.

He stared at Carol then, flat upon her back in the coach. He imagined Opal asking to check the coach once more, one more time, only to find Carol sitting up as Dwight had seen her.

How? How had it happened? What had changed so that Carol could . . . move?

"It's not fair," he said, kneeling in the dirt by the Trail's edge. He grabbed handfuls of earth and rock. "You never moved before! It's not . . ." He rose and went to the coach. ". . . *fair!*"

Then Dwight shoved the stony dirt up Carol's dress, stuffing it by her waist. He went back to the Trail's edge and took some more. This he shoved down the dress's neckline, jamming it under her shoulders.

He got some more.

He stuffed more of it into her dress.

"Try getting up now," he said. *"Try sitting up now!"*

Dwight made many trips to the Trail's edge, bringing more and more earth to the coach. By the time he was done, satisfied that Carol couldn't possibly rise with the weight he'd added to her dress, he adjusted the mirror so that it reflected the coach, the same way Opal had seen it.

On his quick walk to the driver's box, he thought it an irresistible image, Carol with rocks in her dress, as if she were drowning without water.

He grabbed rope from the box, brought it to the coach door, and tied the door closed.

"This isn't fair," he echoed, his voice shaking enough that, had Opal heard it now, there would be more than suspicion in the lawman's eyes. "It's . . . unjust!"

Dwight climbed up into the driver's box and clacked the reins. The steeds erupted into motion.

"What, Martha dear? Who? Why, that's the old friend we're burying tomorrow. That's the last thing we've got to do."

He snapped the reins again. His voice, he thought, sounded like a child's. And it only scared him more.

How would Carol upright have looked to Manders?

To Opal?

To Moxie?

He passed the big homes of Harrows. Passed even his own. Without realizing he'd made a change of plans, he was in the process of carrying them out.

There was one place he needed to go before returning home. In the hope of removing one of the many faces that he still saw upon the head of the stranger he'd woken to.

"One stop, Martha. Trust me." He thought of Carol on her back, rocks and dirt in her dress. "But you always do trust me, don't you? Yes, you do." He touched the new cut on his face. "Where to? Where are we going? Why, her name is Farrah Darrow. And she needs to be reminded who she works for."

Dwight cried out into the coming night, as blood trickled a thin line across his face. As the steeds crushed pebbles on the rocky Trail, and as his wife, weighed down, did not move with the motion of the coach.

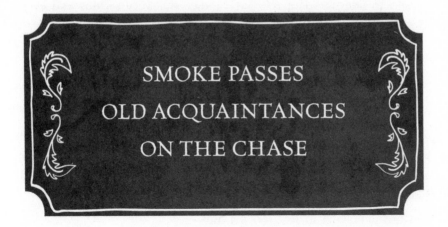

SMOKE PASSES
OLD ACQUAINTANCES
ON THE CHASE

The four of them ate around the small table that greasy-bearded Garr said was more like a stool. They stuffed their faces with rabbit and drank beer that blond Horace had ripped from the cold storage of the town's only tavern. It was evening, the sun had painted the sky the color purple, but there were no windows in the small wood shack and all four of them liked it that way. Overweight Kent had shot the old man who owned the place; his body lay under a blanket outside, beside the hole they shit in. Lewis, the most stable-minded of the lot, was the cook; tonight he turned the rabbit caught in the big woods and the smoke went through a hole in the roof shot through by Kent, too. Horace stood watch, making sure the smoke or smell didn't bring any lawmen, but really he just sat on a stump and smoked a pipe himself. There were no beds in the dirty shack. No bedding. Four days Horace had been putting off going into Albert's Port to get any supplies. He claimed the law in Albert's Port was "ticky-tacky" and would pick a man up for looking confused. The men argued this topic often. Some were getting stir-crazy. Garr wanted to go into town. He growled about men's needs and said there was no reason to live like paupers. But Horace was very serious and even threatened once to turn the others in if anyone went.

It was the trials of traveling with fellow outlaws.

"There's fur on this rabbit yet, Lewis!" Garr said, taking a bite.

"Skin's the best part," Kent answered.

In the corner of the shack, on the dirty wood floor, sat a box of gunpowder the four had stolen two weeks prior. The plan was to sprinkle the stuff in a line around Deputy Pearson's home up near Abberstown and watch the pig-shitter explode. Pearson's men had been tailing the triggermen, and they were getting closer.

But the powder made Garr nervous.

Dead-skulls like you three around and I gotta worry you're gonna drop your smoke right into the box!

"We're gonna need ourselves more beer soon," Kent said, rubbing his belly. "How is it we run out so quick?"

This would pose a real problem and could possibly break the stalemate regarding going into town. Garr's plan was to clean himself up nice with a shave, or to clean Lewis up since he, despite his age, was the baby-face, and send him in as a traveler, someone there to spend his coin. Garr had known tough lawmen in his time and raged at Horace's hyperbolizing the ones in Albert's Port.

"Looks like we'll have to go into town for more," Garr said, looking directly at Horace as he tore meat from the rabbit bones.

Horace knew he had to say something.

"We can go without for a night or so, Garr. We'll steal some on the other side of town."

Garr scowled. "You might do whatever you like, good man. I might do the same."

The wet sound of the men sucking meat from the bone padded the silence between them.

"We done already had this talk, Garr."

"Yes. Many times."

"Many times."

Lewis rose, went to a bucket, and brought back some more rabbit.

"No end to the meat, though," Garr said. "Got plenty of first-rate meat!"

"Pipe it, Garr," Kent said suddenly, grabbing hold of the charred rabbit and tearing a good piece from its neck.

Garr stood up quick and took Kent by the collar. "You don't tell me to pipe anything, understand?"

Horace and Lewis froze. Garr was something like his own big fear . . . the gunpowder . . . all ready to explode . . . just needed a small spark.

"All right, Garr."

"Don't tell me all right!"

"Okay."

Garr let go and sat back down, crashing upon the chair.

"The last time I listened to you three we let a man go we ought to have killed. Had him for dead, had his whole body there before us, and walked away with only his legs."

Horace stared coldly at Garr. Lewis rose and pretended to be minding the meat bucket.

"That's right," Garr said, his mouth full of rabbit. "I'll be listening to myself from now on. And I'm fixing to go into town to get me some things."

The tension was high.

"Do you all smell that?" Lewis suddenly asked, standing by the bucket near the wall. He stuck his nose out.

"And I'll tell you what I'll get when I'm there!" Garr went on, ignoring the cook. "I'm gonna get a damn pillow. A bottle of booze. Some fine pig I can suck on for as long as I want. I'm gonna get a quilt, too. That's right, I am."

"Fellas," Lewis said, stepping from beside the bucket and placing his fingertips against the wall. "Boys . . ."

"A whole rack of lamb is what I'm gonna get! And a good horse, too! I'll find myself the best feed they got and fatten up that horse and ride the beast right out from under their noses, I will!"

"You boys smell that?" Lewis asked again.

Now Garr turned to Horace.

"And whence I do, noble Horace, I'll be sure to send ye a gift box. A box full of rabbit, stale beer, and *pig-shit!*"

Garr cocked his head back and howled delight.

Lewis was at the table now. "You boys smell that?"

Garr stopped laughing.

"Smell what, Lewis?" Horace asked.

"Come here."

The other three got up, and Lewis held out both palms for them to stop moving. "No, wait . . . you can smell it right . . . here."

The men were quiet, their noses in the air.

"All I smell is burnt rabbit," Garr said. "And dirty floors."

"No," Horace said, holding up a hand. "Smells like . . . smells like oil."

Garr scowled. "Now, how in hell's heaven could it smell like oil? I know I weren't lucky when I met you louses and I know we arnt sitting on any oil."

"It is oil," Horace said.

A sudden *boom!* from outside and the wood walls began crackling.

Garr grabbed his guns. Horace ran to the door and kicked it open. Flames rushed in fast, taking Horace by the shirt and hair. He fell to his knees, screaming, unable to put it out.

"It's the law!" Lewis screamed.

"The powder!" Garr yelled. *"The POWDER!"*

Horace was rolling on the wood floor, burning. Kent stepped to the door, an arm protecting his face, and looked into the flames.

It was a path of fire, a tunnel of flames, chest-high, blocking the only way out. The roof was seconds from catching.

"Someone's out there!" Kent screamed, and shot into the fire.

Lewis was beside him now, shooting, too.

The roof caught.

Garr dropped to his knees and dragged the box of gunpowder to the center of the shack. He covered it with his arms, his wild eyes scanning the corners where the walls met the floor.

"There's someone out there!" Kent called again, trying to shy the flame from his face.

Kent was right. There *was* someone out there. Someone they once ran with. Someone they changed forever.

Smoke saw the faces of the men turn black with ash. Men who once stood above him as he woke in an alley, as rain crashed crazy to the earth and did not wash the blood from his severed legs but spread it wide instead: a growing pool of blood at his knees that flowed toward his shoulders with the slight sloping of the ground. Smoke couldn't see them then, couldn't see their faces, just four black ovals appearing and disappearing behind the thick columns of falling water.

Sorry we 'ad to cut you up, fella, Garr said then, the rusted ax still in hand. *But coin is tight . . . and a four-way split is something better than a five.*

Smoke didn't yet know what they had done to him.

And I'll tell you what else, Garr hissed. *I never liked you none and you know it. Too unruly for your own good. Too loud. Men who have secrets don't like loud.*

Smoke couldn't hear him or the others as they called out through the rain that night. He knew something terrible had happened to himself; something like being mangled now, deformed. Things had gone wrong. The world they ran in was ugly, angry, and smelled like pig-piss, and yet well within the lawlessness of that daily life, something had gone terribly wrong.

Smoke felt the blood pooling by his head then. He could smell it. Garr's ax reflected the moonlight and Smoke's hands went to his head first. He groped his chest, his waist, his groin, looking for the reason for that ax.

Try getting up, pig-shitter! Try getting up!

Smoke felt his thighs and knew it before he got to his knees.

Yes, things had gone wrong.

He looked about the alley, frantic. The rain fell chittering from the black sky.

I done warned thee, Garr called. *I done told you I'd chop you up if you didn't settle down.*

Then Garr dropped to his knees and whispered close in Smoke's ear.

Try getting up, pig-shitter. Try getting up.

Smoke saw them then, his lower legs, two yards from his body, beyond the boots of the others. The smell of horror and beer and Garr's bestial odor overcame him and he vomited. It came up fast and hung on his chin and neck and the rain did not wash this away, either.

Garr hadn't just severed his lower legs. He'd sliced him at the center of his knees.

Oh looky! Garr hollered, rising. *The pig-shitter shit out his face!*

Smoke heard their voices leaving him then, boots on wet earth fading, smothered by the volume of the rain. He saw the moonlight glisten once off the ax Garr carried.

Smoke, insane, screamed, *My legs! Leave my legs! You can't have my legs!*

He passed out that way, with the mad idea that he just needed to reach his lower legs, if he could just get to them, then he'd be able to connect them, simple, back onto his body.

But when he woke, the reality of it woke with him.

If he was going to walk again, if he was going to catch the men who hurt him, Smoke was going to need new legs.

Now, standing at the head of a path of flames, he watched.

Vengeful. Motionless. Mad.

Soon the gunshots ceased.

James Moxie was gaining ground, but Smoke wasn't thinking of the legendary outlaw at all.

I got better legs, boys. I got better.

He had.

When Smoke woke again, everything the same, the rain, the darkness, the blood, he started crawling for help.

Someone passed the entrance to the alley and looked inside. There he saw Smoke, dragging his partial body by his fingertips along the rocky wet earth, blood flowing from his knees like oil.

Smoke screamed for help. Black rainwater filled his mouth.

A doctor! I need a doctor! Take me to a doctor!

Now the memory of that doctor cauterizing his split knees was just one of a thousand crude paintings. None of them any good. But tonight some of those paintings, those nightmares, had life to them.

Art.

Smoke did not smile.

Smoke stood.

These legs were better legs indeed.

He watched as the lean-to lit up the early-evening sky. A crown of thick flaming hair, moon-orange snakes fighting over the scurrying rats beneath them. The right wall caved in first. An astonishing splintering of wood that did not echo but played out once, quick and flat. Howls for help erupted from within. Someone was still alive. Begging to be let out. But there was no getting out. The door was a perfect coffin of red raging arms. Smoke saw a figure inside, tearing at his own shirt, ripping off the buttons. Then the left wall fell, and with it the roof.

Smoke's eyes watered.

It was magnificent. It was art.

He just hoped the pig-shitters didn't pass out before burning.

Moxie Moxie Moxie mane . . .

He watched awhile longer but he had somewhere else to be. And he wasn't interested in seeing their bones. Their bones meant the suffering was over.

He took with him the sight of Horace tearing at his shirt, his cheeks already blue with burn.

He limped to his horse, hitched to a tree on the Trail. Behind him he heard an explosion, a little something extra going up in the shack, and still Smoke did not smile. Rather, he recalled the four faces looking down at him in the alley. He recalled the blood. The stink. The fear.

Smoke did not look back.

"Moxie Moxie Moxie mane," he said without singing. "I once crawled legless through the rain." The horse began trotting. Smoke back on the chase. "Moxie Moxie Moxie mat." The darkness, the wind, the Trail. "You can't get away from a man like that."

His horse, stronger than Old Girl, gained ground with every step. As if the legendary outlaw were slowing down, without noticing, without seeing it, without knowing why.

FARRAH AND DWIGHT

"I 'll tell you why I'm not going to that funeral. Whether he's invited people or not."

Farrah was holding the bottle of whiskey she'd been carrying when Sheriff Opal stopped her on the boardwalk. Clyde lifted his glass without speaking and she poured him some more without looking.

Clyde had been worried about her all day. This morning, when they woke, he'd asked innocently if she'd like him to accompany her to the funeral. Farrah looked at him like she might hit him. Clyde didn't mention it again. He rose, got dressed, and left the house for work. When he returned, Farrah was opening that bottle of whiskey and she said, "I saw you coming up the road. Thank hell's heaven it was you."

At first Clyde didn't want to share the bottle with her. He'd had a full day of working (and working off his own drinking), helping to reinforce the wooden beams of Harrows's one theater, the Northern. More than that, he didn't know if Farrah should be drinking so much so fast. And yet they were a quarter of the way into the bottle when she told him she'd talked with Sheriff Opal about Carol and Dwight Evers.

But there was more. Clyde knew. Something else had happened, too.

"The man's up to no good," she told him. Then she looked over her shoulder to the window, and Clyde looked over her shoulder, too, before looking her back in the eye.

"What is it, Farrah?"

Farrah frowned and poured more whiskey. Clyde thought it just about the saddest, most lovely face he'd ever seen.

Farrah rose and went to the front door. She tried the handle, making sure it was locked. Then she stepped to the window and peered out the drapes. Clyde watched her in wonder.

"I'll tell you why I'm not going to that funeral, Clyde."

Suddenly, for the first time all day, there was some life in her eyes. Clyde liked to see this. But he had a bad feeling about the story she was about to tell him.

Sometimes, Clyde knew, the life in someone's eyes was fear.

"When I came back from talking with Sheriff Opal, I set this bottle on the counter and I went into the bedroom and lay down for a spell. I didn't sleep. I don't think I slept. I stared at the ceiling and thought about what I told the sheriff and whether or not I told him enough or enough of the right things. I started to feel like I'd done something wrong. What if Mister Evers is actually just a grieving man? I might have suggested something really awful then. No, if that's the case, if Mister Evers is truly grieving, then I *did* do that. Even worse than that. I stood on a dirt road right there in the middle of all of Harrows and told the sheriff I thought Mister Evers might have played a part in Carol's death. And what does that mean? Clyde? What else could it mean? It means I suggested he *killed* her!"

Farrah looked beyond Clyde then, to the window in the kitchen. She walked quickly past him and peered outside once more. It was dark out. In the glass she saw only the kitchen reflected, Clyde at the table.

"Ah, you don't really think that, do you, Farrah?"

Farrah turned to him quick, her face pale from the whiskey. Her eyes looked crazy.

"He was here, Clyde. I heard him outside. Then I heard him *inside*."

Clyde, stunned, looked over his shoulder to the front door.

"At first I thought it was an animal," Farrah said. "I was in bed, lost in replaying that terrible conversation I'd had with Sheriff Opal, when the sound of footsteps on the grass came through the open bedroom window. I told myself it was a deer. A fox. Something. You would've done the same. But it sounded heavier than any of those and suddenly there was a shape in front of the window, blocking the sun. A black shadow came across me and across the bed and I just about screamed. Someone was there. Someone was *right there* at the window looking in."

Farrah slumped into the other kitchen chair and sipped from her glass. Clyde thought about stopping her, telling her maybe she shouldn't drink so much right now. Had she been drinking when she saw someone outside the window?

"I pulled the blanket up to my eyes and stared at that shape at the window. No, I couldn't see a face. A black silhouette is what it was. I imagined any second he might break the glass. Reach right in. What was he looking for? Who? Well just as suddenly as he came, he was gone. And just as suddenly someone opened the front door."

Clyde stood up now. He walked to the front door and checked the lock.

"Shudders, Farrah," he whispered. "You're scaring me."

"I heard footsteps in the house and I slipped quiet out of bed. I got on the ground and looked through the crack under the bedroom door but I couldn't see anyone. I know our house is small, Clyde, I know it's just these few rooms, but he wasn't in sight. I got so scared, I crawled right under the bed. You might've done the same thing. I crawled under the bed and held my hands in little fists up by my face. I listened to those footsteps. And they were *slow,* Clyde. Like the man didn't want you or me to hear he was inside the house. And then . . . *he said my name.*"

Clyde's face was as white as hers now. He took hold of his glass and downed what was left, then held it out. Farrah refilled it.

"What next, Farrah?"

Farrah stared into the emptiness of the rest of the house before answering.

"Still under the bed, I looked toward the crack under the bedroom door. The footsteps got closer. He called my name again. He said, 'Farrah, if you're here, I'd like to talk with you. It has to do with Carol. Maybe you can help.' On my blood, Clyde, on my blood."

She drank. She went on.

"The bedroom door opened slowly. I saw black shoes at the threshold. I tried not to breathe. He said my name again and I started crying but I didn't whimper. Didn't make a sound. Even when he stepped into the room and knelt beside the bed. Yes, Clyde. Mister Evers knelt by our bed. I heard his knees touch the wood. I saw his black pants, a pair of pants I'd seen a thousand times hanging in a closet in that house of theirs. He knelt beside the bed and looked underneath it. Oh, bless the Lord in hell's heaven, Clyde! I saw his *face*! He had a scratch on one cheek and he stared under the bed a long time in silence then suddenly whispered my name and then I almost did whimper, I almost screamed.

"*Farrah . . .*

"He didn't see me. Bless the time of day. He didn't see me. He rose again, he got up, and . . . and he left."

Clyde got up, too, and went to her. He put his hand on her shoulder and she cried, full and honest. Then he stepped to the lantern and blew it out. In the dark he walked to the window and looked outside for a long time. Farrah was quiet. Clyde walked through the house, checking the other windows, the closets, under the bed. In the darkness he said, "You have to tell Sheriff Opal about this. It don't matter how scared you are, Farrah."

"I'm not going out there tonight, Clyde. And I'm not going to that funeral. Do you understand me? I'm not going near that man."

Clyde nodded in the dark, but Farrah did not see him.

"I'll go when it's over. The moment it ends. I'll pay my respects on my own. But I'm not going near that man."

Clyde heard her sip from her glass in the dark.

"Do you want some more, Clyde?"

He stepped through the house toward her.

"I surely do."

THE CLOCK
ON THE MANTEL

What if she were to wake ... right now? What if she were to come stumbling through the front door ... her hand to her head ... complaining of body aches ... fatigue ... and the things she'd heard within? Oh, the image of Carol in the foyer, the black night beyond her, seen through the open front door! Her hair blown wild by that dark wind, a thousand buried screams ... the blubbering of banshees she was so close to meeting, so close to sharing her story with, the story of her husband and how he tried very hard to bury her alive.

Dwight loosened his tie. An owl spoke outside the parlor window and he jumped and turned to the glass, half expecting to see Carol on the lawn, her comatose eyes open, her hands reaching for him still.

But Carol slept, weighed down by earth and rocks, on the floor of the black coach in the drive.

And yet ...

What if she were to wake ... right now? Hadn't she woken in less time before? And she'd never sat up before ... never *moved*.

Dwight sat down on the edge of the couch. The clock on the mantel sounded flatly in the plush, cushioned room. Seconds ticked. How many more? Thirty thousand more? Too many, more than enough time . . .

Dwight rose from the couch and wiped sweat from his forehead. A few minutes passed before he understood he'd been staring at a throw pillow, fantasizing about smothering his sleeping wife with it.

Another bestial sound from outside. Looking through the glass, he was certain he'd see Carol crawling out of the coach.

Dwight, she might say, *Dwight . . . I'm awake now . . . I'm awake . . .*

He went to the window and put his hands to the glass, shielding the reflected lanterns of the parlor.

The coach door was still closed.

But what if she were to wake . . . *right now?* There was no good reason to believe she wouldn't. That she couldn't. And what would Dwight do then? Shoot her? Smother her? Drown her in the tub? She would go to Opal first. She must. And Opal would listen and console her while loading his gun and taking from his desk the key to one of the cells in the station.

Opal would come for him.

Maybe he was already on his way.

James Moxie is on his way.

Dwight ran a shaky hand through his damp, sweaty hair. What a cruel, unfair disadvantage for Carol to have known one of the Trail's most legendary outlaws! It wasn't right, he felt, to have to worry about this man, this monster, approaching, splitting midnight on a black horse, coming to break open the wood coffin with his bare mythic hands!

"Oh," he said, his voice like a child's. "What if she were to wake *right now?*"

Dwight would hide. Yes, if he heard the creaking of the coach door opening he would rush to the pantry in the kitchen and hide.

The clock on the mantel ticked.

Dwight paced the parlor. The lanterns sent shadows up and down the beautiful room, a room decorated (and funded) entirely by Carol. Each shadow imitated the posture of his sleeping wife, now standing in the doorway, a thousand vengeful spirits beside her, those she met when so close to death. The friends she'd made in Howltown.

Kill her now, he thought.

He looked down to see he had the throw pillow in his hands. His knuckles were white with squeezing.

Yet another sound from beyond the glass and this time Dwight froze. The pillow fell to his feet and he was certain, yes, he heard footsteps. Leaves on the lawn crunching beneath the weight of something much greater than a squirrel, a bunny, a fox. Unthinking, his shoes shuffled backward, to where the lantern did not reach, to the corner of the parlor where just yesterday women whispered about the sad sudden passing of Carol Evers. He did not take his eyes from the glass, though he wanted to very badly. Dwight whimpered, a single girlish hiccup, before seeing the shape of a deer pass ghostlike across the frame.

Pig-shit on Robert Manders and his line of *dead bodies*! Curse the Illness that had come to Harrows, that had granted Carol these remaining thirty thousand seconds to wake!

The clock on the mantel clucked and Dwight stepped to it fast and took hold of it and smashed it against the brick framing of the fireplace.

"Stop it!" he screamed. *"STOP IT NOW!"*

Oh, if Dwight used his hands, Opal would find the marks of murder upon her.

"No marks!" he said. Then he brought a finger to the slight cut on his face. Made by Carol in the coma.

What if she woke, right—

You heard wrong, Carol! Dear! What you heard in there was not true! It was a nasty dream, nothing more! Distortion! Perversion! A nasty dream!

He brought a hand to his chest. He was breathing much too hard. So much planning, *such* good plans . . . all of them . . . for naught . . . if she were to wake . . .

Right now.

Light sparkled outside and Dwight was certain it came from within the coach. The door was opening and his conscious bride was coming to life in some hellish form of light. She would come with the face of the grave upon her, the future dirt and death-smell, the way he *wanted* her to be. But awake! *Alive!* Yes, Carol would come with string-thin hair and black-oil nails and Dwight would cower, chattering, as she approached, her voice level fury, telling him, *They all know they all know they all know Dwight that you tried to bury your wife alive because they all know you couldn't bear the burden of her shadow, her mind, her money. They all know they all know they all know you didn't have the guts to kill her they all know you waited waited waited for her to do it herself . . . for you . . . even this . . . even this you couldn't do on your own . . .*

A sound outside and Dwight cried out, "Stay away, James Moxie! *Stay away!*"

Not just any outlaw, no no, the outlaw who killed a man *without drawing his gun.* The black-magic marvel; a name bigger than any other on the Trail; a Trail littered with the tracks of a thousand terrible men; and he, the biggest, the darkest, the worst, was coming . . . coming . . . coming here . . .

What if she were to wake right now?

Light dazzled through the glass and Dwight curled up into the corner. He shook his head *no no* and knew it was James Moxie, knew it was Sheriff Opal, knew it was *Carol* herself.

The clock, smashed and in pieces on the floor, clucked the seconds away.

Someone *was* coming. The light . . . a lantern . . . someone was coming up the drive.

Dwight shook his head no no and the fingers of fear held him flat against the wall.

Who could it be? Who would come calling at this late hour if not with a mind for murder?

The light grew and Dwight saw the orb pass close to the coach. Was Carol sitting up in there? Could the carrier of the light see her body within?

The light vanished from view.

A knock came at the door.

I was sleeping, Sheriff Opal . . . I didn't hear your knock . . .

I was sleeping, Sheriff Opal . . . I didn't hear your knock . . .

I was sleeping—

"Hello?"

A foreign voice. A voice Dwight did not know.

Timid, trembling, he stepped from the corner of the parlor and his boots clacked against the wood floor and the echo told the person at the door that he was indeed not sleeping.

"Hello! Is there someone there?"

Dwight crossed the room slowly, his teeth clenched painfully, his eyes wet and wide, his fingers contorted into claws.

"Hello?"

Dwight opened the door.

In the light of the held lantern, the traveler saw him and saw that he was the picture of unbalance, that he had perhaps knocked on the wrong door tonight.

"I—I'm sorry to have bothered you, sir, but I—I was looking for a place to sleep. I've been walking some—"

"What?"

The traveler inched back from the door. "I don't mean to bother you, kind sir, I'll just—"

"What are you saying?"

"Sir?"

"What are you doing here?"

The traveler attempted to plead ignorance once more.

Dwight shut the door.

And he stood by the window, watching the orb of light grow smaller once again. As the stranger passed the coach in the drive, Dwight did not gasp. He did not cry out. For he almost expected she would be sitting up in there, her and the thousand spirits she had met so close to death.

they all know they all know they all know

"Lafayette," Dwight said. And his voice was animal instinct. His voice was hardly his own. "Call Lafayette . . . once more . . . get rid of the girl Farrah . . . Farrah knows something . . . get rid of the girl . . . what if she says something . . . what if she says my name . . . what if she says . . ."

Carol.

What if she says Carol is only sleeping?

And what if Carol were to wake from that sleep . . . right now?

CAROL AND ROT

Rot held her hand. Carol saw it in the glass. Saw what looked like a hand made of cowhide gripping her own. She understood, instinctively, that the veil between the real world, the world in which she slept, and this one had slimmed. She also knew it was the doing of the monster that sat beside her on the coach floor.

He leaned close and whispered, "Look, Carol. Out the coach window. Do you see that cardinal rise to the sky?"

Carol did see it. And while the terror she felt for being so close to Rot ruled her, she couldn't help but experience the astonishment, still, for seeing anything of the real world while still inside the coma.

But Rot had given her light. Light to see by. Light to see her own end by.

"That," he whispered, and his breath was meat left out in the yard, "that is how things really look. That is how all things will end."

Carol understood. For, while she could see the bird rising in the sky, it did not resemble the healthy cardinals she'd counted in her gardens at home. Rather, the bird seemed made of red paper, paper left in a puddle of oil, feathers shining wet with the means by which it could suddenly go up in flames.

Beside her, Rot wheezed and held her hand as Carol tried hard not to look at him in the glass, tried hard not to see the bird, either, the rotting thing flying, rising into the sky, believing itself still alive, not aware how much it had already died.

But Carol had little trouble resisting the urge to move now. Dwight had seen to that. And somehow, to her, this was the most terrible thing Dwight had done. Worse, it seemed, even than trying to kill her.

By loading her dress with rocks and earth, Dwight had made it impossible again for her to move in Howltown. A thing she had tried her whole life to do.

There's a difference between bad and evil, John Bowie once told her, his voice slurred with brandy. *Bad is when you ignore the one you love. But evil is when you know exactly what that person wants, what means most to them, and you figure out how to take it away.*

MOXIE

Moxie believed he was going to make it to Harrows by nightfall because if he didn't believe that he'd go mad.

He'd make it. He'd sleep in the graveyard at the lip of the hole dug for Carol. And when the diggers came and asked him to leave, he'd bury them instead. He'd bury the whole town if he had to. If it meant burying whoever had hired the Cripple. Whoever wanted to stop him from breaking apart the funeral of a living woman.

Carol wasn't going into the ground. Not tomorrow.

It's her husband.

Because it had to be. Because only husbands and wives could be so cruel.

The guilt had galvanized, become a solid mass within him. Or rather, had taken the place of his blood, flowed through his veins like oil, slick and sludged.

The husband wouldn't be the husband if Moxie hadn't run away.

The husband hired the Cripple. The man of the house certainly read the incoming telegrams.

He knew Moxie was coming. He knew Moxie knew about Carol.

He wanted Carol dead.

But why?

A figure emerged from the brush ahead and Moxie did not hesitate in bringing forth his gun. The man stumbled and Rinaldo's description of a crippled hit man came scorching aflame to the foreground of Moxie's mind before he understood the man had only been drinking.

Close call. Near death for the drunk.

"Hey there, feller!"

Old Girl continued and Moxie did not respond.

"Hey there . . . hold up now . . . stop for a minute why doncha . . ."

The man stumbled against the trunk of an enormous oak then stumbled back onto the Trail. Moxie and Old Girl were beside him now and the man looked up, unnecessarily shielding his eyes from a sun that was long tucked away for the night.

Later, the man's wife wouldn't believe him. She'd tell him he was drunk and leave him stewing in the kitchen. But ultimately he would know that it was true: that when he looked up at the man on the mare the man looked down at him and the man looked like he had no face, like the only features he had were Guilt and Rage and both were wrapped like gauze tied tight to his fiery skull.

"It's true!" he would holler at his wife, his words slurred, his vision blurred. "Truer than anything I've ever seen. His eyes burned and his face was made of stone. He held his gun between my eyes, he did, and he said something I'll never forget. He said it like I knew what he was talking about, like we were in the middle of a conversation. He said, *She's not going into the earth.* How was I to respond? Hell's heaven, I shivered and fell to my knees on the Trail! Drunk or not, I saw the face of Guilt out there! And I saw the rage it takes to atone for it!"

ALEXANDER WOLFE

Opal was sitting at his desk when the doctor walked in. He was well dressed and his full silver hair was combed back from his forehead, expressing confidence in the striking features of his face. A thick silver mustache highlighted his square chin, and Opal had a feeling he knew who it was before the man introduced himself.

"I'm Doctor Alexander Wolfe." He had bright science in his eyes. "Are you the sheriff then?"

"That I am."

"Care to talk? Do you mind if I sit down? I've driven all the way from Charles. My coachman is sick this evening and I've had to make the trip alone."

Opal extended a palm to the open chair on the other side of his desk.

Outside the sky was already close to black. If Opal opened the window at this hour he would most likely hear some harmless variety of ne'er-do-well on the square, but tonight the doctor from Charles had his entire attention.

"Mister Evers sent me. His telegram was full of much concern. Seems he thinks you don't believe I exist."

"I'm still not sure I do."

Wolfe smiled. "With all due respect, Sheriff, and I *do* mean respect . . . where I come from that sounds like you may have it in for an innocent man."

"That's how they'd see it in Charles?"

"That's how they'd see it just about anywhere, I'd gather."

When Wolfe smiled, his eyes flashed white. His skin tightened to his face.

"And why's that?"

"Why? Because I'm sitting before you is why."

"Any proof you're who you say you are? Any proof you're a doctor?"

"You may have to take my word for it. Though we could talk medicine all night if you need to."

"Maybe I do."

"Very well. Tell me, how can I help my friend clear his good name with you?"

"You can tell me about Carol Evers."

"What do you want to know?"

"How'd she die?"

"It's not that easy, I'm afraid." He tented his long clean fingers above the crossed legs of his suit pants. "I think hers was a weak heart. Dwight told me she was known to complain of light-headedness. I understand she experienced a bout of it the evening she passed."

"I heard the same thing. Where'd you hear yours?"

"Dwight told me, of course. Who else?"

Opal did not respond. He stared hard into Wolfe's bright eyes. Wolfe said, "The man is grieving."

"Yes. That's what he told me."

"And you don't believe that, either?"

Opal dropped his elbows to the desk and leaned forward.

"You're just a walking question machine, ain't you? You dispense questions like they're sugar treats. How about we reverse that lever and you start answering instead."

Wolfe's expression did not change. "Yes, of course."

"What do you think she died of, Doctor, and why do you think what you think?"

Wolfe breathed deep.

"In my opinion, Carol Evers passed from a weak heart. I came to that conclusion based on the fact that she had poor circulation, a symptom of which could have been the dizzy spells. I suppose she could have had a stroke."

"You don't know?"

"No, Sheriff. If I had been her physician through life—"

"Why weren't you?"

Wolfe appeared to be only mildly affected by the question. "I'm not sure. Too far away I suppose."

"But close enough to call the evening she died."

"Death is a much more serious thing than the common cold, Sheriff Opal."

"Who's talking about the common cold?"

Wolfe smiled. "I think what matters here is that she's passed. Your asking for me insinuates you are suspicious of Dwight."

"I'm suspicious of you."

"I understand that. We've never met before. Still, I'm not sure what else a man can do but tell you who he is. It's up to you to believe him or not."

"Why aren't you in the registry?"

A sudden question. Opal watched close for the reaction.

"Excuse me?"

"The ledger of registered doctors."

"Because I'm not."

"Not registered?"

"That's right."

"How's that?"

"You understand more than most that a man has the right to see whatever variety of doctor he chooses. Just like he votes as he wishes and eats as he likes. My methods aren't considered suitable by an archaic volume and you, like those who compiled the book, think I don't exist for it."

"Are you a witch doctor?"

Wolfe smiled. "No. But I believe the spirit can heal most wounds."

Opal leaned back in his chair. This was the best answer he'd had to this question.

"So you're a quack," Opal said.

"Not a quack. A modernist, if you will."

Opal tapped his fingertips on the desk. "A modernist."

"I think this is a classic case of a woman simply being taken too soon."

"You do?"

"Yes. Some deaths are ill timed. All, I dare say."

"How do you feel about Evers keeping the body in the cellar?"

"I'm not sure what you mean."

"Just what I said."

Wolfe considered. "I've known men and women to keep the deceased many places. It depends on what you plan on doing with the body."

"Well, most people deliver the body to the funeral director here in Harrows. Most people would rather it wasn't in their own hands for very long."

"Isn't the funeral tomorrow morning?"

"Yes it is."

"That doesn't sound unreasonable to me."

Opal considered. When Wolfe first entered the station he thought it might be someone Dwight hired. Like everything else with Evers, it was too tidy. But the man was convincing. Wolfe didn't know everything: a trait Opal looked for in a sincere person.

"Quite an illness hit Harrows just four weeks back."

"Of course, I know of it. A deluge of rot."

"Pardon?"

"Many graves, Sheriff. Too many."

Opal paused.

"You think it had anything to do with Missus Evers's death?"

Wolfe considered. "Well, I'm not sure I'm qualified to answer, but I would say no. I really do believe it was her heart."

Opal studied the doctor's face a moment before rising.

"Thank you," he said.

Wolfe stood up as well and attempted to make small talk, summer weather, the view from Harper's Hill. But Opal wasn't biting and Alexander Wolfe took his leave.

Opal watched the man climb up a stanhope and guide a brown horse back up the road from which he'd come. He watched until the carriage vanished into the shadows beyond the Northern Theater, beyond the ice-and-candy parlor, beyond the gunsmith's, too.

When Cole came in to take over for Opal, the sheriff said there'd been a change of plans. He wanted Cole to ride out to Dwight Evers's place and thank him for delivering the doctor. He wanted Cole to take note of Evers's reaction to the thank-you. Write down what he saw. The deputy did as the sheriff asked. When he returned, he told Opal that Mister Evers said not to worry but he hoped things were cleared up. He also said Dwight looked bad. Grieving bad. Opal frowned. Always so tidy, always so clean. Cole shrugged and said, "That's what I saw."

What Cole didn't see was Dwight's face after the deputy left.

Breathing heavy, paranoid, and sweating, Dwight tried desperately to figure out who would have done this for him.

Who would have known to do it?

In the mirror Dwight looked skeletal: his lips far from his teeth, his eyes wide as divots in the Trail. The scratch on his cheek had stopped bleeding. Had become something of a solid purple line.

Alexander Wolfe was an invention of Dwight's splintering mind.

And yet . . . tonight . . .

The figment walked. He talked.

Dwight locked the front door.

The man with the shifting face had woken him, told him to hide his wife.

And now . . . Alexander Wolfe.

Dwight laughed. A single high-pitched shriek. Then he brought his hands to his lips as though it were possible to retrieve it, as if it were terrible luck to laugh now, so close to Carol's burial.

He wanted to feel grateful. He wanted to thank the man, the thing that was helping him. Instead he brought a hand to his heart and trembled, unable to take his eyes from the shadowed corners of his home.

Yes, *thank you* was what he wanted to say, but he mouthed the words

What do I owe you?

instead.

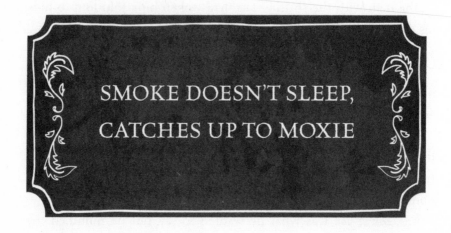

SMOKE DOESN'T SLEEP,
CATCHES UP TO MOXIE

Moxie Moxie Moxie mo
go to where the dreamers go . . .
Moxie Moxie Moxie me
lay thee down and go to sleep . . .

As he sang, Smoke's legs were screaming.

The hole in his upper shin cut into his skin, and the wound was getting worse.

Moxie was in Harrows by now, Smoke knew this.

Oh, Moxie Moxie Moxie mine!
Sweat drips heavy from the vine!
Moxie Moxie Moxie mug!
You're cornered like a common bug!

A match came to life between his fingers, and Smoke saw he'd reached the thick northernmost woods of the Trail. Shades of great pines showed in the scant light. Beasts scurried in the brush. Smoke sang to them.

Beyond the horse's head he saw the tracks he'd been following for two days.

Looked like the outlaw's horse was getting tired, as the hoofprints were closer together now.

A second set of tracks, too. The same Smoke had seen all day. Small hooves. Quick steps. As if someone were riding a dog. Whoever it was, they weren't riding with Moxie, and Smoke relished the idea of a simple civilian, a messenger, an innocent caught in the crossfire.

Fire.

Smoke smiled, but his eyes remained cold white in the darkness.

He thought of Moxie's myth, re-witnessing the conviction held by the small man in Griggsville he'd torched on the shitter.

He started to laugh but the pain cut him short.

Beyond the drone of black hooves clacking he could hear the outlaw's voice, the things the legend would say when Smoke caught up to him. It'd be straight from the Book of Cliché Pleading, the words all the older outlaws used when the End was nigh; words they learned back when phrases were hotter than burning oil. Take that hermit. Had he shot more and talked less Smoke would be dead. But the old outlaws loved the talk.

I'll give you five seconds, Moxie would say.

You better be planning on dying today, he would say.

I hope you said your goodbyes.

Oh, the shibboleths of the Trail.

Smoke tucked his chin low and feigned a deep voice.

"Break a leg, hit man!"

"On your knees!"

"It's gonna be a short fight, Cripple!"

He snickered and brought his boot heels down on the horse. It felt good to laugh. Even a snort. Even as the tin dug into his mangled knee. Both he and the horse propelled by the sting of sharp metal against flesh.

The wind picked up, the beast moved fast, and Smoke felt the town approaching.

"You gonna lose your arms, too, Cripple! Ahahahahaha!"

At last: real, full laughter.

Smoke felt the cool, dark air pass over him. As if he were traveling through a wall of ghosts. The horse was moving fast, dangerously fast, but Smoke didn't care. The horse could fall, could step hard in a divot, break two legs, send Smoke into the brush. Smoke could lose his own legs, lose his oil, but hell's heaven, he could *smell* that shitter town and the nonsense legend that lurked there.

"You done lit yer last fire, Cripple!"

"I'm gonna enjoy breaking the rest of those legs!"

"Ahahahahahaha!"

Tree branches scratched at his arms and chest. Rocks flew from the horse's hooves. Smoke was gaining. Moxie wasn't going any farther than the finish line.

"Ooh-eeeh! We ridin' now!"

He brought his shins down hard and felt the slosh within. Some spilled. Smoke didn't care. Not tonight. Tonight he could finish the outlaw with one drop. That was all he'd need. One drop of oil in Moxie's mouth. One drop of oil in his eye. Smoke felt it coming: the moment, the kill . . .

The burn.

They were past the pines now and the moon lit up the fields beyond them. Smoke knew these fields were the last landmark he'd see before crossing the town's dotted line. Ahead, bathed in moonlight, he saw the town's outline, Harrows's silhouette, the downtown boardwalk and shops nestled at the base of a hill that boasted the finer homes and barns. Far to the right burned the many lanterns that framed the graveyard, making it look something like a ship to Smoke now, tombstones and markers out to sea, bobbing in the blackness.

Smoke imagined. Smoke prepared.

He was going to stand over Moxie and watch the flesh crinkle from his face, curl back black from his hairline and ears. The outlaw's mouth would open with fright; his last scream for life; his *forever-*

howl. He'd like to see Moxie bring his hands to the flames on his face. Oh, what glory to know Moxie's *brain* would burn inside his mythic skull, for inside that brain was the explanation for the Trick at Abberstown and once it was burnt, it was gone, and once it was gone, it was nothing . . . no more.

No legend. No more.

Smoke was going to watch the horse burn, too. Count on that. He'd been staring at the hoofprints forever. He'd *start* with the horse. The outlaw would hear the beast screaming and leap from the whore's bed he shared. He'd rush half naked out onto the balcony and see the good horse jerking its head from the hitching post, rendered ash and bone in the road. Had the great James Moxie ever heard the sound a horse makes as it burns? He would. Then he would know it had begun, that the man following him was now the man who had caught up, and the fire that made the mare scream was the very one coming for him.

> *Moxie Moxie Moxie my!*
> *We can't both get out of this alive!*

Passing the dark, low fields just south of Harrows, Smoke saw a scarecrow that reminded him, in shape, of his mother. Inspired by it, he imagined her burning. He imagined the dresses from her closet . . . the curls in her blond hair . . . the rims of her glasses . . . all of it and everything blistering, bending, burning.

The fire he imagined for her was blue and smelled like childhood. And childhood reminded him of the children he once knew; he imagined a girl named Merrily melted to the shape of a chair, another, Henry, sitting upon her in a classroom.

He'd like to burn them all. Every face he'd ever seen.

Excited now, Smoke saw the mothers of these former schoolmates rushing from their homes, desperate feet pattering on the porch boards, able to discern the smell of their own child burning above all others. Smoke would be there when they came. He'd be there with a piece of meat on a stick.

Dinner over childhood's fire.

Hey, Ma! This meat only gets better the longer it cooks!

Moved, Smoke imagined more.

Men in suits bursting into flame upon exiting church. Families sitting down to eat burnt food, blackened bread, ashen meals upon scalding-hot plates.

Come on, Billy! Eat your fire! EAT YOUR FIRE!

A blazing funeral. A funeral in flames. Shitty Benson caskets lowered into blackened holes. A graveyard of open lids; men and women screaming *help us,* covered in oil, drenched in dread. Heat-thunder breaking open a midnight sky. And Smoke, the minister, walking the rows, dropping a match for each along the way. Plots exploding into . . .

. . . fire.

A combustible wedding next. The happy couple exchanging tongues of white flame. Smoke bringing their parched faces together, kiss the bride, kiss the groom, kiss the ashes upon the broom.

Scalding birth. A lady on a bed of straw, a doctor on his knees, encouraging, push, push, as the hell-howl escaped the mother's mouth and the doctor's face caught *fast* . . . the inferno erupting from all the way within the woman . . . the womb . . . the tin colander every mother nurtures . . .

Doctor! I can't control it! I can't!

Oh, Smoke would assure the young mother, *but look at its face!*

"You set on dying, Cripple?"

"Ol' Magic Moxie gonna make you disappear!"

"I'll give ya ten seconds' head start on those legs!"

"Ahahahahaha!"

Smoke was relishing. Smoke was alive. Smoke was . . . *closing in.*

Moxie Moxie Moxie moo . . .

I'm so bored without you!

At the end of the fields the terrain changed, leveled, and Smoke saw better the torches and candlelit windows of the town called Harrows. His hamstrung legs dangled, numb and pained.

The horse whined for rest. But Smoke wouldn't give it.

There would be no stopping tonight. Tonight Smoke was going to find the famous outlaw James Moxie . . . and torch him.

"Ahahahaha!"

The wood WELCOME TO HARROWS sign looked particularly flammable as he passed it.

Moxie Moxie Moxie may . . .
Where in town might you stay?

Across the border, there were far too many tracks for Smoke to follow. Moxie could be holed up in any shadow, any locked hotel room, any brothel or barroom or bathhouse. The outlaw could be sleeping right here on the side of the Trail and Smoke might miss him if he wasn't watchful.

Could be awake, too.

Asleep. Awake. Asleep. Awake.

Man of magic, why not both?

He guided the horse quietly along empty Main Street. No Harrowsers in sight.

Moxie, he knew, could be anywhere.

But Smoke found him in the graveyard.

He sang no songs. He imagined no fire. Hills became valleys and the valleys grew into fresh hills, and beyond the last of the Harrows homes, down the slope of a grassy hill, he saw the amateur camp he was looking for. The headstones were well lit by a very small fire, probably made an hour ago. The markers seemed to be able to dance with the flickering of the flames, as if Smoke were approaching a living cemetery, where even the stones might point him out, might cry danger. The big silhouette of the funeral home on another hill stood out black against the graying sky. The crosses, wood posts, stone memorials, and one-room chambers of the mauso-leums fanned out beneath it like devotees, all bent at the knees in prayer.

Smoke whispered to the horse, "You make some crazy noise now and I'll burn you, too."

He focused on the fire, seeing now the two shapes beside it. One was the horse, and the other, yes, the other was James Moxie.

He looked smaller than Smoke thought he'd be. But legends had a way of making a man bigger than he really was.

The fire, Smoke knew, meant *sleep*.

Shoulda used one of them mausoleums, outlaw.

The flames were reflected in the windows of the funeral home. But no light came from within.

The horse's hooves were silent on the grass and Smoke could read the names on the markers but he kept his eyes on the outlaw and the outlaw went out of sight as Smoke descended a small hill. He could hear the fire, could tell it was close to putting itself out.

Smoke rode the horse slowly up a last incline and stopped.

From where he observed, the headstones might've fallen from the sky, pell-mell, strangely artful in their chaos.

Lanterns flickered, framing the graveyard, but the only fire Smoke saw was the one by the sleeping man and the hole in the ground be-side him.

Smoke looked long into the trees bordering the cemetery. Looking for anything that didn't belong.

The outlaw didn't move.

Smoke mouthed the syllables *ma-gic* but did not speak them.

The air was cool, the sky was dark, and untethered clouds passed before the moon.

Smoke dismounted, the sloshing in his shins quieter than the fire. He limped four paces and looked to the pit beside the outlaw.

A perfect place to bury a burnt legend.

Fingering the loops in his pockets, Smoke studied.

In a moment this quaint scene would be blazing.

He admired the outlaw's fire. Moxie had done good work.

It reflected in the black of Smoke's eyes, growing bigger, as he limped toward the sleeping outlaw and the grave dug fresh for Carol beside him.

MOXIE AND SMOKE

Moxie heard the oil spilling out of Smoke's boot heels but had no clear idea exactly what was making the sound or how it worked. He watched the man limp quietly, circling the open grave and sleeping horse. The Cripple had his hands in his pockets and Moxie connected that to whatever was happening at his feet. There was something awful about the way he walked, something that went much deeper than an injury.

He'd first seen him standing up on the hill, overlooking the grave-yard, and understood by his dismount that this was the man follow-ing him. He looked lithe—Moxie had expected a bigger man—and he wore no hat and carried no gun.

The Cripple had a big horse, much bigger than Moxie's, and the outlaw guessed he'd made stops of his own along the way. He watched him survey the scene, the thin silhouette illuminated by the full moonlight, up on the hill, looking for movement, looking for some-one hiding.

Moxie was still.

Uneven steps on the soft grass and Moxie couldn't see him on his descent of the hill. Then the man came into view again, his shape emerging from behind a giant stone, peering, pausing before carrying on, quietly, limping, stiff-legged, toward the open grave. The moonlight and stars detailed some of his features—not his face, not yet, but the folds in his shirt, the bulging of his pant legs below the knees, the slope of his shoulders, and the tilt of his hatless head.

Moxie watched the man slip his hands in his pockets and he wondered if the *click* sound that followed would wake the horse. It didn't. He saw the triggerman change direction, carefully, walking no longer toward the open grave but around it.

Soon he understood the man was describing a circle.

The sloshing sound, the oozing of something wet: Moxie couldn't be sure what that was.

One revolution complete, the man began another, a second circle within the first, breaking the pattern to connect the two circles he'd made. He was good at what he did, Moxie understood; at times he couldn't hear the man moving at all.

The second circle finished, the man began a third, an arc that would bring him very close to Old Girl, sleeping soundly yet. He limped slowly, patient. Something a little bit gray was added to the sky and something a little bit black was taken away. He'd passed the mare and was at the foot of the grave when Moxie heard the mare stir and lift its head and look to the limping man. Moxie watched them both.

The Cripple turned his head to the horse.

The horse, docile, made no move and the triggerman continued, not taking his eyes off the beast. His steps got smaller but so did the circumference of the circle, and it took him just as long to complete the third as it had the first.

On the fourth round Moxie smelled it. A wind crossed close to the ground of the graveyard and brought to him the inimitable smell of oil. The man, he understood, planned to burn him and his horse. He looked to the shins again and the picture was almost complete.

Whatever had happened to the man's legs, he'd made up for it.

Moxie did not move.

The Cripple limped to the sleeping outlaw. He balanced on one boot, raised the other carefully, and let the oil drip onto the legend's shirt and pants. Moxie watched the triggerman limp quietly out of the four circles, to the border of pine trees that guarded the graveyard. Moxie heard another soft *click* as the boot heels closed again. The Cripple turned to observe his work.

He reached a hand into his pocket and removed a small box. A flame came to life between his fingertips, and Moxie heard him whisper-sing,

> *This is the Where, outlaw, and this is the When . . .*
> *This is how it looks when you get to the end.*

The he let the match fall to the oil . . .

. . . Smoke stopped when he heard the mare lift her head. He was near the foot of the open hole and he turned to see the beast staring at him. The outlaw was sleeping to Smoke's left and he didn't want the horse to wake him. He held its gaze for a long time before continuing with the fourth circle. What Smoke would like to see was the rickety beast get up and try to run through four rings of fire.

The legend was going to burn and Smoke smiled with some humor. What a thing to wake to. What an end.

Smoke limped to the side of the sleeping outlaw.

The moonlight gave strange contours to the outlaw's face. The fire by the grave was almost out, but it flickered a brief shadow on the outlaw's chin and Smoke mistook it for movement. He waited. A wind came and the fire moved again and Smoke saw it was shadows after all.

The dark face remained still, sleeping.

Smoke balanced on one boot and raised the other slowly, his finger still in the loop in his left pocket. The oil flowed in a thin neat line, and Smoke knew he didn't have much left. It didn't matter. He had enough. What sounded good was removing his shin and pouring the rest down the sleeping man's throat.

The oil circles were set. And they were connected now to the outlaw's shirt and pants. Once he caught, where would he go?

The outlaw didn't wake. Smoke understood that the myths, the legendary stories, had happened back when James Moxie's mind was much sharper than it was tonight. That glory was got a long time ago. The legend, his clothes in oil, his horse too tired to address a stranger . . .

. . . truly . . . in person . . . there was nothing to him at all.

Smoke limped into the shadows of the pine trees that framed the graveyard and turned to look at what he'd made.

It was magisterial.

Moxie would wake aflame and run stumbling into the grave he slept beside. Smoke thought he might just get himself a shovel and bury the myth himself.

He reached into his pocket and took out the small box and brought fire to life off his fingernail.

He whisper-sang a song:

> *This is the Where, outlaw, and this is the When*
> *This is how it looks when you get to the end.*

He let the match fall.

The outlaw sat up long before the first ring caught the second. And there were two more yet to be caught.

"Moxie!" the outlaw called, confusing Smoke, calling out his own name.

There was excitement in the voice. And more . . .

. . . there was an accent.

Vaguely, Smoke recognized the voice. The lilt to the syllables, the clipped syllables that he used.

"Now, Moxie! *Now!*"

Smoke heard movement behind him coming from the pines and he turned to see a man break through the dark. A red shirt and foam-white eyes beneath a tan hat. Smoke stumbled, the fire building behind him, his legs incapable of running.

Then the outlaw, the legend, the myth was upon him.

Smoke had time to think,

Everything about this one is true.

Moxie didn't grab a phrase from the Book of Cliché Pleading. Instead he took Smoke by the blond hair of his head and pressed a gun to his heart and fired.

The horse whinnied as Rinaldo led her away from the spreading fire and the flames howled toward the lightening sky, but Moxie heard none of that. He let go of the Cripple's hair and saw that the triggerman remained standing, balancing, it seemed, on his lower legs, his chin limp to his chest.

"We did it, Moxie!" Rinaldo called, rushing to Moxie's side. "It was ... it was ... *magic!* I fooled him twice! I fooled him twice!"

Moxie watched the blood pour from the triggerman's heart, crimson oil, down his shirt, to his pants, and to the boots and grass at his feet.

The Cripple looked like a man who had fallen asleep standing up, his hands at his pockets, as though trying to

Draw.

When Moxie turned to face Rinaldo, he looked nothing like the man Rinaldo had caught up to only an hour ago.

"How'd you get out of the outhouse?" Moxie asked him, his voice crackling flames.

Rinaldo opened his mouth to tell him, then stopped himself.

"Same way you did the Trick. *Magic.*"

Rinaldo smiled, but Moxie did not.

"The worst trick I ever performed," Moxie said, the flames rising in his animal eyes, "was breaking a good woman's heart." He looked at Rinaldo and Rinaldo could see that the outlaw, his hero, was somewhere far from the graveyard in Harrows. "Thank you, Rinaldo."

Then Moxie went to Old Girl and mounted.

"Do you need me, Moxie? Do you need me to follow? Do you need me to act as your double again?"

"Stay here," Moxie said.

From town, as if crawling between the trees that bordered the graveyard, in the first scant trace of daylight, Moxie saw the morning of Carol's burial approaching.

He rode toward it.

CAROL

Carol started doing the thing she'd heard other people had done when faced with the end. She started listing off the things she was grateful for, the things she had loved, the things that meant something good to her during her time living. For that life, she believed now, was as close to its end as it was going to be and she didn't think she'd find the strength to say thanks once she was buried alive.

It had taken a lot out of her to sit up in the coach. From Howltown, Dwight looked something like a corpse himself. The veil between the coma and the real world had lessened even more: Rot's plan for her to experience her death in full. She screamed, silently, inside the coma, when Dwight opened the door. And she cried out when he pushed her so easily back to the coach floor.

Whatever Dwight had added to her dress made it impossible to sit up again. The weight, the pressure . . . too much.

Rot had been in and out to see her. To hold her hand. To whisper sickening phrases into her all-hearing ears. Rot was the one thing Carol had ever encountered in the coma that was not distorted by it. Rot came as he was. Carol had no doubt that the monster belonged there.

No sheriff in Howltown, no. But perhaps Rot was the closest thing to it.

Dwight had fallen asleep in the drive outside the coach. Carol could hear him breathing. And try as she might to sit up again, the added weight was too much.

But she found enough of it to give thanks.

To Hattie.

To Farrah Darrow.

To John Bowie.

To James Moxie, too.

This last one was hard for her to reconcile. She'd spent so many years angry at him; to think of him now in any other way was foreign to her. Almost. He'd certainly done enough to frighten Dwight. Perhaps that was enough to say *I forgive you.*

It was earliest of morning. She could tell by the songs of the insects and frogs. The wind in the trees that never came with quite as much bravado during the day. She'd been listening to the swaying of the trees for so long that she lost track of the unseen winds of Howltown. The ceiling of the coach rippled, but she hadn't been looking at it. Her mind's eye, it seemed, had finally transcended the coma. Carol was doing something now, at the end, that both Hattie and John had wanted so badly for her to do.

She was finding peace.

Don't give up yet. John Bowie's voice. So clear that Carol half expected him to be standing outside the coach, his bare feet in the gravel drive. *You aren't buried yet.*

But no word from Hattie. No right words that Carol could come up with that might be something Hattie would say at a moment like this.

That's because Hattie was practical, Carol thought. And the meaning of this statement seemed to be the lock that clicked shut on Carol's casket.

She gave thanks to the same people she'd already given them to, pausing again on James Moxie, wondering what might have been had he not run off to the Trail. Had she not foolishly trusted the monster that was Dwight. Had she—

No more of that.

Her own voice. Stronger somehow.

She heard movement from up on the bench and knew Rot had returned from whatever errand he'd been on. The fiend was in the coach with her again. She didn't wonder what he would say, didn't wonder what he would do. Instead, she lived her final moments to the beat of a memory of Hattie constructing a box, the sawing and the hammering, the polishing and paint.

Out of the corner of her eye she could see Rot. Slumped in the corner of the coach bench. As he actually was. His wide-open, unfocused eyes revealed a depression, a sadness Carol was grateful to have never known.

The monster, Carol thought, *looks different when nobody's watching.*

The memory of Hattie at work continued. The vision of James Moxie helping her faded. And the lack of Hattie's words only meant that Mom was still working, of course, in her own Howltown, perhaps, unable to bring herself to say *don't worry* when those words did not apply.

And the sound of Hattie hammering was the sound of Carol's casket closing. As earliest morning became morning in full. As the beast wheezed on the bench above her. As light added details to the inside of the coach, Carol had already accepted that a coach is like a casket, its wheels rolling through the grooves of an individual trail, one for each and everybody, as the legends of their own names rose, then fell, then rose with the terrain again.

She closed her eyes. Peace. The end.

Then, without deciding to keep fighting, she opened her eyes again and looked to the beast wheezing on the bench. His indeterminate face did not obscure his eyes and Carol said, without parting her lips,

I am not you. You are sadness, you are the end of things, you are rot.

Then her heart beat, not one beat per minute, but two.

I am not.

And the terrible thing trained his eyes on her, detecting the second beat, aware of the fight in the woman on the floor of the coach.

And in his eyes Carol saw concern. Worry.

Carol saw fear.

BURIAL

A lready concerned with the gravediggers' complaints of a prowler, Manders, wanting both the Carol Evers and Winifred Jones funerals to be without blemish, woke at daylight and walked the grounds close to the home. He traveled the main floor quietly then took the stone steps to the basement, where Norm dressed the bodies. All was quiet and all was as it ought to be. There had been no break-ins, no defamation. As he took the steps back up to the foyer, his shoes sounded crisp against the stone. Then they echoed off the parlor's shining floor. He exited under the recently painted white trim of the front doorframe, and walked quietly past the plot directory to the graveyard itself.

Before he came close enough to tell what it was, he knew the prowler had come the night before after all.

Something was on the ground surrounding Carol Evers's grave. It was a big black something that at first looked like tossed garbage, but was soon unmistakable.

Manders passed under the wood arch proclaiming official entrance to the cemetery.

It was a burn was what it was.

The grass was charred to ash and the exposed dirt was hard under his black shoes. Whoever the prowler was, Manders noted a purposeful design: Four black circles surrounded the plot, connected by a single black path. He knelt to the grass and pinched some of the soot between his fingertips, letting the ash fall and wiping the morning dew on the hem of his pants. He smelled oil. Burnt oil. And he wondered what kind of man thought it prudent to waste oil on something like this.

A cult, he thought, rising.

Manders didn't like this at all. A cult meant more than one member and a cult meant rituals that might come again, annually, monthly, *daily*, who knew. This could become a serious problem. Nearby he spied the remains of a small fire and he pieced together the scene from the night before.

Worshiping the grave, he thought, wiping his hands together. *Who knows what they may have sacrificed . . .*

He walked to the grave's edge and nervously peered within but saw it was as clean and empty as Lucas and Hank left it.

And that was nice. The sort of thing he needed to see. The diggers would arrive shortly and Manders would see to it they made the grounds as presentable as possible for the morning's ceremonies. It was a small relief, finding the grave empty.

The director turned and looked across the graveyard to where Winifred Jones would be lowered. He detected no foul play, no black oil circles, and felt hopeful that what he'd found was the only damage done.

He left the unsettling scene and passed back beneath the wood arch and up the grassy hill. In his office he made preparations for Carol Evers's ceremony and looked out the window consistently, hoping the diggers might pick today to show a bit earlier than normal, knowing it was a big day . . . the lowering of two prominent Harrowsers before noon.

Now, Manders thought nervously, on top of their usual duties, they had a mess to clean, too . . .

. . . Opal arrived before the diggers did and Manders was surprised to see him. He left the office and met the lawman on the circle drive at the foot of the funeral home steps. Opal was still upon his horse.

"Mornin', Manders."

"We had a prowler last night."

Opal raised an eyebrow. "How's that?"

"Somebody burned circles in the grass surrounding Carol Evers's grave."

"You see, Manders, that makes me suspicious all over again."

"Were you not anymore?"

"I was paid a visit by the one and only Doctor Alexander Wolfe."

"Really?"

"He corroborated Evers's story."

"Story, Sheriff?"

"He gave the same reasons for Carol's passing as what he'd stated in the letter you read."

"Well," Manders said. "That's at least *some* good news."

"Turns out he's more of a fruit-doctor than an imaginary one."

"You mean a spiritualist?"

"That I do."

Opal looked toward the cemetery. Even standing among the white lilies framing the home's front walk, he could make out the desecration in the grass.

"Take a look at the body when she comes in," he said, without turning to Manders. "I'm not asking you to examine her, but give her a look. Anything jump out at you, let me know."

Opal tipped his hat and turned the horse.

Manders climbed the steps and entered the house.

The sheriff rode under the cemetery arch and stopped the horse a few feet before the vandalism. Young sunlight against his back cast his shadow across the hole in the earth. He dismounted and studied the circles for a long time. He didn't like it at all. None of it. Didn't like the way it made him feel. The images of Farrah Darrow with the unopened whiskey, Dwight Evers in the shadows of the willow trees on the Trail, and Alexander Wolfe in the station were all superimposed ghostlike over the fresh black rectangle in the grass. He hoped to hell's heaven a traveler had done this. A passer-through. It wasn't the first time someone had vandalized Harrows's one graveyard, but it was perhaps the most significant.

Opal didn't like the circles. Didn't like that they framed Carol Evers's grave.

On his horse again, Opal headed for the graveyard arch. He would go to Cole's house. He'd ask the deputy if anybody, strange or otherwise, had ridden into town last night.

He heard a shuffling in the trees.

Opal stopped the horse and squinted into the shadows. Whoever it was, he was doing a poor job of hiding himself.

Opal drew his gun and fired it into the foliage left of the figure. He heard a shriek.

"Come on out, then," Opal said.

Without much hesitation a small, soot-covered man emerged from the shadows. Opal gestured *come here* with his gun.

"I'm not the bad man," Rinaldo said, raising his arms, as if to show the sheriff there was nothing up his sleeve. "I fooled the bad man twice."

"Didya now. Why don't you come a few feet closer and tell me the story."

Rinaldo did as he was told. Opal noted the genuine smile on the suspect's face.

"I fooled him once with the outhouse, and again as a double. Have you read Doberman's book on doubles? I have."

"Uh-huh." Opal removed the cuffs from his belt loop.

"Liliana tells me I'm not good at magic. And maybe she's right. But today . . . today I was."

"Magic, huh. What's a double?" Opal gestured for Rinaldo to come closer yet.

"It's how you make a man disappear, then reappear somewhere else. Unless you know real magic, you use a double."

"I see. And so who did you double for?"

Rinaldo was beside the sheriff's horse now. "The great James Moxie."

Opal held the suspect's eyes for the duration of five breaths. "You helped James Moxie disappear, huh?"

"Yes!"

"And then reappear, too."

"Yes!"

"Uh-huh. And where did he disappear from and where did he reappear to?"

Rinaldo looked over his shoulder, to the rooftops of Harrows.

Opal looked to town, too. Then back at Rinaldo. "James Moxie is here? In Harrows?"

"That's right. And I helped him."

"Uh-huh. Well while we're on the subject of magic . . . how good are you at getting out of handcuffs?" . . .

. . . Farrah woke beside Clyde and quietly slipped out of bed. Despite the fright she'd had under the bed, the fact that Mister Evers had been inside their home, she did not think to wake her husband.

Just then she needed to grieve alone. Carol's burial was at hand.

As she quietly dressed in the hall, she found herself hoping Sheriff Opal had found something wrong with Mister Evers. It was a terrible thing to long for. She decided she'd visit the sheriff after paying her respects. She'd tell Opal of the shoes she saw while under the bed, and the voice she knew very well, the one that whispered her name.

And if Opal wanted to dig Carol back up at that point? So be it.

As she pulled on her boots, she considered moving somewhere like Griggsville: a town where the people were young, the work was plenty, and she could grow up without the ghost of Carol's body asleep in every cellar she entered. Clyde's insistence that Time was grief's only

cure sounded like pig-shit to her last night and horse-shit this morning. Griggsville ... distance ... these words felt like an all-new kind
of truth. Words she could live by.

Standing before the mirror, she saw she did not look well. The pain
of losing Carol was evident in every feature. She looked at her lips
and imagined them talking to Opal yesterday. She'd visit him again
today. Right after she paid her respects. And after seeing the sheriff,
she'd ask Clyde if he wanted to move to Griggsville. She was a woman
who cherished good feelings, and for her there were none of those left
in Harrows.

Dressed and washed, she looked into the bedroom again and saw
Clyde in the same position she'd left him. She silently thanked him
for trying and left quietly out the front door ...

... Dwight left Carol's body in the coach all night for two reasons:

First, he hoped the cold air might further the appearance of death.
Second, the phantom (the friend?) that woke him yesterday morning
was right when it told him to hide the body.

Waking up on the gravel drive, the morning of Carol's burial finally upon him, he checked the coach, found Carol still at rest, and
thought of Alexander Wolfe. The fictitious doctor had somehow visited Sheriff Opal last night. Dwight tried not to let this impossibility
crack him, but it was hard work. It was one thing to want so badly for
everything to go right, but there was certainly a "right" way of things
going right.

Wolfe's visit was perhaps too right.

Yet he believed nothing birthed by his fissured imagination could
sour the incredible sense of coming relief, the arms of happiness that
would surely envelop him when his wife's casket was finally lowered
into the earth.

He'd fallen asleep to thoughts and images like these; feelings he
hadn't known in a long time. Freedom from Carol.

But there was still the horrifying reality of the inevitable transference; the handing off of Carol's body at the funeral home; the one moment in which Carol must be out of his control, when Manders and his staff would have her body to themselves.

Sleep still fading from his mind, Dwight cursed the unfairness of life. Even a man with a righteous, foolproof plan had to worry. Everything accounted for, everybody fooled, all holes filled, he still had to worry.

It wasn't right.

He looked once across the large front lawn before examining Carol closer. She looked good. She certainly looked dead. He touched her arm and then her neck and thought, yes, the cold night air had done its job. Then he turned back to the house and

(*what if she woke right now?*)

entered the house and walked upstairs.

In the master bedroom he put the final touches on the look he ought to have for the burial. There wasn't much to do; he had slept outside. But it was a look he'd considered many times, even named; the Numb Widower. Using Carol's vanity, he purposefully ruffled the appearance of the Numb Widower even more.

How terribly sad, he thought, mimicking the voices of the townspeople. *Evers is so distraught he forgot to comb his hair.*

Dwight had explicitly asked that there be nobody at the funeral. But you couldn't be sure with a woman like Carol.

People liked her . . . so very much.

And still, there was Manders to see. Possibly Opal. And certainly those he might encounter soon after Carol was buried.

Buried.

The word sounded sweet. Like dessert.

He splashed water under his eyes and tugged on the flesh of the Numb Widower's face. He rehearsed a handful of expressions in the glass. This was the Numb Widower recalling a private moment with his wife; a half-blind distant gaze, his chin to his neck, his lips fishlike and unsmiling. *This* was the Numb Widower recalling a favorite joke of hers, something clumsy she had done perhaps. And *this* was what he looked like accepting the severity of the ceremony, her departure; a humorless granite stare into the future, years to be spent alone, without the love he'd so cherished.

Satisfied, Dwight rose and split the drapes covering the nearest window. He could see the coach below in the drive.

"Do not wake," he said. "Please, Carol, *do not wake.*"

Then, after forcing himself to inhale and exhale steadily for a minute, he left the master bedroom, the second story, and the house.

On the ride to the Manders Funeral Home, Dwight wondered if the black providence watching over him might continue this very important morning. The shroud who woke him, the imaginary doctor visiting the very real sheriff. Would this ghastly fortune persist? Might not this helper be there when the apex came, the moment of deliverance, the handing off of her body?

Hide your lady.

Indeed. But what advice would the shadowy savior give him when he couldn't hide her? When he had to carry her out under the bright sun for all to see?

If Smoke hadn't stopped Moxie, if Moxie were somehow alive in Harrows (*now*), Dwight would need all the black magic he could get.

He cracked the reins.

These thoughts persisted, yet none of them were quite powerful enough to crack the ecstasy of the momentous occasion ahead.

"Do not wake!" he called over the thunder of the hooves. "My dearest, my love . . . *today is your burial!*" . . .

. . . Carol did not wake. But her heart beat three times a minute. And the wheezing creature slumped on the bench looked out the coach window, not as if observing the passing landscape, but as though able to see much farther, to all of Harrows itself, even into the detectable hearts of all those in town . . .

╰⧉ • ⧉╯

... After disposing of the man who had been tracking him, Moxie rode under the cemetery arch and stood at the head of the funeral home drive. He'd wait, here, for Carol's casket. When it was brought up the street, he would remove his gun, introduce himself, and tell them to open the box. If they didn't, he would shoot them.

But long before anything like that happened, a woman called his name.

From the far side of the graveyard, beyond the view of the funeral home windows, a woman's voice traveled the wind like dust, like flakes of skin, like ash.

Rinaldo, hiding in the woods, did not indicate that he heard it.

Moxie, his eyes still reflecting the dying flames as if they'd reached a new zenith, took his gun from his holster and turned to where the voice came from.

His face was black with soot.

"James," a woman called from far across the markers. *"Come here..."*

Moxie led the horse toward the sound, back under the arch.

"Moxie," Rinaldo called, "where are you going?"

"Jaaaaaames... come... come here, Jaaaames..."

The tombstones obstructed his view, but Moxie thought he saw her waving, the outline of a woman, black hair tousled by no wind.

The gesture was familiar, the voice, too, and Moxie held his gun waist-high.

Molly...

"Come here, James... come heeeeeeeeere... meet my friend, Carrrr-rolllllll..."

"Molly?" he said, the craziness in his face softening.

"Moxie?" Rinaldo stepped toward his hero and, without looking, Moxie trained his gun on him.

Rinaldo stopped.

"I'll wait here," he said. "I'll guard the grave."

Moxie rode Old Girl to an old stone whose letters had evaporated over time.

"Come here, James . . . meet my friend . . ."

The woman's hair and forehead were visible above a wide marker, but she vanished quickly.

Moxie followed. She showed and hid, showed and hid behind other stones.

Moxie followed.

He caught her behind a mausoleum.

"Come here . . . I want to introduce you to my friend . . ."

It was Molly. She was undressed. But it was not Molly as she looked the day he met her, the day she introduced him to Carol in a tavern.

It was Molly as she looked now, dead for so many years.

Moxie gripped the reins.

Her black hair looked like string woven into the wrinkles of her scalp. Her face, it seemed, had shrunk with death, her eyes far from her ears. She spoke his name and he could smell the individual letters. As she smiled, the bones of her face tore the garlic-thin skin that remained.

"Molly?"

She gestured for him to follow her. Something moved within her sagging gray breasts.

Moxie followed.

"Molly? Are you taking me to Carol?"

The guilt. The memory. The moment he met Carol.

Molly turned and for a breath Moxie saw that both her eyes were in one socket, the other empty and dark.

"I've always brought you to Carol . . ."

Like Moxie had acted childish for asking.

They passed the last of the graves and Molly continued ahead, into the pines that framed the grounds, then into the sunless forest that stretched from the grassy grounds to the homes of Harrows.

"Molly," Moxie said, blinded by remorse. "I don't want to meet her, your friend. I'll do her wrong. I'll hurt her."

Young laughter from inside a tavern erupted, and the first real sign of the sun arrived.

"Come, James . . . you're going to fall in love with her . . ."

Moxie led Old Girl around solid stumps and fallen logs. Molly led them both.

She's taking you to Carol, he thought. *Carol's the reason you ride again. Go to her . . . follow Molly . . . go to Carol and wake her . . . tell her you're ready to help her now . . .*

The space between the trees grew smaller and Old Girl had trouble getting through. Molly blurred ahead, visible, then not.

Moxie called to her. "Wait!"

A crisped shoulder, the bones of her spine. Partial images shown, then taken away.

Moxie could still smell her, but he could see her no more. His name echoed off the bark of a thousand trees: the sweet singsong voice of the dead woman, asking him to follow, come on, come meet my friend, love awaits thee. As he cried out, sweat coursed down the sides of his open mouth, rivulets in the soot.

The sun was rising. The burial was soon. So soon.

Was Molly taking him to Carol's box?

She must be. She must.

But as Moxie guided Old Girl between a pair of maple trees as thick as the columns of the Mackatoon Courthouse, as he entered a blossom grove, he saw there was no box in the clearing at the foot of the black cherry trees.

It was Carol herself instead.

She looked as she looked now: twenty years since last he saw her, since the day he carried the owlfly in a jar away from her house. Her bare feet crunched pine needles on the forest floor.

She looked so intelligent. So strong. So totally alive.

"Carol," Moxie said, riding slowly toward her. "Carol, you're awake."

Carol smiled. Her face, her expression, the strength in her eyes, the independence in her posture: It was everything Moxie would have hoped she'd become.

He smiled, too, as he dismounted. Old Girl neighed and Moxie patted her on the side, as though telling her, *We made it. We've reached the end.*

Moxie stepped toward Carol.

Then Carol collapsed . . .

. . . When Manders showed him the Bellafonte, Dwight just about screamed. He thought something had gone wrong or was about to go wrong or that Manders was feigning niceties but ten lawmen were about to come out from the back room and shoot him without asking why.

"Incredible," Dwight said, trembling, gaping at the ornate box displayed in the funeral home's foyer.

"Any idea who it's from?" Manders asked. He noted the thin line of a scratch on Dwight's cheek.

Dwight turned to him, wide-eyed, then back to the Bellafonte. He didn't know who sent it. And the existence of the thing scared him. Deeply.

"Well," Dwight said, "it's a beautiful piece of work. It's . . ."

Don't let them use it, Dwight thought.

Lucas and Hank walked in carrying a stretcher between them. Norman entered, too. Manders politely explained to Dwight that it was time to transfer the lady from his coach to the casket. Dwight agreed because he was afraid to say no. He followed them outside. As the diggers opened the coach door, Dwight held his breath.

He'd removed the rocks and earth from her dress only minutes ago, just prior to pulling in to the funeral home. What had weighed her down, what had given Dwight some piece of mind, was now scattered just beyond the evergreens that framed the head of the drive.

Without the weight . . . could Carol rise again?

But Carol was on her back. Thank the sky, Carol was on her back.

The diggers lifted her out of the coach and Dwight saw some of the dirt from the Trail fall from her shoulders. Norman watched from the top of the funeral home steps.

This would be a bad time, Carol, Dwight thought. *Please, for me . . .*

Manders was explaining more about the casket, its uniqueness, its beauty, its weight. The diggers were discussing the best way to move her. Manders said he'd never seen a Bellafonte exactly like it. The diggers said it was gonna take eight men, or four horses. Manders said—

Everything was escalating too fast for Dwight.

Fresh sunlight painted the half-circle drive a bright orange.

So many details.

The dirt in the wrinkles of the knuckles of the diggers' fingers.

A smudge at the bottom of the right lens of Manders's glasses.

Each pebble of the drive.

Every blade of grass.

The rise and fall of Carol's chest.

"Manders!" Dwight yelled, reaching for the director.

"What is it?"

Did she look dead? Or did she look like she was sleeping? Like she could easily open her eyes and say, *Him . . .*

Dwight searched his mind, frantic for something to say.

"Is the casket . . . is it . . . is it good enough?"

"It's a casket worthy of a queen," Manders said, his final words on the Bellafonte.

Dwight needed to sit down. He wanted to curl up on the stone steps. He wanted to leap up into the driver's box and ride until the legs of the steeds turned to dust.

This was the apex: the unfairness of life; the part of his plan he couldn't control; the final pass before Carol would be forever underground, beyond the reach of suspicion, beyond the guns of the lawmen.

Beyond the guns of the outlaws and triggermen, too.

"Look here at this lid, Mister Evers." Hank the gravedigger might have been trying to distract Dwight. To ease the horror of seeing his wife in such a way. "It's solid cebil wood, the strongest in any forest on earth. It'd take a small explosion to pry it open again."

Dwight faced the digger.

"What . . . what did you say?"

Hank repeated himself.

Dwight smiled as a wave of calm carried him toward something more peaceful.

Yes, of course, the casket had been a gift . . .

"You can see for yourself," Hank said, "no dirt is going to scratch this lid."

. . . a gift . . .

"If you don't mind," Dwight said, hiding his growing confidence, "I'd just as soon get her safely inside. I'm not a man of prolonged emotion, beleaguered as I am . . ."

"Go on inside," Manders said kindly. "Go into the office and Hank will bring you a glass of water. Let us take care of moving her for you."

Dwight adopted one of the many faces he'd rehearsed.

"That'd be nice," he said. "Water."

"Lucas," Manders said. "Bring a shot of whiskey for the gentleman, too."

The diggers walked Dwight inside. In that moment he felt himself free falling; a man whose entire future lay in the slippery hands of other men. But he did not mind; Dwight willingly fell. The belief he now held of who had sent the casket bolstered his sense of justice: He had numbers; somebody on his side.

It'd take a small explosion to pry it open again.

The shape-shifting stranger was helping him. Again.

In that moment, madly, Dwight didn't even care if they caught him.

In the office Hank pulled out a chair for him and Lucas came in with the whiskey. Hank brought him water. Dwight sat and smiled, feeling himself on freedom's front porch, and drank the alcohol from the small glass.

"Thank you," he said.

Outside the office, in the parlor, Manders and Norman lifted Carol carefully from the stretcher and set her within the Bellafonte. She was as radiant as the box. The director leaned forward and studied her closely. Not only was there no sign of foul play, but Carol looked cleaner than anybody who'd ever been carried through the front doors of the Manders Funeral Home. He looked once to Norman and saw awe in the makeup man's face. They did not speak, but both might have said she looked to be living. Without considering how silly it might appear, Manders removed a small hand mirror from his pocket and, checking the parlor door once, placed it just below her nose, keeping it there a full twenty seconds before bringing it to the blooming daylight coming through the open front doors.

There was no mark, no fog, and Manders nodded, assured that lifeless lungs meant Missus Carol Evers was indeed deserving of a burial.

Manders closed the lid and felt great relief. He had nothing foul to report to the sheriff.

He entered the office.

"Mister Evers," Manders spoke as gently as he would to a child who had lost both parents to consumption. "We can begin." . . .

. . . Moxie carried her body through the forest.

He told her not to worry, he could feel her heart beating. She was alive, he told her, *alive.*

Soon he could see the town through the trees. The rooftops and chimneys were welcome sights. People lived there. Carol lived, too. He walked faster, the mare a memory, left behind, untethered in the woods.

When he exited the forest he felt like he'd broken through it, an unseen barrier, as if he and Carol had taken major steps toward something better, toward reconciliation, toward forgiveness.

Stumbling upon a dirt road, homes on either side of him, Moxie's boots and breathing were the only sounds. Faces appeared in the windows but nobody stepped outside to help him. He was, of course, just another dangerous man from the Trail, a man certainly to be avoided, with his ashen face, his shining eyes, and the way he walked like he was carrying something, or *thought* he was carrying something, though his arms were clearly empty.

Ahead, Moxie saw Silas Hite in the open door of what looked like a stable. It wasn't Silas as he looked behind bars in Albert's Port, not how he looked when Moxie once woke him, carrying Carol, years ago, but as he looked now, after so many years of rotting.

"Silas!" Moxie called. "She just fell! I need to get her to a doctor!"

The sun pooled dull in the indentations in Silas's face. His teeth looked made of corn.

"Silas?"

White hair clung to Silas's misshapen head, and when he spoke, his voice was not sweet like Molly's.

"I know a doctor, James . . . an excellent man of medicine . . ."

The thin texture of Silas's hair sparked detailed memories for Moxie . . . of Jefferson's home . . . of the jail cell in Albert's Port.

Of Abberstown.

But these memories were not connected to anything solid in his mind. Only pictures with no frames.

"Where is he, Silas?"

Silas smiled, and when his lips parted Moxie took a step back. Something foul escaped his throat. Something not all laugh and not all language, either.

He pointed farther up the road. Toward town.

"A doctor you say?" Moxie asked. "Will he be there?"

Silas nodded. The Adam's apple sank lower, too low, in his throat.

"Do you like how she walks?" Silas suddenly asked.

Moxie, already walking toward Main Street, responded without looking back at him.

"She's fallen, Silas. Thank you for—"

"Does she smell like the lamb's wool to ya?"

Moxie could smell it again. The compost of rot from Silas's body. As if Silas slept in the morgue.

The smell of Molly.

The smell of Silas.

And now . . . something else . . .

Moxie looked down at Carol and shook his head no.

"You are alive," he said . . .

. . . By the continued light in Howltown, a light that began with a flickering candle in the storm room of her home, a light no doubt lit by a monster that wanted her to see in full the events of her premature death, Carol saw a horribly distorted version of Robert Manders remove a mirror from his pocket and place it under her nose. The mirror, too, was distorted, and the woman she saw reflected in it was screaming, *Help, I am not dead, I AM NOT DEAD!*

And beyond her own pleading face, reflected, too, she saw the very monster floating, wheezing, eyes bright in a face exhausted with change. And as Manders checked Carol for unlikely, improbable life, the monster spoke.

It's too late, Carol. You may wake yet, but you will wake in a box.

Then, as Manders removed the mirror, she saw the terrible thing float away, as if concerned with something else, here, in Harrows.

Then Manders closed the lid of her casket. And to Carol it looked like a living wall of stone falling dead, forever, upon her . . .

. . . When he reached Main Street the sky was bright with streaks of orange, reminding Moxie that it was, despite the sense of it being one unbroken nightmare, a new day. And yet the few early risers populating the dirt road looked upon him as they might their own death. His face and hands were covered in soot from the oil fire, and he wore the blood of Smoke across the chest of his red shirt. Carol's body lay malleable as clothing in his arms. His hat was partly burned, and one onlooker, a cook, told his boss there was a maniac in the street who smelled something like decay. Moxie's eyes and teeth flashed through the dirt and ash, and had Sheriff Opal been on the street instead of at the Manders Funeral Home, he would have stopped the outlaw on principle alone.

He found the doctor immediately.

In an empty storefront window with no sign declaring its purpose, Moxie saw the doctor who had first seen Carol some two decades past. He, too, looked to have been yanked from the grave. His muted-blue suit was marred with dirt and stains from what looked and smelled like garbage. His thin brown hair appeared glued to his shriveled head.

String, Moxie thought. Like Silas's hair. The stringy coif of the dead.

The doctor held open the door for Moxie to enter.

"Doctor," Moxie said, confused by the memories (hadn't he seen this man by the fire?), "she's fallen. Will you look at her?"

The doctor gestured for Moxie to bring her to a cold steel table. His fingertips were black.

Moxie set her down gently.

As he watched the doctor study her, he held one bloodied shirt-sleeve over his mouth to block the smell of the man.

"I want to help her this time," Moxie said. "I'm ready."

The doctor shook his head no.

"I don't want to turn my back on her this time."

The doctor shook his head no. Dust rose from the top of his head.

"She's alive, Doctor. I felt her heart beating myself."

When the doctor started to say no once again, Moxie grabbed him by his blue suit and thrust him against the wall.

The doctor turned to dirt in his hands, thick earth sliding down the wall to the floor.

Moxie, gripping only the stained suit now, heard the front door open and close. He turned to see the back of Carol leaving, going quickly past the storefront's cracked window.

She was no longer on the table.

"You see! She lives . . ."

Moxie moved fast, following her out the door. Crazed, he looked up and down Main Street. He grabbed strangers by their wrists.

"Have you seen her?" he shouted. *"Have you seen her?"*

People backed away from him. One called out for Sheriff Opal.

Moxie saw her standing in a second-story window of the Corey Hotel.

His boots thundered across the planked boardwalk and he entered the building, splintering the door as he did.

"Can I assist you, sir?" a voice called from deep within the fog, from beyond the images of four fiery circles, a heart exploded, dirt piled tall as the pines, and eyes opening to find themselves in the dark, in a box, buried.

Moxie climbed the hotel stairs fast and, gun drawn, kicked open the door to the second floor.

Rot stood at the window at the end of the hall, facing him.

The voice from the barbershop, from the cell in Albert's Port, and from the other side of that fire, too, greeted Moxie.

The voice that encouraged him long ago to leave Carol.

"James Moxie. What a joy to have you here. Here . . . and not in the graveyard where you'd rather be."

Moxie understood.

He fired.

The form did not recoil.

Moxie ground his teeth and fired again.

"You won't stop me," he said. "Not today."

"Do you really think you would have chosen differently this time had I let the illusion persist?"

Moxie fired again.

Nothing.

"You were at the barbershop, beneath a towel."

"Yes."

"You were behind the bars in Albert's Port."

"Yes."

"You spoke from the other side of the fire."

"Yes."

"And you were there, in a tavern, long ago. You told me to leave her."

"Yes."

"Are you death?"

"No. I am *Rot*."

"I'll give you someone else to rot."

The eyes grew wider, trembling disks in a vague face.

"You were going to kill the husband no matter what deal we make."

"Take the Cripple then. We're even."

The form laughed.

"The Cripple? I already got more from the Cripple than you can imagine. No, Moxie. The Cripple isn't fair trade."

"You won't stop me. Not today."

"I already have."

Moxie turned back to the door through which he'd come and saw it was no longer there. In its place was the same length of hall, the same form at the far end of it, Rot, standing before the same window.

"Tell me who you want."

"I want Carol Evers, Moxie. You know that."

"Why her?"

"Because she's come so close to rotting so many times. Because she mocks the end of things. Because she's been places nobody else has."

"She's not dead."

"Do you think I don't know whether or not she is dead?"

The lines of the thing's face moved independent of one another. His skin rippled like goat's milk. For a brief, horrific beat, Moxie saw Rot as he truly was. Sickly, balding, slumped; fueled by the power of lust alone. Then he was indeterminate, vague once more.

"There's no funeral happening today."

"Isn't there? A casket has been sent."

"I'll break it apart."

Moxie stepped forward again but the length of the hall did not change. He turned and saw the man still there, hovering by the second window, a reflection of the first.

Moxie said, "Let me go."

"But that's not what I want to do."

Moxie could sense a clock ticking. Time running out. Carol in the casket.

"Let me go."

"But that's not what I'm *going* to do."

"She's not dead."

"Oh?"

"You wouldn't be here with me if she was."

Moxie moved, but the lengths of the hall before him and behind him did not change. And Rot at both windows did not change but for the black dirt writhing in the wrinkles of his face . . .

. . . Farrah truly planned to avoid the burial when she left the house, but realized she'd been walking toward the cemetery after all.

She thought of Mister Evers on his knees by the bed.

She turned around.

She didn't know exactly what time the burial was set for and she hadn't realized she didn't know this until now. What with the rash of the Illness that came to Harrows, she knew Manders had his hands full; Carol could be lowered at noon or at six and how was Farrah supposed to know when to go there?

You're supposed to go there all day.

The thought was a bad one. Guilty as hell's heaven.

And yet . . . Mister Evers must have decided on a very private ceremony because nobody in town was talking about it and everybody in town liked Carol Evers very much.

This, Farrah thought, more than a little crazed, was because Dwight had killed her. It had to be that. *Everything* pointed to that. Carol would never have asked for a closed, unannounced send-off.

Farrah thought of that conversation she'd overheard, so long ago now, when Carol told Dwight to *let her in*. To let Farrah in on . . .

. . . *what?*

Was there a link between what Carol was trying to tell Farrah before she collapsed and the argument she'd overheard that same night?

A light flickered in Farrah's mind . . . something fuzzy, deep in her brain.

Then it was vanquished. Then it was gone.

Farrah believed she was walking without direction again, but discovered she was actually walking toward the sheriff's station. It was time to tell Opal about Dwight coming into her home. It was time to tell Opal that no matter what conclusion the lawman had come to, Dwight Evers had played a part in the death of his wife.

She'd walked half the distance to the station when a woman too big for the vest she wore stepped out of an alley and blocked her way.

"Farrah Darrow?"

She was smiling and Farrah didn't like her smile at all. Didn't like her face or the ponytail that hung like an eel over her shoulder.

"My name's Lafayette. I was hoping you wouldn't mind accompanying me for a spell."

Farrah had heard of this woman before. Mister Evers did business with her. Carol did not.

"I'm sorry, Miss Lafayette, but I don't—"

But Lafayette grabbed her by the arm and took her anyway . . .

. . . "There was once a day when you held all the space in her world in the palms of your sooty hands, and you took it, pocketed it, robbing her and leaving her to sweat it out in the claustrophobic horror of true darkness and decay. You sent her to sleep in a box, Moxie. It's truth. It's regret. And no man is allowed the chance to pretend it is not."

"I was young."

"It is too late. They lower her into the earth already . . ."

❦ • ❧

... They were, indeed, lowering her into the earth already.

Lucas and Hank rolled the big wood wheels slowly as Dwight and Manders watched the rope. It was a crude process, and the creaking of the pulley was heard with every revolution. The weight of the Bellafonte tested the strength of the diggers. Hank and Lucas dripped sweat to the grass. Carol was in the hole now, and the men had only to set the gorgeous box carefully on the grave floor. Manders crossed his hands and solemnly waited. All parties were silent. Dwight performed the expressions he'd worked on at home—the Numb Widower was certainly present—but really the diggers were occupied and Manders's eyes were on the box. Once they had her safely positioned at the bottom of the hole, Lucas removed the rope from his side and then Hank did the same with his. Manders asked Dwight if he had anything to say and Dwight, staring at the lid, did not.

The funeral director and the men stepped silently to the side of the pulley and began taking it apart, placing the pieces on a wheeled platform. When all three had their backs to him, occupied as they were, Dwight knelt quickly to the grave's side and pulled his watch chain from his pocket. Attached was a penknife; he snipped the bell-string swiftly. Shoving both the knife and the string in his pocket, he rose. Lucas turned as he got up and Dwight wiped false tears from his eyes, feigning such horrible grief that Manders had to escort him up the hill and back to the house.

When the pair passed under the cemetery arch, the diggers began filling the hole ... and the heavy thud-thudding of the black earth falling upon the steel lid soon gave way to the softer sound of dirt upon dirt.

With the sound of so much dirt, Manders paused, a hiccup in his step, and he stared blankly ahead, the way a man stares into a memory.

Dirt, he thought. Yes, he'd seen a trifle of dirt near the neckline of Carol's dress as he clandestinely checked her with the pocket mirror for breath. At the time, her being deceased and him being a funeral director, the sight of some errant dirt appeared natural. The woman's funeral was today after all. And dirt and dead bodies went hand in hand.

And yet, walking Mister Evers to the funeral home, it struck Manders that a woman ought not to have dirt upon her body until *after* she's buried.

"Is something the matter, Robert?"

Manders wondered, briefly, if there was. He thought again of the scratch on Dwight's cheek and distantly thought one word: *struggle.* Then he recalled the diggers removing Carol Evers from the floor of the coach and breathed a sigh of relief. Dirt accumulates, of course, on the floors of coaches just as it does on the floors of funeral homes. No matter how hard one cleans.

"Absolutely not," Manders said. Then he continued to escort the widower up the hill . . .

. . . "He's telling the truth, Sheriff. I seen him myself."

"Cole, it's part of your job not to be as crazy as the prisoners. That's basic policing."

"No, Opal. I seen the man myself. He looked like he'd been dropped from hell's heaven. Looked like he passed through some pig-shit on the way."

Opal frowned.

"Why didn't you stop him?"

"On what grounds, Sheriff?"

Opal searched for an answer.

"I don't know, Cole! Mystery!"

"I don't even know what that means, Sheriff."

Opal felt like he was running out of time on something he wasn't sure existed . . .

... Farrah was in an alley and the woman Lafayette had just said to her, "I've got to make sure it looks like an accident."

Her heart beat hard and she pined for Clyde or anybody else to come running into the alley and find this woman who had her cornered. She'd already tried asking why she'd been brought here, but she knew the answer. And the woman didn't give her any other one. She stood before her, her big frame blocking most of the way out, as she absently wiped a razor on a razor strap.

"It's gonna be sad to cut you up, Missus Darrow. You seem like a nice girl."

Farrah wanted desperately to run, but there just wasn't enough room. Lafayette blocked the exit whole.

Useless concerns cluttered her mind:

Was Carol already buried? Was this woman Lafayette somehow involved?

"So," Lafayette said, her voice direct and cold. "You worked in the Evers home?"

Farrah did not answer.

Lafayette set the razor down on a stack of wood boxes and ran her fingers through her hair. She adjusted her ponytail and looked up to the sun. When she looked back, Farrah had already begun swinging her arm. The blade shimmered in the sunlight and Lafayette gasped and believed Farrah missed her. She opened her mouth to say something like *you're quick* but her throat wouldn't let her. She brought her hands to her neck and observed in wide shock as the color red ran down the length of her fingers. She looked down at her shirt and saw blood like a baby's bib covered in lobster sauce.

Farrah watched as Lafayette fell to a side of the alley. Then she dropped the razor, stepped over her, and ran ...

... *Illusions,* Moxie thought. *Like Molly and Silas Hite. Tricks.*

He recalled Rinaldo shouting two syllables:

Magic!

"After she dies, I will come for you, Moxie. I will come for you in the crowded street in the bright burning daylight. I will be under every bed you lie upon and within every closet you open. I will be in the food you eat and I will be beneath the water you wash with. I will be in every mirror you gaze into and I will be with you when you realize it is not yourself you see. I cannot kill you Moxie, I cannot take, but I know those who can."

Moxie fired at the window where the second shroud stood and the glass shattered and the hall came at him, fast. He shielded his face but felt nothing hit. When he lowered his arms he found that the dimensions of the hotel had returned. He whirled and the man was already coming at him, his eyes insane, many faces alive. Moxie fired but the bullet passed through him and shattered the glass there, too. He stepped back and fired and stepped back and fired and the fiend was upon him.

Moxie felt the broken glass of the window cut into his back, his arms, his hands. Then he was falling out the window, toward the dirt street below.

A lady screamed as Moxie landed hard. Rot hovered above him, his face no longer a face at all, now only features pell-mell, many eyes, many mouths, and the deep overwhelming wheezing of what sounded like a sick sky.

Then, as Moxie made to inch back, Rot suddenly became whole again, a singular face, looking beyond Moxie, horror in his eyes.

"What is it?" Moxie said, knowing it had to do with Carol. Knowing the only thing that could frighten this fiend was Carol.

Then Rot was gone. And the space above Moxie was only blue sky, the unfair morning of a funeral for a woman who did not deserve one.

Moxie, his legs pained from the fall, dragged himself onto the boardwalk, to where horses rested at hitching posts. Standing, he untied the nearest and used the stirrups to pull himself up.

Harrowsers called out for Sheriff Opal. But Moxie was already getting away . . .

᪥ • ᪥

. . . Can you imagine if they buried you alive? he'd once asked her.

I used to worry about that. But I'm past that now.

Moxie rode fast by the finer homes of Harrows. Then through the forest where he'd left Old Girl, where he'd followed Molly's corpse. The graveyard in sight, he brought his heels down hard against the horse, traveling quick down the long slope of trail that would take him to where the Cripple stood his last stand.

Was Carol in the earth?

Was she?

Moxie reached the border of the cemetery and stopped the horse. He was afraid. Afraid to go on.

Not because there was no wind, no heat, and no sound. Not because the cemetery was empty of all people and not because it meant that the funeral was over, passed, and that Carol was indeed buried out there.

Moxie stopped because the entire graveyard, the whole expanse of lumped earth, was moving.

The stones trembled as if shaken by hidden men. The dirt between every marker, the marble walls of the mausoleums, and the very gates themselves . . . the ground breathed . . . like the folds of the face of the fiend . . .

. . . No more light in Howltown. Whether the veil between the coma and the real world had been stripped entirely or not, there was no light because, Carol knew, there is no light in a box that is already closed.

And yet . . . she was not alone.

Her heart beat ten, fifteen times a minute, and the hoarse breathing of a second person inside the casket led to words from lips she could not see.

"Wake," it said. *"Feel this moment . . . wake . . ."*

Her heart beat twenty, twenty-five beats per minute.

She was waking, yes, just as the monster wanted her to. Waking in a buried box.

Carol tried to scream, tried to push him away, but there was no room, no space between them. She felt something wet upon her ear; his lips perhaps, his breath, the tip of one of his many noses, or wholly him, all of him, attempting to slip within her.

Or maybe it's the wet decay of your own ear, Carol thought, unable to cry, unable to cry out. *Maybe this is the beginning of rot . . .*

. . . The earth split near the horse's hooves and worms poured forth like foam.

Moxie kicked the steed and rode him hard over the uneven ground as it rose, swollen, then dipped six feet deeper than it'd been. Moxie, focused on the scorched earth ahead, the site of Carol's burial, was not prepared for the sudden stop as the horse he rode sank into the earth mid-stride, its front legs stuck at once.

Moxie rolled from the horse and stumbled toward Carol's grave. On foot, wounded, with broken bones he did not yet know he had, Moxie crossed hills of rotting grass. The markers came at him, the scares in a traveling carnival's house of horrors, so many tombstones, it seemed, sprouting from the earth. More than one cut him and blood flowed, forming dark paths in the soot from Smoke's fire.

Ahead, Carol's grave rose and fell with the waves.

Rot, Moxie knew, trying to stop him still.

A wooden cross came at him and Moxie ducked, fell to the ground, and felt the worms suddenly upon him, so many fingertips, the infinite hands of Rot.

As the graveyard bucked, as the worms blinded him, Moxie crawled to Carol's grave.

He felt the fresh dirt beneath his fingers.

In the delirium of effort, hope, and hopelessness, too, Moxie understood clearly that this time he had not turned his back on her.

"Carol!" he cried.

He thrust his blackened hands farther into the dirt.

And the earth split easy.

Beneath him, at his knees, the worms spilled forth. Moxie crushed handfuls at once, Rot's many faces showing between the small bodies, like eyes flashing between the flames of a campfire. When he saw the lid of the casket, so clean beneath the dirt and worms, Moxie brought his fists down against the wood.

There was no give.

New worms gushed upon the casket from the walls of the fresh grave. Moxie lowered himself into the hole, on his knees on the lid, and pounded with black fists made of guilt, made of rage.

Someone was near, the voice of a woman above, but Moxie did not hear her.

Moxie's fist broke the wood. Then a chip became a break. And the break, a hole.

A figure blocked out the sun above, a woman's voice again, and Moxie fired his gun without looking and the figure disappeared.

Magic, Rinaldo called it. The way things disappear and then appear again.

Moxie tore at the wood and became, there, the legend he was said to be. A man capable of killing with no gun, a man capable of destroying a Bellafonte with his bare hands alone.

He cracked the wood apart even more, tearing open a hole big enough for his arm. He reached into the box and felt for her, for Carol.

But felt no body.

Instead . . . gears . . . a crank . . . rope.

The entire graveyard seemed to rise and then flatten at once, as Moxie saw into the box . . . saw the open black space . . . the upholstery . . . the craftsmanship . . . Moxie saw . . .

Saw that the box was empty.

No Carol within.

A woman's voice again and Moxie closed his eyes.

No Carol.

The graveyard stopped moving.

The worms (*It was a good trick! It was a great one, Moxie! Magic!*) had vanished. And the legendary outlaw was upon his knees on a broken casket in an ordinary grave, under an uncaring sky of blue.

The sun was high in Harrows.

A dirtied hand clasped Moxie's shoulder and he turned quick, insane, to see a face he hadn't seen in twenty years looking back, looking into his own deranged eyes.

"James Moxie," she said. "You're as unhinged as the box beneath you. Come . . . fast."

And Moxie understood that yes, he himself was James Moxie, the mythic outlaw, the legend of the Trail, the man who had performed the Trick at Abberstown.

He *was* James Moxie.

Only this time, he hadn't run away.

CAROL AND HATTIE

When Carol was five years old her mother, Hattie, pointed to a mess in the corner of the playroom and told Carol to climb in. Carol, looking at all the toys Mother had just dumped onto the ground, wasn't sure which toy Hattie was talking about.

"The chest, Carol," Hattie said. "I'm telling you to climb into the toy chest."

Carol had long loved and trusted her mother. She crossed the playroom, avoiding the wooden toys and wooden wheels, and stepped into the open red toy chest.

She stood that way, knee-deep, waiting.

"Now lie down in it, Carol."

At five, Carol had no concept of death and therefore had no way of knowing what Mother was asking her to do.

Play dead.

Carol got to her knees in the box. She held the edge with her small white fingers.

"Lie down, Carol. All the way now."

From where Carol knelt, Hattie looked a bit crazy. The second-story hall fanned out behind her, along which were the closed doors of the home's many bedrooms. Carol wondered if Bess the maid might show up in that hall, might peek into the playroom, might ask Hattie what she was thinking to do.

But Hattie had sent Bess home early that day. And this, Carol understood vaguely, was why.

"Lie down now. On your back."

Carol did as Mother said. And from her back she saw the powder-blue ceiling as though it were the sky. Then mother's face eclipsed the sky.

Hattie took hold of the toy chest's lid.

"Don't be afraid," she told her daughter.

Then Hattie closed the lid.

And locked it . . .

. . . By ten years old Carol was able to complete her studies, lying on her back, as Hattie tinkered with the Box, the idea she'd had for five years but had yet to perfect. Carol lit a small candle and brought it into the large box (much larger than her toy chest; Carol was glad those days were behind them) and she read the classics as Mother hammered against the wooden sides that made it so dark in there in the first place. Often the lid would pop open and Mother would reach inside, adjusting a knob, a lever, attempting to make final changes before what she called the test run.

"Put the book down, Carol."

"Hang on, Mother."

Because Carol liked to read. And she wasn't going to put the book down in the middle of a paragraph.

Hattie waited.

"Okay." Then Carol would do as she was told and Hattie would explain what to do, how the box worked this time.

"Spring-loaded," Hattie said once as Carol looked up into her mother's intelligent, focused eyes. "So when you press this button here, the lid should fly right off the box."

"Even if it's nailed shut, Mother?"

"Even if it's nailed shut."

Carol imagined it would have to be a very powerful spring, to do something like that.

Hattie shut the lid.

Carol, in the box, heard her mother's muffled command.

"Press it, Carol."

Carol pressed it.

Nothing happened. Just the loud sound of mangled metal. As if the springs had nowhere to go but back into themselves.

Hattie pried open the lid. She was frowning.

Carol picked up her book and started reading again.

Hattie tinkered some more . . .

. . . At fifteen Carol had long since joined in with the tinkering, though it was clearly always Mother's project. The Box. Carol's interest came from a more scientific place. Hattie's was obviously born of grave concern. It wasn't that Carol wasn't afraid of her condition or the fact that she fell into deep multiple-day comas, but she was still only fifteen, and mortality felt assured.

"If I die," Hattie said one evening, as the pair greased the gears of a strong steel wheel, "there may be nobody to say you're still alive. Do you understand?"

"Of course."

But Carol didn't like talking like this. *Let's figure this out, yes, let's build the Box already, yes, but do we have to talk about being buried alive?*

"Even if everybody in town knows you have this condition, Carol, they might mistake it for the real thing. But a mother knows. Always. A mother knows. So we need to be sure you've got a . . . plan B. Just in case."

"I won't be buried alive," Carol said, her face the campaign button of youthful confidence. But she was scared of it. "That would be just too . . . awful a thing."

"Yes, well, the world *can* be unfair. And all the money in Harrows cannot correct that."

Once the gears were greased, Hattie reached into the Box and began turning the crank of the wheel. The lid slowly lifted above it.

Carol clapped.

But Hattie's enthusiasm was reserved.

"Now the dirt," she said.

Carol and her mother carried four forty-pound sacks of dirt across what was once the playroom but had become the workroom long ago.

"Get in, dear."

Carol got in.

Hattie closed the lid and then Carol listened patiently as Mother dumped 160 pounds of dirt onto the lid.

"All right," Mother called.

Carol turned the crank.

The lid did move. But hardly any at all.

Once Hattie had cleared the lid again and Carol was up and out of the Box, Hattie said, "We're close. Whether we think we are or not. We're close." . . .

. . . When Carol brought James Moxie to meet her mother, Hattie knew he must have meant something special to her. Carol had never brought a man home before. At just eighteen years old, Carol probably wasn't thinking marriage yet, but you never knew. When Carol and James were on their way over, Hattie began the laborious task of cleaning up the workroom, then opted not to. There were plenty of other rooms for the man to see, and besides, a young man had no place being upstairs at Carol's.

At the front door, when she saw James for the first time, she said, "You're a gentleman outlaw if I ever saw one."

Not because he was one. He wasn't. Not yet. But because the young man had an energy to him that spoke of leaving, rushing, running out to experience the Trail and all the shadows it offered.

Hattie had seen that energy many times in her life.

Instead of showing James Moxie the Box that was only a floor above him for the duration of his stay (she would never show anyone but Carol), Hattie talked about horses and hooves, hats and belts and gloves.

When Moxie left for the night, Carol wanted to know what her mother thought.

"What do I think? I think I figured it out finally."

"Mother, I'm talking about James."

Hattie shrugged.

"Come upstairs," she said. "The Box is more interesting than any young man you bring home."

She said she thought she'd figured it out. But she hadn't.

And really no box was more interesting to Carol than this young man . . .

. . . Long after Carol married Dwight Evers, Hattie got sick with croup and died. By then Carol was no longer living under the same roof as her and so wasn't there to test out the Box that Hattie certainly never gave up on. At her mother's burial, Carol couldn't help but think of the bizarre bond they'd shared over caskets. As Hattie was lowered into the ground, Carol felt a crazy urge to get up and check the craftsmanship of the box, to make sure that her mother was sleeping in a casket worthy of her work.

She didn't get up. Instead she gripped Dwight's hand and Dwight said it was going to be okay. Days later, after Carol woke from a coma Dwight insisted was induced by the stress of losing her mother, Dwight was far south in Baker, dining with friends of his from his youth. Carol looked out the window to see an elderly man approaching on horseback. The man's white hair highlighted his kind eyes. Up close, though, his eyes were more than just kind, they were truly sympathetic, and Carol understood it had something to do with Mother.

The man, Carol discovered, was there to read her mother's will, and along with the considerable amount of money that had been left to Carol was a stipulation the lawyer had never encountered before in all his years of public service.

"She's asked that, upon *your* death, Carol, a certain casket be delivered to the funeral home that will be handling your burial. Morbid thoughts, I suppose, but consider it a final gift from her ... to you. She included a note with these instructions, a note for you." He shuffled the pages in his hand and cleared his throat. Then he handed Carol the note.

Carol read it.

> *My dearest Carol,*
>
> *I've done it. I've perfected it. I don't call it by its rightful name here (TB) because I don't believe anybody ought to know about it but you. It's an emergency, if you will, and so long as it's in my will and the knowledge of it only exists between the two of us, we can successfully eliminate the possibility of a third party muddying up the affair by arguing the thing is too heavy. Too big. Anything of that sort. I've fashioned it after a Bellafonte, as though to disguise it. But mark my words, it's no Bellafonte. It's a Hattie original. Priceless, I daresay, and certainly capable of lifting much more than a mere 160 pounds of dirt ...*

... All this, this history, Carol told Moxie as the two held each other in the pines framing the cemetery at the Manders Funeral Home. Farrah sat on a stump nearby but routinely rose to come touch Carol's arm. Carol also described finding the lever behind the upholstery, just where Hattie had explained it would be. She also retold how the lid slammed down after Farrah had helped her crawl out. How, if she'd been half a minute longer in escaping, it might have crushed her.

"Hattie almost got it perfect," she said. "But I'm not complaining."

She told Moxie how she and Farrah repacked the dirt, how and why she didn't want Dwight knowing she was alive yet, and how she was fortunate nobody but Farrah was in the cemetery to see it all.

Then Moxie said what he'd been wanting to say for a very long time.

"I was a fool."

"You were chicken-shit is what you were." Then, after a pause, "But not today. Thank you."

Moxie stepped closer to her. Farrah tried to look away but couldn't.

"He was in the box with you?"

"Yes." She shuddered.

"How did you get rid of him?"

Carol laughed and it was the laughter of an intelligent mind, having played a part in outfoxing betrayal.

"I woke up. And I pulled the lever."

Then Moxie kissed her. And Farrah, not only unable to look away, clapped.

Carol turned to her. "You!"

And when she looked back to Moxie, she saw he was staring seriously toward town. She knew he was thinking about Dwight.

"I can do it," Carol said.

Moxie shook his head no.

"If it's between you or me . . . it's me. The one who took to the Trail. The one who can live, easily, with what's about to happen."

Carol nodded. They stared into each other's eyes for a long time. Then Moxie, covered in soot from Smoke's oil and blood from Smoke's heart, left her standing in the woods.

She didn't need to ask where he was going any more than she needed to ask if he'd return.

The bell-string hanging from his dirty right hand, walking with a limp toward the horse he'd stolen from downtown Harrows, James Moxie looked every bit the outlaw Hattie had once predicted him to be.

If you ask me, John Bowie had once said, curled up on the wicker chair on the front porch, holding a red rubber ball, *I think you should steal away one night and find your way to Mackatoon. There's a man there who, when you bring him up, your eyes get as bright as the sky.* He sipped his drink. *I have half a mind to go fetch the outlaw myself.*

Then John closed a fist around the ball, and when he opened it again, it was gone.

Love vanishes, he said. Then he got up out of the chair and clasped his hand in Carol's. Carol felt the rubber ball appear in her palm. *But it has a way of coming back.*

MOXIE AND DWIGHT

Dwight maintained his grieving visage the entire ride home. He parked the coach in the drive and patted the gray horses sympathetically, as if even the beasts might detect disingenuous sorrow. Upon entering the house, *his* house now, he loosened his tie and set it over the back of a parlor chair and walked quietly upstairs. He was tired. In his bedroom he removed his shoes and lay upon the bed.

Carol was buried and Opal was satisfied and hell's heaven it was an easy thing to get away with, murder, when your wife's condition made it so.

A sense of overwhelming completion swept over him. It was a big enough wave to send him into a heavy slumber.

He woke to a man standing at the foot of his bed.

"Do you see these guns?" the man said, his face as black as greasepaint for the stage. "You move a finger and you trigger every one of them."

Dwight blinked twice and saw the man had blood all across his chest and neck. Despite the warning, he made to move but felt something tugging on each of his ten fingers. He looked to his hands and saw that all ten fingers were curled unnaturally, held taut with string he might have missed had he not looked as closely as he did. He blinked again and saw that the ten lines of string extended beyond the bed, to the dresser, the vanity, the wardrobe. Ten guns, indeed, set up around the master bedroom, held in place with more string.

The man at the foot of the bed stood in the center of the web as if they were an extension of himself. As if he had the power to create them out of thin air.

Like magic.

"What is this?" Dwight cried.

"You knew she was alive."

Dwight now knew who this man was. "What? Who? Who's alive?"

"You should've smothered her."

Dwight, unable to move, only mustered a muttered response. "I . . . who . . . I . . ."

"You hired the Cripple."

"Alive? Are you talking about my wife?"

Terror shook the words from his mouth.

The man stared at him out of the blackness of his face. A devil risen from a writhing graveyard, a Trail that got no sun.

"I buried my wife today! I'm grieving!"

"You buried your wife alive today."

The man looked to the scratch on Dwight's face. For Dwight, it felt something like the man had caught him naked. Dwight shook his head frantically.

"Alive? Who? Carol? Is she? Why . . . that would be *wonderful*. Alive you say?"

Dwight, wide-eyed, sweating, looked to his fingers. The string was taut, too taut.

When he looked back at the man he saw he was holding something and heard the soft jingling of a bell.

"The string was cut," the man said.

Dwight said suddenly, "How did you get that?"

Then Moxie tossed the bell-string to him and Dwight, unthinking, went to catch it.

THE PIG-SHIT
MESSENGER-THIEF

Three young men sat on a couch in a second-story apartment in Charles and talked about the local women. One of the men said he was going to quit going to the cathouse because word spread in a town this size and he didn't want his hopeful to hear about it. The youngest said he wouldn't stop going to the cathouse for any woman and damn be pig-shit if she didn't like it. The third simply belched.

The front door to the small apartment was kicked open and wood splintered at the hinges. The young men called out as the outlaw stepped inside and turned to the three frightened faces on the couch. His features were sharp, his clothes were dirty, and the face he wore bore no forgiveness.

The outlaw looked at the third. Then spoke.

"You have something of mine."

The young man stammered a response and the outlaw pulled his gun, cocked it, and trained it on the young man's chest.

"You have something of mine."

Trembling, the young man said, "I sold it."

"Buy it back."

The young man nodded yes, hurriedly, and rose from the couch.

He left the apartment.

The outlaw waited, holding the other two at the end of his gun.

It's him, one of them wanted to say, but couldn't. Couldn't bring himself to speak. *Holy hell's heaven, that's James Moxie . . .*

. . . Opal had many things on his mind as he climbed the stairs of the Evers home but only one was a question.

You know your wife's still living, Dwight?

He had his gun out and he walked cautiously. As far as Opal understood, there was no reason to knock this time, no protocol at all. After Carol Evers had been buried, and long after the cemetery was cleared of its grievers, Robert Manders had come running into the station, insisting someone had "dug Carol up." Opal rushed to the cemetery. Hank and Lucas told a wild story. Said they found a dug-up grave with a busted Bellafonte only the Bellafonte was some kind of trick kind, with strange gears and levers. Opal asked where Carol's body was now and the gravediggers pointed to the dirt, to the bare-foot prints beside two other sets, one made of bigger boots. Dwight's name came forth from the confusion and Opal wasn't surprised when Lucas said, *You don't think Mister Evers tried to bury her alive, do you?*

"Mister Evers . . . Sheriff Opal here . . . about to open your bedroom door . . ."

The mess at the graveyard had tipped Opal right over. Manders's original suspicion had set him up but that pig-shit mess at the graveyard just tipped him right over.

Why did Lucas ask if Mister Evers had attempted to bury his wife alive? Why did *everybody* in Harrows have a bad feeling about Dwight?

But Opal knew this answer.

Where there's smoke . . .

"My hand is on the knob now . . . about to enter, Evers . . ."

Opal didn't have his hand on the knob. He stood four paces to the right of the door and aimed his gun about chest-high.

"That's it, Evers . . . I'm coming in."

Maybe he's sleeping, Opal thought. *Maybe he's hiding. Maybe he's a quarter of the way to Griggsville.*

More than once in his career Opal had been asked to act with acumen in a world washed of reason. Now he reached through all the morning's irrationality and turned the master bedroom doorknob.

Then he kicked the door open and almost fired because the body on the bed was bent in a way to suggest it may have been pointing toward the door.

"Hog-lords . . ."

Opal held his pose a full minute, scanning the room, the windows, the corners, returning to the misshapen form of Dwight Evers and the ten bullet holes that disfigured his face and body.

Finally Opal stepped farther into the room and lowered his gun.

"Lord of all hogs and pink piglets . . ."

The first string caught him by surprise, touched his shoulder, and Opal instinctively lifted his gun before understanding what it was. He brought his fingers to it and followed it to a pistol wedged between the dresser and the wall. The gun was held in place by more string. Then he followed the first string back toward the dead man and saw more string yet, so much and so apparent that it was astonishing to him that he'd missed it all the first time. Opal swallowed hard. The closer the string got to Dwight, the more red it became. From where Opal stood, he saw ten red lines extending forth from Dwight's chest and stomach . . . as if the shots had come from within him . . . his passing petrified . . . a three-dimensional rendering of his death.

Opal had some difficulty looking Dwight in the face.

He ducked under the strings and crawled to the other side of the bed. There, on his knees, he brought his fingers again to the string.

He studied.

"Well, holy pig-shit," Opal said. "Abberstown."

The oddball Rinaldo had claimed to be helping James Moxie. And

Cole had seen Moxie himself earlier in the day. Said he'd looked the part of a vengeful cacodemon from heaven's hell.

Opal rose when he heard the front door below and a woman's voice call from downstairs.

"Sheriff Opal!"

"Don't anybody come up here!" he called back.

"It's Farrah Darrow, Sheriff Opal!"

"That's fine," he called, stepping under the string and heading for the bedroom door. "Don't anybody come up here!" ...

... Opal sat with Carol at a table in a tavern at the end of Main Street.

"I don't mean to be bothering you," he said, placing his hat on the table. "And I don't mean to ask anything that might be sour for you to be remembering, but ... is that true you could hear what was going on about you?"

"Yes, Sheriff. That's right."

"Well, shudders, Carol. That sounds about as ugly a thing as I can imagine."

Carol smiled and Opal thought it amazing the woman was able to do so.

A waitress stopped by and asked if the pair were all right and Opal looked to Carol and Carol said yes she was all right. Opal said the same.

"You've got an admirer it seems." Opal pointed to a glass case containing a blue owlfly on the table. The light through the window seemed to cut the beautiful thing in half ... one wing in the shadows ... the other as kaleidoscopic as Carol's garden. Carol looked at it, then to the sheriff.

"He went and became something of an outlaw, huh," Carol said, musing.

"James Moxie?"

"That's right."

"That's right, he did. When I first started here in Harrows, his photo was still up in the station. From what I hear he wasn't so bad. Wasn't so bad in the graveyard anyway."

Carol nodded. "Are you going to take him in?"

"For what now?"

"For Dwight."

Opal paused. But he'd already thought this through.

"No, ma'am. I don't plan to. Seems to me he's taken care of my business for me. If it was him that done the taking care of it."

He winked.

Carol was quiet before speaking again.

"Sheriff, this is the second time in my life a man has acted insane because of my condition. Why do you think that's so?"

Opal shook his head. "Can't say I know that answer."

But Carol thought she did. "It must be hard," she said, "being that close to death. Even the phony kind."

"I don't know," Opal said. "Ask Manders." Then he paused. He looked Carol long in the eye. "Where is he now?"

"James?"

"Yes."

Cole had already told Opal that James Moxie had been spotted twice leaving town. Both times with Rinaldo. Once they'd come back with this very owlfly. And the second time? Cole said they'd headed south. That's all he knew. But then, everything was south from Harrows.

"Mackatoon," Carol said.

Opal wanted to ask if he was going to stay there. But he didn't.

Farrah entered the tavern and, smiling, sat beside her lady.

"I don't know how much you're talking," she said. "But I know that you're talking too much." Then, turning to Opal, "You're the one making her do it. My lady needs a break. What say we do this another day?"

Opal nodded and looked at Carol. "I agree," he said.

"Now, Farrah," Carol said, taking her friend's hand in her own. "The last thing I want is rest."

"Oh, Carol!" Farrah said, suddenly gripping her lady's hand. "I knew something was wrong! I *knew* it!"

Opal rose and put his hat on his head. He addressed Carol.

"You planning on staying in Harrows?" he asked gently.

Farrah burst out, "She doesn't deserve to have to wake in Harrows one more morning."

But Carol answered differently.

"You asked where James Moxie was," she said. "But you didn't ask whether he was coming back."

Opal waited. So did Farrah.

"Well . . ." Opal said. "Is he?"

Carol smiled.

"I think he's certainly proven he deserves . . ." She looked to the owlfly. Something beautiful, something simple, passed over her eyes. "Another chance. I think we both have."

"Well," Opal said at last. "I respect you for that, Carol. I respect you for many things. It's a good thing we all know about your condition now. We'll keep a good eye on you from hereafter." Then, "And the other eye on James Moxie, if you don't mind."

"He's coming back?" Farrah asked. "You two are gonna . . ."

Carol patted Farrah's hand.

"Don't rush it," Carol said. "Love is more complex than just coming and going."

Opal tipped his hat. Before leaving the tavern he asked, "You might know anything about a cripple? A man with only half his legs? Anything to do with all this? Your boyfriend's friend didn't tell me much about him. Only that he fooled him . . . twice."

Carol looked to Farrah and then back to Opal.

"No, Sheriff. I certainly don't."

"The strangest thing . . ."

Opal left then, and shortly thereafter Farrah helped her lady up and the two stepped out of the tavern together. Arm in arm they walked, Carol carrying the glass case with her free hand.

"You know what I'd like to do?" Carol asked.

"What's that?"

"I'd like you and me to walk through the garden and you can tell me all about Clyde."

"That old hog? All he does is sleep and snore!"

Carol smiled. "They all do."

"Truth is," Farrah said confidentially, "I love him very much."

"I know you do."

Carol thought of the many variations on love and the myriad ways it was shown. She recalled Hattie in the workroom, John Bowie on the porch, and James Moxie on his knees in a grave, staring into an empty casket he'd broken open himself.

Arm in arm they walked, and talked about Harrows, about Clyde, and about the days Carol and James Moxie met at a tavern and tried their hands at union, and how those days had circled back, like the Trail, in a way, from north to south and then back north again, all a bundle of shadows and unknowns, places without sun, places where things might hide, and yet the life-force, the throughway, the vein of all this life and living.

The Trail.

"I liked that," Farrah said. "What you said about love."

"What did I say?"

"You said there's more to it than coming and going."

Carol nodded. Her boots crushed pebbles on the boardwalk.

"That's right," she said. "There's the air we breathe, heading in either direction, too."

ACKNOWLEDGMENTS

Vast, eternal thanks to Wayne Alexander, Candace Lake, and Ryan Lewis who read *Unbury Carol* a bit ago and gave me seriously priceless advice. Candace especially had to teach me the difference between things like a hitching post and a fence. Without them I'd look like what I am ... a writer who probably too often values enthusiasm over research.

Thank you, Kristin Nelson, for being a super-agent, an endless support system, and often more like a sister to me than anything else.

Tricia Narwani, Mike Braff, Del Rey, and Penguin Random House ... where does a writer begin in thanking the people who take his book from his office to the shelves? I'll begin right here, thank you all. And I'll keep letting you know how grateful I am every time we speak.

And Dave Simmer, forever, my friend, for opening a door.

ABOUT THE AUTHOR

Josh Malerman is an internationally best-selling, Bram Stoker Award–nominated American author and one of two singer/songwriters for the rock band The High Strung. His debut novel, *Bird Box,* was published in the United Kingdom and United States in 2014 to much critical acclaim. He lives in Ferndale, Michigan, with his best friend/soulmate Allison Laakko and their pets Frankie, Valo, Dewey, Marty, and the fish.

Facebook.com/JoshMalerman
Twitter: @JoshMalerman
Instagram: @joshmalerman

ABOUT THE TYPE

This book was set in Caslon, a typeface first designed in 1722 by William Caslon (1692–1766). Its widespread use by most English printers in the early eighteenth century soon supplanted the Dutch typefaces that had formerly prevailed. The roman is considered a "workhorse" typeface due to its pleasant, open appearance, while the italic is exceedingly decorative.